Praise for *Beautiful Invention: A Novel of Hedy Lamarr*

"Chock full of Hollywood royalty, the golden age of the silver screen is brought to vivid life in this extensively researched novel about the less heralded accomplishments of Hedy Lamarr, one of its brightest luminaries. Margaret Porter paints an indelible portrait of the reluctant starlet, focusing a klieg light on her many other fascinating facets—as immigrant, inventor, and fierce patriot."

~ Leslie Carroll, author of *Notorious Royal Marriages*

"Set against the backdrop of World War II, including a heady mix of Hollywood stars, this book provides an insight into the life of one of the film greats. An exceptionally well-researched account of the life of this actress. Those interested the early days of Hollywood glamour will love this book."

~ Amanda Rofe for *Readers' Favorite*

Praise for *A Pledge of Better Times*

"Porter's ambitious novel of 17th-century England is brimming with vivid historical figures and events . . . rigorously researched and faithfully portrayed."

~ *Publishers Weekly*

"A true delight for fans of monarchy . . . Porter does a sensational job portraying the time period."

~ *The Examiner*

"Porter winningly captures both the dramatic societal upheavals and the sparkling wit and court life of the time . . . . A very rewarding reading experience—I highly recommend it."

~ *Historical Novels Review*

"A richly evocative peek into a world long gone, with political and ideological maneuvering and romantic entanglements . . . Porter explores friendship, marriage, parenthood, and loyalty as she tells the story of people who were celebrities in their time."

~ *New Hampshire Sunday News*

BEAUTIFUL INVENTION

a novel of Hedy Lamarr

by

MARGARET PORTER

GALLICA PRESS

Beautiful Invention: A Novel of Hedy Lamarr/Margaret Porter—1st Edition
ISBN 13: 978-0-9907420-3-6

In memory of my father, admirer of Hedy, historian of World War II, and movie fan.

For my mother, who taught me to read and led me into the wonderful, magical world of books.

For my husband, with endless gratitude.

And for all whose talents, creativity, and contributions are insufficiently acknowledged.

"All creative people want to do the unexpected."
~ Hedy Lamarr

PART 1: 1932–1937

"Hedy Kiesler is the most beautiful girl in the world."
—Max Reinhardt

Chapter 1

The tiny shadows cast by the branches dappled her pale flesh. The breeze whispering against her shoulders and caressing her bottom also tousled her hair, but she wouldn't risk exposure by reaching up to smooth it. One arm shielded her bare breasts, and she splayed her fingers between her thighs. Sheltered and concealed by the surrounding trees, she waited nervously while the director conferred with the camera operator.

At the click of the clapper board, she sprinted towards the lake. Wincing as sticks and pebbles scraped the soles of her feet, she dodged the slender birches in her path.

"Too fast," Gustav Machatý called to her, his voice amplified and altered by his megaphone. "No one pursues you. You are hot from riding, wanting to feel cool. Again, please, Fraulein Hedy."

For her next attempt, she followed his instruction. She stifled a gasp as the frigid water enveloped her and began to swim, careful to keep her head up.

"Shift onto your back."

An experienced swimmer, she flipped her body, holding herself afloat with gentle kicks. The midday sun seared her face, and she tried not to squint.

"Now you discover your horse ran away."

She contorted her features in a panicked expression and cried out, then paddled vigorously to the bank. When she emerged from the lake, her drenched, unclothed body was fully revealed to the director, the sound technician, and the cameraman. Turning, she fled into the woods.

"No, no. Along the shore where you can be seen. Back into the water and come out again."

And again. And again.

Breathless, her arms and legs aching from exertion, she covered herself with a robe and bound her dripping head with a towel.

Her rise from lowly script girl to bit player in insignificant pictures to leading actress was swift—dedication to her craft combined with her desire to please had garnered her directors' respect. When offered the primary role in this highly prestigious picture, she hadn't been deterred by the required nudity. If the story was simple, it was also filled with conflict and passion and heartbreak. Hedy's sympathy for her character, the virginal and unhappy bride, found its way into her performance, for she shared Eva's yearning for independence and sexual fulfillment.

Everyone who sees this movie will remember Hedy Kiesler, she assured herself.

⬦

When the light faded, a thick mist rose to curtain the Carpathian peaks. The production convoy returned to Dobšiná, a sleepy Czechoslovakian village.

As they were driven to their inn, Hedy leaned against her co-star's solid frame. "You already knew how I look without clothes. Today the whole crew saw me naked."

"Don't bother your pretty head about those Czechs," Aribert replied. A German, he was disdainful of other Europeans.

"They gossip about me."

"True," he conceded. "Earlier today Machatý told me something about you. He says you're seventeen."

"I won't be after November."

Her age wasn't the only fact she'd kept from him. She had four Jewish grandparents, something she wasn't comfortable admitting to a fervent admirer of Hitler and Germany's National Socialists.

"How could your parents let you come here by yourself?"

"They didn't like it, but I was able to persuade them." Only after protracted debate and copious tears. "I'm sure Mutti and Papa are praying for me." Her parents, like many of their social class, were Catholic converts, her father nominally and her mother devoutly. Hedy, brought up in that faith, had begun her education in a convent school.

How shocked those grim old nuns would be, she reflected, if they knew I was naked most of the day, in view of camera and crew as I swam in a lake and chased a runaway horse.

Her parents had been slow to accept her choice of profession, and today's scenes would revive their objections.

I'll tell them I was unaware of the camera's position, she decided. It's no lie. The sun was in my eyes, and I had to concentrate on what the director told me to do.

Aribert, ten years her senior and with several movies to his credit, played her lover in the German and Czech versions of the script. A French actor portrayed Adam in a third version.

"Pierre likes you. You like him. I've seen you laughing together."

"He pronounces my name 'Eddie,' no matter how many times I correct him. He can't say 'Hay-dee,' because of the 'h' sound. I was teaching him—'huh, huh, huh.' It was funny."

Beneath her skirt, his hand skimmed her bare leg, sliding up to her thigh. Like her, he was thinking of the mutual pleasure they would find when he joined her in bed.

"You don't mind," she murmured against his ear, "my age?"

"During our last film, you said hardly a word to me, or anyone else. You seemed so shy. Now I know better."

As reel after reel of film was shot and canned, Hedy participated in several on-set debates about certain aspects of her performance. With firm conviction, she proclaimed that her nakedness was no more scandalous than unclothed females in the Old Master paintings on display in Vienna's Belvedere galleries or the classical statuary in Berlin's Altes Museum.

When the company left Prague for Vienna to shoot interiors at Schönbrunn Studios, Hedy returned to her parents' elegant apartment in Peter-Jordanstrasse, thankful for home comforts after her summer of gypsy living.

<hr />

After its Prague premiere, *Ecstasy* was lauded as an impressive achievement in filmmaking, and Czech critics hailed it as Machatý's masterpiece. In a letter to Hedy he quoted reviews extolling her photogenic face and expressive performance. But references to her nude scenes and on-screen orgasm meant she couldn't share these affirmations with her parents.

In the weeks before her film's Vienna release, she received frequent interview requests from curious arts journalists. What would be her next role? Was she planning to marry Aribert Mog? Had her swimming scene and the on-screen lovemaking helped or hurt her career?

On a wintry evening she accompanied Mutti and Papa to one of several cinemas screening *Ecstasy*. A society dressmaker had designed her gown for the occasion, and she carried the fur coat she'd purchased herself with beauty contest prize money. Before taking her seat, she scanned the crowd but didn't see Machatý or anyone else from the production.

Surely her parents, so proud of her elevation to star status, would appreciate the quality of the filmmaking and the director's innovations. Their tastes were sophisticated and progressive. In her own way she followed in the footsteps of the Kiesler family's most famous member—Cousin Friedrich was a world-renowned theatrical designer and modernist architect, now living in New York City.

The audience buzzed with anticipation when the lights dimmed and the music started. The letters of the title faded in, superimposed over Hedy's indistinct face. In the opening shot, shiny black shoes stepped onto a doormat, and hands fumbled with a set of keys. After a comic struggle, the aged bridegroom struggled to carry his much younger bride across the threshold.

Her mother expelled an appreciative sigh. "A lovely wedding dress and veil!"

"You are exquisite," her father whispered.

The camera maintained an ominous and symbolic focus on certain objects—the decaying bridal bouquet, a house fly in its death throes. The cinematography and imagery were painterly. Cottony clouds floated above a Carpathian mountain vista. Fronds of grain swayed in the breeze.

Eva deserted her disinterested, impotent husband, seeking solace at her family home in the countryside. Clad in an impractical white silk garment, she guided a horse along a tree-lined avenue.

Hedy's heartbeat accelerated, and she twisted her fingers together. The swimming scene was about to begin.

After a tracking shot of branches and quivering leaves, she emerged naked from the woodland and ran to the lake, plunging into the water. When she floated on her back, her breasts were visible, their nipples a darker contrast to her pale, sun-blanched skin.

Mutti seized her hands, squeezing hard. "Hedl, how *could* you?"

Her cheeks burned when her naked figure loped along the shore. "It's artistic, the same as a painting. And *avant-garde*."

An eruption of laughter, derision, and shock drowned her whispered words. Her bare breasts had filled the screen, an instant before she turned to chase her fleeing horse across a broad field.

Papa stood, hat in hand, and grasped Mutti's elbow. "We will go. Now!"

Hedy reached for her fur coat and hurried up the aisle, but her passage was blocked by others making a swift departure. She looked around, curious to know how much of the audience remained to watch her performance. Gray heads wagged in dismay. Young men grinned. Young women stared open-mouthed. Hisses and catcalls followed her into the lobby.

"The camera was placed at a great distance from me," she told her parents when she caught up with them. "How could I know it had a zoom lens? Nobody told me."

At least they were spared the sight of Eva—of their daughter—writhing in her lover's arms as she experienced her first orgasm.

No more film roles for me, she mourned. After tonight Mutti won't take me to Hollywood, and Papa will never permit me to travel there alone. To continue as a professional actress, I'll have to find stage work.

And keep my clothes on.

———◇·◆·◇———

Hedy attempted to mollify her outraged parents with impeccable behavior. She played chess with Papa and piano duets with Mutti, and card games with both of them. She whiled away her solitary hours with word puzzles, or the Märklin mechanical steamship she was trying to repair.

On bright days she bundled up for invigorating walks in the nearby Türkenschanzpark or the Vienna Woods. Occasionally, she visited a café popular with theatrical friends, former classmates from Max Reinhardt's acting academy at the Schönbrunner Schlosstheater, to exchange gossip and share aspirations.

She accepted an offer from Theatre an der Wien to be Paula Wessley's understudy in the Marischka brothers' popular operetta *Sissi*. The promise of eventual promotion to the title role reconciled her to singing in the chorus and appearing in crowd scenes. Paula, one of Reinhardt's most successful protégées, wanted a film career, and Hedy looked forward to replacing her as the hoydenish young aristocrat who unexpectedly won Franz Josef's heart to become Austria's beloved Empress.

The production's technical aspects fascinated her. When she begged the light board operator to teach her about the controls, he responded with an incredulous snort.

"You're an actress, Fraulein. Why should you care about such a thing?"

"I'm interested in mechanics. As a child I took apart my music box and was able to put it back together, without any help. Papa and I collect our neighbors' broken-down clocks so I can try to repair them."

"Do you succeed?"

Laughing, Hedy confessed, "I've never made one run again. But the parts are in such a sorry state, it's no wonder." Her forefinger hovered over one of the levers. "This one you call a dimmer—is that right? Which light does it connect with?"

"I'll show you."

She tipped her head back as he pointed at the array of light cans positioned above the stage, angled to brighten different areas. They produced the *helligkeit*, he explained, the broadest illumination. He described the merits of modern Fresnel lenses. He compared the improved spotlights to the outdated carbon arc lights. They returned to the board for a tutorial, and she proved so quick a pupil that he told her to come early to the theatre tomorrow, before the other technicians and performers arrived, to perfect her new skills.

That night she spent her backstage hours sketching the electrical circuitry and making a diagram of the light grid.

Upon Paula Wessely's departure, Hedy was distressed to discover that her former schoolmate Rose Stradner, another promising product of Reinhardt's acting academy, was taking on the star role. Burying her resentment, she blithely asserted to fellow cast members that Rose was the better singer. Their assurances that she was more beautiful and closely resembled the real Sissi were meager consolation.

After a month as Rose's understudy, she was called to the director's office. Hubert Marischka's glowering face didn't prepare her for his brusque declaration.

"Fraulein Kiesler, the management has terminated our agreement with Fraulein Stradner. From tonight you are the new Sissi. This after-noon we will rehearse you. Go to the wardrobe mistress for costume alterations. You're thin as a lamppost, and all the gowns need taking in. Tomorrow you pose for publicity pictures and lobby placards. The announcement for the press is prepared."

Dazed, she read through the contract he presented, and signed it. A reduction in box office receipts since Rose joined the cast must have convinced him that the *Ecstasy* actress, already familiar with the part, would be a more profitable option.

A wardrobe assistant's experienced fingers pinched and pinned the waist and bodice of the frothy gowns Hedy had yearned to wear, fitting them to her newly svelte figure. After seeing her entire body exposed on the screen, she'd followed a rigorous slimming regimen.

"My breasts are even smaller than they were before my diet," she told the woman regretfully, studying the tape measure that circled her chest.

"Don't fret, *liebchen*. You have a face to compensate for what you lack below."

In her parents' eyes, her portrayal of teenaged Countess Elisa-beth of Bavaria removed most of *Ecstasy's* lingering taint. This was a respectable role, and they were proud of her success. Press and public praised her performance, and reviewers judged her versatility and talent as generously as they did her appearance.

Night after night every theatre seat was sold. Newspapers and theatrical journals printed Hedy's photograph. Numerous admirers gathered at the stage door, waiting to see her when she exited. Her dressing room overflowed with floral tributes, each of them accom-panied by an engraved card bearing the *Friedrich Alexander Mandl*.

One night during curtain call, an army of ushers carried enormous baskets of flowers to the stage and placed them at her feet, a spectacle that was equally embarrassing and flattering. Marveling at her admir-er's persistence, she returned to her dressing room. A sturdy, dapper figure stood at the door.

"Herr Professor!" She kissed Max Reinhardt on each cheek. "Did my performance please you?"

"Very much," he replied. "You made me believe the character, and you sang well. I'm not surprised to hear that the most beautiful girl in the world might go to Hollywood," he added, following her inside.

"Paramount Pictures offered a contract, but I haven't accepted it. Not yet." Thus far, parental objections had proved insurmountable.

"I wonder what those prudish Americans make of *Ecstasy*." He tilted his curly head. "Did you know about the nudity beforehand?"

For the first time she admitted the full truth. "It was in the script. But Machatý assured me the scene would be tasteful and very brief."

Max bent over a basket of flowers to read the card. His cheerful expression gave way to a grim one. "Be careful, Hedy," he warned. "Fritz Mandl is no man to trifle with."

"I've never met him."

"Surely you know who he is. And what he is." His voice was edged with contempt.

"Rich enough to afford all these flowers," she said airily.

"My dear, Mandl manages munitions factories, and his fortune is one of the largest in Austria. He associates with Austrofascists. He funds the *Heimwehr* militia and is the chief supplier of arms to Mussolini. Herr Hitler, Germany's new chancellor, is probably a customer. Mandl is ruthless in business, unconcerned with legalities or established treaties."

"I'm not political."

"No, not yet, because you're young and idealistic. Jews are being struck down and murdered in Berlin's streets and all over Germany. Their creations—books and music—are fuel for bonfires. You must know that."

She bowed her head in acknowledgment of the anti-Semite atrocities committed over the border. Adolf Hitler's ascent had driven many film and theatre professionals from Berlin to Vienna.

"When the foulness afflicting Germany oozes into Austria—already it begins—anyone whose birth was recorded as Jewish will have much to fear. I know you profess a different faith from that of your ancestors. It will make no difference. Our race, our very blood, is hated." He held up Fritz Mandl's card and waved it in the air. "He's as vulnerable as we are. His wealth and power won't protect him."

"What an excellent actor you must have been, Herr Professor."

His melodious voice lightened when he said, "Enough of dark matters. Come to our festival in Salzburg this summer. Bring your parents. We can make plans. Tonight, you convinced me you can be the fine actress I always imagined."

His cautionary words about Fritz Mandl whetted her curiosity. The next time she received a note requesting a meeting, she didn't send it back with the usual refusal.

At the end of the performance she rose from her final curtsy and rushed to her dressing room, so crammed with vases and baskets that she had difficulty moving about. After the dresser helped her out of the elaborate gown and crinoline and set the heavy braided wig on its stand, Hedy gave her a bouquet of roses to take home.

She changed into her street clothes, wishing she had time to remove her makeup. When the knock came, she was frantically brushing her hair. "Come in."

Her visitor was no taller than she was. His broad, satisfied smile was slightly angled to the left. "I'm delighted to meet you at last, Fraulein Kiesler. Every night for weeks I come, only to have my hopes dashed."

"You are kind to send so many flowers."

He leaned down to pluck a white orchid from an arrangement and inserted the stem into the lapel of his tuxedo jacket. "I invite you to be my companion at a private supper I've ordered for us. My chauffeur and limousine are waiting."

He expected her to be available—or to make herself so. Annoyed by his presumption and his confidence, she replied crisply, "Not tonight, Herr Mandl." Offering no apology, she retrieved her handbag from the dressing table.

"Another time, then. I look forward to becoming acquainted. I daresay you've heard about me."

"Nothing good," she retorted.

Smoothly he responded, "Then you really must give me a chance to repair your poor impression."

"That could take a very long time. I don't have any to spare."

He blocked her only path to the door, preventing the regal exit she intended. His amused expression annoyed her. Determined to avoid physical contact, she aimed her foot at a flower-filled urn and delivered a mighty kick. As it toppled over, it took down several similar obstacles. On leaving the room, Hedy was pleased to see Fritz Mandl surrounded by a swelling pool of water and broken blossoms.

Chapter 2

Hedy placed a cushion from one of the wicker armchairs on the veranda's hard floorboards and sat down to inspect the object she'd brought home from the theatre. Inside the battered wooden box was the military field telephone the light technician had used during the Great War, for secret communications in the trenches. Hers to keep, he'd said, and to disassemble. She studied the instructions and diagrams printed on the label glued inside the lid. Age and regular use had scarred the dark leather padding around the handset's earpiece, and the cord was frayed. Tentatively she turned the hand crank. After a brief resistance, it moved.

Music poured through the parted drawing room window as Mutti's accomplished fingers hammered the keys of her grand piano. Her choice of composer was always a reliable indicator of her mood. When contented, she chose Mozart. For melancholy moments she preferred Chopin. Hedy wondered which problem had prompted the booming rhapsodies by Franz Liszt—so jarring for poor Papa, kept from his office by a migraine. The actress daughter who bared her body in a scandalous movie? Her ailing husband, striving to restore his bank to solvency amid economic crisis and threats of nationalization?

Mutti's father, a Budapest musician, had overseen her training as a concert pianist. She relinquished her dream after marriage and the arrival of her only child. An attentive and devoted mother, she dispensed criticism instead of hugs and kisses, believing excessive affection could spoil a girl. To stifle vanity, she never complimented Hedy's appearance and instructed her to avoid mirrors.

Papa compensated by showering her with endearments. She was his Princess Hedy, so clever and creative. In her childhood, he'd joined in her games and read aloud from favorite fairy tale books. During long walks through the city, he'd patiently answered every question. From him she learned about the mechanics of automobiles and streetcars. He recited the history of the magnificent buildings and statues they passed, in their beloved Vienna and the other European cities they visited on holiday. He provided her with an allowance so she could purchase the movie magazines she craved. At Swiss ski resorts, they competed in daring contests on the slopes.

Both parents worried that *Ecstasy* had ruined her chances of providing them with a rich and respectable son-in-law who would cure her impetuous behavior and penchant for drama. If she didn't intend to put her curiosity and intellect to good use by continuing her formal education, they regularly told her, she needed to marry.

The doorbell's clang interrupted Mutti's playing.

"The gentleman's card," said the parlor maid. "He came in a limousine."

After a brief silence, Papa responded, "You may send him in."

His position as manager of the Creditanstalt Bank, founded by the Rothschilds, placed him at the summit of Viennese society. Prominent businessmen visited him in Döbling, and on occasion the Kieslers had received minor royalty. But never at this hour of the morning.

Hedy's most determined admirer possessed a limousine.

After his visit to her dressing room, Fritz Mandl had obtained her address and telephone number. When he called her at home, she wouldn't speak to him, nor did she respond to the messages he left with the servants or staff at the theatre. Yesterday he'd sent a magnificent bouquet to Mutti, a stratagem that prompted prying questions for which Hedy had no easy answers.

She moved closer to the drawing room window, careful to keep out of view.

"Herr Kiesler, I'm very pleased to meet you," Fritz Mandl said. "And you, Frau Kiesler. I hope I don't intrude at an inconvenient time."

After thanking him for her roses, Mutti offered coffee and cakes. His prompt acceptance ensured that his visit would be lengthy.

"I wish you might persuade your daughter to see me again," he said. "Although I met her only once, very briefly, I am eager to know her better. Everyone speaks highly of her. And beyond doubt, she's the most beautiful creature I've ever seen."

Mutti said apologetically, "Our Hedl suffers from shyness."

"I don't object to your becoming better acquainted with her," Papa responded, "as long as you keep in mind that she's only eighteen. What is your age?"

"Thirty-three. I must admit that I ask more than your permission to call on her and take her out. To put it more plainly, I wish to court her. And eventually, to make her my wife."

His declaration stunned her parents into silence. Hedy, overwhelmed, leaned against the wall.

One of Europe's richest men, with the reputation of a heartless seducer, was stating honorable intentions in no uncertain terms.

Papa broke the silence, saying soberly, "In that case, Herr Mandl, I require information of a personal nature."

"Certainly. My father was a Hungarian, and a Jew. My mother, a household servant, was Catholic. They didn't marry till I was ten, and by then he'd converted. During the war his munitions company flourished, but the aftermath was ruinous. He went bankrupt and was forced to sell the firm my grandfather founded. After years of hard work and extensive negotiation, I restored Hirtenberger Patronen-fabrik to our family. Because we manufacture necessary commodities, we remain profitable despite shifting political winds."

"You are fortunate. The banking business suffers, as do many Austrian enterprises. The collapse and dissolution of our empire has been disastrous."

"I, too, was born in Hungary," Mutti volunteered. "Emil, isn't it exciting? You'll give your consent, of course."

"I see no reason not to."

Perplexed by their willingness to entrust her future to this bold and persuasive stranger, Hedy crept down the steps to the garden. She wouldn't see Mandl today. In her white blouse and flowery dirndl, smudged with dust and dirt from the field telephone, she resembled a girl, not a rising star of stage and screen. At their next meeting—apparently inevitable—she must appear older than her years, not younger.

At most, she thought, he'll be a social acquaintance. Nothing more. Nobody can make me marry him if I don't want to.

⸺◆⸺

Two weeks. Within that brief time, Fritz Mandl melted Hedy's initial resolve to deny him all that he demanded—her time, her attention, and her affection.

Hedy, whose wealthy parents fulfilled her every desire, was astonished by the vastness of Fritz's fortune. He owned properties all across Europe, filled with valuable antiques and art. He employed dozens of servants. His circle of friends included princes and prime ministers and potentates, and he frequently referred to gatherings that included Prince Ernst von Starhemberg, Chancellor Dollfuss, or Benito Mussolini of Italy.

However fierce he might be in his business dealings, when escorting her to restaurants or nightclubs, his manners were formal and rather old-fashioned. She relished being driven around Vienna in his black limousine, redolent of leather and wood polish. Receiving the attentions of a man so brilliant, so important, was novel and flattering. The scope of his knowledge and his worldly experience impressed and awed her.

On a bright Easter Sunday, she and her mother returned home from Mass to find his car in front of their house. Fritz leaned against it, smoking a cigarette, his face shaded by the brim of his Tyrolean hat. Beckoning to them, he lifted the car boot to display a woven basket the size of a shipping crate. It held covered dishes, neatly stacked, and an upright champagne bottle wrapped in a cloth, the neck glistening with moisture. Folded blankets cushioned the contents.

"I'm taking Fraulein Hedy into the hills for a picnic," he announced in his assertive fashion.

"Only if I can change out of my dress first." She'd grown accustomed to his commanding habit, but complete submission was not in her nature.

Wearing trousers and a thin cashmere cardigan more appropriate for this country excursion, she returned to the car and climbed in. The driver maintained a respectful speed through Döbling's Cottage District. Fritz wouldn't reveal their destination. Surprise was an essential component of his courtship, and he derived pleasure from holding her in suspense. Her assumption that the drive would end somewhere in the Vienna Woods turned out to be incorrect.

She felt sure they traveled southward. Yellow flowers brightened the green meadows—coltsfoot and primroses and celandine—and white and purple crocuses bloomed beside the farm cottages. Cattle and goats grazed the roadside fields. After Baden, wooded hills gave way to rugged Alpine peaks.

Fritz regaled her with tales of his stag hunting and deerstalking exploits, naming different types of rifles and offering a detailed assessment of their capabilities. No wonder he liked blasting guns. One of his factories, she'd learned, produced cartridges.

"You have experience in the sport?" he asked.

"Not enough to know whether I'm a good shot."

"I can teach you to shoot targets or game, whichever you prefer. You will have your own gun, one suitable for a woman."

Hedy laughed.

"What amuses you?"

"Europe's famous arms dealer wants to arm an actress."

"You will enjoy it."

Would she? Perhaps. She imagined him standing behind her, his hands cupping her elbows as he showed her how to improve her aim, and suddenly craved physical contact.

"I have many horses, so we will also ride together." He reached into his coat pocket for a gold case and lighter. After she declined his offer of a cigarette, he lowered the window on his side to release the smoke. "Döbling parish church must have been full this morning. Easter Mass draws those who rarely attend."

"The singing was beautiful, and the altar had as many flowers as my theatre dressing room." Her smile faded. "Pastor Johann urged us to contribute generously to our archbishop's relief fund for Ukraine famine victims. All those starving people have deserted the countryside for the cities in hopes of finding food. They die in the streets, hundreds of thousands of them."

The extent of the tragedy was incomprehensible. Born in the first year of the Great War, Hedy remembered nothing of it. From parents and grandparents, she'd learned about its horrors and numerous casualties. Too many of the soldiers who marched off to fight the enemy were slain on the battlefield. This was peacetime, yet ordinary people in a nearby country suffered and perished from crop failures and lack of food.

"Soviet officials turn a blind eye to the agricultural failures," Fritz responded, "evidence of the faults in their collectivist system. Where food suppliers and manufacturers are permitted to thrive, they can successfully serve their markets."

The politics underlying the disaster mattered less to her than the agony and death it caused. Turning to him, she said, "We who can afford to assist, must do so. Papa joined the relief effort. I hope you will."

"You're a compassionate creature, Hasi."

Little bunny, his favorite endearment. Baby rabbits were delightful, but they were also completely dependent and lacked personality.

"Compassion is worthless unless supported by action," she declared. "I can't help by moaning and wringing my hands. I wish I could do something besides make a monetary donation."

She lacked the botanical expertise to develop her solution to the problem. Crops failed from drought or excessive rain, from too much heat or dangerous frosts. If seeds and plants could be hybridized to flourish in any weather, food shortages would be eradicated. Her theory was sound, she was sure, but how to develop it?

"You know so many prominent men. Are any of them plant scientists? Or botanists?"

"I don't think so," he replied. "I trained in chemistry."

"The only class I never skipped. I loved our laboratory sessions. Measuring the liquids and heating the test tubes over the burner."

"A pretty girl in her school uniform, mixing love potions."

Even if she hadn't seriously considered a career as a chemist—her ambition had been firmly centered on performing—those hours in the school lab had proved her skill for precision and concentration.

A sidelong glance at her wristwatch told her they had traveled more than an hour. In order to receive holy communion, she'd skipped breakfast. Fortunately, the low rumble of tires on the roadway drowned out her empty stomach's moaning. A marker informed her that they were entering Schwarzau-im-Gebirge, an unfamiliar village in mountainous territory.

"We've reached the Höllental, Hell Valley. For many, many years the River Schwarza has supplied Vienna with water. From now on, when opening your taps, remember that. And think of me."

Farther along, he rapped the glass panel separating them from the driver, and the vehicle came to a gradual stop. Fritz got out and walked around to open Hedy's door.

The air at this altitude was crisp and cool, scented with fir from the nearby wood and smoke from a peak-roofed cottage. An appliqué of soft white clouds decorated the pure blue sky.

They crossed a meadow of swaying grasses and wildflowers to a spot that overlooked the valley. Fritz spread blankets on the ground. The chauffeur set down the food basket and opened the champagne before departing.

Fritz filled two glass beakers. Hedy waited for the hiss and the bubbles to subside before she sipped. She really must tell him she disliked the beverage he deemed so essential—even for the most casual outing. He let her arrange the salads, pastries, fresh fruit, and cheese. She was hungry enough to stuff her mouth but plied the silver cutlery with a ladylike delicacy that would have pleased Nixy, her childhood governess.

During the meal he enumerated the various game animals that inhabited the surrounding mountains. He described the excellent fishing the river afforded. The region was ideal for riding and cross-country walks. That he intended her to be his partner in these pursuits was perfectly clear, though not explicitly stated.

As soon as they finished eating, he drew her to her feet. He led her along a narrow path into the shadowy forest where the air was chilly. A woodpecker darted from tree to tree, shattering the silence as it drilled each trunk.

"Do you know where this track leads?"

"We won't get lost."

Their gradual descent brought them to the edge of the woodland. A dozen or so horses cropped the tender new grass in a pasture. The limousine was parked beside a large stable, one of several outbuildings.

Fritz pointed to the grandiose mansion. "Villa Fegenberg. The largest and most historic of my hunting lodges."

Their journey to Schwazau had taken on an unexpected significance. The picnic spot hadn't been chosen at random. She suspected he owned the ground upon which they had dined. And the forest.

His country residence contained antique furniture and Persian carpets. Its windows framed mountain vistas or colorful gardens. Glass-eyed hunting trophies—stags and bucks and goat-like chamois—stared sightlessly from the walls. In an alcove a great brown bear stood on its hind legs, teeth bared in a menacing snarl.

"Did he live in your forest?"

"I took him during a hunting trip in the Alps. Perhaps in Switzerland, but possibly in Italy. We were crossing from one into the other with almost every step. Fear not, Hasi, you're in no danger of being devoured. Not by any bear," he added, squeezing her forearm.

He visited his villa at intervals, yet the wood surfaces and silver candelabra and crystal sconces gleamed.

"The staff are vigilant," he explained when she commented on the caretaking. "I might turn up at any time, and often with important guests. I employ a butler and a housekeeper, several maids. Gardeners and stable workers and men who manage the kennel. My chef is excellent—I pay him and all the kitchen staff very high wages."

He took her to a sun-filled room with a porcelain stove in one corner and French doors that opened onto a terrace. Beyond it was a swimming pool.

"When you are my wife, we will share all that you've seen here. And so much more."

Lifting her head, she studied him. "Perhaps. Someday."

"You *will* marry me. Say yes, Hasi. I can give you anything—everything—you desire. Money and jewels and beautiful clothes. Houses all over Europe, with servants to manage them. Our life together will be wonderful beyond your dreams."

"How can you be sure I will make *you* happy? We've spent so little time together. We haven't even . . . " She hesitated.

"After our engagement, if you want, I will take you to bed. But when I formally ask your father's permission to make you my wife, I must do so as an honorable man. Not as your seducer."

"I've had lovers, Fritz."

His hand clamped down on her shoulder, the thumbs pressing her collarbone. "Don't! It tortures me to hear that. You will belong to me and no other. Say it!" His genuine dread of rivals revealed an insecurity at odds with his characteristic bravado.

"If we marry, I will be only yours."

"You already are." Now both hands were in her hair, tipping back her head to receive his kiss.

His insistent lips and his fingers against her scalp evoked dizzying sensations. No less surprising than his ability to arouse her was the extent of her arousal. If his very evident desire moved him to lay her down on the velvet settee, she would let him.

He stepped back, not quite releasing her. "I should take you home."

Dazed, and somewhat disappointed, she nodded.

Throughout their drive back to Döbling, he was in an expansive mood, planning future travels and sporting excursions about which she made no comment. The surge of passion was dissipating, and she needed solitude to think about whether she wanted this man for her husband. She hadn't verbally accepted his proposal, but obviously he regarded her kisses as tacit consent.

Her parents were in the garden, surveying clumps of flowering bulbs. Mutti, her dark hair neatly coiffed, looked so tiny next to Papa's towering figure.

"Did you have a pleasant time?" he asked.

"Fritz showed me his hunting property in the mountains. He wants to marry me," she blurted. Confronted by beaming faces, she clarified, "I didn't give him an answer."

Mutti's frown carved a crease between her eyebrows. "Hedl, why ever not?"

Impossible to explain what she couldn't quite comprehend. "It's such an important decision. And I had to find out if you approve. Now that you know him better."

"We do approve," Mutti answered. "Don't we, Emil? Tell her!"

Papa pulled his pipe stem from his lips. "In these uncertain times, money and influence are great advantages. Mandl is hard-working and well-connected."

"And so thoughtful," her mother added. "Sending flowers every day, here and to the theatre. He's devoted to you."

"He is," Hedy agreed.

"Don't make him wait too long, Hedl. You're lucky he's willing to overlook your scandal. Not many men would."

She looked to her father. "You think I should marry him to repair my reputation?"

"It would be beneficial." He added significantly, "For all of us."

His frankness wounded her. "This isn't my first proposal," she reminded them. "And I can't be sure I'm more prepared for marriage than I was the other times."

"How difficult will it be?" Mutti asked. "Surrounded by luxury, with an adoring husband, and plenty of servants to wait on you hand and foot."

Her parents' pragmatism wasn't as disheartening as the unsubtle, unhelpful pressure they applied. Climbing the veranda steps, it occurred to her that they hadn't asked whether she loved Fritz.

I must. When we were kissing, I felt quite sure.

A man so determined to succeed in all things would satisfy her sexually. His personality challenged her. His intellect and his knowledge were a good match for her curiosity.

He had a past. After his divorce he'd had a highly publicized affair with his second cousin, an actress. When he expressed reluctance to marry again, she'd committed suicide, the ultimate proof of her troubling instability. Hedy was haunted by a similar tragedy—a few years ago, a lover had killed himself when she rejected his proposal. Franz's act had shaken and scarred her, and ever since she'd avoided involvement with emotional young men. Shared loss and the residual remorse could only strengthen her bond with Fritz.

When she imagined life as Frau Mandl, it matched the picture both Fritz and her mother had drawn of mansions, servants, trips, recreation. Her upbringing and her training in the social graces ensured acceptance by Viennese society, and her parents had often received important people—politicians and captains of industry like those who formed Fritz's circle of friends.

Her professional prospects, she mused, might improve. After months of playing Sissi, repeating the same scenes and songs every night, she was eager for change. Supported by the Mandl fortune, she could be selective when accepting roles. Film production in Vienna was increasing with the influx of refugee directors and scriptwriters from Germany.

Her capitulation came during a late supper at Fritz's favorite restaurant. After their plates were cleared, he removed a small leather box from his coat pocket. He opened it and slid it across the tablecloth. "It's time for you to wear this,"

The ring was set with an excessively large aquamarine flanked by diamonds. Was it impulse or decisiveness that prompted her to slide it onto her fourth finger? It didn't matter. They both recognized the significance.

He signaled to a waiter, who carried over two glasses of champagne already poured in anticipation of the happy moment.

"To our love," Fritz said, raising his glass. "To our future." He drank. "Your parents must announce our engagement at once. Tomorrow you will leave the theatre."

"I have a contract."

"And I have lawyers. The very best. They'll deal with the management."

"No!"

"Why delay the inevitable? You can't go on with being an actress after you become my wife."

"Why not?"

"As Frau Mandl, you will be far too busy for rehearsals and performance nights. I need you to serve as hostess for my dinner parties, be my dancing partner at society balls. On opera nights we shall sit together in my box. Business often requires me to travel, and sometimes you will accompany me."

Clearly, she would be unable to combine matrimony with a stage career. Struggling to accept all that he'd said, she discovered that her love for Fritz was far more potent than her ambition, more durable than long-cherished dreams of stardom. He'd marched into her life at a time when her highly-praised portrayal of Sissi had begun to eradicate the scandal of *Ecstasy*. Ever since intruding into her dressing room, he'd demonstrated his ability to provide unimagined comfort and security—and excitement. It was far too late to turn away from it all. And her heart, no longer fickle, now belonged entirely to him.

With a faint but valiant smile that barely concealed her regret, she said, "At least I retire as a success."

He came around to her side of the table, saying, "We will spend our honeymoon in Venice, on the Lido. My secretary will book a suite at the Excelsior." When he bent to kiss her, his display of affection delighted the other diners, whose applause made her acutely aware of how much she would miss it.

Two weeks separated Hedy's final stage performance from her wedding day. On a warm August morning, one of Fritz's drivers delivered her and her parents to the Karlskirche. She'd always dreamed of marrying in her Döbling parish church, with Pastor Johann conducting the ceremony, but Fritz insisted on a more magnificent venue. As a compromise, he reluctantly assented to wed in the chapel rather than the baroque columned sanctuary.

Her mother's wish to see her wearing white satin also went unfulfilled. Hedy wouldn't revive memories of *Ecstasy* in a gown similar to the one she'd worn as the adulterous Eva. She arrived at the cathedral in a sophisticated black and white print dress from her Paris trousseau and carried a large bouquet of white orchids in place of the fragrant nosegay of lilies and roses and fern fronds she'd envisioned.

She linked arms with Papa and entered the chapel. Except for relatives, most of the two hundred guests were strangers. Max Reinhardt, seated at the back, was the only theatrical friend deemed sufficiently reputable for the occasion.

She and Fritz spoke their vows as instructed, and he placed a gold band on her finger. After the priest's blessing, they withdrew to the sacristy to sign the register.

The Grand Hotel—not the familiar old Sacher, Hedy's preference—was the venue for their wedding luncheon. She clung to her new husband when his father, Alexander Mandl, welcomed her into the family. His sister Renée Ferro and her Italian husband kissed her cheeks, murmuring polite and subdued felicitations. Her Litchtwitz cousins from Budapest gathered around to bestow hearty hugs, chattering in Hungarian. Champagne flowed, and the elaborate meal began with a series of toasts.

Fritz escorted her from their table to circulate among their guests. While he received congratulations from his close friend Prince Ernst von Starhemberg, she slipped away to speak with Max.

"I'm so glad you came."

"The stage suffers a loss today, but society gains," he said wryly. "You worked hard and well, this year. A pity to waste your talent and experience." Pitching his voice low, for her ears only, he added, "When you weary of your *hausfrau* role, come to me."

She would. Fritz adored her, and eventually she would persuade him that she should her resume her career.

At the conclusion of the festivities, she and Fritz ascended the grand staircase. Moments after they shut themselves away in their wedding night suite, he told her to remove her ring.

"I don't want to take it off so soon," she protested.

He seized her hand and pried it off. Pressing it into her palm, he said, "Look inside. Read the inscription."

She carried the tiny circle of gold to the nearest lamp and held it under the light.

You are my love

"And you are mine," she declared. "Now put this back where it belongs, if you want me to get into bed with you."

Chapter 3

Married life turned out to be the romantic adventure Fritz had promised. Not for his bride the hotel water taxi. He hired a private launch for day trips from the Lido to Venice, and a gondola when they arrived. Lounging against velvet cushions, her hand in her husband's, Hedy floated dreamlike along the shimmering Grand Canal and beneath the shadow cast by the Rialto Bridge. Any shop goods she admired, he purchased—lengths of Venetian lace and Italian silk, a set of Murano glass perfume bottles, a triple strand of pearls. In the afternoon they returned to the Excelsior to wander its beachfront at sunset and drink cocktails in one of its Moorish-style lounges. After dinner they danced across the gleaming wooden floor of the Sala Stucci, an ornate ballroom, before retreating to their suite.

As expected, her bridegroom's lovemaking was highly proficient. The first time she initiated sex, he scolded, "You are my bride, not my mistress." Curbing her boldness, she ceded control to him and waited to be seduced.

She especially enjoyed dining on the elevated terrace that overlooked the tennis courts. One day, before their first lunch course was served, a young man bearing a racquet approached their table. Fritz, absorbed by a German-language newspaper, failed to notice until a hesitant voice addressed Hedy.

"Fraulein Kiesler, I saw *Ecstasy* in Vienna. Three times. You're my favorite star of the cinema, and . . . " He swallowed. "I hope you'll soon appear in another film."

Down came the newspaper. "Show some respect for my wife's privacy." Fritz's voice was as cold and hard as a glacier. "She is no longer an actress."

Her admirer's shoulders sagged, and he stammered an apology.

Hedy intervened. "I appreciate the compliment, but as my husband says, I've retired from performing. Are you enjoying your stay here?"

"Indeed. Thank you. Good day to you." He made a quick escape. As he hurried down the broad stone staircase, he struck one of the crouching lion statues with the head of his racquet.

"You should wear dark glasses," Fritz grumbled. "And a hat."

"I dislike hats."

"Then why do you buy so many?" He folded his paper. "It must be shocking, that travesty of a film."

"You didn't see it?"

He shook his head. "I will not watch objectionable scenes featuring my wife."

"We didn't even know each other then," she pointed out.

He stood up. "Let's go inside."

"What about our food?"

"They can deliver it to our rooms. You've been sitting in this sun too long. I mustn't let you burn."

The rest of their itinerary was a mystery, because he liked surprising her. She was learning to enjoy the present and ask no questions about the future.

From Venice he swept her and her trunks of new clothes and their two servants southward to Capri, a dry and rugged island surrounded by the bluest of seas. Then he took her north to Lake Como, where the sapphire water and dramatic peaks were more to her liking. On France's Côte Basque, she ventured into the famous salt baths that

Empress Sissi had frequented. She shopped at Biarritz Bonheur.

But resort living and an unvarying routine of pleasure-seeking was no longer novel, and her enjoyment was waning. The sun's constant glare sparked headaches. Late summer was the ideal season in Austria's forests and lakes and mountains. If only Fritz would put down his phone and take her home to familiar places, where she could feel more like her true self.

I ought to be grateful, she acknowledged. He's generous to a fault, and I've never been so indulged and cossetted.

His preoccupation with impending disarmament discussions kept him tied to the Hotel du Palais.

"We cannot permit Germany to re-arm," he told her when he concluded another of his lengthy telephone conversations. "It poses too grave a danger to Austria. The Nazis are already among us, lying in wait."

"I thought our government prohibited party membership."

"Officially, yes. But the threat remains. Hitler bides his time. Which is why representatives of France, Britain, and the United States are about to meet in Paris. Next month they will present proposals at a larger conference in Geneva."

Repeatedly he instructed the operator to connect him to Austria's Chancellor Dollfuss, to Prince von Stahremberg's Vienna palace, to Mussolini's villa in Riccione. None of the ensuing discussions satisfied him.

"Mussolini fears that Hitler might remove Germany from of the League of Nations," he reported. "He is furious at the prospect."

While he sought additional intelligence from his highly-placed sources, Hedy sat on the balcony and paged through *Vogue* and *Marie Claire,* studying the skillful cut and intricate detail of garments created by Chanel and Schiaparelli. She disliked the models' static, vapid faces, rendered identical by *maquillage* that obliterated any evidence of personality. Who were these pale, artificial women, joylessly cavorting on city streets and beaches, seated at café tables or floating across a ballroom? Why would any sensible female aspire to be a lifeless *mannequin*?

Her husband joined her, drink in hand. "I want to take you to the Côte d'Azur. And after a few days in Cannes and Nice, on to Paris. Where every honeymoon couple should go."

And where, he'd admitted earlier, disarmament talks would take place.

He formed plans and made arrangements without consultation, and to preserve marital harmony, she refrained from debate. But she couldn't maintain this passivity indefinitely.

On Fritz's orders, the maid packed Hedy's suitcases, and his valet supervised the transfer of the luggage to a limousine. Their little party boarded a private plane at midday and reached Cannes in time for dinner.

Examining her artistically arranged plate, Hedy doubted there was any type of fish or seafood she hadn't consumed during this protracted pleasure trip. It was a wonder she hadn't sprouted gills and a tail. She went swimming so often that both would be useful.

"What makes you smile?" Fritz asked.

"A funny thought."

"Share it."

"It wouldn't amuse you." He might regard it as criticism.

Swiveling in his chair, he surveyed the room. "Which one?"

His query perplexed her.

"The two men, staring at you. You smiled at one of them. Do you know him?"

For the first time she noticed their fellow diners, tanned and exceptionally handsome in their evening attire. "He's a British actor. I can't remember his name. The other might be also."

"Look at me," he demanded. "Promise you will avoid them. Such men cannot be trusted, Hasi."

Waiting until he finished his cognac and smoked the rarest available cigar down to a stub, she was careful not to let her attention stray to any other table.

Easy enough to behave with discretion, but she had no power to regulate male behavior. How could she avoid recognition while dining in a hotel, or deflect the sort of admiring glances she'd encountered ever since reaching adolescence? Fritz had married her in part for her beauty and, she believed, to stir envy in other males. As a man of the world, he ought to recognize the uncomfortable consequences of marrying an actress associated with a notorious film.

For the rest of their stay in Cannes and later in Nice, she took pains to be circumspect. On leaving the hotel she wore a concealing broad-brimmed hat and dark glasses, despite her conviction that they made her more conspicuous than not.

She expected a less challenging time in Paris, a city she'd sometimes visited with her parents. Unfortunately, Fritz didn't share her fondness for morning excursions to galleries or strolls through the lush parks. His mornings were devoted to telephone conversations, conducted in German or simple Italian. At his request, she remained in their rooms until he returned from his various lunches and afternoon meetings. At night, he took her to the most celebrated restaurants before visiting his choice of club or casino.

"Poor Hasi," he said one day, "your patience deserves a reward."

It was a short taxi ride to the celebrated shopping district. At one end of Rue Faubourg St. Honoré, he encouraged her to order evening gowns at Monsieur Rochas's atelier. She bought day dresses and a bottle of perfume in Maison Chanel, tucked into the Rue Cambon, and acquired other items at various establishments between the two. And he took her to the Cartier boutique at 13 Rue de la Paix.

"At the Paris Opera tonight, you must sparkle," he said as they stood before the window display. "Choose something. Anything."

Looking past her own reflection in the glass, she eyed the array spread across dark velvet, jewels sufficient to adorn a dozen women. "The pearl bracelet matches the necklace from Venice."

"True. But the diamond tiara would complement the earrings I gave you. Shall we inquire?" He drew her towards the arched entrance.

The doorman performed his duty. The shop's elegantly dressed clientele spoke in reverent murmurs, as though in a church. A male member of staff moved to greet them but was forestalled by a female who wore her hair in a chignon. The bony face, as expressionless as a Vogue model's, relaxed slightly.

"Monsieur Mandl, a pleasure to see you once more."

"The treasures in your shop window are so enticing that my wife cannot choose just one. She will have all of them."

Hedy burned with embarrassment. How greedy she must appear, and except for the tiara and the bracelet, she couldn't even recall the contents of the display.

If Mademoiselle was astonished, she hid it well. "The items will be removed at once. Would you like to try them on, Madame Mandl, to see if any want re-sizing?"

"Of course." Fritz never failed to answer for her.

After a brief colloquy with an underling, Mademoiselle Toussaint ushered them into her office for a private examination of their purchases. In addition to the sole piece Hedy had considered, she was gaining the tiara, a ruby-encrusted platinum bangle, pearl drops, a wide gold band etched with a Greek key design, a watch with a rectangular face and narrow black leather strap, a pair of diamond clips, and a diamond necklace.

And a ring, the likes of which she'd never seen—or imagined.

"The very finest of large stones." Mademoiselle proffered the case. "Eleven carats. An eighteen-karat gold setting."

"Here, Hasi." Fritz removed her aquamarine and placed the diamond next to her wedding band. "Your new engagement ring. A perfect fit."

"As if made for her," said the lady jeweler. "The other purchases will be packed and sent to Madame at . . . at Le Bristol?"

"The Ritz."

Evidently Fritz had made other visits to Cartier, doubtless to purchase a pricey bauble or two for a mistress.

The delicate diamond crescent made its debut at the opera. Ascending the Palais Garnier's grand staircase, Hedy self-consciously fingered her new necklace. As her hand slid up the cool marble balustrade, the *torchières* drew fire from her massive ring. She didn't doubt that

Fritz derived greater satisfaction from the evidence that he'd spent a fortune on her adornment than he would from the performers' vocal artistry.

———◁•◆•▷———

Benito Mussolini was coming to dinner.

This was no state visit. Italy's leader came to Vienna for a dual purpose: to continue a private negotiation with Fritz for weapons produced by Hirtenberger Patronen-fabrik Industries, and to confer with influential Austrians about his faltering relationship with Chancellor Dollfuss.

"Dining room diplomacy," Fritz explained to Hedy, before reeling off names of the politicians on his guest list. "We will use the gold dishes, the most splendid in all Europe. Il Duce's press attaché will make arrangements with our staff and impress upon them need for complete secrecy."

"What am I to do?"

"Very little," he assured her. "Look ravishing and charm our guest of honor. Wear a Paris gown and many diamonds."

Mutti's pet name for her was Snow White, for her resemblance to the ebony-haired, white-skinned, forest-dwelling heroine of the Brothers Grimm fairy tale. Now Fritz had transformed her into Cinderella, a princess with many castles, dining on golden plates and wearing gowns and jewelry that royalty might envy.

Her new home was a ten-room room apartment in the Ofenheim Palace, overlooking Schwarzenbergplatz. Like all Fritz's properties, this one was filled with antiques and carefully maintained by the seven household servants who received his orders. Hedy had no housekeeping role. Her responsibilities were few—serving as her husband's companion when he was at home, acting as his hostess when he entertained, and pleasing him in bed. The last she performed with expertise and genuine pleasure. But in the grand drawing room and at his long dining table, she played a part.

She selected a velvet gown of darkest blue and piled on the diamonds before she presented herself to Fritz for inspection. He examined her closely, while his valet applied a brush to his black tuxedo coat.

"No tiara?"

"Too much for a dinner at home. It's not the Opera Ball."

"I can always rely on your excellent judgment about what's appropriate. One of the reasons I married you." Gently he kissed her powdered cheek.

"I'll wear the diamond star that belonged to your mother. And my diamond clips."

Seated before her dressing table mirror, she watched her maid create a left side part in her dark hair, to which the starry ornament was attached.

An elaborate gown and all the diamonds couldn't disguise the fact that she was still in her teens. A little girl playing dress-up, that's how she would appear to Fritz's impressive company. Her ignorance about international affairs put her at a disadvantage, and she dreaded their disdain.

Mussolini, the first arrival, was accompanied by the Italian Ambassador Preziosi and an attaché. With his large head, lack of hair, and determined expression, he could be Fritz's father. When Hedy greeted him in Italian, he smiled approvingly.

"Signora Mandl, they tell me you're a famous actress. I have a fascination with the theatrical arts," the Italian leader declared. "Sit beside me during dinner."

She nodded, wondering how this command affected the careful seating plan Fritz and his butler had devised.

"How good of you to receive us at short notice. No doubt your husband explained we come in support of Austrian independence and autonomy. I will always oppose Hitler over the *Anschluss*. I'm determined to prevent an annexation by Germany, as I told your Chancellor Dolfuss when he came to my villa in Riccione last summer." There was an undercurrent of animosity when he uttered the name. Moderating his tone, he continued, "You and Mandl must also visit me there, Signora. My family and I will be delighted to welcome you."

She went to Fritz and said urgently, "Mussolini wants me next to him during the meal. He is interested in theatre, he says."

Fritz huffed. "Most of his mistresses have been actresses. Don't worry, Hasi, he won't try to seduce you. I am the supplier of what he most desperately wants—and it's not another woman."

Guns and bullets, she surmised. For what purpose?

Last year Fritz had stirred universal outrage by illegally supplying the Hungarian fascists with Italian weapons reconditioned in his factory, contravening the Treaty of St. Germain. He'd never mentioned the disgraceful incident to her, and what little she knew had been confided by Prince Ernst Rüdiger von Starhemberg, Fritz's friend and political associate. Leader of the Christian Socialist Party, Ernst was as fiercely anti-Nazi as Dollfuss and Mussolini. The cache of contraband rifles and machine guns, he'd explained, had been provided to Austria's home guard, the *Heimwehr,* primarily supported with Mandl money. An adequately armed military force was necessary to repel a German incursion. Therefore, what was roundly condemned as an international crime was in fact a national necessity. Far more disgraceful than the Hirtenberger weapons scandal, the prince declared, was Hitler's dangerous re-arming of Germany in violation of various treaties.

At the moment, Fritz's crafty brain was busy with matters of etiquette. "Mussolini will sit on your right," he told Hedy. "Ernst can go on your left side."

As a hereditary prince, prevented by law from using his title, Ernst retained an aristocratic polish singular in a politician. Hedy found him attractive, despite his beaky nose. The downward sloping mouth lent him a weak and wistful aspect at odds with his vigorous political machinations. After making small talk with the others, she gravitated to his side.

He followed up an exchange of pleasantries by asking, "Are you acquainted with the actress Nora Gregor of the Burgtheatre?"

"Not well. Max Reinhardt introduced us before she went to

Hollywood, but I haven't seen her since she returned."

His eyes narrowed slightly. "We're seeking a place of privacy—such as the home of a mutual friend—where we can be comfortable together, out of the public eye. I've no wish to expose Fraulein Gregor or my wife to hurtful gossip. Might we rely on you and Fritz? You'll find Nora compatible, and you've got the acting profession in common. Like you, she cares not at all for politics."

Skilled negotiators, Hedy was learning, invariably pointed out benefits to the person with whom they negotiated. "We'll invite both of you to dinner. And you may join us at Villa Fegenberg whenever we're there."

With his customary courtliness, he clicked his heels together and bowed over her hand.

Oh, these powerful married men, and their actress mistresses. Fortunate for her that Fritz began his pursuit long after his divorce and with matrimony in mind.

When they all gathered in the dining room, Mussolini waved Ernst aside and pulled out Hedy's chair.

"*Grazie mille,*" she murmured, taking her place.

A centrepiece extended the length of the table, a blue river of violets—difficult and expensive to obtain in winter interwoven with contrasting orchid blossoms. Gobelin tapestries covered the walls, and the heavy curtains were parted to reveal antique stained-glass windows. The *hors d'oeuvres*—paté and caviar—arrived promptly. For the fish course they had Lobster Thermidor, followed by *coté de veau milanais,* most likely to compliment the Italians.

Hedy divided her attention between her nearest companions, spewing simplistic responses to every commonplace remark. There was no substance to the conversation. The men talked of hunting and motorcars and sporting prowess. If she weren't present, no doubt they'd boast about women they'd bedded. Mussolini, on her right side, chewed vigorously and with evident enjoyment. Ernst, impeccably polite, was more attentive to his hostess than to his food. She ate sparingly of the rich food and cheeses, and by the time individual *pots de crème* appeared, she was full. And the fruit course had yet to arrive.

"Mandl, your chef's skill is as impressive as your wife's beauty," Mussolini declared at the conclusion of the meal.

Hedy's father mistrusted authoritarianism in all its forms and would deplore her husband's furtive association with these men. Because Papa's health, no longer robust, had deteriorated since her wedding day, she and Mutti conspired to shield him from unpleasantness. Nothing distressed him as much as the gathering danger the Nazis posed within Austria and beyond her borders.

In the drawing room, where masculine talk resumed, Mussolini reminded Fritz, with ill-concealed impatience, "We are here to discuss our concerns about Dollfuss."

The Italians nodded. Fritz and Ernst stared into their after-dinner drinks, thinking hard but saying nothing. Conscious of rising tension, Hedy wondered what political scheming would occur this night.

A meaningful glance was her husband's signal that she should leave. Obediently she excused herself.

"Signora Mandl, I look forward to meeting you in Italy this summer," Mussolini told her. "Before then, I mean to view *Ecstasy*."

The prospect of this man leering at her nakedness brought a flush to her face. Fritz clenched his jaw but stifled his evident displeasure, for Mussolini was too important a client to offend. He shepherded Hedy to the door and shut it firmly behind her.

The solid wood didn't quite block Mussolini's laborious German, and Hedy leaned close to listen.

"Prince von Starhemberg, I should think your chancellor's near-assassination would persuade him to support your *Heimwehr*."

"We trust he will," Ernst replied. "He intends to retain power by any possible means. We can ensure it. But if he alienates younger folk and others who are easily swayed by rhetoric and propaganda, they'll align with the Nazis instead of the Austrofascists."

"That would be fatal," Fritz asserted. "Hitler makes avowals of support for Austrian independence, but his intent is obvious. The *Heimwehr* is our best bulwark against his ambitions. But it is essential to maintain alliances with other nations. Italy. Hungary. Possibly even France and Great Britain."

Mussolini asked, "Would Dollfuss be open to overtures from Germany? From Hitler? If so, consider replacing him."

"With whom?" Ernst asked.

"Someone dependable, who will repel any attempt at an *Anschluss*. Fulvio, brief our friends on your meeting with the Führer."

The next speaker's tone was so low that Hedy couldn't make out his words, but she'd heard enough. Whatever ill wind blew in the Chancellor's direction, from Germany or Italy or elsewhere, Fritz and Ernst would protect Austria's interests—and their own.

———◦◆◦———

In every town from Salzburg to Vienna, men in Nazi uniforms crowded streets and squares. Their banners, marked with the garish swastika, were draped across public buildings and village halls. An alarmingly well-coordinated demonstration, Hedy realized, unsanctioned by Austria's government. She saw none of the violence that had plagued Vienna early in the year, but as the Mandl limousine approached the capital's suburbs, her apprehension increased.

She nudged her drowsing companion, seven months pregnant with Ernst von Starhemberg's child. "You'll be home soon."

Nora Gregor brushed a dangling lock of hair from her brow. "Already? How long did I sleep?"

"Since Vorchdorf, I think."

"I'm sorry. I should've been cheering you up."

"Impossible." She sighed. "Max said no director will employ me without my husband's consent."

To win Fritz's permission for the journey, Hedy persuaded him that refreshing mountain air would be more beneficial to Nora than the heat of the city. She hadn't mentioned her plan to consult her professional mentor, or that friendship with an actress had sparked a desire to resume her own career.

"Next month," she went on, "Max is staging the *Merchant of Venice*. In Venice, within the courtyard of the Campo San Trovaso. He wants to me to play Jessica, Shylock's daughter."

"Shakespeare is perfectly respectable. Fritz couldn't possibly object."

"I expect he will." She removed her compact from her handbag, intending to reapply her lipstick.

The car came to a sudden, jarring stop.

"Roadblock," Nora observed. "Could it be another insurrection?"

Martial law had been imposed during the February uprising, a brief period of gunfire and bloodshed and dead bodies lying in the streets, followed by thousands of arrests and many executions. In the aftermath, Chancellor Dollfuss was denounced for his ruthless reprisals and the reinstatement of the death penalty. But his unprecedented demonstration of strength and force won high praise from Mussolini, thawing the frostiness between them. Dollfuss presented a revised constitution with fascist overtones, similar to Italy's. In the spring, he and Mussolini and the Hungarian Prime Minister signed the Rome Protocols. Bolstered by this tripartite solidarity against Germany, Mussolini summoned Hitler to Venice—and regretted it. The Führer's behaviour hardened Il Duce's dislike and mistrust.

A pair of soldiers, each bearing a rifle, approached the chauffeur's side. Hedy, seated directly behind him, lowered her window. "Are we permitted to pass?"

One of the men leaned down to address her. A glossy curl of a black feather was attached to his *Heimwehr* cap. "Depends who you are. And where you mean to go."

Chapter 4

Hedy's heartbeat accelerated and her eardrums pounded. "I'm Frau Mandl, and this is Nora Gregor, the actress. We're on our way to my residence in Schwarzenbergplatz."

"You are related to Herr Friedrich Mandl?"

"My husband."

The taller soldier nodded in recognition. "You can prove your identity?"

She reached into her handbag and felt for the gold case that held her calling cards. The black onyx lid was inlaid with tiny diamonds forming her initials, HM. She handed it over.

He extracted a card and returned the case. "Excuse me, Frau Mandl, while I consult the officer in command."

When he was gone, she said, "Ernst is the leader of the *Heimwehr*. I should've explained that your safety is of great importance to him."

"We can't have any scandal." Nora's breath emerged in short gasps. "That's why he went alone to Italy."

Hedy pressed her friend's hand, coming in contact with a damp palm. "You can't faint till I can get you home. Lower your window and breathe the fresh air."

The soldier returned with a superior officer whose jacket was decorated with bars and badges. Leaning in, he surveyed the car interior, noting the ladies' handbags and a leather dressing case on the floor. "Our apologies, Frau Mandl, for the inconvenience to you. Tell me, please, from where you traveled."

"Salzburg."

"Not a good time to be on the roads. A rebellion broke out yesterday."

Her voice emerged as a feeble croak. "The Nazis. We saw groups of them, marching."

"They breached the arms depot and seized control of radio transmissions. Over a hundred invaded our Chancellery while the cabinet was meeting."

Nora collapsed against her.

Ernst, the Vice Chancellor was in Venice, far from present conflicts, but danger awaited him if he returned. Curling an arm around her friend's shoulder, she said shakily, "Fraulein Gregor needs immediate medical attention. Can I take her to my house?"

"This far from the city, we have no trustworthy radio reports. I'm not able to guarantee your safety if you proceed beyond this checkpoint."

The Mandl residence sat outside the Ringstrasse, the Chancellery was well within. She decided to take a chance. "I understand. If we encounter difficulty, I absolve you of any fault."

"I can provide an armed guard for your protection, and a jeep escort." Facing the other man, he uttered curt commands. "Sit with the driver. Keep this window down. Hold your service revolver and your rifle at the ready."

"Yes, Colonel."

The barrier opened and the limousine slowly moved through. After a sharp right turn, the soldier advised increased speed to keep pace with the jeep. Nora, propped against Hedy, uttered a faint moan.

Hedy used her handkerchief to fan the ashen face, but her attention was locked on the activity in the streets. In the distance a group of policemen leaned from a window to remove a swastika banner. Clusters of well-armed *Heimwehr* soldiers stood at intersections.

Which faction controlled Vienna? Who was in charge of the government?

And where was Fritz? His fortune had provided the weapons their guards carried, and surely one of his factories had assembled them.

Their strange journey ended at the Ofenheim Palace. Hedy offered heartfelt thanks to their uniformed escort, who joined his comrades in the jeep.

She supported Nora, conscious but weak, across the threshold and up the staircase. On the upper landing she fumbled with her keys—the door had multiple locks, and her hands were unsteady. She inserted the wrong one more than once, until the bolts were drawn from inside and the heavy door swung open.

"Is Herr Mandl here?" she asked the butler.

"In the library."

Fritz sat slumped in his favorite chair, clutching a brandy glass. She wrenched it away, splashing liquid onto the Persian rug, and gave it to Nora. "Sit down. Drink!"

The wireless hummed in the background, but no speech issued from it.

Fritz sounded dazed as he said, "When I telephoned the Salzburg house a servant said you were gone. Whatever possessed you to leave?"

"I didn't realize what was happening until we saw the brownshirts. They were everywhere." She sat down on the sofa next to Nora. "The *Heimwehr* soldiers we met at a barricade told us Nazis occupied the Chancellery. And the radio station."

"They issued a bulletin, stating that Dollfuss resigned in favour of Anton Rintelen, that traitor bastard. Whether this is true or not, I have no way to know. I doubt he would, unless extreme force was applied. The Cabinet received advance warning minutes before the raid. Von Schuschnigg and the rest escaped to the ministry office. But Dollfuss was trapped."

"Can we send for a doctor? Ernst will never forgive us if harm comes to Nora or the child."

With a semblance of steadiness, Nora said, "Don't worry about me. It's Ernst and his colleagues who deserve our concern. Have you heard from him?"

Fritz nodded. "We spoke briefly, but hasn't established contact with his fellow ministers. President Miklas is already heading back here from the Carpathian mountains. In Klangenfurt he stopped at a radio station long enough to make a broadcast declaring any and all rebel pronouncements null and void. By his decree, Schuschnigg is provisional chancellor until Dollfuss's fate is determined. If Ernst had been in the country, that title would've been his. He'll be here as soon as possible—Mussolini is providing him with a transport plane."

Nora twisted her handkerchief. "He should stay in Italy until the rebellion is put down."

"His country needs him. Now more than ever," Fritz asserted.

"You ought to have food," Hedy told her.

"I couldn't eat anything."

"Lunch was hours ago. Ernst will expect you to take good care of yourself, and your little one."

Leaving the room, Hedy found their suitcases stacked in the hall. She instructed the butler to place Fraulein Gregor's belongings in the best guest room and requested sandwiches and salad.

They passed the evening in agonizing suspense, united in fear. Neither Hedy or Nora wanted to go to bed. They sat silently on the sofa, their needlepoint in their laps. Fritz, insistent on keeping the phone line open for calls, refused to let Hedy contact her parents.

The book-lined room felt airless, but he wouldn't open a window. Hedy wondered whether he'd read all, or even some of the cloth- and leather-bound volumes on the shelves. She was doubtful. It appeared to be a museum-like display, and the contents must be valuable. A smaller bookcase in his private study held his collection of well-worn chemistry texts and various political tomes.

When the telephone pierced the silence, Fritz grabbed it before the second ring. "Mandl."

For several seconds he listened, pressing a hand to his brow all the while, as if warding off whatever news was being communicated. At length he said, "Italian troops are amply supplied. We were wise to take that step. We're fortunate to have Mussolini as the guardian of Austria's independence. By positioning his army at our border, he sends a clear warning to Hitler." For a few moments he listened. "Nora's here. She and Hedy were driving back from Salzburg while hell was breaking loose. Will you speak to her?"

As the actress embarked on a tearful dialogue with her lover, Fritz crossed to the sofa and took the empty space next to Hedy. Bent double, he pressed his fists against his temples.

"They shot Dollfuss. He bled to death, begging for a priest. Those murdering Nazi dogs hadn't the decency to let him have last rites. His family are at the Mussolini villa in Riccione, waiting for him. The Duce had to tell Alwine that she is suddenly a widow and her little girls are fatherless. He'll send them back to Vienna in one of his planes. He might accompany them. Ernst wasn't sure."

Moved by her husband's vulnerability and sharing his sense of loss, Hedy leaned over to embrace him.

The Nazis who repeatedly terrorized Austria with their demonstrations and their bombs—and this political assassination—were determined to overrun the country. If they succeeded in infiltrating the government and imposed the same anti-Semitic laws prevailing Germany, neither her husband's wealth nor his powerful cronies would stave off persecution.

⎯⎯⎯◇•◆•◇⎯⎯⎯

The Film Festival of 1934 coincided with the Mandls' holiday in the place where their honeymoon had begun a year ago. Producers, directors, exhibitors, and actors converged on the Lido for the second Bienniale. This year its director and board had instituted a competition and would award prizes in various categories. Gustav Machatý was present, with *Ecstasy* as his entry, and Max Reinhardt would stage his Shakespeare production in the streets of Venice.

Hedy preferred the antique grandeur of the canal city, with flowing ribbons of water and ornate *palazzi* rising from the murky depths. She longed to sit in the Piazza San Marco, watching people and pigeons, but

Fritz favored the Excelsior's frantic revelry and fashionable clientele. The baroque glories Hedy craved lay across the water from the sunlit strand lined with bathing huts. Her husband haunted the casino and she avoided it, disliking the click of the ball in the rotating roulette wheel and the gleeful shouts of lucky players.

True to form, he spent much of his time conducting arms sales via telephone and cable and keeping Ernst company. Nora, in the last weeks of pregnancy, remained in Vienna.

As a result of the Dollfuss assassination, Kurt von Schuschnigg had been elevated to Chancellor. Ernst, Mussolini's preferred candidate, retained his Vice Chancellorship and was designated Minister of Public Security. Tens of thousands of Italian troops were massed along Austria's border, signifying to Hitler that an incursion would be forcefully repelled. Mussolini publicly denounced him as a murderer and a degenerate.

Film screenings took place after dark on the grounds of the Excelsior. Because Fritz spent his evenings plotting and planning with Ernst, or secretly conferring with Mussolini, rumored to be in or near Venice, Hedy enlisted Max Reinhardt or Gustav Machatý as her escort.

After her ordeal last month, and her increasing apprehension about Austria's future, she welcomed the lighthearted entertainment provided by the American pictures. Machatý accompanied her to *It Happened One Night,* featuring Clark Gable and Claudette Colbert. The Czech director agreed that it was a clever romp, though far removed from the high art of European directors. She also admired the adaptation of *Little Women,* a novel she knew from her girlhood. Jaunty Katharine Hepburn brought tomboy Jo March to vivid life. Joan Bennett, a pretty blonde, was well cast as Amy. The American actresses were accomplished and experienced, exuding confidence. Though they were attractive and photogenic, Hedy regarded none of them as exceptionally beautiful.

She'd discarded her chance to compete with them for starring roles, refusing the Paramount contract in order to marry her millionaire.

She was his pampered doll, moving with him from one luxurious dollhouse to another, occasionally displayed to a select few. Her old dream of seeking Hollywood fame lay dormant, but it hadn't quite died.

Why not?

I'm rich beyond my wildest dreams. My husband adores me, He's brilliant and successful, relied upon by Europe's most powerful leaders.

And yet, she acknowledged, theirs wasn't a truly companionable marriage. Her parents, despite their age difference, were so well attuned that they finished each other's sentences. Confident in their connection, they freely aired their opinions and never shrank from arguments. Mutti managed the household and servants and the social calendar. To relieve the stress of running the national bank, Papa organized family excursions and holidays, and when in good health, he enjoyed hiking and skiing and tennis.

Fritz gave Hedy no responsibilities whatsoever. When she asked about his work, he discussed it in general terms. Although she sometimes offered advice, he never sought it.

One night they crossed the water to attend *The Merchant of Venice*. Watching the pretty and affecting actress Max had cast as Jessica, Hedy suffered a fresh attack of professional jealousy.

When she asked Fritz if they might attend the *Ecstasy* screening, he firmly declared he would rather not. He instructed her to remain in their suite while he and Ernst dined with a visiting dignitary—unnamed—promising to take her to the casino afterwards.

From a window, she watched the lowering sun cast its golden rays upon distant spires, wishing for her watercolors and art paper. When darkness closed off the view, she turned to the unfolding tragedy of Thomas Mann's *Death in Venice*. The power that physical beauty exerted upon susceptible persons, and its unfortunate ability to corrupt, fascinated her, but it was disturbing to contemplate.

Applause drifted through the half-open door of the private terrace. How gratified Machatý must be. And so was she. Deep down, she didn't regret playing Eva. In retrospect, shedding her clothes and feigning an orgasm didn't seem so outrageous. *Ecstasy* was lasting proof that she was a talented actress.

Fritz returned at midnight, his eyes glassy from hours of drinking and cigar smoking and staring at cards.

"Your movie received a standing ovation." He unfastened his gold cufflinks and dropped them onto a table.

"You saw it?"

"Only the conclusion—the railway station, and the final montage. But I do mean to see the whole of it."

"There are scenes you'll dislike, you know."

He pushed down the straps of her negligee, baring her torso so he could squeeze her breasts. "Come to bed, Hasi. So many brazen women hanging about tonight, their hints and their smiles offering everything. But I wanted nothing to do with them, I was so eager to be with my own beautiful little bunny wife." He placed her hand over his erection.

Responding to his silent demand, and the rush of sensation between her legs, she unbuttoned his trousers to stroke his rigid flesh. Mutual desire should have been an equalizing force in their relationship, but for Fritz the sex act was the most pleasurable method of exhibiting his power over her. She followed him into the bedroom, leaving behind her thin silk garment.

She stood before him, her head bowed, awaiting her cue. His gaze, more alert now, roamed her naked body. Before slipping off his waistcoat, he removed the heavy gold stopwatch that guided his every waking moment. He took off his tie and shirt, shoes and socks, trousers and underclothing. He stretched out on the bed.

Plucking out hairpins, she uncoiled her dark locks.

"Turn around. Good. Now face me again."

His burning gaze seared her bare flesh. Hundreds of festival attendees had seen as much of her body as he did now. They had watched her face in close up, eyes shut and lips aquiver, during the lovemaking scene.

"Come to me. Let me show you how much I need my Hasi." In his advanced state of arousal, he took her readiness for granted.

She hadn't inserted her rubber cap.

Fritz didn't know she used one. Before marriage they'd never made love, so she hadn't needed to assure him, as she had other lovers, of her care in avoiding conception. A pregnancy fright during an affair with a wealthy young Bavarian had taught her the necessity of taking precautions. Whether or not Fritz wanted children was as much a mystery to her as the volatile substances that went into his bullets and bombs. She only knew that she hadn't yet experienced maternal urges.

Thinking quickly, she produced a little cough. Before she climbed onto the bed beside him, she made a faint choking sound. "My throat is dry. I need water."

"Be quick."

She ran the sink taps full blast, and with speedy efficiency performed the necessary task. Pleasing her husband meant submitting to his wishes and desires. But this most personal matter was hers to manage, without his knowledge or interference.

⸺⧫⸺

According to Ernst, three hundred members of the press were covering the festival. After the *Ecstasy* screening, they pursued Hedy day and night. Photographers trailed her whenever she emerged from the Excelsior, flanked by Fritz and Ernst, and she needed no reminder to wear dark glasses. The enthusiastic response to her film—never before seen in Italy—was more exhilarating than she dared admit.

"The Pope objected to your movie being shown, did you hear?" a journalist shouted one morning when she stepped onto her balcony.

That evening a studio executive sought her out at and invited her to dance. "We're casting *Bride of Frankenstein* at Universal. Come to Hollywood, we'll test you for the lead." When she rejoined Fritz, she didn't mention the flattering and tantalizing offer.

"Mr. Alexander Korda of London Films wishes to make your acquaintance, Miss Kiesler." She accepted the card the English publicist pressed on her and tucked it into the lining of her dressing case, where Fritz would never find it.

"You're a sensation," Max Reinhardt declared over afternoon drinks, "the festival's most sparkling and sought-after star. More than ever I want you for my fairy queen. As Titania, you'd pack the Hollywood Bowl!"

"I believed you to be a visionary artist, Herr Professor. Not a showman."

"It's necessary to be both," he replied. "Come to Salzburg for our festival. Bring your husband. Together, you and I can work a magical feat worthy of Oberon. We'll convince him that you should perform in my next Shakespeare play. I'm expecting a very distinguished American guest. I won't say who, but he's a person you ought to meet. Mandl, too. He likes to associate with prominent people."

On the festival's final day, Fritz entered their suite to find a reporter lying in wait. Hedy's maid, recipient of a lavish bribe, was duly sacked for this act of disloyalty.

"You can interview for a new maid in Paris," he comforted Hedy. "You ought to have a Frenchwoman."

This statement was the first indication that he was postponing their return to Vienna.

Before their departure, the festival awards were announced. Fritz escorted her to the ceremony, his face as expressionless as a rock as she received compliments on her performance. *Ecstasy,* so often maligned by press and public, had found a highly appreciative audience, and Gustav Machatý took the Silver Lion as Best Director. Katharine Hepburn was named Best Actress and Wallace Beery the Best Actor.

The Mandl airplane carried Hedy away from the scene of her greatest professional triumph. Soaring above the glistening Adriatic, she gazed upon the golden strand far below and the sun-bathed islands, where a lost piece of her identity had been restored. She was an actress still, and always would be.

The pilot slowly banked the aircraft, tipping her upward into the clouds. Hedy clutched the armrests, conscious of a shift in her equilibrium that was more than physical.

Chapter 5

Hedy's introduction to the world's most famous studio mogul was staged in Salzburg, with the same care and deliberation as any Reinhardt production. With strategic nonchalance, Max mentioned to Fritz that German industrialist Gustav Krupp was in residence at Blühnbach Castle. Exploiting her husband's hunger for business talk and his distaste for theatrical conversation, she encouraged him to drive to Werfen. She remained at Schloss Leopoldskron, Max's lakeside palace, nervously awaiting his illustrious guest.

From the moment Fritz departed, Max drilled her in English. At school she'd studied the language for only one term, and her comprehension barely exceeded her ability to converse.

Dressed in a smart ensemble from Elsa Schiaparelli's Paris atelier, she sat in the formal terrace garden, studying Titania's lines. When the glass and wrought iron double doors parted, she stood.

"Hedy, my dear, I'm pleased to present Mr. Louis B. Mayer. Of the Hollywood studio Metro-Goldwyn-Mayer."

She'd imagined a towering giant, his height commensurate with his worldwide reputation. Even in flat-soled shoes, she topped him by at least an inch. His head was the shape of a potato, with a thin covering of once-dark hair frosted with gray. Round-rimmed spectacles perched on his beaky nose. If not for his tailored suit, silk tie, and matching pocket handkerchief, he would resemble an ordinary shopkeeper.

His stubby hand shot out and his thick fingers grasped hers. "Delighted."

"You might know Frau Mandl by her professional name, Hedy Kiesler. She stars in *Ecstasy*, which received a prestigious award at the Venice Film Festival."

"You're the nude girl?"

Not a promising start. In careful English, she responded, "I was very young, Mr. Mayer."

He nodded. "Many an actress makes stupid mistakes early in her career."

"MGM won several awards at the festival," she continued. "Clark Gable's movie. And another with the actor Beery, about a Mexican."

"That's David Selznick's picture. My son-in-law."

From the way his mouth pursed she deduced that there was no love lost between them. She cast about for an appropriate compliment. "I am liking Mr. Gable very much. In all his pictures."

Mayer's expression softened. "A great guy. All men like him, all women love him." He turned to Max. "You've got an impressive spread here, Reinhardt. At my studio, we strive for splendor in our sets. But nothing compares to the genuine article."

Hedy wondered what else she could contribute to the conversation.

Max, ever supportive, came to her rescue. "Hedy trained at my theatre schools in Berlin and Vienna before acting professionally, on stage as well as in film. Her talent is much commended by the critics."

"She's definitely a looker."

The term was unfamiliar. Was he saying she was observant?

"Kiesler. Mandl. So, you're Jewish? Such shame the families must feel about your nudie movie." Turning to Max, the studio head declared, "I'd like to look your place over, if that's okay."

"Certainly," Max replied. "I must make a trunk call to Los Angeles, to discuss my Shakespeare production. Hedy will show you the grounds."

"If your Hollywood Bowl stunt succeeds, maybe we'll make it into a picture," Mayer called after Max's departing figure. His dark eyes raked Hedy from head to toe. "Are you Reinhardt's mistress?"

His directness appalled her, but she mustn't let it show. "I'm a married woman, Mr. Mayer. To me, Max is Herr Professor. Almost another father."

"I also take a fatherly interest in my actresses. So, where's your husband?"

"Visiting an acquaintance. He will be glad to meet you when he returns." It wasn't true. Fritz detested filmmakers. And Americans.

"Where do you live?" Mayer asked as they walked beside the mirror-like lake.

"In Vienna. We have also some hunting lodges, in the mountains."

"Do you keep horses?"

"At Villa Fegenberg, yes. And seventeen dogs."

A lengthy silence ensued.

"I'm lousy company," he said gloomily. "This European trip has been a disaster from start to finish. Put me in quite a funk."

Another mysterious word. From the context, she perceived a funk was a negative thing. In a cheery tone she responded, "But you are now here with Max, at his beautiful *schloss*. And tonight we are seeing his festival play *Everyman,* a popular annual event in Salzburg."

Fritz came back later than she expected, in a mood so foul she was unsure whether to question it or ignore it. Deciding on the latter, she summoned her maid so she could prepare for the evening.

In Paris she'd hired a statuesque brunette who had worked as a dresser at a lesser fashion house. Broad hips and large breasts precluded fulfillment of Laure's ambition to become a *mannequin,* so she accepted the position of lady's maid to an elderly countess who had died. She admitted that offer of employment from a young and socially active millionaire's wife, with a Vienna mansion and other properties scattered across Austria, was providential. The salary was large, and she enjoyed travel to interesting places.

If English presented myriad challenges, Hedy's fluency in French was a point of pride. She communicated to her new servant the necessity of impressing the man from Hollywood. Although she preferred a simple hairstyle, she encouraged Laure to devise a more elaborate coiffure. They were admiring the result when Fritz barged into the room in dinner attire.

With a nod, Hedy dismissed the maid. "What happened to upset you?"

"Taffi Krupp. Who is no Krupp at all. He was born a Halbach and was made to take Bertha's surname after their marriage was arranged by Kaiser Wilhelm. Taffi lives like an emperor in that castle where poor Franz Ferdinand led his life of debauchery. At heart he is a firm monarchist, but out of loyalty to Germany he chooses to support the Reich. It causes strife between him and Bertha and the rest of their family. True-blooded Krupps regard themselves as a fraction less imperial than Hapsburgs. Hitler, that lowborn Austrian house painter, is anathema to them."

"Not only to them," Hedy murmured.

Taking a turn around the room, Fritz continued heatedly, "Taffi sacked every Jew serving on the board of Germany's Industry Federation. If Bertha's father were alive, he would approve. He was a staunch proponent of eugenics. I wanted to discuss Panzer tanks, but for hours I listened to Taffi spew Nazi rhetoric. And to preserve our partnership in certain enterprises, I had to stifle my outrage. And then . . . " He fell silent. "You don't need to hear the worst of it."

"I'm your wife. You can tell me anything."

"That *schwein* Alfried, the son and heir, followed me into the courtyard. And after he admired my motorcar, and my choice of wife, he made a hideous proposition."

"For armaments?"

"No, my dear. For *you*," he growled. "Half a million in jewels, he offered. Whatever you desire. Diamonds, rubies, emeralds, pearls. Not that he'd make good. Taffi keeps him on a strict allowance."

"You speak in riddles."

"A fortune in jewels in exchange for one night of 'ecstasy' with you."

His clenched fist banged a tabletop. "That infernal film. It follows us everywhere. And I hate that I haven't seen what has caused such an extreme reaction in other men."

When they descended the polished stone staircase, she reached for his hand, but he shook her off. They joined their fellow guests in Max's two-tiered, wood-paneled library for pre-theatre cocktails. This was her favorite room in a castle containing many magnificent ones, but in her concern about Fritz she was oblivious to its grandeur. Their host moved about the room, exchanging words with his friends, taking down one of the valuable books for a fellow bibliophile to examine. Shattered by her husband's outburst, she yearned to rest her head against Max's shoulder, as she would do if Papa were near.

Mr. Mayer stood next to the columned fireplace in conversation with a giant of a woman, a famous patron of the arts, whose jutting bosom almost grazed his balding pate. Hedy maintained her distance, trusting Max to promote her interests.

All is not lost, she comforted herself. He and I will persuade Fritz that a quality Hollywood production will erase, or at least mitigate, any damage *Ecstasy* did to my reputation.

Max's *Everyman,* reprised at every Salzburg Festival, was performed outdoors with the majestic cathedral as the backdrop. Its characters entered from adjacent streets, their movements halting and their poses reminiscent of antique woodcuts. With a theme of death and divine judgment, it was a fantastical and allegorical depiction of human frailties. Everyman, soulless and unsympathetic lead, was like no one Hedy had met. But Mammon, all greed and acquisitiveness, reminded her of Fritz, an unflattering comparison that she refused to dwell on.

He constantly fidgeted with his gold stopwatch, revolving it between his fingers and twisting the chain. She knew better than to correct his behavior when he stewed in wrath.

Mr. Mayer, seated in front of them, exhibited a similar anxiety. In scenes of intense drama, he clutched Max's forearm, and he spent much of the evening hunched forward in his seat. The play began in daylight, continued through sunset, and concluded in darkness. The banquet scene, with roistering and dancing, gave way to gloom and remorse and the dire pealing of the bells. When unseen spirits keened woefully, calling Everyman to his death, Mayer sat up straight as if he was the one being summoned.

"Outstanding. Unprecedented," he declared after the finale. "Bring it to Hollywood. New York has the highbrows, but we appreciate spectacle. It will be a sensation, like *The Miracle.*"

"I'll consider it. After I've finished my *Midsummer Night's Dream,*" Max replied, with a conspiratorial glance at Hedy.

Returning to the *schloss* in the same caravan of cars that had conveyed them to the cathedral square, they dined in the Venetian Room.

Hedy, separated from Fritz, was placed opposite Mr. Mayer. Each time she caught him eyeing her, she beamed at him.

Noticing this byplay, Max seized his opportunity. "Mr. Mayer, I've known Frau Mandl since she was my most promising pupil. In our country she's an established star of theatre and film. How would you rate her chances of success in America?"

Mayer placed his fork on the edge of his plate and wiped a streak of wine sauce from his chin. "No chance at all. I couldn't risk putting her in a picture. None of my competitors would either."

His bluntness was a blow. Beneath the table, Hedy mangled her napkin.

"This *Ecstasy* movie. I know all about it. She ran around stark naked, not a stitch on. That's improper. Immoral. And, I hear, there's a very smutty sex scene." The eyes behind the round glass lenses shifted to Hedy. "You're gorgeous. Aristocratic. But American audiences want to see wholesome American girls when they go to the cinema. Girls who keep their clothes on. And speak clear English."

Be calm. Keep smiling. Prove to him and everyone at this table that you're a lady—and a superior actress.

"I regret to be a disappointment, Mr. Mayer."

"Not at all. Glad I met you. Here in Europe you'll do just fine."

Fritz joined in the conversation, saying, "Reinhardt's question was hypothetical. My wife has no ambition to become one of your starlets, Mr. Mayer. Nor would I permit that. My position is enviable, for I needn't purchase a cinema ticket to admire her beauty."

Their host abruptly changed the subject, proposing a morning boat excursion.

"We leave for Vienna after breakfast," Fritz declared.

At an early hour, he ordered their servants to stow the luggage in the car boot and commandeered their host's study to make a telephone call.

As Hedy waited in the great hall, Max told her quietly, "I regret exposing you to Mayer's gracelessness last evening. And in front of so many people."

"It was him you exposed. He's a boor. And a bore. You're too nice to say it, but I'm not."

"This is a troublesome time for him. His wife had an emergency operation in Paris and had to remain there. At the same time, he learned from a detective that his mistress was having an affair with someone else. By the time he arrived at the spa in Carlsbad, she'd married the someone."

"He preaches morality and has a mistress? That makes him a hypocrite."

"Hollywood has many studios," he reminded her. "Improve your English. Don't be discouraged."

"Fritz is a bigger problem than Mr. Mayer's prudishness. I don't dare ask him if I can be your Titania." She extended a gloved hand. "But I'll always be grateful, Herr Professor, for your faith in me."

———◦•◆•◦———

The stack of film cans on Fritz's desk proved that he could get anything, everything he wanted. Somehow, he'd obtained a print of *Ecstasy*.

"A select group of friends will attend my private screening," he announced. "Ernst. His brother Ferdinand. Some Hirtenberger executives."

"I'm going to Nora's," Hedy said. "I've got a christening gift for baby Heinrich."

"You'll stay." His commanding tone forestalled any attempt to dissuade him. "You can thread the film in the projector. I know you like to."

Not this time, she thought grimly, snapping the empty pickup reel into place and unspooling several inches of celluloid.

Watching her parents watch her nude scenes had been hard enough. Sitting through her performance surrounded by her husband's friends was an even greater mortification. The man who professed to love her had imposed a harsh and senseless punishment for what could not be undone, and it shriveled her affection for him. Through the haze of unshed tears, she beheld the infamous lovemaking scene and was surprised to find it as tender and moving and atmospheric as Gustav Machatý intended.

After her final scene at the train station, Prince Ferdinand von Starhemberg leaned close to whisper, "A lovely performer. And a touching performance."

She studied him in the semi-darkness. His lips quirked ever so slightly in a smile that conveyed understanding. He was younger and more attractive than his brother Ernst. She welcomed her flutter of interest, a distraction from pain and helpless fury.

"We ought to know each other better." His tone was soft and intimate.

Concerned that Fritz might overhear, she offered no response.

The room was steeped in silence throughout the closing credits. None of the executives acknowledged her before departing. The two princes remained.

Fritz glowered at the blank screen. "I'll purchase every print of this damned film. All of them! I don't care what it costs. My office will contact the cinema owners. The distributors. The press. Gustav Machatý can name his price for the negative." He moved to the window and parted the thick curtains. "Ernst, I rely on your assistance."

"No."

"No?"

"It's a waste of your time and energy and funds when we have more urgent matters confronting us. *Ecstasy* has been exhibited across Europe. Many journalists have reviewed it favorably. In Venice it received much acclaim and won a prestigious prize."

"It is disgusting."

"Not at all," Ernst maintained. "Don't say things so hurtful to your wife."

Fritz rounded on his friend. "Get out. Both of you. Now!"

Hedy and the von Starhembergs stood like statues, staring at him. "Did you hear me? Go!"

Ernst clicked his heels together, bowed slightly and turned away.

Ferdi boldly took Hedy's hand. "Good day to you, Frau Mandl. I assure you I meant everything I said," he told her before making his exit.

Reaching for the brandy snifter, Fritz said, "Ernst is no longer welcome in my houses. Neither are his mistress and their little bastard. Or his brother. We will not associate with them. Do you understand?"

She inclined her head obediently, doubting that his edict would last. He had too many enemies and too few real friends to maintain a permanent rift. Or so she hoped.

Fritz was planning a lavish celebration of her twentieth birthday. She would let him figure out how to rescind the invitations already posted to Ernst and Nora. Her Swiss finishing school education hadn't covered so unlikely a situation. She'd considered including Ferdi von Starhemberg and one of his lady friends to keep numbers even. A man that good-looking must have plenty.

She placed the film reels in their containers and pressed down the lids. "Do we dine out tonight or here?" She knew the danger of berating her husband for his rudeness, or echoing Ernst's objections to his mad plan. Going to a restaurant would force him to restrain his temper and behave normally for a few hours.

"We are staying in."

She went to her room to change, knowing that tonight an effort was required. She chose a simple dark dress and instructed Laure to pull her hair back into a conservative chignon.

"No jewelry," she said when the maid carried the tortoiseshell case that housed her less valuable *bijoux*. The rarest and costliest pieces were secured in a concealed safe set into a bookcase in Fritz's study. To pacify him, she must present herself as a penitent. Gleaming gemstones would mar the effect.

By the time she joined him in the dining room, his anger had subsided, and he'd fallen into depression. The servants' presence inhibited conversation, and she was glad. Neither of them ate much of the roasted chicken, or any of the other dishes the chef had prepared.

Setting down his cutlery, Fritz informed the butler that they would take their coffee in the library.

The servant arrived with the requested tray and promptly withdrew.

When Fritz approached her, Hedy stood her ground.

His hand cupped her chin, the thumb and forefinger pressing her jawbone. "He took you to bed, didn't he? The German actor."

"We agreed never to discuss people from our past."

"The director, Machatý. Was he also your lover?"

"No."

"Why else would you perform for him like that?"

"Because of the script. I'm an actress." Realizing her mistake, she amended, "I mean, I was then."

"You want to be again. It was obvious when we were at Reinhardt's. Like a pimp, he paraded you in front of that vile Mayer."

"Stop insulting our closest friends," she shot back. "First Ernst and Nora. Now Max. You're the one behaving like a pimp. You invited all those men over here, knowing they would see me naked. Did you want them to envy you?" His averted gaze told her she'd guessed correctly. "You forced me—your wife—to sit with them as they watched. Worse than that, you're treating me like I am a whore."

"You looked like one, with that actor rubbing himself against you. I daresay you enjoyed it. Your face had that passionate look I know so well. I've heard that your lovemaking was real. That there was footage so depraved that it couldn't be used."

"All lies! You want the truth? Machatý crouched out of camera range, poking me with a pin until I made the facial expression he wanted. It was a performance. And today, for the first time, I appreciated the beauty of that scene. By shaming me, you've made me less ashamed. Your behavior, not mine, is deplorable."

"I will not tolerate your speaking to me that way," he raged.

"And I dislike your scolding and bullying. I won't live with a brute. I'd rather go home to Mutti and Papa. They love me. I've wondered whether you do, ever since Salzburg. Maybe even before that. And now more than ever."

Her icy admission wiped the tension from his face. His shoulders slumped. "Oh, Hasi, I do love you. That is why I could not bear seeing all that I saw."

"My movie is more important than you realize. A masterpiece, some call it. And if I want to make another, or act in one of Max's plays, why shouldn't I?"

"Because it isn't necessary. Whatever you want, I can provide it. Isn't that why you married me?"

"I fell in love. So deeply that I sacrificed what was most important to me. My career. I've never asked you for jewelry or clothes or motorcars. Fritz, please don't deny me the one, the only thing I've ever requested."

He sat down at his desk and regarded her with the expression of a monarch receiving a troublesome supplicant. "You'll outgrow this childish desire."

"My parents believed that. I proved them wrong. I ran away."

Calmly he replied, "You know you cannot run from me. We'll remain in Vienna till New Year's. Afterwards I'll be traveling a great deal with important business. While I'm away, you will live at Villa Fegenberg. I can join you there on weekends. Your parents can stay with you. Your father needs a holiday. A dose of country air will do him a world of good. He hasn't looked well lately."

Fritz would relent. He had to. Christmas and the New Year were weeks away. By then he'd be in a happier frame of mind. And if not . . . .

Their marriage was increasingly an obstacle to contentment rather than a source of it. His insensitivity, his temper, and his bullying wounded her. And so did his determination to stifle her artistry and her ambitions.

That night, for the first time, she locked her bedroom door.

Within minutes, she discovered that her husband had his own copy of her key.

Chapter 6

From an upper window, Hedy waved goodbye to her Litchwitz cousins before the Mandl limousine drove them to the station to catch the Budapest train. All of the mourners had departed, and the Kiesler house in Peter-Jordanstrasse was unnaturally silent.

She turned to her mother, also dressed in funeral black. "I'm glad you had relatives at the service to comfort you. I hope they understood that I simply couldn't bear to go. Papa would have, I think."

Mutti blotted her eyes with her handkerchief. "With his final breath, he spoke of you. So lovingly."

"I wish I'd been here."

"It came all of sudden, his attack. You couldn't have done anything."

"When he suffered that odd spell at Schwarzau, he refused to see a doctor. We should have insisted."

"He didn't want to add to your troubles."

"But I added to his," she acknowledged with a pang, "when I told him I'd rather not stay married to Fritz."

Financial reverses had required the shedding of household staff, but Papa refused her offer to pay the salaries of the extra maid, the manservant, and the gardener. He wouldn't be beholden to the man who was making his beloved daughter miserable. And now his death deprived her of the emotional and financial support she would need when she sought a divorce.

"We trusted him to take care of you and make you happy. For a time, it seemed that you were."

"Fritz changed. When we met, he convinced me that he was a charming prince. But all along, he was the ogre." With a half-smile, she added, "Remember how Papa would read folk takes, doing the different voices?"

Mutti nodded. "He let you play under his desk, acting out stories you made up. Even then you dreamed of being a film star."

"He got so angry when I cut my hair to make a Clara Bow fringe. And whenever I ran away from school."

"Three times, from the one in Lucerne."

"Our headmistress was horrid. She fed us bread rolls as hard as rocks, and every night at supper we had rhubarb, which I loathe. On the night I escaped, I had only a few coins. I could hardly afford a third-class seat, with nothing left to buy food. I was starving. And my train caught fire."

"The second time, you slipped out to enter that beauty contest."

"And I won."

"The last time, you were meeting some boy."

Mutti never quite forgave and hardly ever forgot, often reciting the ever-thickening catalogue of transgressions. Always the harsh disciplinarian, the constant critic.

Now Fritz assumed that role, compounding her depression with each recital of her faults and failings. According to him, she was irredeemably sullied by *Ecstasy*. He complained that she was unsociable, then removed her from society by sending her to the country house. Accusing her of extravagance, he cut off her credit at the shops and restricted her to a cash allowance, doled out monthly.

Instead of making purchases, she hoarded her funds. In the past six months she'd deposited a sizeable sum into the secret bank account she shared with her maid Laure.

Hedy moved to the sofa and sat beside her mother. "Papa often told me, 'Think with your heart.' Even if it seemed to lead me in a wrong direction, he said, all would turn out well in the end. I hope so. Because my heart urges me to leave my husband."

"Hedl, *liebchen,* whatever steps you mean to take, I don't want to hear. I must be able to tell Fritz truthfully that I know nothing." Mutti stood up and squared her shoulders. "Dry your face and comb your hair. Soon the car will return to take you home."

"Today, my home is here."

Passing along the corridor to her room, she traced her father's final steps. Overtaken by faintness, he'd staggered to her bed, crying out for Mutti. His heart stopped before the doctor arrived. Tears flowing, she hugged the pillow that had supported his head when he drew his last breath.

Here was the floral wallpaper she knew so well, and the chintz curtains. Long before she ventured into the world to experience it, she'd lounged on the window seat, reading books or sketching or daydreaming. In her imagination she played important roles and engaged in passionate love affairs. She hadn't envisioned a future that included an internationally scandalous movie or a marriage that would founder within weeks of her first anniversary.

Her entire life was steeped in blackness. The color of bereavement was equally symbolic of shattered hopes and matrimonial demise.

She had no friends. Fritz didn't permit visits to Nora Gregor and refused to receive her—he wouldn't risk any encouragement of unseemly professional aspirations. His prohibition against Ernst hadn't lasted. Their collaboration and influence with the government were in Austria's best interest. And Mussolini's.

According to Laure, Fritz had ordered the servants to report Hedy's activities to him, and they listened to her telephone conversations. He replaced her personal chauffeur with a man of undoubted loyalty, a former truck driver for his factory in Hirtenberg. He increased Laure's salary, unaware of her intense devotion to Hedy, and together they concocted false scenarios to convince him that his spy was worth her pay.

As Mutti could attest, Hedy was an experienced and successful runaway. She was also an actress. She'd play the obedient wife while she plotted and planned for the day when all her skills could be used to her advantage.

⟶⌖⟵

As much as possible, Fritz avoided the resident British, so strenuously opposed to fascism in all its forms. To Hedy's astonishment, one evening he presented an officer as their dinner guest. Captain Ryder Young was handsome in the English fashion, with sandy hair and light eyes that lingered on her with evident appreciation.

Hedy listened to the men's discourse about Mussolini's war in Ethiopia, aware that Hirtenberger Patronen-fabrik had supplied the Italian soldiers with their weapons. During their martial talk she faced the window, relishing the cool spring breeze and the birdsong that wafted into the drawing room.

When the men spoke of Austrofascism, her husband's verbose defence received a forceful rebuttal from his guest.

"Your branch of the movement is destined to become entwined with the German National Socialists. Britain will not only stand firm against the authoritarianism that has overtaken much of Europe. She will repel it."

"An unaffordable luxury, your democracy. It is best suited to prosperous times, which Austria does not enjoy. In this extreme financial crisis, we prefer the strongest of leaders."

"Yours was murdered in cold blood. By Nazis." Captain Young extinguished his cigarette in a Bohemian glass ashtray. With a smile for Hedy, he said, "Frau Mandl, you must find this political talk terribly dull."

"She's accustomed to it," Fritz answered for her. "All our top men come to this house. Chancellor Schuschnigg. Prince von Starhemberg, our Vice Chancellor."

"Can they keep anarchy at bay? For how long?"

"Indefinitely. You know of last month's conference at Stresa?"

Nodding his fair head, the captain smiled. "I piloted Sir Walford Selby and our British delegation."

Their discourse immediately shifted to the mutually fascinating subject of aviation, and a detailed comparison of aircraft types. Fritz proposed a factory tour, an overture that was accepted. On moving to the dining room, they talked of shooting sports. As Captain Young boasted of his exploits in the hunting field, Hedy suspected him of exaggerating to impress her. Feigning attentiveness, she pondered how she might benefit from his apparent susceptibility.

They returned to the drawing room to smoke and drink whisky. Rather than excuse herself, as she typically did, she steeled herself for another bout of uninteresting masculine conversation.

Young pried open his cigarette case. "Blast. I'm empty."

"I've got plenty in my study," Fritz volunteered. "I'll get them."

"Don't trouble yourself, Mandl."

"No trouble at all. I should also make a telephone call." He emerged from the corner, where he'd tweaked the controls of his Radiola machine. "Excuse me, I will be away but a short time."

Hedy hadn't been alone with any other man for months. Leaving her chair, she beckoned to the captain and led him to the open window. Her voice low, she said in English, "I need help. I want to leave my husband."

After a momentary confusion, his smile returned. "I forgot you're an actress. Are we rehearsing a scene?"

"No. Oh, how to make you understand?" she cried in frustration. "He won't let me perform. I'm little better than a prisoner here, and our servants report my every move to him. My father, who could have rescued me, died in February." When she reached for his hands, he stepped back as though electrified by the contact. "Do you stay at your embassy?"

"At the Hotel Regina."

Not nearly far enough away—but she wouldn't remain there very long. "Tomorrow I will ring you. I ask only that you take me away from Vienna." Stepping away, she returned to her chair.

I'll board a night train to Budapest, she decided. I'll stay with my cousins until I can take an apartment. Mutti can visit me. And eventually I will travel. To anywhere I wish.

Fritz returned with a handful of cigarettes. "You should find these to your liking, Captain. I purchase them from an English tobacconist here in Vienna."

Hedy hoped he wouldn't notice the tremor in Captain Young's hands as he refilled his case. He'd smoked only half a cigarette when the clock chimed the hour. Bounding up, he declared that he must not linger.

When preparing for bed, she reviewed the necessary tasks to be performed in the morning, as soon as Fritz left for his office. She would pack her clothing and as much jewelry as she could while Laure withdrew her savings from the secret bank account.

A heavy rap interrupted her mental list-making. "Come in." She no longer bothered locking the door.

"I want you to hear this." Fritz, in his silk dressing gown, held up a vinyl record. "We'll listen to it together."

"Can't it wait till tomorrow?"

"No."

When he used that tone, protest was useless. She slipped her feet into satin mules and followed him to the drawing room.

These are our last moments together, she realized.

He placed the disk on the turntable and adjusted the controls. A Strauss waltz spilled from the speaker, as slow and soothing as a lullaby. After a popping sound, the music stopped.

"I need help." The words were English. "I want to leave my husband." The voice was high-pitched and thickly accented.

"I forgot you're an actress." Captain Young's words were clipped and clear. "Are we rehearsing a scene?"

Fritz had set his Radiola to record, capturing her conversation with the captain. Desperate to shut it off, she struck the needle arm, carving a gouge into the black vinyl. She pried up the disk and smashed it against the windowsill.

He laughed softly. "By now your knight in shining armor has

received my very direct message. I warned him to keep his distance, or I would inform the British ambassador of his attempt to steal away my wife, a revelation that would be ruinous. I trust both of you learned a useful lesson tonight."

She'd learned that he was as devious as he was ruthless. And to free herself from him, she must emulate him.

<hr>

Fritz atoned for unkindness with expensive gifts. Although his fleet of motorcars was extensive, he ordered up a Mercedes limousine for Hedy's use. She preferred jewelry, having discovered the ease of converting it into cash. In the days before his departure he treated her with uncommon tenderness, but he hadn't revealed his destination. Until he returned, she would be stuck at Villa Fegenberg. The weather precluded outdoor pursuits like riding or swimming, and she was resigned to entertaining herself with needlework and reading. She'd brought her drawing materials, thinking she might design a flower garden to surround the spring-fed pool.

Staring at the moisture-dotted window of her sleek black vehicle, she imagined herself opening its door and jumping out. Apart from the likelihood of a grave injury that would hamper mobility, she was too pragmatic to run off on foot into the Vienna Woods without money. If they stopped for lunch, she could add a few of her sleeping pills to her chauffeur's coffee to render him senseless. Although she rarely drove herself, she was confident she could reach the border of Hungary. But the opportunity never presented itself.

Every visit to Fritz's country home reminded her of her first one. Of their meadow picnic and woodland stroll and his marriage proposal. On that memorable, crystalline afternoon, so unlike this dreary and damp one, she'd been filled with youthful optimism. She'd believed every one of his lavish promises but hadn't understood his character at all. Was it any wonder their relationship had disintegrated so dramatically?

The butler greeted her by announcing, "Prince von Starhemberg telephoned from Venice. He left no message."

Supposing that Ernst and her husband were in Italy together, she was puzzled by his attempt to contact her. She began to worry that he was delivering bad news. Because Fritz enjoyed Mussolini's protection, it was unlikely that he'd been arrested. Had he suffered some accident, was he injured? Although she wanted to be free of him, she wished him no harm.

When the phone rang, she was surprised that the caller was Ernst's brother, Prince Ferdi.

"I have an urgent need to speak with Mandl. Is he with you?"

"I'm afraid not. I can't say where he is," she confessed. "Possibly in Austria. Or else in Italy. Or maybe Switzerland. Or France. Is something the matter?"

"There's been a motor crash, a very bad one. The Chancellor was injured, not seriously, but Frau von Schuschnigg was killed outright. Their boy is in hospital with cuts and bruises. It's not certain that this was an accident. Sabotage of the vehicle is naturally suspected."

"Where is Ernst?"

"Flying his plane back from Venice. He'll meet Schuschnigg and accompany the coffin to Vienna."

She leaned back in the desk chair. "Too often when he's in Italy, tragedy strikes our leaders. One time, poor Dollfuss was murdered. Now, Schuschnigg's wife is dead."

"It is on Austria's behalf that he goes there so often." His voice dropped to a near whisper. "And you? You are well?"

"I'm lonely." She gripped the receiver with both hands.

"A beautiful princess shouldn't be all alone in her castle. She ought to have a companion."

Whenever Ferdi had flirted with her, out of Fritz's earshot, she hadn't taken him seriously. In case the household informants were listening on the extension, she continued in French, "This one is surrounded by spying servants. But when she returns to the city, she could perhaps evade them. She'd try. If a handsome prince asked her to."

"You have brightened a very dark day," he responded.

"*Au revoir,* Ferdi."

"*Au revoir,* Hedy."

They were treading dangerous ground.

Her gaze landed on the antlered trophy on the opposite wall, a chamois buck—another of Fritz's unhappy victims. She returned its glassy stare, pondering whether to ask Ferdi to remove her from this confined and frustrating existence.

Intending to pen a condolence letter to Chancellor von Schuschnigg, she searched the drawers of the large desk for writing paper but found none. The broad central one didn't budge.

Picking locks was a skill she'd developed during her mechanically-minded youth. The silver letter opener was too large, so she took a metal fingernail file out of her handbag and inserted its tip into the keyhole without success.

A bent hairpin worked perfectly. She tugged at the drawer.

No stationery, only a single large envelope, unsealed and stamped "CONFIDENTIAL." She reached inside to remove the contents.

The first page, a typed letter bearing the signature of Hellmuth Walter, referred to the development of an experimental torpedo. The name was unfamiliar. Hedy couldn't recall Fritz mentioning him as an associate or an employee, and she was certain she'd never encountered him at a dinner party. The enclosure consisted of pages of diagrams, annotated with text, and lengthy technical descriptions.

For two years she'd listened when Fritz advised dictators and chancellors and generals about expanding their arsenals. They would be interested in this new torpedo, but he had never presented it to them.

Knowledge is a weapon, she told herself. By far the most powerful.

After reading the entire report, she went through it again more slowly. Wire guidance, frequency selection, electronic jamming, remote control. Meaningless terms at first, but she soon connected the images with the detailed specifications.

She tore a sheet from her sketchpad and hastily replicated the images, scribbling brief explanatory descriptions. If necessary, she could use this confidential report to bargain with Fritz—her silence in exchange for her freedom. To prevent her from sharing this discovery with the French or the British, competing with his clients for new technology, he'd agree to anything. Wouldn't he?

She shut the drawer and once more put her hairpin to good use, manipulating the tumbler into the locked position.

Fritz, the chemical engineer, builder of bombs and tanks and warplanes, would never realize how completely she'd gained advantage over him with this small, simple tool. And her female ingenuity.

Chapter 7

To build anticipation for the Summer Games to be held in Berlin, Germany's leaders staged an Olympic torch relay through nations highly suspicious of Hitler's ambitions for territorial expansion. In late July, the flame's arrival in Vienna ignited robust demonstrations by Nazi partisans who swarmed into the city from all regions of Austria. Swastika flags sprang up near government buildings, and the Nazi anthem was sung openly. With their shouts and jeers, the agitators drowned out Ernst von Starhemberg's formal address.

In August, Fritz took Hedy with him to the Lido, keeping her close by even when he took meetings with other men ostensibly on holiday. A year had passed since she found the plans for a wireless torpedo, and because he'd never spoken about it in her presence she had no idea whether he was building it or not. Throughout those twelve months he'd been a model of husbandly devotion—excessive, at times. And she had perfected her role of complaisant wife, all the while devising a scenario that would ensure her eventual liberation.

His munitions plants had never been busier, as the threat of invasion demanded increased arms production. It was no secret to Hedy that with Taffi Krupp, whose firm had created the relay torch, he was anonymously negotiating the purchase of majority shares in Austria's largest metal manufacturing enterprise. Located in Berndorf, convenient to Fritz's Hirtenberg works and his Enzesfeld artillery factory, it produced brass and other materials for cartridges. The Austrian government, preferring to nationalize the armaments industries, opposed the acquisition.

When Hedy and Fritz returned to Vienna in September, the Union Jack decorated facades throughout the city to welcome Britain's King Edward VIII. They had the opportunity to do so in person by accepting the invitation to a reception at the Belvedere Palace, the Austrian Chancellor's residence.

In the Biedermeier salon vestibule Hedy paused to speak to the Chancellor's motherless son.

"Kurti, shake hands with Fraulein Kiesler and Herr Mandl," the governess prompted.

"Do you remember us, Kurti?" Hedy asked with as much cheer as she could muster. "My husband and I met you when you were living at the Kriegsministerium."

"Why is your name different from his?" the boy wanted to know. He indicated Fritz's departing figure.

"Kurti, don't point and don't ask so many questions. Mind your manners."

Hedy lowered herself to the level of her interrogator. "Actresses are called 'Miss,' even after they marry. Some people still call me by the name I had when I made movies."

"This is my autograph book." Kurti thrust it at Hedy. "Fraulein Alice and I collect famous people. Will you sign, please?"

She went down on one knee, balancing the volume on the other one. The fountain pen was attached with a string. Uncapping it, she asked, "Which of my names shall I write?"

"The actress one. You're very beautiful, Fraulein Kiesler. So was my mother. Her hair was blonde." After she completed her signature, he took back his book, saying, "I've been in hospital a lot. I had double pneumonia. *And* scarlet fever!"

"He recovered," the governess hastened to explain.

"Being ill is horrid, isn't it? I imagine you were an impatient patient." Hedy pinched his upturned nose.

He responded to her playfulness by lightly slapping her bottom. He patted it again, crying out in surprise, "Oh! You're hard like a stone back here. What are you wearing under your dress?"

She laughed. "A lady's undergarment. Ask Fraulein Alice about it. Later."

"Would you like to see my train sets?"

"Another day," said the governess. "Your papa and King Edward are waiting for you."

In the salon, the two leaders occupied a green-and-white striped sofa. A full year as a widower and the strain imposed by his position had diminished Schuschnigg. His bespectacled face was thin and lined. Though he wasn't yet forty, his head was graying.

The guest of honor invited Kurti to sit on his lap. "You've grown since last year," the King observed. His German was excellent.

"Did you bring your crown?"

"It stays in England when I'm on holiday. Like you, I've got a home called Belvedere. Mine is called a fort, not a palace like yours. Nor is it so grand."

The boy presented his autograph book, pointing to an entry. "You wrote this when you were a prince. Now that you're a king, would you please sign again? Here's a space beside Fraulein Hedy Kiesler."

Leaning close to Hedy, Fritz murmured, "Entertaining little imp. By this time we should have had a son of our own. My sister recommends an excellent doctor who successfully treats females who can't easily conceive. I'll make an appointment. Contentment will come with motherhood, Renée tells me—and I feel sure she's right."

Hedy's sister-in-law, Fritz's senior by a year, was a meddler. A plain, thick-browed widow who, she was certain, resented her beauty and her attractiveness to men.

Her husband crossed the room to converse with Sir Walford Selby, the British Ambassador, no doubt angling to be presented to the King.

Both von Starhemberg princes were in attendance. Ernst, as Vice

Chancellor, was seated near Schuschnigg, his superior.

Ferdi was daring enough to approach Hedy. "Have you decided on the day?"

"We can't talk about it now. Fritz mustn't see us together. Laure will get a message to you."

She abandoned the crowded salon and exited the palace, preferring the shrub-lined alleys of the Belevederegarten to the buzz of many voices. She sat on a bench and fished in her handbag for her platinum cigarette case.

"Fraulein Kiesler?"

A small and extremely slender woman stood on the other side of the low hedge. A large-brimmed hat shaded her bony face, a long pale oval that was striking in its symmetry. A bump of a mole marked a spot just above her chin.

Waving her cigarette holder at the palace, she asked, in a blend of English and American accents, "Was the King enjoying the reception?"

Comprehension dawned. This was Mrs. Simpson.

In halting English, Hedy replied, "Before I am out of the room, he had the Chancellor's son on his lap. Will you sit?"

"Walk with me. Easier to evade photographers if I keep moving, and these hedges are wonderfully shielding. Your journalists are prohibited from declaring my presence, but I don't trust them."

Rising, she discovered that she was taller by half a foot. "My English is bad."

"My German is non-existent. I envy David's, that is, His Majesty's fluency." Mrs. Simpson's eyes were icy blue, set beneath plucked arches. She angled her head, revealing sleek dark hair bundled into a chignon. "Thank heavens you're too young for him. Though somewhat older than you appear in your film, which we screened." Her lipstick and her nail varnish were the same vibrant red. Her dress, mono-chromatic and unadorned, fitted beautifully, its material hugging her narrow hips and drifting down past her calves. "I wonder if you might help me, Fraulein."

"I will try."

"During our . . . during the King's cruise on the Dalmatian coast, he fell out of a dinghy. Seawater got into his ear, and now there's an infection. He needs medical attention, from a very discreet doctor who has society's trust and approval. Do you know of anyone?"

"My parents took me to Dr. von Neumann whenever I had earache or sore throat. He's in the same building as Café Landtmann, near the university and the Burgtheatre. Everyone knows him, he has much respect."

"I'll arrange it. The King doesn't want to sicken while we're with the Rothschilds."

"You are invited to Schloss Enzesfeld?"

Mrs. Simpson nodded.

"We attend shooting parties there. My husband has a factory and a villa not far from the Rothschilds."

"I might've guessed a creature as lovely you are is married. To whom?"

"Fritz Mandl." Hedy released a smoky breath. "In Austria he is like royalty. Our newspapers call him 'the munitions king.'"

"Just the sort of person Da—the King would want to know. He's quite interested in industry."

"Do you miss America?"

"The people, yes. The attitudes, often. British people are so stuffy and judgmental. Their royal family is afflicted with a pack of court-iers who simultaneously revere them and hem them in. However, my life is tied to Britain. The King won't hear of my leaving." Hastily she added, "Nor would my husband, of course. Whatever happens, I can rely on his understanding and advice. He's a Canadian, and wonder-fully pragmatic."

That a husband could be amenable to his wife's affair with another man—who was a king—was incomprehensible. A cyclone of ques-tions, none of which she could utter, revolved in her mind.

"I've grown quite familiar with your country," Mrs. Simpson continued. "Last winter, we came here to ski. I disliked it. David was a disaster on the slopes. Last month we attended the big festival in

Salzburg. I don't dare admit it to David, but I much prefer Austrians to Germans. He has so many alarmingly Teutonic cousins." She placed her hand on Hedy's forearm. "I'm glad to gain a Viennese friend."

Her brittle cheer and outward confidence and elegant appearance cloaked an insecurity that Hedy recognized, and shared. She didn't admire her new acquaintance's hairstyle but was tempted to copy her center parting. As a brunette with similar coloring, she believed she could wear a lipstick as richly red as the sophisticated Mrs. Simpson's.

The sapphire eyes were studying her closely. "Tell me, where did you find your delightful frock?"

"Mainbocher designed it for me," Hedy answered.

"Not in his usual style."

"I like to wear the dirndl and asked him to make one in silk and velvet."

"Have you tried Vionnet? Lately I'm mad for her. And Elsa Schiaparelli for evening gowns."

"And for suits. In Paris I go also to Mademoiselle Chanel."

"You must be Vienna's best-dressed woman."

"My husband insists upon it," Hedy admitted. "But I would wear trousers all the time, if he let me."

"Last week when David hunted partridges, he insisted on doing it in Tyrolean dress. Most unflattering. Even worse than his kilt." In response to Hedy's confusion, Mrs. Simpson added, "The plaid wrap skirt that the Scotsmen wear."

The next day Baroness Kitty Rothschild telephoned from Schloss Enzesfeld.

"Wallis Simpson asks me to invite you, Frau Mandl. And your husband, of course. It's to be quite a mixed group. The Duff Coopers. Lady Diana, you know, was a Reinhardt actress. Lord and Lady Brownlow. Some people called Rogers. A few others, Americans and English. Can you come?"

In order to socialize with royalty and aristocracy, Fritz readily discarded whatever prior plans he had formed. On the appointed day, their Mercedes limousine joined the convoy of Rothschild guests. The medieval *schloss,* created over many centuries, boasted a turret and a tower. The company gathered in a vast high-ceilinged chamber hung with tapestries.

Baron Eugene Rothschild, whose family was closely connected with the Creditanstalt Bank, kissed Hedy's cheek in welcome.

"I remember how you and Frau Kiesler entertained us with duets on the grand piano. We spent many pleasant evenings in your home. Your father's experience and knowledge of banking are much missed in these difficult days. How sad that the stress of his directorship took so great a toll on his health. My dear, let me present you to our guest."

England's ruler was only slightly taller than his mistress, discounting her high heeled shoes. He was adept at small talk, and his smiles alternated between mere courtesy and outright impishness.

He expressed a desire to tour the nearby Hirtenberger factory. "My interest in industrial innovation and labor practices is keen, Herr Mandl." He turned his tawny head in Hedy's direction.

Don't, she pleaded silently, mention *Ecstasy.*

"Frau Mandl, I'm grateful for the introduction to Dr. Neumann."

"I am glad."

With a grace indicating much practice, he passed her over to Lady Diana Cooper. The renowned English beauty had toured America in Max Reinhardt's famed production of *The Miracle.* In French, their common language, she asked Hedy for news of the director.

A light lunch was served. Hedy, as usual, was the youngest person at the table. The revolving topics of fashion, scandal, and sport were just as uninteresting to her when discussed by the elite of various countries. As the afternoon wore on, the American ladies formed one subgroup, the Englishwomen another. There was no such division among the men. Struggling to hide her boredom, she cultivated Kitty Rothschild's dogs, planted on either side of her chair.

When the British King and his entourage departed Austria, the Union Jack banners came down from Vienna's buildings. Journalists resumed their dissections of the Chancellor's attempts to strengthen his military and avert the *Anschluss,* while also maintaining good relations with Hitler.

Fritz was moving money into neutral Switzerland, buying property there and in France, and as far away as Argentina. This redistribution of assets indicated that he was not as sanguine about the future as he wanted Hedy to believe.

Germany's Nuremberg Laws had deprived Jews of citizenship, and Hitler would impose the same legislation on Austria if there was ever an annexation. Austrian film producers no longer employed persons of Jewish blood, and the outflow of directors, actors, and technicians had increased. Hedy's ancestry was no secret in Vienna, or across the border, and Hitler cited it as his reason for banning *Ecstasy* from German cinemas. If he seized her homeland, she and Mutti and Fritz, son of a Jew, might well join the hundreds of thousands consigned to the concentration camps.

To revive her acting career was her dream. Ensuring her survival was a necessity.

With Laure's assistance, she'd begun a secret correspondence with a former colleague from Vienna's Sascha studios who had found work in Budapest. Encouraged by reports of employment opportunities there, she wrote one of her cousins expressing her desire to visit sometime before Christmas.

Like last year, her birthday celebration was muted. Not even Mutti, unable to conceal her discomfort around Fritz, was present.

After dinner he produced a miniature box covered in gold-flecked leather. Another ring.

"I asked King Edward where he purchased Mrs. Simpson's giant emerald. This one is even larger than hers. Twenty-two carats, a carat for every year of your life. It was mined in Columbia. Mademoiselle Toussaint at Cartier supervised the design."

The chandelier highlighted each facet of the green gemstone. "Magnificent," she murmured.

"You'll wear it when I take you to bed tonight. And nothing else."

He no longer wooed her with words or caresses. He used her body for his pleasure. And to make her pregnant.

"Our son," he panted in the dark prying his damp flesh from hers, "is going to have my brains and initiative, combined with your looks. I'll send him to the best schools in the world. And when he's old enough, he will join me in managing my companies."

He'll never exist. And this, she vowed, is the last birthday I will spend in this house, with this man.

——◁•◆•▷——

Wrapped in a full-length fur coat, a matching round hat perched low on her forehead, she stood on a platform at Vienna's Sudbanhof. A pair of suitcases held clothing. Her dressing case contained jewelry and personal necessities. Before leaving for the train station, she'd cut a slit in the silk lining and inserted her handwritten notes describing the secret torpedo, its control mechanism and trajectories.

Ferdi von Starhemberg opened the door of their carriage and helped her up the step. After handing up her luggage, he boarded with his single valise. When their belongings were stowed, they settled into their seats for the eastbound journey to Budapest.

The final stop inside Austria was the Nickelsdorf station. At Hegye-shalom she and Ferdi presented their passports. As the train chugged deeper into Hungary, she began to relax and let the numbing hum of iron wheels on the rails lull her to sleep.

When she woke, their compartment was thick with cigarette smoke, and its windows were squares of evening murkiness. Her neck ached after sitting so long with her head at an angle. "What time is it?"

"Almost seven. We're about an hour from Budapest. They'll be serving in the dining car."

"I don't know if I can eat anything."

"Why not decide once we're there?"

The cold air and jolting at the junction of the carriages blasted away the lingering effect of slumber. She ordered cheese on toast, a child-hood favorite, and ate several bites of a strudel that Ferdi finished.

In the lavatory she applied powder to her face and refreshed her red lipstick and combed her hair.

During the last stage of the journey, she felt calm enough to take her needlepoint from her handbag.

"How alike you and Nora are," her companion observed. "Besides both being actresses, you're seldom without your embroidery. She was sorry she didn't have a chance to say goodbye."

Hedy froze. "When did she say that?"

"Yesterday, when we took my nephew Heinrich to the Tiergarten Schönbrunn to see the wild animals. He's a delightful little—"

"You *told* her I'm leaving Fritz?"

"Certainly not."

"I hope you didn't mention Budapest."

"I said only that you wish to inquire about film or stage work. Which of course she understands. She thinks Fritz is most unreasonable."

It wasn't only that quality that had prompted Hedy's flight into Hungary. Unsure of how to instigate her divorce in a different country, she'd rely on Ferdi to explore her legal options while she consulted theatre and film producers. By the time Fritz returned from Rome, she intended to have an attorney and a job.

The train's whistle signalled their arrival at the Keteli rail yard. Ferdi removed their luggage from the rack and handed over her dressing case.

"I'll never forget how helpful you've been," she told him. "Making the arrangements. And coming with me."

He couldn't remain in Budapest indefinitely and before long would return to Vienna. For her, this city was the first stop in a much longer journey. If luck favored her, it would someday carry her as far away as America.

With a squeal of breaks, the train slowed. They joined the line of passengers in the corridor. Ferdi exited first with her suitcases, and she passed him the dressing case and his valise.

Before her feet touched the platform, she saw her husband.

Chapter 8

won't cower. He despises weakness.

But not as much as disloyalty.

Fritz marched up to Ferdi and drew his hand from his coat pocket. Not to deliver a blow, but to hold up a slip of paper.

"Your ticket to Bucharest. You will stay at the Grand Hotel, and I will cover your bills. I don't give a damn how long you stay in Romania or what the hell you do while you're there. Never approach my wife again. Whatever friendship existed between us is dead."

Through gritted teeth, Ferdi responded, "Don't hurt her."

"I never have. I never will. Not that it's any business of yours."

Biting her lower lip, Hedy watched her would-be rescuer abandon her. He didn't look back.

"Only two suitcases?" Fritz observed. "You surprise me."

"I'm visiting my cousin."

"Ernst suspected otherwise. After Nora told him you'd taken the afternoon train to Budapest, with his brother, he cabled me in Rome. My pilot and plane are at the airport. There will be no scandal. Do you understand?"

He didn't speak to her again until they were on board and belted into their seats.

"You aren't in love with Ferdi, so don't pretend that I've disrupted a grand romance."

Thankful for the engines' roar, she offered no denial or defense.

"Ernst is wholly dependent on me, and my goodwill is more essential to him than his brother's. Before the dissolution of his *Heimwehr*, I supplied their guns and ammunition. For years I have supported him financially. He lost his government position, so without my assistance he couldn't maintain Nora and the child."

For a man whose wrath could be volatile, Fritz was strangely calm.

"Would you have followed me," she wondered, "if I'd left on my own? Without Ferdi?"

"To be perfectly honest, I'm not sure."

In victory, he'd acknowledged a small measure of defeat.

After the Budapest fiasco, speculation about Hedy's relationship with Ferdi von Starhemberg consumed upper class Vienna. Fritz insisted on an expedient retreat to his hunting estate. Rising before dawn, he spent the morning hours stalking large game animals with his factory managers. Twice a week, Madame Marton, his personal secretary, brought his correspondence and contracts and other paperwork from the Vienna office. She was extremely attractive. Her easy familiarity with Fritz and their many hours behind the closed door of the library made Hedy wonder whether the relationship purely professional. If her husband was carrying on an affair, it would bolster her case for a separation.

In early December, King Edward VIII of England abruptly gave up his throne. As Duke of Windsor, the former monarch deserted a kingdom in crisis and sought refuge at nearby Schloss Enzesfeld.

When Baroness Rothschild telephoned, Hedy steeled herself for an onslaught of uncomfortable questions about her marriage. Luckily, Kitty was preoccupied with the unexpected impact of the abdication.

"Nobody in England expected this—Eugene's relatives over there are prostrate with shock. The King can't meet Wallis until she divorces Mr. Simpson. Her next husband shifts from relief to despondency and back again. He misses her most terribly, and he's one who relies on female companionship and stimulating conversation. I'm hoping you and Herr Mandl will join us for dinner tonight. It might cheer him."

Hedy doubted that Fritz would seek the company of the Duke of Windsor as avidly as he'd courted King Edward of England. However, his shared business interests with the banker Rothschild compelled him to accept the invitation. Like any hostage, she said or did whatever was necessary to render her captivity easier, and excused herself by falsely pleading queasiness.

"You will go with me," he insisted. "Wear the emerald ring. I want the Duke of Windsor to see it."

How unkind and insensitive he was, flaunting his wealth and his wife before a king who had just given up his kingdom and was deprived of his beloved.

"I left it in Vienna, in the safe." She added, "I feel extremely unwell. You wouldn't want me to miscarry."

"If you're pregnant, you'd better pray the child has Mandl features and not von Starhemberg ones."

She fled to the bathroom and locked herself in.

He went to Schloss Enzesfeld without her.

His mood was no better when he returned. He barged into Hedy's room—she was reading in bed—to air his complaints. Heavy rain and fog had clouded the road. A cadre of reporters lurked at the gates with their flashing cameras. The chill of night permeated the stone walls of the Rothschilds' *schloss*. The Duke of Windsor seldom spoke, and when he did it was in drawling English rather than crisp German.

"He cradled his terrier, very likely for warmth as much for comfort. Louis Rothschild offered to host a hunting party at Waidhofen. Hardly a flicker of interest. The duke only cared whether the telephone exchange there was better than the Enzesfeld one. The phone line cuts out whenever he chats with his woman. I told him the difficulty was probably on the French side."

"I'm glad I didn't go," Hedy murmured.

"Our meal was dismal, unworthy of Baron Eugene's kitchen. Why doesn't he import a Paris chef to go with the Bordeaux and the Roquefort and the Brie? The Triesting River teems with fresh fish, the forests are filled with venison on the hoof. A table surrounded by Jews, and he served us pork cutlets!"

"Why does that matter? We were raised in Christian households. Our families never followed their ancestors' dietary rules."

"Are you feeling better?"

"My monthly cramping started. I took an aspirin."

Dashing his dream of an infant Mandl was punishment for his accusation that Ferdi von Starhemberg had been her lover.

Hedy and her widowed sister-in-law Renée Ferro were joint hostesses at the annual Christmas party for Hirtenberger managers. Fritz spared no expense on food, drink, decorations, and music. With the steady flow of alcohol, the festive crowd grew louder and livelier.

"Fraulein Kiesler." The stranger, whose accent identified him as a German, added uncertainly, "Or should I address you as Frau Mandl?" His eyes, dark and intense, were set beneath coal-black brows.

"That's preferable, on this occasion," she answered.

"I'm Hellmuth Walter. My wife, Ingeborg."

The creator of the secret torpedo plans in Fritz's desk. "What's your title?" she inquired. "How long have you worked for my husband?"

"With him rather than for him," he corrected her. "I'm a propulsion engineer."

"What do you propel, Herr Walter?"

Smiling ruefully, Frau Walter murmured, "You'll wish you hadn't asked."

Hedy encouraged him with a nod. "I'm quite interested."

"I develop technologies for gas-powered submarines and build prototypes at my testing facility in Kiel."

"Submarines," she repeated. He hadn't mentioned torpedoes.

"We also pursue innovations in rocketry. Herr von Braun is in charge of aircraft technology."

"You don't manufacture weapons?"

"Oh, we do. On behalf of our Navy, we're devising a more reliable remote-control system for torpedoes. Which led to our collaboration with Herr Mandl."

If Fritz had involved himself in a German naval project, he was working for Adolf Hitler. The enemy of all right-thinking Europeans. A threat to neighboring nations. A murderer of Jews.

Concealing her resentment, she said, "My husband, I suppose, provides the shells for your torpedoes. And you determine how to direct them from the submarine to the target."

"Precisely."

Ingeborg Walter stared at her. "For a film star, you catch on quickly. Hellmuth's concepts are very complex."

Her spouse smiled. "I haven't even got to the complexities."

"Please do. You can tell me about it during dinner."

"My pleasure," he replied.

She found places at the main table, at a distance from Fritz and the other Mandls and the senior staff.

At the start of his opening address, Fritz acknowledged his father Alexander Mandl, son of the company's founder. He identified managers of various divisions and their products: small arms ammunition and the metal components used by client companies for their tanks and airplanes. He boasted of the current year's successes and favorable prospects for 1937.

Hedy pondered certain facts that he failed to mention. The market for weaponry produced by the Mandls, the Krupps, and their competitors had increased because European nations were arming themselves for the next war. After several years of demonstrations and riots in Austria and in neighboring countries, Nazis infiltrated and destabilized governments in preparation for German incursion.

The products created by her husband, and his employees, and

the pleasant man seated beside her caused death and destruction. Bullets, bombs, grenades, landmines, tanks, warplanes. Did these rich, well-dressed people ever consider the bloodshed or the destruction their creations caused? Were they haunted by images of maimed bodies and ravaged landscapes?

Her satin and velvet gowns, the jewels and furs, expensive motorcars, servants, the luxurious houses—all her possessions flowed from the merchandizing of weapons.

Everything I touch, she mourned, is tainted.

After a series of celebratory toasts, Hedy resumed her conversation with the designer of torpedoes that could shatter and sink ships at sea. She followed Hellmuth Walter's finger as it moved across the tablecloth to illustrate his guidance system.

"To avoid detection, we must ensure that the torpedo leaves behind no wake when approaching its target. For propellant, we use hydrogen peroxide mixed with a lesser amount of lime catalyst. Because the resulting mixture isn't visible in seawater, the path is invisible. Unfortunately, the torpedo's fuel capacity is small, so it can't travel very far. In time, we'll overcome that limitation."

"Before dinner, you referred to remote control. How is that different from the way you guide your torpedoes now?"

"They receive operator signals through a wire connected to the launcher. Your husband is keen to employ a different type of communications. Missiles dropped by aircraft are controlled by radio waves. Each bomb has its own unique frequency and is guided separately from the rest. It prevents signal jamming."

"As with radio broadcasts," she said.

He nodded. "Anyone who disturbs the signal would disable the missile. It's called interference. Despite our best efforts, we can't yet control submarine-fired torpedoes remotely. The radio frequencies don't pass through water in the same way they do through the air."

"Your wife spoke the truth. There's much complexity in your work."

"Perhaps this time next year, I'll be able to announce our success."

"I look forward to that."

She wouldn't be there to hear him.

———⊃•◆•⊂———

To quell persistent gossip about the state of their marriage, Fritz and Hedy attended the Vienna Opera Ball, highlight of the winter social season. She enhanced the regal effect of her plum-colored velvet gown with the crescent tiara and a large diamond brooch. Fritz, who always looked his best in white tie and tails, escorted her to their loge in the middle tier. From this elevated situation, she counted the dignitaries assembled beneath the soaring oval roof: Chancellor Schuschnigg, Foreign Secretary Schmidt, Sir Walford Selby from the British Embassy, and others. In years past, she'd enjoyed this gathering of the powerful and the privileged. Tonight, she took no pleasure from the orchestral music or the singing or the dancing.

"When can we go?" she whispered to Fritz.

"At any time."

"I want to walk."

"It's awfully cold."

"I've got my fur."

The air outside the Opera House was bracing but not unbearable. In a gallant gesture of husbandly care, he fastened her chinchilla cape to cover her neck and chest.

How strange, this sense of privacy as they strolled along a busy street at night. At home, servants were always within earshot. In a motorcar, their chauffeur was on the other side of the glass partition. At a restaurant or dinner party, watchful eyes searched for evidence of the estrangement they sought to hide when appearing together in public.

She clutched the sleeve of his greatcoat. "I need a mountain holiday, in a place where I can ski. In wintertime Papa often took Mutti and me to St. Moritz. I want to go there. Without you."

"How long would you stay?"

"A few weeks."

He paused beneath a street lamp to light his cigar. The breeze played with the flame of his lighter, reducing it to a spark.

"Let me." She took the lighter from him, cupping her hand around it.

He expelled a smoky breath. "I might agree, with certain conditions. Your mother goes along as chaperone. I will telephone your hotel every day. I might decide to join you at any time, without advance notice. You had best be there." He tapped his cigar against an iron railing.

Watching the ash drift down to the pavement, she readily agreed to his terms.

"I miss the time when we were friends, Hasi," he said unexpectedly. "Have I made you hate me?"

She shook her head. On this night, she didn't. She wouldn't think about being spied upon by servants and having her movements restricted. Or that German torpedo. Because at long last he was willing to acknowledge the failure of their marriage.

"My secretary will take care of your reservation. First class train carriage. A suitable hotel, convenient to the slopes."

When Hedy arrived at the resort, her spirits soared as high as the snow-clad peak of Piz Nair, visible from her room. The fresh air was scented with evergreen. The sky was as perfectly blue as the Blessed Mother's robe. A pristine layer of snow covered the ground. Their fellow guests looked cheerful and relaxed.

Mutti's mood was brighter, too. "Emil loved this place. It brings back happy memories."

They spent their days outdoors, skiing or skating. Twice a day they worked up an appetite for the hearty Swiss fare by walking Chérie, Mutti's coal-black Scotch terrier puppy. They drank the iron-rich spring water. The cable car carried them to the Olympic stadium, which they saw being built almost a decade ago.

When Fritz telephoned, she received a detailed report about the Duke of Windsor.

"Baron Eugene and Kitty decamped to Paris," he reported, "leaving their guest at Schloss Enzesfeld. When I called on him, he said he wanted to spend his honeymoon in that ghastly ruin. He counts the weeks until his mistress obtains her final divorce decree."

Hedy's athletic pursuits interested Fritz less than her accounts of the celebrities who were present. When rattling off names of authors and directors, actors and actresses, she withheld the most meaningful one.

She'd wept over Erich Maria Remarque's war novel *All Quiet on the Western Front* and sobbed throughout the cinematic version. His sensitive depiction of the battlefield, his somber intelligence, and his dark good looks combined to arouse intense interest. Her sympathy was stirred by the author exiled from his own country, reviled by the Nazi government that orchestrated the public incineration of his book and its film. Gazing into his dark eyes, shadowed by a soldier's sadness, she ached to console him. When he admitted that his battle wounds rendered him nearly impotent, she was eager to discover the extent of his malady. And their affair began.

"My husband has no morals," she confided to him in the hotel bar, after her nightly telephone conversation with Fritz. "Fighting and even killing to support a righteous cause might be justifiable, in a case of good versus evil. But his loyalty belongs only to his companies and his bank accounts and investments. Profit is everything to him."

"He sounds monstrous."

"He infuriated Mussolini by supplying arms to both sides in Spain's civil war. He received top secret documents from a German engineer who makes torpedoes and airplanes and submarines." The cognac was hot and fiery against her throat. "He's a traitor."

"If the Germans invade Austria, your husband stands to lose all the things he values. Their munitions factories are nationalized, controlled by Hitler and Goebbels and the rest."

"The *Anschluss* would be ruinous. For all of us." She drew a sharp breath. "I can't bear thinking about it."

Erich gave her a copy of his latest novel, with an inscription too personal to share with Mutti.

From soul to soul, calling to one another. E.R.M.

"I want you to play Patrice when they make the film of *Three Comrades*," he told her as they sat smoking on his balcony, wrapped in blankets. "It's as though my imagination conjured you before we met. You and she are beautiful and tragic, from similar backgrounds. Your suffering will give depth to your performance, as mine informs my books. We are artistic to our very core. That's an aspect of your character that your husband cannot comprehend." His lips merged with hers. "To be true to your real self, you must sever yourself from what you hold dear. Your mother. Your country. I wonder if you're prepared for that."

"I am."

"You need a strong heart to live without roots."

She placed his hand on her breast. "Feel how powerfully this one is beating. For you."

Starved for a relationship built on mutual desire and dependence, she was quick to love him. Erich understood her. They shared an appreciation of books and music and the dramatic arts. He didn't seek to control or constrain her.

The next time Fritz rang, he announced that he would arrive in two days. His perception and his possessiveness were equally acute. If he discovered her liaison, he'd be less likely to consent to divorce. Or— even better—an annulment, so she could remarry in the church. Was Erich religious? She knew only that he'd had been raised in a Catholic family and his early marriage to an actress ended after several years of strife.

"Don't bother. I'm bored to death. And Mutti says she's ready to return to Vienna before the pup has an accident on one of the hotel carpets."

"I'll send a car to meet you and Trude—and the dog—at the station."

Unaware that Hedy spent her nights in Erich's bed, her mother believed the Alpine air and the mineral waters had refreshed and invigorated her. Boarding the train that would carry her away from her lover, she rejoiced in the knowledge that her longed-for freedom wouldn't be as lonely, or as friendless, as she'd previously feared.

Think with your heart, Hedl, and you'll win in the end.

She intended to follow her father's advice.

Chapter 9

"I didn't expect to find you here, Frau Mandl."

Hedy regarded her visitor curiously, then glanced at the card he'd presented. "Do you have business with my husband, Herr Sobotka?" The name was vaguely familiar, but she couldn't think why. There was nothing especially memorable about his appearance. His dark hair was receding from a prominent forehead, and he wore glasses with black frames and thick lenses.

"I'm an architect. I also design interiors. And furniture."

"I envy you," she confessed. "I trained in design, before my marriage. You must be acquainted with my father's cousin, Friedrich Kiesler."

"Not well, but we've corresponded a few times in the years since he went to America. Perhaps one day I will follow him into academia."

Smiling, she responded, "You know more about him than I do."

He held up his briefcase. "I've brought the plans Herr Mandl commissioned."

"Plans? For what?"

"You make this very awkward for me, Frau Mandl. I'm responsible for the improvements to his hunting lodge. The new guest accommodations and the . . . the nursery wing."

It was pointless to pretend she had knowledge of this. "I'd like to look at your designs, please."

"Certainly."

She took him to Fritz's study.

He spread the renderings across the broad desk and showed her the exterior elevation as well as floor plans for a large, multilevel addition. "The children's wing is here. The guest rooms, there."

"When did you visit?"

"Last month he invited me to look over the property. My daughter Ruth was there as well, hoping to meet you. Your performance as Empress Sissi gave her a taste for the stage. She's studying dance with a star of the Vienna Opera House company. But that day Herr Mandl had his—his other lady with him."

"Madam Marton, his secretary?"

Shaking his head, he replied, "She had a title. Countess, baroness— I can't recall. Her hair was blonde. She's the next Frau Mandl, yes? She said I should make the nursery very large because she wants many babies."

Damn Fritz. When she'd described him to Erich, she hadn't even realized the depth of his amorality.

If he'd already chosen her replacement, he must want a divorce as much as she did. What deeper game was he playing?

"You can leave the plans here," she told the architect.

"If Herr Mandl requires any alterations before construction begins, he may contact me. They are included in my fee. The cover letter serves as an invoice for payment."

She nodded absently, her mind too busy for details that didn't concern her.

When Fritz returned, she confronted him with the architect's revelations. All of them.

With no sign of remorse, he said accusingly, "You have broken trust with me so many times. Why wouldn't I seek the companionship of a woman who appreciates all that I can offer? One who will be quite content to bear and raise my children. And don't pretend that you've been entirely faithful, because I won't believe you."

When she announced that she'd be leaving for Carlsbad that evening, he made no attempt to stop her.

"Do as you please. I'm traveling to Marienbad tomorrow."

To join his mistress, she supposed. And she didn't care if he did.

———◦·◆·◦———

Hedy's refuge from her enigmatic, straying spouse lay west of Prague in the Bohemian territory designated by Germany as Sudetenland. As in Austria, military personnel and recently erected fortifications at the border were bulwarks against Hitler's encroachment. The Hotel Imperial loomed above the spa town and afforded a panoramic view of surrounding tree-clad hills, vibrantly green beneath the June sunshine.

After a month's separation, Fritz joined her. She doubted he had come to soak in the famous thermal baths.

He commandeered her suite for a meeting he described as important.

"Dr. Joeden will be dining with us."

"Are you ill?"

"Kind of you to inquire, dear wife," he replied with heavy sarcasm. "I've never felt better." Turning back to the table, set for the midday meal, he tucked a gleaming golden object inside the starched napkin.

"What's that?"

"A present for my guest." He unfolded the fabric to reveal a cigarette case.

While he was in his bedroom with his valet, changing out of his travel clothes, she eased the cigarette case from its hiding place and pried it open with her fingernail. Inside was a check for many thousands of francs, drawn on Fritz's Swiss bank account. Excessive for a medical consultation. A bribe?

Curious about this visitor, she answered the knock at the door.

"Dr. Johann Joeden. So very pleased to meet you, Frau Mandl."

He was German.

As he bowed over her hand, she asked, "Are you an engineer, like Herr Walter?"

"Ah, no," Joeden replied, "although I reside in Kiel, where his factory is located. I'm a director at Krupp Enterprises, serving the firm in a legal capacity, related to finance."

That Fritz conferred with an employee of the Krupp munitions companies wasn't surprising, given their joint manufacturing projects within Austria. But Krupp's German branch was far more sinister, being so closely allied with the Reich.

Hedy detected nothing damning in the two men's dialogue. Fritz offered an optimistic picture of Austria's recovery from its financial crisis, joking that his extravagant wife was largely responsible for the change. His guest boasted of the surge in German manufacturing during Hitler's chancellorship.

Waiters arrived with trolleys of food and swiftly departed.

Dr. Joeden continued, "Demand for armaments far exceeds supply. The Krupps are willing to join your syndicate for the purchase of the Berndorf works, provided we can agree on the division of shares."

"One third to Hirtenberger Patronen-fabrik. Another third or more, if they insist, to the Krupps. The remainder for Koenig, who managed Berndorf before the Creditanstalt Bank took it over."

"Your Enzesfield factory has the monopoly for artillery ammunition. What will be produced at Berndorf?"

"Semi-finished and finished brass for cartridges."

"And now to the most essential point. Your estimate for the overall cost of our enterprise."

"Ten million schillings." After a pause to re-calculate, Fritz amended, "Possibly eight.'"

"I trust the Creditanstalt would regard the offer as acceptable."

"Austria's former Minister of Finance, one of our Hirtenberger directors, can inquire. The syndicate's membership will remain confidential."

Joeden nodded. "Far better, from the German perspective, to keep your name out of it. As long as we can."

Fritz waved a dismissive hand. "My involvement in our transactions will be entirely lawful. Hermann Goering himself bestowed on me the special status of honorary Aryan."

He was more closely aligned with the Nazis than Hedy had guessed. After Hitler, Goering was the most powerful man in Germany.

When she abruptly excused herself, both men rose. Courtesy was observed, she reflected bitterly, even in the midst of conspiracy.

She went to her bedroom, where Laure was mending the ruffled cuff on a blouse.

"I'm returning to Vienna. Please have our suitcases brought here from hotel storage so we can pack at once. Where's my passport?"

Laure was already on her feet. "In your bureau drawer. I'll get it."

When the luggage was ready, the maid arranged for it to be taken to the hotel's Customs officer for immediate inspection.

Fritz and his guest had carried their coffee outside to the balcony. Hedy doubted they would hear the bellboy's knock. She and Laure had to wait their turn in the Customs office, but the questioning and examination were swiftly completed. They exited to find Fritz in the lobby, standing beside a potted palm with his arms crossed.

Hedy was prepared.

She plastered on a smile. "So thoughtful of you to see me off."

"Where do you think you're going?"

"Home."

"I don't believe you."

"Ask the desk clerk who changed my money. Or the Customs man. I don't tell lies to government officials. Can you say the same?" When he reached for her arm, she evaded him. "The Nazis are beasts. Their leaders are the most inhumane men on the face of the earth. There's no honor in letting them call you an honorary Aryan. It's a disgrace!"

"You are hysterical. Come back to the suite."

His menacing tone dissolved her composure. With both hands she shoved at his chest, hard enough to knock him off balance. "Enough!" she cried. She pushed him again, more forcefully.

A teenaged girl standing nearby laughed, loudly. Her mother, an American, shushed her.

He loathed public scenes, but Hedy was thankful for so many witnesses. Everyone was staring at them—society people from Vienna and Berlin and Budapest, international celebrities on holiday.

She lowered her voice. "There's no love between us now. No tenderness at all. Let's end this sham of a marriage as quickly as we can."

Tonelessly he replied, "You're a Catholic."

"An annulment, then."

"On what grounds?"

"Your first wife charged you with cruelty. To that, I can add infidelity. And insanity, based on your association with a murderous, warmongering dictator. The same man you vowed to keep out of Austria. That makes you a traitor." She turned her back on him.

He didn't try to stop her when she made her way to the door. Laure was waiting outside with a taxi that took them to the station.

After a long and tiring train journey, she entered the white mansion in Schwartzenbergplatz. Despite the late hour, she went to the telephone in the library and dialed a number, once familiar and unforgotten.

"Nora, it's Hedy. I hope I haven't interrupted your dinner. Can I come by, please? Tonight?"

———◦•◆•◦———

"Ferdi cared about you," Nora Gregor told Hedy. "More than you realized."

Almost a year had passed since their abrupt parting on the Budapest railway platform. She hadn't seen him since then.

"I didn't betray you," the actress added. "When I mentioned to Ernst that his brother was accompanying you to Hungary, he drew the obvious conclusion and felt duty-bound to inform Fritz. He regarded Ferdi's behaviour as a blot on the Starhembergs' family honor."

"It doesn't matter now. Sometime this summer, either Fritz or I will travel to Riga for a speedy divorce. And I'll consult Cardinal Innitzer about an annulment."

"It takes forever," Nora pointed out. "Ernst has been trying for ages."

Hedy leaned forward. "He means to marry you?"

"As soon as he's free. He wants to legitimize Heinrich."

"Fritz hasn't breathed a word about it. Did he tell you he's planning to remarry?" She described how she discovered the existence of his future bride, and their plans to procreate. Stabbing the ashtray with her cigarette stub, she said, "Let's not talk about him. I'm ready to work again. Either at the Burgtheatre, or with the Josefstadt company."

"I'll do whatever I can to help. I owe you that." Nora sifted through a stack of bound scripts and handed one to Hedy. "*The Women*—a new play, from a director at Max's theatre. An all-female cast. In New York it was a great success, and Helmuth Lothar has adapted it. His wife will have a plum part, you can be sure. If the Burgtheatre releases me, and Fritz lets you, we could perform together!"

"I'm not asking permission." It would be advantageous to present him with a *fait accompli* whenever he returned to Vienna.

"Where will you live after your divorce?"

"I suppose I'll rent a flat between the theatres." She imagined upper floor rooms with a street or courtyard view, cozy and bright, and decorated to her own taste. Until she was called to Hollywood to star in Erich's *Three Comrades,* she'd support herself on her earnings as an actress and reserve her accumulated savings for the future.

Her initial meeting with Director Horch of the Josefstadt buoyed her optimism. He remembered her performance in *Sissi,* and her assurances of a forthcoming recommendation from Max Reinhardt found favor.

"Rehearsals don't begin till late September, but I'm hurrying to put my players under contract." Her prospective employer grimaced. "That motion picture man Mayer is here again from Hollywood, poaching talent for his studio. Nora Gregor tells me you've seen the script. Would the role of Crystal be acceptable?"

After playing ingenues, the selfish and greedy mistress would be an interesting challenge. Exploiting her sexuality was a risk, because of *Ecstasy*, but the part he proposed was rich with caustic dialogue.

By the time a curiously subdued Fritz reappeared, she felt even more confident of an offer from Horch. Judging it best to say nothing, she kept her expectations to herself.

One evening, as they faced one another across the long expanse of the dining table, she asked, "Which of us is going to Riga?"

"I'd prefer a holiday in Antibes. But I don't imagine you'll go with me."

"I can't imagine why you'd want me to," she replied. "I'm accepting Max's invitation to the Salzburg Festival. Toscanini will conduct Wagner. The Mozart celebration has Ezio Pinza performing both Figaro and Don Giovanni. And Captain von Trapp's family will sing choral music."

"Are they any good?"

"We saw them last year. They won the amateurs' contest." Reaching for the antique silver grape scissors, she sliced small branch from the cluster.

"I'm not keen to see *Everyman* again."

She paused before placing a grape in her mouth. "I thought you disliked the festival. You're always so reluctant to attend."

"It's an important feature of national life," he responded. "Choose whatever August dates suit you, and purchase the tickets you prefer."

His surrender of responsibility for planning was as unprecedented as his indifference about details. Pondering his reasons for accompanying her, she assumed he intended to meet with dignitaries— German ones, perhaps.

During their stay in Salzburg, she and Fritz attended concerts and the evening parties where illustrious visitors gathered. When they were alone together, he maintained a glassy civility that would probably shatter if she raised the subject of divorce.

At a time when Max had so many demands on his attention, Hedy was grateful for his invitation to join him at a café.

"Horch tells me you're doing the new play at the Josefstadt. My dear, I beg you to be more careful about dubious backstage visitors than you were during your previous theatrical engagement."

"You needn't worry about that. The man I love isn't dubious, and he's nothing like Fritz. You've heard of him—you might be acquainted with him—but I won't reveal his name. His latest novel is being produced in Hollywood by MGM. He says I'm perfect for the heroine."

"Interesting. Perhaps that's why Mr. Mayer inquired about you when I saw him."

His declaration startled her. "He's here?"

"In Carlsbad, for the water cure. Very effective, I gather. Every night he dances the rumba with the Hungarian soprano, Ilona Hajmassey. She'll probably earn herself a contract."

"Her English can't be any worse than mine," she commented acidly, recalling the ill-fated dinner party when the studio head heaped humiliation upon her. "Horch is afraid he'll steal all the best actresses in Vienna and take them back to Hollywood."

"When does he begin rehearsing you?"

"In a few weeks. By then I hope to be divorced from Fritz. Nobody will be shocked. The newspapers already predict it." For a long moment she stared into her empty coffee cup, then looked over at him. "To keep you in Germany, didn't the Nazis offer to designate you an honorary Aryan?"

"I refused. So must you, if they succeed with annexation."

"Fritz accepted."

He shrugged. "Industrialists are highly valuable to the Reich. More so than theatre directors."

"But blood is blood. As you told me, years ago, we all have the wrong kind to live fearlessly in a German state. He says he'll be safe. But if he were so sure, he wouldn't have transferred so much of his fortune into Switzerland and Argentina."

When Vienna's newspapers reported that Hedy Kiesler would play Crystal in *The Women*, Fritz threatened legal action against the theatre and the play's director. His wife, he declared, could not enter into a theatrical contract without his permission. The offer of employment was immediately withdrawn.

Furious and devastated, Hedy related these developments in a lengthy letter to Erich, residing in Venice. As soon as she could, she would join him there.

His reply contained none of the passion or tenderness that had pervaded earlier letters. If she was intent on divorce, she should remain in Austria, because in Italy it was nearly impossible. He was sorry about her professional disappointment but trusted that opportunities would surface after she severed her marriage. Their time together in St. Moritz would live on in his memory, he concluded, but he no longer envisioned a shared future.

Hopelessness descended. With no play to keep her occupied and no lover to console her, life as a single woman would be lonely and dull.

She was quietly weeping over the letter when Fritz entered the drawing room.

"What's wrong?" he asked.

Reluctant to show weakness, she tucked the sheets into her skirt pocket and blotted her tears with her handkerchief. "I'm miserable. And terrified. Hitler knows I've got Jewish family, it's why he kept *Ecstasy* out of Germany. If the Nazis overthrow our government, they won't make me an honorary Aryan. They'll probably send Mutti and me to a camp."

"It won't happen," he insisted. "Even after the divorce, I'll look after you."

"I'm fearful for you, too. Mussolini cast you off. Why wouldn't Hitler do the same?"

"He wants what my factories produce. Nevertheless, I'm prepared for all contingencies. I deposited twenty million francs in Switzerland and invested nearly as much in Argentina." His lizard-like smile faded when he told her, "Tomorrow I leave for Hungary with Ernst and a few more. It's a hunting party. I expect to be away for at least a week, perhaps longer. When I return, we will decide the terms of our separation."

She lifted her head. For the first time he'd indicated complete acceptance of the inevitable break. "Terms?"

"Financial arrangements. Your domicile. The amount of maintenance I am willing to provide."

"I don't want anything, Fritz."

Freedom, tantalizingly close, would be enough.

"Nevertheless, you should take legal advice."

Lawyers and negotiations and settlements. Added together, they resulted in delay. He had his own reasons for agreeing to the divorce—a blonde noblewoman and the prospect of creating more Mandls. But his interference at the theatre was all the proof she needed that he wouldn't readily cede control over her future. And as long as she remained in Vienna, in Austria, he would stand as an obstacle to her wellbeing and her peace of mind.

"Have a pleasant journey," she said.

Those four polite words, she decided, were the last she would address to him in person.

———————⊂•◆•⊃———————

From an upper window, she observed the group gathered around the blue Rolls Royce Phantom III roadster, sent from Germany last month and paid for with Reichsmarks. Ernst von Starhemberg helped Fritz raise the hood to reveal the engine. With them was the Mandl's Belgian banker, Hugo Marton, husband of Fritz's trusted and very beautiful secretary. They all climbed inside and he lowered the fabric hood before driving off. The Mercedes limousine, driven by the chauffeur, followed with luggage, gun cases, and the valet.

She returned to her room to resume her own packing.

Fur coats, their pockets stuffed with gemstone necklaces and bracelets, went into one of the large trunks. Laure was filling another with evening gowns, layering paper between them to reduce creasing. A smart suit, several dirndls, and day dresses went into a third. Shoes and a selection of hats and handbags filled a suitcase. Still tucked beneath the inner lining of her vanity case were her notes on German weapons manufacture and sketches of Hellmuth Walter's torpedo.

She made room for a few mementoes. An album of family photographs. Her gold compact, a gift from Mutti, with *Hello, Darling* engraved on the disk that protected the cake of powder. From her dressing table she removed a double frame. In one picture she smiled up at Papa on the veranda of the house in Peter-Jordanstrasse, in the other she stood beside Mutti. She couldn't leave behind her two music boxes—the wind-up clown with the pointy red hat, and the porcelain ballerina who spun to the *Blue Danube* waltz. Her beloved dolly Beccacine, a favorite companion during her solitary childhood, was also going with her.

To rid the house of spying eyes and ears, she gave the servants a holiday. Undetected, she and the maid transferred the luggage to the vehicle the staff used for errands and transporting household supplies. With a growl of gears, Laure drove off in the direction of the Südbahnhof.

For the first time, Hedy was completely alone in the vast apartment where she'd received princes and playboys and politicians. Her four years as nominal mistress of her husband's domain certainly didn't inspire nostalgia. She took up her purse and gripped the handle of her vanity case. She descended the staircase for the final time and exited the Ofenheim Palace through its broad central door.

Striding along Prinz-Eugenstrasse, Hedy joined the flow of her fellow Viennese going about their daily business, darting in and out of shops, gathering at the cafés. Dimming daylight lent a surreal quality to the landscape and its inhabitants.

She thought about Mutti, who had promised to pray for her morning and night, and light a candle in the parish church. When would they meet again? And where?

"The porter took your luggage," Laure told her when she arrived in the station waiting room. "I bought some magazines. Here's your ticket. The train's not due for a while yet."

"You needn't stay."

"Did you leave a note for Herr Mandl?"

Hedy smiled. "Like a runaway wife in a novel? No. I'll telephone him when I reach the Riviera. Or from Paris. If he behaves badly, my mother will house you until you can arrange your travel. All the things I've left behind are yours, if you want them. Goodbye for now, Laure."

"*Au revoir,* Madame. *Bonne chance.*"

Instead of remaining in the lounge with first class passengers who might recognize her, Hedy made her way to an empty bench on the platform. She was conscious of the weighty items beneath her ruffled blouse—multiple strands of pearls and gold chains strung with her most valuable rings. The magazines lay unopened on her lap.

She was struck by the familiarity of her situation, almost identical to her final scene in *Ecstasy.* She could remember the glow from a lamppost, contrasting with the surrounding darkness, and the hardness of the bench. Her facial expressions had conveyed her remorse and her responsibility for her estranged husband's suicide.

"Tell him . . . tell him nothing," she had said to the station master, before she deserted her sleeping lover and boarded the wrong train.

I told Fritz nothing.

Up to this moment, her life and Eva's had run in parallel. Pampered daughter of a rich family, she'd married a wealthy older suitor with whom she had too little in common, who was consumed by other interests. She'd found sexual satisfaction with another man. She was deserting her husband.

Her train was here.

Unlike Eva, she knew no guilt.

PART 2: 1937–1940

"Suddenly everybody gets excited and I am important.
This I do not understand."
—Hedy Lamarr

Chapter 10

Arriving for her appointment with a London talent agent, Hedy's spirits lifted at the sight of a familiar face from Vienna.

"I forgot you lived here," she told Walter Reisch before they kissed cheeks.

"Lisl will be jealous when I tell her I was with that other most beautiful creature from Austria!"

"Is Mrs. Schulberg your agent?"

"My matchmaker. I'm to develop stories and write scripts for Metro-Goldwyn-Mayer. In Hollywood. At the end of the month, Lisl and I sail to America on *Normandie,* with the studio head himself. Our honeymoon voyage."

After congratulating him on his marriage, Hedy said, "Mr. Mayer is in London now, isn't he?"

"Only to sleep, I suspect. He spends most of his time overseeing a production at Denham Studios, the MGM outpost here. Where are you staying?"

"The Regent Palace."

"I'm meeting Bob Ritchie, Mayer's talent scout, for drinks at the Café Royal—across from your hotel. My little ballerina can join us for dinner. And Herr Mandl, of course."

"I traveled alone. Fritz is in . . . " She shrugged. "I don't know where he might be. Later I will explain," she added as the inner office door swung open.

"You're early, Mr. Reisch," said the woman in the doorway. "Miss Kiesler, so pleased to meet you. I'm Adeline Schulberg. Everyone calls me Ad. We have mutual friends. Reinhardt. And Remarque."

"You know Erich?"

"Marlene Dietrich was one of my first clients, and he's her current *amante*. MGM is adapting his novel *Three Comrades,* and Remarque insists that she will play his heroine. They're forever ringing me from Venice to discuss it. When they aren't snuggled together in a gondola."

A wounding barrage of information. At a moment when she needed to project invincibility, she received a double blow. Erich had discarded her to take up with Marlene Dietrich, and she'd lost her chance to play Patrice.

"Come with me," Ad invited. "Mr. Reisch, I'll be with you shortly."

Film posters, citations, and photographs decorated the office.

"I am improving my English," Hedy said. "Ever since Mr. Mayer told me I'm bad at it."

"I gather he met you at Max's."

She nodded.

"I help refugee artists when I can, especially Germans and Austrians. But I'll tell you straightaway, if you're headed for Hollywood, you're better off with an American agent than with me. L.B.'s schedule might not accommodate an interview, but I can put you in touch with Bob Ritchie, one of his scouts."

"I'm meeting him this evening," Hedy interjected.

The agent eyed her with approval. "You work fast. In case Bob doesn't tell you, L.B. has a chronic dislike of anything scandalous. Max says you're divorcing your husband. Any children?"

"No."

"You'll want to be careful. I can recommend one of the women's clinics I established in California. I was more concerned about a less fortunate class of female than movie starlets, but anyone who needs preventatives can get them. Oh, dear, I've shocked the shocking *Ecstasy* girl."

Hedy summoned a perfunctory smile. Would she ever get used to the Americans' blunt speech?

"The MGM publicity machine is powerful enough to wipe your slate clean. My advice is to charm the socks off Bob Ritchie. If he and I work on L.B., you'll probably get an offer. Should you choose to stay in London, I'd be glad to represent you. Avoid Herbert de Leon, who badly botched Greer Garson's salary negotiations. L.B. offered her a mere five hundred dollars a week. Clever girl, she wouldn't settle for a penny less than one thousand. Are you Jewish?"

"Adolf Hitler says so. And it's printed on my birth certificate. But all my life I've attended Catholic mass, and I had a convent education."

"L.B. is a Jew but doesn't let his actors be. Not publicly, that is. Well, good luck to you, Miss Kiesler. Let me know how things turn out."

Hedy returned to the Regent Palace, a few steps from busy Piccadilly Circus. The white stone building filled an entire block and boasted more rooms than any other hotel in Europe. The façade's aged splendor cloaked a startlingly modern lobby and restaurant. Staff members were accommodating, and the cashier patiently explained the various confusing denominations of English currency when Hedy changed her French francs.

Her trunks and suitcases made her room appear even more compact. The nearest lavatory was in the corridor, an arrangement she regarded as inconvenient and uncivilized. Her husband would have commanded a suite in the supremely elegant Ritz, or at Claridge's, but hoarding her money was more essential to her than luxurious surroundings. The Regent Palace was close to the theatre district, and the agents' offices were located in nearby streets.

She passed the afternoon laboriously reading a London newspaper and resting her feet. She walked everywhere—her limited English hampered communication with taxicab drivers, whose accents and vocabulary were incomprehensible. If she had no appointments she explored Regent Street and Oxford Street, admiring window displays but only purchasing inexpensive necessities.

Deprived of Laure's skills, she relied on a hotel maid to iron the creases from a green silk dress. For ornaments she selected a pair of diamond clips and diamond drop earrings, hoping elegance would compensate for her deficiencies in language.

The Café Royal entrance hall was more palatial than she'd expected, very much in the European style.

A tall and smiling gentleman stepped forward to meet her, hat in hand. He was good-looking, with a high forehead and dark hair. "Welcome to London, Miss Kiesler, from another newcomer. No need to wait for Walter and his wife to have our first drink." He guided her to a room filled with small tables.

"I saw *Ecstasy,*" Bob Ritchie announced after they were served.

"Where? It's supposed to be forbidden in America."

"Yes and no. A severely edited version popped up in independent cinemas, in defiance of Joe Breen and his Production Code. I saw it in Paris, and don't see what all the fuss was about. You're wonderfully photogenic."

"Jan Stallich is a fine cinematographer. Since several years he works in English films."

"And you want to make more pictures."

"In Hollywood, if I can."

"Before I left my office, Ad Schulberg phoned, insisting that you see L.B. before he sails. She says, and I agree, you could make a big splash in American cinema. Her opinion carries a lot of weight with him because of their, um, past relationship. Do I need to spell it out for you?"

She made a sound somewhere between a yes and a no. Splashing and spelling? His vernacular mystified her.

"Ad was L.B.'s mistress."

"Is she the one who married somebody else? At Max Reinhardt's *schloss* a few years ago, he was in a low mood because of it."

"That was Jean Howard. A damned hard blow for him. Why the hell didn't he snap you up then? Offer you a contract, I mean."

"My husband wouldn't permit it." She preferred not to mention Mayer's distaste for her on-screen nudity. "Mr. Mayer has many women."

"Honey, he can't keep his paws off them. When I was Jeannette Macdonald's personal manager, we were . . . close. *Very* close. I handled all her business affairs, accompanied her on tours. Until L.B. interfered. He'd visit her on the set, which he almost never does. Made her sit on his lap when she signed her contracts. Got her to do more than that. Next thing I know, I'm dumped as her manager and shipped over here as a talent scout. Fat lot of good it did L.B., because along comes Nelson Eddy to make him jealous. And vindictive. He forced poor Nelson to sing at her wedding to Gene Raymond. I'm not sure she knows her bridegroom's big secret, but I bet anything L.B. does. Jeannette loves her husband, she says, but it's not a passionate thing. Some pansies perform okay in the sack with a woman, but it's pretty rare."

"But Mr. Mayer has a wife, doesn't he?"

"When does that stop a man from taking what he can get? Margaret Mayer's practically an invalid. Out of loyalty, she keeps up appearances, which makes him feel twice as guilty about seducing starlets and dancing the night away in clubs."

Bob's breezily crass revelations were as informative as they were unpleasant. His depiction of a lurid, sex-obsessed Hollywood clashed with her vision of stars who were as glamorous, witty, and genteel as the characters they portrayed. She was relieved that the Reischs' arrival curtailed the gossip session.

From the heights of a gold-painted box seat, she'd often watched Elisabeth Handl pirouette on the stage of Vienna's Imperial Theatre. Bending low to kiss Lisl's porcelain cheeks, she felt like a giantess. The dancer—so blonde, so perfectly formed, so petite—resembled the ballerina figurine on Hedy's music box.

Apologizing for their tardiness, Walter pulled out a chair for his wife.

"No matter," Bob Ritchie said. "We made the most of our time alone."

"Was Bob singing MGM's praises?" the scriptwriter asked.

"I know more than I did," Hedy equivocated.

"I missed my chance to make Hedy a star," Walter continued. "Several years back, I wrote *Unfinished Symphony*, a musical film about the love affair between Franz Schubert and Countess Ester-hazy. Ah, she remembers! She was my choice for the heroine. But the producers weren't convinced that her singing could match her beauty, and they cast Paula Wessely."

"When I replaced her in *Sissi*, I proved I can sing."

"And you snared a millionaire husband. Who made you leave the stage."

"In Paris, I tried to un-marry him. Even though he's already picked out his next wife, a blonde baroness, the judge said *I* was the deserter. He refused to help me."

"In America," Bob said, "it's easy to get divorced. A few days in Reno, and you're single again."

Lisl gripped her hand. "It's good that you got away. As much as we miss Vienna, we feel safer here."

"Hedy and I were born on the same street," Walter said. "A decade apart, but I regard it as a form of kinship."

"Tell me about your background," Bob invited her.

"My father was manager of Austria's national bank. He died. Mutti trained as a concert pianist but stopped performing to care for me."

"Be sure to tell L.B. He's susceptible to tales of maternal devotion and worships his mother's memory. You need a theatrical lawyer. I'll put you in touch with Paul Koretz. He works out of Vienna but he's in town now. Maybe you've met him."

"The name I know." Turning to Lisl, she said, "Your English is very good."

"After four years here, I hope so. But still I dream in German."

"You could find work in Hollywood," Bob told Lisl. "Dancing. Acting."

A broad smile spread over Walter's square face. "I'm no Fritz Mandl. I prefer a wife with professional ambition. And earning power."

They abandoned their empty glasses and proceeded to a dining room. Throughout the meal, Bob entertained them with tales of Hollywood and its celebrated inhabitants.

Hedy, struggling to follow the conversational flow, retreated into silence, as she'd done so often during her husband's dinner parties. She recognized similarities between Austria's political and social hierarchy and that of the moviemaking realm. Power was everything—gaining it, holding on to it, and wielding it against competitors and enemies alike. Success ensured it. Failure threatened it. Repeated failure destroyed it.

"He hated Thalberg," Bob was saying. "He was consumed by envy of the boy wonder and couldn't let it show. A great judge of talent, L.B., and quite the actor when it suits his purposes. Oh, the crocodile tears he shed when Irving died. The funeral was a spectacle, he made sure of that. Sent Gable and Fairbanks as pallbearers. Comforted Norma Shearer, the grieving widow. Gloom descended over Culver City, it felt like the end of the world. Irving was a genius and a visionary. L.B. is a showman. Can he sustain our past success? We want to draw in even bigger audiences—and their dollars." With a smile for Hedy, he said. "I'll bet you can help us. Fresh talent. A new sensation. Somebody who'll excite the people. And the press."

Chapter 11

"L.B. is a sucker for glamour and class. The pearls are the perfect touch," Bob Ritchie said when Hedy, in a dark Chanel suit and Paris hat and black gloves, arrived at Claridge's for her appointment. "Meet Paul Koretz," he continued, leading her across the geometrically patterned carpet. "He's your legal advisor. And your translator."

"My pleasure, Fraulein Kiesler," said the other man. "I well remember your fine performance in *Sissi*."

Mr. Mayer's suite, a tribute to Art Deco design, doubled as his business office. Stacks of newspapers and fat envelopes covered the surface of every table, and some of the chairs. The studio head muttered into a telephone, an unlit cigar protruding from one side of his mouth. He gestured towards a white sofa.

Sitting down, Hedy removed her gloves and tucked them into her handbag. She wanted her impressive diamond ring to be visible.

"No time to read the book," he growled. "Give me a synopsis when I get back." Briefly he was silent. "Did the papers report that? Sure, I yelled at Michael Balcon. He already picked that Vivien Leigh nobody for the second girl in *A Yank at Oxford*. I nixed her and said I wanted a big name. After Bob pitched my choices, Balcon called him a bloody fool, implying that I'm one too. That's when I blew my stack, so loud everybody at the Denham offices and on the soundstage could hear me. Bob Taylor likes the British broad a lot, but I've still got my doubts." He ground his cigar between his teeth. "That's right. I'll be in touch again before we sail." He put down the receiver.

"Ida Koverman is his assistant," Bob explained to Hedy. "How is she, L.B.?"

"Busy. Bossy. Fiercer than Leo the lion."

Bob grinned. "Nobody sees L.B. without getting past Ida."

Mayer moved to the middle of the room. "Let's have a drink. Bob, three glasses of scotch." The puffy eyes behind the round spectacles fell on Hedy. "So, you ditched your Nazi-loving husband. Good move."

From Bob she accepted a glass of amber liquid and ice cubes. Warily, she sipped and immediately regretted it.

Mayer settled into a curved-back chair. "Somebody tell me why I would give a contract to a girl who ran bare-ass through the woods? It goes against everything Metro-Goldwyn-Mayer stands for."

Lowering her head in contrition, Hedy said. "The director had much power and told me what to do. I was very young."

"In Europe," Paul Koretz interjected, "*Ecstasy* is regarded as an artistic masterpiece. At Venice it received a cinematography award."

"You keep telling me. But in America—" Mayer broke off, shaking his head. "Banned for indecency."

"I am a serious actress, Mr. Mayer. Leading roles in motion pictures and on the stage. If not for my husband, I would now be rehearsing *The Women* at Vienna's Josefstadt Theatre."

He stroked his chin. "We make clean pictures, you see. We require our actors to lead clean lives."

"My family is very proper."

"Her father was Austria's most important banker," Bob declared. "Her mother trained as a classical musician."

"I attended a Swiss finishing school," Hedy interjected. He didn't need to know she'd run away from it, several times. "I am fluent in five languages."

Mayer shook his head. "You'd better not count English as one of them."

"C'mon, L.B.," Bob said. "Dietrich wasn't born speaking it. Or Luise Rainer."

Hedy directed her most brilliant smile at the studio head. "Austrians are more clever than Germans. I will very soon be speaking good English."

"You're a stunner, there's no denying it. But not, ah, buxom."

"Don't forget, Hedy can really act," Bob reminded him. "And she photographs beautifully. Better than Greer Garson, and you were keen to sign her."

"Miss Garson is ladylike. So is her mother."

"Mine is also," Hedy insisted. "My heart breaks to leave her in Austria. War may come to Europe. If I make money in America, I can put my Mutti in safety. You could make it possible, Mr. Mayer." How she disliked playing the supplicant before this tough, rude little man.

"What's her name?"

"Gertrude. Trude. From Budapest, when Hungary and Austria belonged to the Empire. Mutti could have been a concert pianist, but she preferred a private life taking care of me and Papa."

"You're a lucky young lady. A mother's devotion is more valuable than your big diamond ring and all those pearls." Mayer subsided into thoughtful silence. "All right. A six-month contract, option to renew. One hundred twenty-five dollars a week. You pay your own passage to New York. After you have English lessons and slim down, we'll give you a screen test."

Bob Ritchie looked pleased. Paul Koretz scribbled notes.

"No." She rose from the sofa. "Your offer is too small. I don't accept."

Bob and Paul stared up at her.

Mayer tilted his head back, saying, "Miss Kiesler, I can make you an international star. My studio is the world's best. Our pictures gross millions."

"I'm a star already," she stated coolly, "in many nations. A few years ago, Paramount offered me better terms than you, and they have a

London scout. So does Warner Brothers. Also, Alexander Korda of London Films wants to meet me. Mrs. Schulberg told me to come first to you. I would like so much to work for MGM. Perhaps I shall, when you buy me from another studio. Thank you for seeing me."

"Who the hell does this broad think she is?" Mayer exploded.

Paul, who had followed her to open the door, turned to say, "Her husband's a millionaire. She's used to bigger numbers."

Bob added, "And she knows you offered Greer Garson five hundred from the start."

"Why didn't you tell me? Her face is fantastic. We could give her better tits."

For days afterwards, Hedy doubted the wisdom of walking out. Fritz, the hard-dealing businessman, never accepted a first offer. His initial refusal was a necessary start to negotiations. Bob Ritchie had described MGM's star-making machine, but she suspected it wouldn't benefit an actress in whom so slight an investment was made. What sort of build-up could she expect if she accepted such unfavorable terms?

Bob urged her not to contact rival studios until Mayer had more time for reflection.

While waiting for her future to be resolved, she wandered the green and leafy expanse of Hyde Park. Dotted with canvas lounge chairs, it was populated by small children with their nursemaids and many Londoners with well-behaved dogs of various breeds and sizes. She joined the crowd outside Buckingham Palace's gates to watch the stiff, red-jacketed guards at their maneuvers.

The Duke of Windsor had lived here as King, she reflected. He and his duchess must regret being banished from its splendors.

With Lisl Reisch, she attended a matinee performance of *Old Music*, a Victorian-era melodrama at the St. James's Theatre in the West End. Greer Garson, Mayer's darling, portrayed a scheming murderess. Her performance was highly skilled. Her face was attractive—rosy complexion, reddish hair, light eyes—and her speech was graceful and distinct.

During the interval, Hedy and her companion sipped French wine and chatted in German.

"Walter was sorry not to see you before our sailing," Lisl told her. "I left him to finish the packing, but I don't trust him to fold my things properly."

Hedy choked on her wine. "You're going soon?"

"*Normandie* sails on Thursday. From Le Havre."

Gripped by panic, Hedy was tempted to race to Claridge's and demand to see Mr. Mayer. But when the bell rang, she followed Lisl into the auditorium for the final act. Earlier admiration of Greer Garson gave way to an envy so piercing that she couldn't concentrate on the acting, or the staging, or the drama's conclusion. Before she knew it, the players were taking their bows, and the curtain descended.

After bidding Lisl farewell in the lobby, she darted to the box office and begged the attendant for use of the telephone. She dug into her handbag for Bob Ritchie's card, and in her anxiety had to dial his number twice before getting it right.

"Hedy! You got my messages?"

"No. But I must see Mr. Mayer."

"Too late, honey. He's gone."

"Impossible. The ship hasn't sailed. Lisl Reisch said so."

"A few days ago, L.B. crossed the Channel to receive the *Légion d'Honneur* from the French President. By now, he and Margaret could already be on their way to Le Havre to meet the ship. And me."

"Please, get me a ticket. I'll pay." She was unsure of the cost or whether she had enough money for a one-way fare. She didn't care. If necessary, she'd sell her jewelry. All of it.

"I'll do my best. No promises, though."

Returning to her hotel, she crammed her belongings into the trunks and suitcases that had accompanied her from Vienna to Paris to London.

When Bob telephoned, his tone was despondent. "First-class state-rooms arc fully booked. If you travel by second or tourist class, you won't be admitted to the upper-class sections."

"I want to be where Mr. Mayer is."

"I know. I can try and squeeze you into the luxury level. First, I've got to track down a client. Ever heard of Grisha Goluboff, the teenaged violinist?"

"He performed last year in Salzburg. Hitler took away his Stradivarius, and a rich American gave him another."

"One of the very richest—Henry Ford. Nice kid, Grisha. He's eighteen, but his parents make him travel with an adult companion. You could take my place as his . . . I don't know what. Nanny? Governess? Watchdog? You'd keep an eye on him in exchange for a first-class ticket, wouldn't you?"

Breathless with relief, she said, "You are so good to me. I am very grateful!"

"Don't thank me yet. I've got to work this out with the booking office. And you must have your fare and be ready to leave the instant I give the go-ahead."

"I will," she assured him.

"What's the name on your passport?"

"Hedwig Mandl."

"When you see Mayer, let him make the move. He knows his offer was less than you deserve. If you can, cozy up to his wife Margaret. And the other MGM executives in L.B.'s entourage. Benny Thau. Howard Strickling."

Apprehension that Bob's plan would fail and she'd miss her chance to travel to America kept her awake much of the night. To ward off pessimism, she devised any number of scenarios, every one ending with Mr. Mayer extending an abject apology for his stinginess, with pleas to accept many hundreds of dollars a week instead of the paltry one hundred twenty-five.

In the morning, she ordered breakfast in her room, too fearful of missing Bob's call to eat in the hotel restaurant. Sorting through her cache of jewelry, she assessed each piece. She decided to relinquish the large aquamarine Fritz produced on the night she accepted his marriage proposal. Her twenty-two-carat emerald ring, larger than

Wallis Simpson's, should fetch a large sum. She needed only one pair of diamond clips.

The next time Bob contacted her, he reported cheerily, "Everything's settled, provided you've got hundreds of pounds to pay the tariff. Grisha's waiting for you at his Paris hotel. The boat train from Gare St. Lazare will take you both to Le Havre. Okay?"

"Okay," she echoed, already feeling like an American.

"Good luck, Hedy. *Bon voyage.*"

Cramming a fistful of valuables into her handbag, she set forth to dispose of the glittering relics of her marriage. In exchange, she received sufficient funds to place an ocean and a continent between her and Fritz.

Chapter 12

Currently the world's fastest luxury liner, *S.S. Normandie* had proved herself capable of reaching New York in just under four days. Launched into service two years ago by the French Line, she was as popular with elite travelers as her British rival, the Cunard Line's *Queen Mary*. From the quay Hedy studied the towering black hull and pristine white superstructure, topped with red and black smokestacks. She marveled that the mammoth ship could move at all.

When she said as much to her young companion, he replied, "The propellers are enormous. That's why she won the Blue Riband trophy for swiftest transatlantic crossing. If she improves her time, this will be a history-making voyage." Since boyhood the violin prodigy had toured the globe, and though a seasoned traveler he was by no means a jaded one.

Excited by the intricacy of the great ship's mechanics, Hedy asked, "Is it possible to visit the engine room?"

"Sure. I'll take you there."

Six years her junior, Grisha exhibited the maturity of one who had been a professional from childhood, surrounded by adults—his parents, his teachers, his manager. Hedy liked him. What's more, the hours he devoted to violin practice meant he wouldn't depend on her for amusement. Her duties as enumerated by Bob Ritchie were simple enough. She was supposed to send him to bed at a reasonable hour and ensure that he turned out his light after an hour of reading. Also, she must prevent him from drowning in the swimming pool or falling into the ocean.

"The food is delicious." With a bony hand he tried to smooth his tuft of dark hair. His extreme thinness, Hedy had discovered on the boat train, belied his hearty appetite.

Her pulses throbbed in anticipation when she stepped onto the first-class gangplank, clutching her vanity case and a handbag containing just under a thousand American dollars. She wore a plain gray suit, as befitted a temporary governess, unconcerned that the chinchilla cape draped over her arm detracted from the effect.

Hedy and Grisha were assigned to adjacent single cabins in the central portion of the first-class section. Her available luggage consisted of the single suitcase waiting in her stateroom. In Paris, on boarding the boat train, she'd surrendered her trunks and two suitcases to a porter. Marked *Not wanted on voyage*, they were consigned to the ship's vast hold for the duration of the crossing.

After inspecting their quarters, Hedy and Grisha made their way to the nearest deck railing for the launch. The engines moaned, the giant propellers were engaged, and at mid-afternoon *Normandie* eased away from the quay. Her passengers waved to the spectators far below.

Grisha took Hedy on a tour of the first-class decks, sharing expert advice on shipboard life. They encountered other passengers exploring the premises. Bellboys in scarlet uniforms glided along the corridors, assisting with luggage and responding to requests.

On the C Deck, towering greenish-bronze doors opened onto the threshold of the opulent *salle á manger*. According to Grisha, its various sections contained tables and chairs for all seven-hundred first-class passengers. From top to bottom, the walls were decorated with opaque glass. Several dozen Lalique *torchières* augmented the light cast by two large chandeliers. A gilded female statue representing Peace gazed sightlessly upon these beauties. A separate space accommodated private banquets. One level down they found the children's dining room, decorated with murals of Babar the elephant king.

When she saw the luxury class swimming pool, Hedy voiced regret that she lacked a bathing suit.

"You can buy one," Grisha assured her. "There are lots of shops in the promenade."

An elevator carried them up to a series of salons and lounges. Drawn to the grand piano, Hedy sat down to play a favorite Brahms piece and earned compliments from Grisha.

"We'll play duets," he said, beaming down at her.

"I'd enjoy that. If you can be patient with me."

"Nothing too difficult," he promised.

In her stateroom she stretched out on her bed to study the passenger list and other printed material: a diagram of the ship, instructions for lifeboat drills, and information about meal times. The steady drone of the engines, many tiers below, lulled her to sleep.

As *Normandie* steamed into Southampton, her blaring horn roused Hedy from a strange dream in which Fritz exhibited his lip-locked lizard smile while holding an infant. She sat up, desperate to banish the disturbing image, and heard the bustle and chatter from newly-boarded passengers.

Dinner would be served while the ship was docked. Because luggage was still being transferred to the staterooms, Grisha had explained, the travelers dressed informally on the first night of their voyage. She selected a brightly-colored frock and with a careful application of lipstick and powder prepared to face the little man with the power to alter her fate.

She and Grisha descended the broad staircase, attracting curious glances from the hundreds of first class passengers gathered in the antechamber. The great bronze doors remained closed, blocking entry into the main dining room.

"Do you recognize anyone?"

Promptly he replied, "There's Douglas Fairbanks, Jr. And Sonja Henie."

The Norwegian skater turned film star chatted with Adeline Schulberg and a matronly brunette.

A man stepped towards the threesome, his jovial greeting loud enough to reach Hedy. "Margaret, how splendid you look."

Determined to gain proximity to Mr. Mayer's wife, she asked Grisha, "Wouldn't you like to meet Miss Henie?"

"I suppose." His indifference was striking, his shyness inconvenient.

"Well, I do. Come with me."

The blonde greeted them warmly and conversed in an animated fashion that matched her lively and athletic screen performances.

"A pleasure to see you again, Miss Kiesler," Ad Schulberg murmured. "This, Margaret, is Austrian actress who refused L.B.'s contract."

Mrs. Mayer regarded her curiously. "A pity. As a foreigner, living very far from home, you'd benefit from Metro's family atmosphere."

Walter Reisch, with Lisl on his arm, was the next person to hail her. "Hedy! We didn't guess you'd be joining us on board."

"It's Bob Ritchie's doing."

"Wonderful! Is he here?"

"I took his place," she replied in German. "I am supposed to take care of young Grisha."

"He doesn't look like he'll be much trouble," Lisl commented.

The tall doors parted, and the luxury class passengers swarmed into their gold and crystal dining room. Glowing clouded glass light fixtures enhanced the magic of their surroundings, drawing stares of admiration from first-timers.

Tables in the first section were reserved for residents of the costliest suites, a select group that included Mr. Mayer and his entourage, film stars, and other luminaries—Cole Porter, Ezio Pinza. Hedy and Grisha and the Reischs established themselves at a table decorated, like hundreds of others, with a vase of gladiolas. The roar of a multitude of voices reverberated from the uncarpeted floor and hard surfaces of the paneled walls. Hedy's sense of displacement was acute.

The Chief Purser, his face grim, dimmed the festive mood by announcing a propeller malfunction and an immediate return to Le

Havre. Captain Theroux, the ship's commander, apologized for the unanticipated delay. During the re-fit everyone would remain on board, he explained, and the French Line would ensure that every amenity was available to its valued guests.

Instead of setting out into the Atlantic that night, *Normandie* retraced her path across the English Channel to Le Havre, reaching the repair quay several hours before daybreak.

In the morning, when Hedy left her room to purchase a swimsuit, she could hear Grisha's violin. Later she and Lisl met at the D Deck pool. After their swim, they spied opera star Ezio Pinza on a rowing machine in the gymnasium.

"Not many weeks ago, Fritz and I attended his Mozart performances in Salzburg. It feels like years have passed since then," Hedy confided.

For her first formal dinner, she wore an intricately draped sea-green chiffon gown designed by Parisian couturier Alix. Grisha's gangly form looked almost elegant in his performance tuxedo.

"Such a grown-up gentleman tonight. I needn't send you to the room with Babar on the walls," she teased.

After the meal, Grisha excused himself and retired to his room. Hedy accompanied her Austrian friends to the Grand Salon for cocktails.

"I worry that boy will fall in love with you," Lisl told her.

Walter's lips twitched in amusement. "Every lad becomes infatuated with his teacher. At his age those youthful passions obtrude."

"You're both very silly," Hedy chided. "I always wanted a brother. While we're traveling together, that's exactly what he is to me. He cares more for his music than romance. Anyway, I am too old for him."

Walter touched her arm. "That man coming towards us is Howard Strickling. MGM publicity. His opinion counts a lot with Mayer."

"Handsome," she murmured.

"At last, the lady I've longed to meet." Without further preamble, Strickling took the chair beside her. "More gorgeous in life than on the screen."

"You are a flattering man." The wines served at dinner had dissolved concerns about her fractured English.

"I'm a truth teller. You've got acting experience, I'm told. Not that it matters." He grinned. "We can teach anybody how to p-p-perform in movies. Dogs. Children. Beauties." He twisted around to scan the room. "Benny Thau wants to meet you, too."

"We will be a long time on the ship," she pointed out.

"Too damn long, which is bad luck for the studios. David Selznick is crazy to get Doug Fairbanks back to p-promote *The P-prisoner of Zenda*. Twentieth Century Fox is waiting for Sonja to show up so they can start her next ice skating movie."

Lisl spoke up. "My husband can write scripts anywhere. Even on the sea."

"I wouldn't think of it. This is our honeymoon trip, remember?" When the laughter subsided, Walter nodded at Hedy. "This one has led a far more adventurous life and might not be content with swimming and ping pong."

"The ship has a shooting gallery," Howard said.

"I'm an excellent shot," she declared. "My husband taught me."

"If he's as big a jerk as I've heard, you must've been tempted to p-p-put a bullet in him. Did he really try to p-p-pur . . . to buy all the *Ecstasy* copies and the negative? Or was it a stunt to get more p-publicity for you?"

"He is a very jealous man. Machatý, my director, wasn't making a scandal. He was creating art. People misunderstand the nudity." She spread her hands, palms raised. "I am an actress. I do what I'm told."

Howard laughed. "That makes you a rarity."

The next day, she received a handwritten note from Mrs. Mayer, inviting her to an after-dinner party in the MGM suite. She rang the beauty shop for an appointment and asked the maid to press her wine-colored *crèpe de Chine* evening dress.

Grisha was far from pleased. "The conductor said I could play with the ballroom orchestra tonight, for the dancing."

"If Mr. Mayer likes you, he might put you in a film."

"I was in one. It's boring. So are parties." His shoulders heaved in a sigh so deep it seemed to end at his toes. "But if you want me to go with you, I will."

The Mayers' grand suite at the rear of the ship had a panoramic view and doors that opened onto a private promenade deck. In their dining room, uniformed waiters mixed and served drinks. Margaret Mayer, wearing a corsage, circulated among her guests. Her husband, penguin-like in his black and white formal attire, stood in the center of the room, waving his unlit cigar as he spoke to the semi-circle of men gathered around him. He was talking about Hitler.

Howard Strickling joined Hedy and gestured towards a young woman looming over Cole Porter. "Do you know Ilona Hajmassey?"

"From her performances at the Vienna State Opera."

"The Hungry Hungarian, I call her. She p-p-practically starved in the streets. Says she never ate meat till she was seven years old. We're changing her last name, of course. She'll be billed as Ilona Massey. Her English isn't much better than yours, but we'll fix that. You should meet her."

Ilona was the same height as Hedy but in coloring her opposite, blonde and blue-eyed. Hedy greeted her in Hungarian.

"How do you know my language?"

"My mother was born in Budapest. I've often visited my relatives there."

Dancing the rumba with Mayer in Carlsbad had proved advantageous. A former dressmaker who abandoned her trade to become a singer and actress, Ilona was promised a role in MGM's musical *Rosalie,* with Nelson Eddy and Jeannette MacDonald.

"Mr. Porter wrote the songs," she declared, "and already he's teaching them to me."

Aware that Mr. Mayer watched them, Hedy flashed a smile.

She conversed in French with Danielle Darrieux, who had starred in *Mayerling* as tragic Marie Vetsera with Charles Boyer as Empress Sissi's suicidal son Prince Rudolph. When Ezio Pinza approached, she switched to Italian. The women admired her diamonds—earrings, necklace, shoulder clips, and bracelets. Men were drawn to her for other reasons. Careful to remain in her host's vicinity, she forgot about Grisha.

During her conversation with Walter Reisch, in German, a stranger came over and whispered, "Miss Kiesler, you'd better rescue your protégé from Cole Porter."

"It is good for him to meet a famous composer, yes?"

"His interest in young men has little to do with music, I'm afraid."

"Oh!" His implied meaning wasn't lost on her. "We will be leaving, then."

"Howard Strickling claims that you like gunplay. Is it true? Looking at you I'd never have guessed."

"Meet me at the shooting range tomorrow," she said, "and I'll prove it."

"What time?"

"I will telephone. What is your name?"

"Benny Thau. Head of casting at MGM."

"Are all the studio men on this ship?"

"It must seem so. During the voyage we'd like to get acquainted with you."

"I wonder if there ever will be a voyage," she said.

"By the time you wake, you'll see the Atlantic Ocean. I have it on good authority."

She found Grisha, whose eyelids were sagging. With a gaping yawn, he admitted he was ready for bed.

"What did Mr. Porter say to you?"

"He gave me a drink. But I put it down after just one sip. I swear."

"You mustn't drink spirits," she warned. "A little wine with dinner, but nothing more. Never enough to make you tipsy. Promise?"

"I promise. Don't worry about me, Fraulein Governess. Goodnight."

The morning brought confirmation of Mr. Thau's assurances. *Normandie,* after a two-day delay, was steaming her way towards America.

Chapter 13

Hedy's hands swept across the ivory and ebony keys, striking the notes of Beethoven's *Moonlight Sonata.* This grand piano in the Grand Parlor, newer than Mutti's, produced a fine, pure tone. As her final notes dissipated, she thought about her parent and duet partner. She'd posted one letter to Vienna but had no idea when it might be delivered to the house in Döbling.

The MGM men ambled in her direction, intruding on her nostalgic reverie.

"We've searched every inch of the ship for you," Howard Strickling informed her. "The Winter Garden. The swimming p-p-pool. The cinema. Even the hairdressing salon."

With calm deliberation, Benny said, "L.B. wants to see you. He just left the *salle de fumoir.* Margaret won't let him smoke cigars in their suite. He's heading there now." Howard examined her with a critical eye. "Better change into something more feminine. He's not so keen about trousers on a lady."

They accompanied her to her stateroom and waited in the corridor while she put on the gray suit she'd worn to board the ship. Then they ushered her to their boss's quarters. Mayer sat in an alcove, reading telegrams by the light of the broad window.

Placing the slips of paper on a side table, he said, "Too bad we couldn't reach an agreement last week, Miss Kiesler. As you know, many of the performers I interviewed in Budapest and Vienna and London are joining our MGM family. Ilona Massey will be our new Dietrich, blonde and statuesque, with a terrific singing voice. Greer Garson, a lovely English redhead, arrives in Hollywood after her West End play closes. Howard says introducing a trio of foreign actresses will make a great story. I need a brunette."

Benny Thau interjected, "With proven talent."

Mayer went on, "You're adrift in the world. No father. No husband. Your mother's in Austria. Hollywood's no place for a young woman on her own. Not a looker like you, with scandal attached to your name. My studio can build you into a star, and that's no exaggeration. You'll have the best make-up artists and photographers. Howard knows the columnists, he'll get Hedda and Louella and Sheilah on your side from the start. Benny will find the best scripts. Eventually, you'll work with our finest directors."

He hadn't mentioned money. "If the salary is what you told me last time," she said, "you know my answer."

"Five hundred and fifty dollars a week. If we exercise our option and renew at six months, it increases to eight hundred a week. We're offering our standard seven-year contract, with the same requirements as before. You'll have English lessons, and you'll lose weight. Do you speak Yiddish?"

Hedy shook her head.

"Hollywood actresses can't be Jewish. Now remember, our agreements contain a morality clause. No more public nudity, on or off the screen. Also, we're changing your name. You may be Austrian, but Kiesler is too, ah, foreign for these times. Mandl is impossible, for reasons you must understand. His known connections with Hitler and Mussolini are distasteful to Americans. And we can't risk his interference in your career."

"I accept."

When he held out his hand, she took it. Squeezing her fingers, he said, "Young lady, you drive a hard bargain. Our New York office will draw up the paperwork so you can review it when we get there. The formal signing will take place in my Culver City office."

He wouldn't, she hoped, make her sit on his lap to sign her contract, like Jeanette Macdonald had to.

"On the train from New York to Los Angeles, you'll see America in its entirety. The West Coast office will arrange your housing. Plus everything else you need."

"My name, what is it to be?"

"We haven't figured that out," Howard admitted. "Before the ship docks we will."

With a toothy smile, Mayer said, "I want you to go shopping, and you can charge all your purchases to the MGM account. Dresses, shoes, jewelry, champagne. Anything."

In her absence, a huge floral bouquet had been placed on the table in her stateroom. Ordered in advance by Mayer, certain that she would agree to his terms? There was an accompanying card: *We are pleased to welcome you to the MGM family and look forward to your future success in films.*

She telephoned the Reischs but had to leave a message with the switchboard. Grisha's room was also empty. Eager to share her news, she sat down at the desk to write another letter to Mutti, and one to Max Reinhardt.

Eventually, she would inform Fritz that she was able to thrive on her own. She intended to dissolve their marriage after she was settled in California, by the quickest method available.

She regretted that she hadn't emerged from their union as the same idealistic, trusting girl she'd been on their wedding day. Of necessity, she'd made drastic choices—occasional untruthfulness, subterfuge, spying. Even infidelity. Gaining her independence had been paramount, more important than honor or honesty. Fritz had decreed where she lived, what she ate, how she traveled. After enduring so much for so long, she was in charge of her own destiny. With Mr. Mayer's help and his executives' guidance, she could make up for lost time.

Her new status conveyed certain privileges. In the company of a ship's officer, she visited the radio station and telephone room, where sea-to-land connections were made. He took her onto the navigation bridge—for her, the vessel's chief attraction. Its area was large enough to accommodate a large staff of technicians and every type of speed and directional indicator, as well as the telephone and telegraph equipment that enabled communication with the engine room far below. An elevator shunted her down to the very depths of the ship where the main engines drove the propellers and the generators producing electricity. The printed cross-section she'd studied so often hadn't fully prepared her for the giant boilers, or the twenty-four enormous fans that dissipated the heat produced by the equipment.

At her dinner table that evening, the mood was buoyant despite an increasingly rough sea and warnings of more severe weather ahead. Not only did Walter and Lisl and Grisha congratulate her, several luminaries stopped by to wish her well.

"You'll take Hollywood by storm," Douglas Fairbanks predicted, and Gertrude Lawrence inclined her head in agreement.

Overnight, the ship's constant shudder inhibited sleep. Stepping onto the deck, Hedy confronted an iron gray sky, buffeting winds, and whitecaps. For the first time since boarding, she recalled Papa's description of ill-fated *S.S. Titanic* and the iceberg that shattered its hull. But that tragedy had occurred in the darkness, during a colder season and in a more northerly location. Fate couldn't cruel enough to send her to the bottom of the ocean just when her dreams were coming true.

Taking Mr. Mayer at his word and hoping the ship's movement would be less obvious on the lower levels, Hedy made her way to the shopping promenade. There was scant competition for the saleswomen's attention. When she showed indecisiveness about a dress too roomy in the bust, she was assured that the tailoring shop would perfect its fit. All purchases, the evening shoes and lacy underthings and dresses for every sort of occasion, would be sent to her stateroom.

"Is Madame in the pictures?" the clerk inquired when directed to bill MGM.

"In Europe. Soon, in America."

"I'd ask for your autograph, but we aren't allowed."

Just as well. She didn't yet know her new name.

The great vessel was pitching more noticeably. Concerned about Grisha, she rapped on his door.

He wore an undershirt and his trousers were unbuttoned and unbelted.

"Are you seasick?"

"Queasy. I couldn't eat breakfast."

"I wish I hadn't," she confessed. "Better go to bed."

"The rolling is just as bad when I'm lying flat as when I stand. Closing my eyes makes it even worse."

Alarmed by his pallor and the dots of perspiration on his forehead, she recommended a cold compress. "I'll come back later," she offered. "I have sleeping pills, if you want them. I rarely use them. Although I did consider drugging my husband when I was desperate to get away from him."

Grisha's sharp laugh was followed by a grimace and a groan. Abruptly he shut the door. His muffled retching made her own gorge rise, and she quickly returned to her own cabin.

While she struggled to decipher an English-language magazine, her telephone chimed.

"Howard here. Can you join us in the smoking room? L.B. chose a name for you, and we've convinced him that you should be consulted. He and Benny and I were brainstorming all morning, at the ping-pong table."

Afraid that the rising elevator would compound her bodily distress, she took one of the staircases.

Dear God, she prayed as she passed the bronze statue of a French peasant girl, don't let me fall sick in front of those men.

The familiar combination of cigarette smoke and cigar aroma struck her nostrils without adverse effect, although they carried unwelcome reminders of Fritz's evening parties. Most of the leather armchairs were vacant, proof that many gentlemen passengers remained in their staterooms.

Mayer bobbed his silvery head. "I see you're a good sailor. I'm a yachtsman, so these little squalls don't trouble me at all."

She thanked him for the bouquet of roses.

"Howard is planning your introduction to the New York press. Reporters and photographers will be waiting at the dock, like vultures, hunting for stories."

"We can't change your identity," Howard said. "Nobody at MGM wants to mention Mandl, but we can't stop his name showing up in feature articles. When asked about him, simply say you were incompatible."

"Can you pronounce it?" Mayer asked.

"Incompatible. My husband and I were incompatible." She felt like a child being taught a lesson.

"If you get questions about *Ecstasy*," Howard continued, "tell them what you've told us. You were young and inexperienced."

"I was. And in Europe, the tastes are more sophisticated than—"

"No!" the publicist objected. "No comparisons between Europe and the United States. Youth. Inexperience. That's all. We'll work up a more complete narrative, in case it's needed."

"It will be," Mayer said grimly. "Hedda and Louella will be all over this."

"Keep her away from them," Benny suggested. "And vice versa. No interviews until her English improves. We'll save lots of trouble that way."

"Good idea," his boss responded. "She stays under wraps."

Howard nodded approvingly. "That'll build up anticipation. And mystery." Turning to Hedy, he asked, "You understand our plans?"

"I am to be the mystery woman. Is my name to be a mystery also?"

"That's settled," Mayer replied. "Hedwig is out of the question. Too Germanic. But Hedy is all right."

"Hay-dee," she corrected him.

"Americans will pronounce it the way it's spelled in magazines and newspapers. To them, you'll be 'Heddy.' Get used to it."

Howard spoke up. "Or she could be Heidi, from the kids' story."

Mayer frowned. "Twentieth Century Fox is releasing a film adaptation. We can't have people confusing her with Shirley Temple."

The publicist grinned. "No danger of that, L.B."

"My other name, what is that to be?" she inquired.

"Lamarr," Mayer announced.

"Le mer," she repeated. "Because I accepted the contract while on the sea?"

"La-marr. Hedy Lamarr."

Suddenly the ocean liner dipped, and the floor shifted beneath her feet. Clutching the chair arms to steady herself, she repeated, "Hedy Lamarr."

"My wife says it suits you. Barbara LaMarr was a dark beauty."

"Practice writing it," Benny advised. "Your signature could be in demand one day."

"We'll do our part," Mayer said, "but you've got a hell of a lot of hard work ahead of you."

"I am ready."

"In Vienna," he went on, "you had many privileges. Money. Servants. Me, I was born in Russia. My parents settled in New Brunswick, a Canadian province. At twelve I left school so I could help my papa support the family. I gathered up scrap metal in a handcart. I was mocked for being just another pauper Yid. But I was proud. And polite. Whenever I had a couple of free hours, I went to the vaudeville theatre. That made me ambitious, determined to rise in the world. I saved up to buy a movie house. Later I acquired a string of them."

He talked on, pausing periodically to puff on his cigar, recounting his journey from deprivation and obscurity to power and fame. His stubborn pursuit of success and his insistence on quality filmmaking impressed Hedy. His speech was self-congratulatory but inspiring nonetheless. By joining his MGM family, she might help him deliver worthwhile entertainment to a world greatly in need of it.

———◦·◆·◦———

The storm subsided. For the closing stretch of the voyage, shipboard life returned to normal.

On their final night at sea, after Grisha joined his friends in the orchestra, Hedy danced with Howard. In his arms, gliding across the ballroom, she hoped to meet someone just like him, handsome and good-natured.

"Are all the Hollywood men as nice as you?" she wondered. "And as fond of their wives?"

"Some. Unfortunately, I deal with the worst ones. Or the most careless. My job entails tasks that aren't at all nice."

"What does that mean?"

"I hope you never find out. I'm a fixer. If somebody at the studio, usually a movie star, gets into serious trouble, I manage the cover up. Keep the p-p-press in the dark. If they do find out, I make them kill the story. Actors and actresses exhibit all the human weaknesses. They make mistakes. Occasionally, they commit crimes. But L.B. wouldn't like me telling you about the seedier aspects of our community."

"There will be no crime by me. I promise." The music ended and they returned to their table. Sinking into a plush orange chair, she broached a topic that confused her. "The clause of morals Mr. Mayer demands. What does it mean?"

"You're required to behave."

"May I not have a lov—" she caught herself. "No boyfriend?"

"You can't shock, insult, or offend the community, or ridicule morals and decency."

"Some of those words you must translate."

"I'll can give examples. You're not supposed to live with a man who's not your husband. Or cause anybody's marriage to break up. No babies out of wedlock. Drunkenness in p-public, taking illegal drugs, breaking the law, or consorting with known criminals—*verboten*. I've got enough influence with the columnists to shield minor infractions.

You won't have to live like a nun. But a significant scandal will destroy you."

"I attended convent school," she told him. "For four years I was married to Fritz Mandl. I follow rules. When I must."

"Good. Cleaning up messes is less appealing than introducing our newest stars. You and Illona and Greer are a p-publicist's dream. Talented. Stunning. L.B. says he'll bill you as the world's most beautiful woman."

An echo of the accolade Max Reinhardt bestowed when she was a teenaged aspirant. A girl no longer, within weeks she would turn twenty-three.

Douglas Fairbanks barged through the doors to the promenade deck. "Come outside!" he shouted. "The Lightship Ambrose!"

Howard set Hedy's fur stole over her shoulders, and together they stepped into the brisk night air. Passengers gathered at the rail, applauding and cheering. On the horizon the lightship's twin beacons pierced the darkness, marking the entrance to the channel and the conclusion of Hedy's three thousand-mile voyage.

Chapter 14

I n defense against the onshore wind, Hedy tied her hat securely beneath her chin and pulled her fur closer. A heavy corsage of white orchids, provided by the shipboard florist, was pinned to her suit jacket. Howard's advice for her first encounter with the American press was to dress well, wear makeup, smile constantly, and give brief, polite answers to questions.

Normandie's crossing, delayed at the start and slowed by the storm, wouldn't enhance her reputation for speed. Freed from quarantine hold at Staten Island, she steamed into New York harbor. The Statue of Liberty, bathed in sunshine, diminished with the vessel's progress. As tugboats maneuvered her into position at the designated pier, passengers assembled at the rail and waved to the waiting crowd below. A motor launch carrying photographers pulled up alongside.

"Hedy! Over here!"

Howard was flanked by two men, one holding a camera. "Hedy, meet Howard Dietz, officially our Director of Advertising, P-publicity and Exploitation. Our mascot was his idea, so remember him whenever you see Leo the Lion roaring at the start of our movies. He traveled all the way from the West Coast to help you."

"Pleased to meet you," Mr. Dietz said as he scrutinized her from top to toe.

Were all MGM publicity men, she wondered, called Howard?

"We're allowing the newspapers to photograph you."

The man with the camera said, "Welcome to the United States, Miss Kiesler."

"Lamarr," Dietz corrected.

"Sit on your suitcase, ma'am. This won't take long."

Hedy perched on the top edge of her luggage. When instructed to cross her legs, she hooked one knee over the other.

"Gimme a smile. That's it!" Light burst from the flashbulb. "Hang on, one more." He licked his fingers, removed the bulb and tucked it in his coat pocket. After he screwed in a replacement, he asked, "Ready?"

Another explosion. Hedy blinked repeatedly, trying to clear her eyes of the searing after-image.

The photographer said to the publicists, "Thanks for letting me see the *Ecstasy* girl in the flesh. So to speak." He grinned.

"Is this the one?" The male voice came from behind her. "The Kiesler girl?"

"Miss *Lamarr*," Dietz repeated. "You are?"

"Robert Wilder, *New York Sun.* Getting a jump on the competition."

"No interviews today, but your photographer can get his shots. Mr. Mayer's about to give his press conference. Your editor won't want you to miss it."

A second cameraman told her to pose sitting on a window ledge, with her legs crossed. "Show us how happy you are to be in America!"

She smiled brightly. This attention seemed excessive. She hadn't done anything yet.

Dietz escorted her down the gangway, cupping her elbow with a steadying hand. A group of men in overcoats and hats crowded in on them, notepads and pens at the ready.

"What's your response to the ban, Miss Kiesler?"

"I don't understand," she whispered.

"A mayor in a New Jersey town refuses to let theatres there exhibit

Ecstasy," Dietz clarified in an undertone. In a carrying voice, he announced, "Miss *Lamarr* is still learning English. She disassociated herself from that film long ago."

"Is it true that Fritz Mandl is coming to get you?"

Impossible, she assured herself. He doesn't even know I'm here.

Dietz said helpfully, "Miss Lamarr isn't in contact with Mr. Mandl at present."

Another man shouted, "What does Mr. Mayer think about all those nude scenes?"

Dietz laughed. "What makes you think he's seen them?"

Emboldened, Hedy replied, "Why should he care? Men all the time are undressing women with their eyes."

Tightening his grip to forestall further comment, Dietz told her interrogators that Miss Lamarr was just one of several European artists whose talents would be valuable to Mr. Mayer and MGM.

Ilona Massey, hovering in the background with her aunt and cousin, glared at Hedy, clearly displeased at being ignored by the publicity men—and the press.

Dietz reunited Hedy with the rest of her luggage, and a limousine swept them from the pier along skyscraper-shaded streets clogged with traffic. While he outlined her westward itinerary, she stared at the modern structures, newer than those of European cities and tall enough to block sunlight.

"Here, your train tickets. You're at the Plaza tonight. In the morning I'll take you to the MGM office and we'll phone Paul Koretz in London to review contract terms. After that, you'll have time for sightseeing. In the evening, you board the Twentieth Century Limited. A junior publicist travels with you as far as Chicago, to ward off any reporters or curious passengers. He'll instruct you about studio protocol. In Chicago, your Pullman car will be transferred to the incoming Super Chief. Three days later it reaches Los Angeles, arriving at 9:00 a.m. An MGM employee will meet you at the station."

"What, please, is Pullman?"

"A sleeper car with private bedroom compartments. You'll be

very comfortable. All our stars travel on the Super Chief." He leaned against the seat.

"Will Mr. Mayer be angry when he reads the newspaper stories? Those men will print rude words about *Ecstasy* because they have no artistic appreciation. In Europe, it's not so scandalous."

"I haven't seen it. You're completely naked?"

She nodded. "Swimming in a lake. And running across a meadow."

"Do you look good?"

"*Naturellecht.* And my acting was praised."

"Americans, especially those in the film business, care about success more than anything. If you could be a success swimming and running in the nude, you're ahead of the game."

<hr />

America was astonishing in its vastness and geographic diversity. After Hedy's train rumbled out of the temple-like Grand Central Station, it sped past cities of varying size, dairy farms, and great stretches of woodland. Waking, she found herself in flatter terrain, the tracks cutting through broad fields of ripened maize. Her map depicted Chicago as a metropolis bounded on one side by a huge lake. Seen from afar, it was a cluster of skyscrapers.

Her publicist companion wished her good luck in her MGM career and disembarked to board an eastbound train. Helpful without being obtrusive, he'd provided her with movie magazines that showed how she would be presented to the public through studio photography and carefully managed interviews. He described Metro's training program and star system and responded to her questions. Her ability to communicate in English was tested, and it improved only slightly during her journey's initial stage.

Rolling out of the great Midwestern city, the Super Chief covered endless miles of agricultural land blanketed with waving golden wheat and cornstalks. It wound through mountains unlike European ones, craggy and rock-edged and nearly treeless. Beyond them lay a region of steep gorges and red stone outcroppings, and after those came dry and barren desert.

At Albuquerque, the halfway point, American Indians sold turquoise trinkets to passengers who left the train. Their hair, dark like Hedy's, hung straight or in long braids, and their complexions matched the ground they sat upon and the walls of the distant dwellings. The air, hot and dry, permeated her carriage. After leaving the station, the train sped past dusty green cactuses covered with pale bristles.

By then she was accustomed to the crew of efficient and scrupulously polite black waiters and porters. At times she had difficulty understanding their speech, and she struggled to make herself understood.

Isolated by her foreignness, she studied everyone—their faces and fashion and hair and voices. Her car contained few females and children; the majority of travelers were male. Businessmen peered at her over their newspapers. Salesmen rearranged their sample cases. An elderly lady, pale from too much powder, never removed her fox stole. Did she know the rust-colored creature was missing one black glass eye? A woman in mourning black got off in Winslow. These anonymous passengers might someday read articles featuring Hedy Lamarr, just as she pored over profiles of current screen celebrities.

After the California desert, irrigated farmland was a refreshing sight. Citrus groves and orchards seemingly extended for miles. Houses were stark white or painted in pastel colors, crowned by rippling clay tile rooftops.

When Hedy arrived at her destination, her appearance was sleeker and more sophisticated than when she'd boarded the train. A flowery clip held her hair back from her face. Following the publicist's advice, she wore a light-colored suit instead of a dark one and had packed away her fur. Her corsage, held in cold storage since Chicago, looked fresher than she was feeling.

Descending the steps of her Pullman car, she spotted a single photographer and one reporter on the platform. The sun's merciless glare made her long for dark glasses, but she'd been specifically instructed not to cover her face.

As Howard Dietz promised, the studio publicist was waiting. He handed over a bouquet of long-stemmed roses and a note of welcome signed by Mr. Mayer, who had returned to California by airplane.

"I'm Don," said the young man, reaching for her vanity case. "L.B. told me to look for the most beautiful creature on earth. I'm taking you to the studio to sign your contract right away. And you get a tour. But first, we give the guys their photos. They always meet the Super Chief because the movie stars are usually on board."

She posed as directed, seated on the baggage trolley with her stack of trunks and suitcases. The reporter bombarded her with familiar questions, but the coaching she'd received enabled her to give the concise, prepared responses. Don guided her through the palatial, marble-paved station to a limousine. Her luggage would soon depart for the Chateau Marmont without her.

After nine days in transit, exhaustion had set in—her excitement and anticipation had ebbed somewhere on the open range. She'd prefer a civilized period of rest and refreshment before her next encounter with Mr. Mayer. But in America, she'd discovered, breakneck speed and ceaseless activity was the norm.

Pasting on a smile, she righted her drooping corsage and cradled her roses and climbed into the sleek black car. The streets were straight as a ruler. Grass either grew sparsely or lushly, so did the shrubbery. These palm trees were taller than the ones on the Riviera.

Throughout the lengthy drive from station to studio, her escort pointed out landmarks.

Metro-Goldwyn-Mayer sprawled across a flat stretch of land with a distant backdrop of low, bare hills. The limousine slowed when it came to a colonnade with three arches, each fitted with a metal barrier. A uniformed guard nodded, waving them through the one that was open.

"You'll be issued an employee pass," Don told her. "But the officers recognize all the actors and actresses and greet them by name. There's the Lion Building, where I work."

They were deposited in front of a gleaming modern façade. One group of workmen planted young saplings at the edge of a pristine walkway while another crew unrolled sod to cover the bare earth.

"Newest building on the lot," Don explained. "It'll be dedicated to Irving Thalberg, who died last year. Norma Shearer's husband. He's a legend here, you'll hear a lot about him. Very different from Mr. Mayer. Construction isn't quite finished, but the executives and important producers and directors and the head writers already moved in."

They entered the new Thalberg Building through a side entrance. Hedy's heels clipped the floor of the lobby as they crossed to an elevator. On the third floor the doors parted. They followed a tunnel of closed doors ending at an alcove of desks occupied by secretaries, clicking away on their typewriters.

A silver-haired woman came out of her office, a sheaf of papers in her hand. "Miss Lamarr? I'm Ida Koverman, Mr. Mayer's assistant." The eyes behind the glasses were keen and all-seeing. "Until you lose weight, you ought to wear slacks. They can be quite slimming. Just don't do it around Mr. Mayer." Glancing at her nearest associate, she said, "Inform Mr. Strickling that Miss Lamarr has arrived."

"Yes, Miss Koverman."

The woman adjusted the sweater draped over her shoulders. After a tap on the door, she opened it. "Sir, Miss Hedy Lamarr has arrived." She grasped the publicist's arm before he could follow. "You stay here." Pressing her hand between Hedy's shoulder blades, she said, "Go in."

Behind an enormous white curved desk raised high on a plinth sat L.B. Mayer. Four white phones were lined up beside him. Everything else in this bastion of power was white—the carpeting, the textured walls, even the piano.

"Do sit down," he invited her. "We spared no expense getting you here, so you should've had an easy journey."

"It was long." Unsure what to do with her roses, she placed them in her lap.

"The food on those trains is good, they say, but I hope you didn't eat too much of it. We need to slim you down before putting you in front of the camera, because the lens adds pounds to a woman's figure. Ida can give you a diet sheet."

At that moment she was experiencing intense hunger, and the prospect of limiting her meals sounded like a punishment.

Howard Strickling joined them, bending to kiss her cheek. He sat down beside her.

"As we've discussed, you'll be having English and diction lessons," Mayer continued. "You'll enroll in an exercise class. Might as well have dance lessons, too. As soon as possible, you should get a Hollywood agent. Have you read the morals clause in your contract?"

"Yes."

"We make clean pictures. We want clean actors. It's important that you do nothing to undermine our efforts on your behalf. Right, Howard?"

"That's right, L.B. Unless somebody from my department is with you, Hedy, don't speak to reporters or columnists, or have your photo taken."

"I won't."

"When we've created your biography, we'll assign a p-publicist," Howard said.

"Am I not to make the biography? It's my life."

The two men exchanged glances. "When introducing a newcomer to the p-public," Howard said, "all the information must be favorable. In your case, we need to explain why you've left your husband and your country."

"To make movies." It was too obvious to require explanation.

"True. But a p-publicity campaign requires considerable finesse."

"I won't tell lies."

"You'll shade the truth, just a little. We'll tell you what not to say. It's in your own best interest."

"You may come and see me," Mayer added, "whenever you have concerns or questions. And if there's a serious problem, Howard will fix it." He shoved a stack of papers across the gleaming white desktop. "Your contract. Here, use my pen. It'll bring you luck."

The typed words ran together, clause after clause after clause, all in English. Printed beneath the blank lines on the last page was her legal name, *Hedwig Kiesler Mandl*.

She signed, instantly altering her status from refugee to employee.

Howard witnessed the contract and passed it back to Mayer, who added a hasty and illegible scrawl.

"When do I begin working?"

"After you've had lots of lessons," Mayer replied, "we'll assess your progress. We'll take care of housing you. You'll be paired up with another of our contract players, or be provided with a bungalow of your own. Tell me, what do you think of Hollywood?"

"Flat and dusty and brown. Not pretty."

Her frankness made him frown. Then he smiled. "You'll change your mind when you've seen our soundstages and our sets. We're the Tiffany of studios. Our pictures exemplify quality and beauty and class."

"That's the reason we signed you," Howard added, climbing to his feet. "I'm going to give you a tour. We'll have lunch in our commissary."

"The chicken soup is the most popular item on the menu," Mayer told her. "My wife's recipe. And it's kosher." He indicated a row of framed family photos behind him. "My other family." He pointed to a framed photograph on the wall. "My mother watches over me. From her I learned how to be a loving parent."

His sentimental streak was a startling in one reputed to be ruthless, and she welcomed evidence of his gentler side.

She didn't much care about exploring the studio, but Howard was so eager and so gallant, and refusing would be rude. And it was a chance to see famous faces—Clark Gable or Joan Crawford or Norma Shearer.

"There's Reginald Gardiner," Howard said, gesturing at a black-haired man with a neat moustache. "He joined us last year. Amusing fellow. L.B. has a particular liking for English performers. Better trained and less troublesome, and they lend sophistication to a picture. They're an insular group, with their four o'clock tea parties and their cricket club."

Feeling conspicuous with her corsage and bouquet, she trailed

Howard in and out of the Lot 1 buildings that housed the wardrobe and makeup departments. In the portrait studio photographers and art directors created the glamourous public images of male and female stars. He showed her the warehouse-sized structure where props were made and stored and took her inside one of the twenty-three sound stages. Lot 2 contained the streets of houses and storefronts and parks that appeared in so many movies. He pointed out trolley system that transported crew members to the more distant backlots. Altogether the MGM complex covered more than one hundred acres.

The commissary was packed with bit players and extras in costume. Hedy stood in line with a cowboy, an old lady wearing a bustle dress, and several showgirls bedecked with sequins and feathers. Obedient to Mr. Mayer's wishes, she ordered his chicken soup. The closest she got to Clark Gable that day was the steak sandwich bearing his name. Howard advised her to eat the apple pie because it was Mayer's favorite dessert, and he would ask whether she enjoyed it. Seated at a table with his department colleagues, she observed the odd way they managed their utensils.

It's an adult boarding school, she realized. Mr. Mayer is the all-powerful headmaster. These publicists are the monitors, noting infractions and possessing the authority to erase demerits. The rest of us are the pupils.

When they finished eating, Howard surrendered her to young Don. Her next limo ride, also longer than expected, ended at the Chateau Marmont. She was almost drooping from weariness as she stood at the reception desk, and her brain was so fuzzy that when signing the hotel register, she couldn't recall whether Lamarr was supposed to have one or two r's at the end.

But I'm here, she reassured herself when at last she was closeted in the luxurious suite provided by the studio, surrounded by her trunks and suitcases. I crossed an ocean and a continent. I've signed a contract with the best studio in Hollywood. And someday, I will have a part in a motion picture that will be seen all over the world. Even in the places where *Ecstasy* is banned.

Chapter 15

The conveniences of hotel living had grown stale during Hedy's years with Fritz, and she repeatedly asked Howard Strickling when she could leave the Chateau Marmont. The influx of European performers, he explained, had reduced the number of available studio-owned bungalows. She had to wait her turn and be thankful she was staying in a classy establishment.

"Besides, if the ground starts shaking, you're in the safest spot in all Los Angeles," he stated. "The Chateau was built to withstand earthquakes."

After English class, she and Rose Stradner, the actress she'd supplanted in the role of Sissi, exchanged harsh criticisms of the Duke of Windsor, who was touring Germany as Hitler's guest. Hedy had respected him for surrendering his crown in order to marry his lover. Exiled from her own country, separated from her mother, she'd pitied his banishment from Britain and his ruptured family relationships. Now she despised him for consorting with Nazis. He and his duchess demonstrated an appalling insensitivity to the cruelties and deprivation that European Jews and so many others were suffering.

Learning that Ilona Massey was moving into an apartment, Hedy sought her out one day at Mrs. Roberts's class to offer herself as roommate until she could find her own place. Ilona, glad to have someone to share her rent, agreed.

They made a pact to speak English together, but only during daylight hours.

Ilona received positive press. Hedy was the target of spiteful commentary from columnist Louella Parsons, annoyed that she couldn't interview with MGM's mystery starlet.

"It's not my fault," Hedy defended herself to Ilona. "The other day that woman sent a spy who followed me to Howard's office. As soon as he realized what had happened, he took me away in a hurry. He's so desperate to keep me apart from journalists that when I go out at night, he makes someone from Publicity go with me. I had enough of that when I was Frau Mandl. I'm about to be twenty-three years old, yet I'm being treated like a child!"

Exactly a year ago, she'd vowed to escape Fritz before she had another birthday. Disregarding her diet sheet, she celebrated her achievement with a large piece of chocolate cake in the apartment, far from the watchful eyes of Mr. Mayer's informants.

Her first month in California was a busy one. She spent mornings at English class, followed by a rigorous exercise session. After lunch in the commissary, she received additional instruction. She enjoyed studying dance. Movement lessons tested her ability to stifle her giggles, as she glided around the room with a book balanced on her head. On free afternoons she went to movie matinees, her preferred method of absorbing her new language.

Ilona, performing the second female lead in the musical *Rosalie,* was permitted to skip lessons. The film starred Eleanor Powell as a princess of the fictional Romanza, attending Vassar College incognito.

"Brenda is not the name of any lady in a European court," Hedy protested when helping Ilona practice her dialogue. "It's American. And princesses don't tap dance."

"Hollywood musicals are fantasies."

No script, let alone one with major stars attached, had been offered to Hedy, and her envy was acute. In addition to helping Ilona with her lines, she imparted the content of the daily language lesson—with less than favorable results.

Flinging the vocabulary text to the floor, Hedy declared, "I'm murdering English. And you're burying it."

Mr. Mayer's clear favorite among his new acquisitions required no improvements to her speech. Greer Garson, the statuesque redhead with perfect diction and a cheerful smile, was being groomed for stardom at a faster rate than any of the Europeans lured to Hollywood by identical promises and far less money.

Hedy sought out the Englishwoman in the commissary to compliment her performance in the London play she'd attended.

"I'm so very glad you enjoyed *Old Music*," the other actress responded. "It's the reason I'm here. How did Mr. Mayer discover you?"

She attempted an explanation of Max Reinhardt's involvement and a description of her negotiation during the ocean voyage. "But Mr. Mayer didn't give me as great a salary as yours. I'm sorry my English is so bad."

"I understood every word. Are you working on a film?"

Hedy responded with a regretful shrug. "I've not even had my screen test. They take many photographs and make me exercise to lose weight. All the time I am hungry."

"So am I." Greer pointed to her salad plate and soup bowl. "How I shall survive, I can't imagine. Where do you live?"

"I share the apartment of Ilona Massey. I would prefer a little house of my own. I've never had much privacy, you see."

"That will be far harder to come by, if Hollywood turns you into a star," her new acquaintance pointed out.

"Ilona and I are seeing a preview of *Snow White and the Seven Dwarfs* this evening, if we don't kill ourselves during the driving lesson we are made to have every week. Would you join us?"

"May I bring Mother?"

"It will be a pleasure. I miss my Mutti and wish so much that she would come here. But she won't leave our home in Vienna, and her friends there. When I was a little girl she called me her Snow White, from the old tale by the Brothers Grimm that my papa often read to me."

"If you're Snow White, I'm Rose Red." Greer tugged a strand of coppery hair.

Mutti's next letter carried news of Fritz, who had invited her to coffee. Without rancor, he'd inquired about Hedy's progress at the studio and asked whether she had enough money to live on. And he'd requested her telephone number. He would soon travel to Argentina in connection with his investments there. Vienna society speculated about the outcome of his ongoing affair with Baroness Herta von Schneider-Werthal, and whether he was divorced from his runaway wife.

In Greer Garson, Hedy found a sympathetic listener, and they soon discovered how much they had in common. Their marriages had taken place at about the same time, resulting in similar unhappiness. Like Fritz Mandl, Alec Snelson turned out to be a possessive and jealous husband who had opposed his wife's theatrical career.

As they dined together at the Brown Derby one night, Greer revealed details of a past that was all too familiar.

"During our wedding trip to Germany, my bridegroom berated me in restaurants when other men looked at me."

"That happened to me, on our honeymoon," Hedy told her. "Everywhere I went with Fritz. In Venice. On the Riviera. In Paris. And it got worse."

"I'd risen through the ranks at the Birmingham Rep, and felt ready to try my luck in London. Alec was given a posting to India and insisted that I go with him, but it would've been ruinous at that stage of my career. He said he might let me perform in amateur dramatics in the garrison, with the other officers' wives. I refused to leave England, pleading an illness that was genuine. He's on another continent now, but I'm still his wife. He refuses to let me divorce him."

"Fritz and I are still married. But the publicists make it seem as though we're not."

These shared experiences created an instant bond. Her new friend confided another secret. Greer was thirty-three years old, a full decade Hedy's senior. For the sake of her career she'd shaved four years from her birthdate, a fiction incorporated into her studio biography. She was fascinated by Hedy's years as a Vienna hostess, and her encounters with such diverse figures as Benito Mussolini and Max Reinhardt, and most especially the former King Edward VIII and Mrs. Simpson.

On the night of the abdication, Greer had performed in London.

"Suddenly, in the middle of a scene, we were told to stop. Never shall I forget sitting on stage with the rest of the cast, and all the audience in their seats, listening to the wireless. Afterwards we had to carry on with the play. It was dreadful. People were so shocked, and many were in tears. But we got a better king out of it."

Her confidence bolstered by weeks of driving lessons, Hedy bought a used car. She also hired a plain upright piano, a poor substitute for the grander ones she'd played in her parents' drawing room and on *Normandie*. In her eagerness to make music, she could overlook its deficiencies.

On a weekday outing, she and Greer visited the nearest plant nursery. In addition to pansies and petunias, Hedy acquired a colorful set of miniature garden statues, Snow White and all seven dwarves. Her friend chose a goose with several goslings.

While helping Hedy pot up her flowers and place them around the patio, Greer said, "Mother and I furnished our home with antiques from a re-sale shop, quite inexpensively, and now we must fill the empty spaces on the walls. I've heard Laguna Beach is the place to purchase paintings directly from the artists. Let's go there on Saturday. I can practice driving on the right side of the road and drill you in English at the same time."

Their southward journey along the coastal road revealed the beauties of California's landscape. The sky was a clear, cloudless blue, and the cool December breeze was invigorating. Beach towns were easily accessible, with no sign of the fashionable throngs that crowded the

Côte d'Azur. Ordinary people, casually dressed, drifted in and out of shops and along the shore. In Laguna, Hedy and Greer explored the art galleries, seeking affordable canvases.

A modernist seascape in shades of blue captivated Hedy, despite the cost.

"Buy it," Greer encouraged her.

"I will," she decided. "Even if I must live on bread and cheese for the rest of the month."

"If it comes to that, Mother and I will feed you."

"Mr. Mayer doesn't want me to eat at all."

The tall, black-haired Englishman wrapping her purchase glanced up and said, "We work for the same slave driver. In the credits, I'm Reginald Gardiner. Reggie, to you." With a smile, he added, "I spotted you on your first day at the studio. You were with Howard Strickling. Later, I chased him down to find out your name." To Greer he said, "Yours, I know. In London I saw *The Golden Arrow* at the Whitehall Theatre. You and Larry Olivier made a good team."

"I should've listened to him," said Greer. "He warned me against coming to Hollywood. His experience here was dismal, and he whinged about it incessantly. He prophesied that either I'd be left on the shelf or be utterly miscast."

"In which way was he correct?"

"The shelf," Hedy replied glumly. "For both of us."

Greer expelled a small sigh. "We call ourselves the Neglected Imports. Mr. Mayer lured us to his studio but doesn't give us parts. I gather you've been more fortunate."

"I'm doing a comic role in *Everybody Sing*, with Judy Garland and the great Fanny Brice. In the new year, I'll begin shooting Norma Shearer's long-delayed *Marie Antoinette*." He stroked his neat mustache, saying ruefully, "I daresay I must be clean-shaven to play a French courtier of the *Ancien Régime*. When not in front of the camera, I'm a carpenter. And a painter."

"So am I," Hedy told him. "When I have time."

"I also happen to be the very best picture-hanger in Hollywood. It would be my pleasure to install your new purchase."

"That's very kind."

In a teasing tone, Greer said, "Don't make assumptions, Mr. Gardiner. Hedy only cultivates Limeys to improve her English."

"Delighted to assist with that as well."

On their first date, Reggie drove Hedy into the mountains for lunch at a rustic roadside lodge. She discovered that his outward charm, piercing wit, and lively humor cloaked a serious, sensitive side. A product of the Royal Academy of Dramatic Art, his performances in revues and plays and films in his own country led to a stint on Broadway. Like her, he was intent on divorce. His estranged wife remained in England.

Unlike Greer, content to spend her evenings at home with her mother, Hedy and Ilona Massey tentatively ventured out into the Hollywood social scene. The publicity department arranged double dates, promoting the Austrian as the new Garbo and the Hungarian as the new Dietrich. By cooking up a fictional rivalry between the two actresses, they created an actual rift.

When Hedy complained to Howard Strickling, he assured her that this was a common ploy, and that the next natural step was a reconciliation and an even stronger friendship that could be touted in the fan magazines. This manipulation frustrated her.

Ilona, returning one afternoon from a photography shoot, blamed Hedy for their flat's untidiness.

"I was working today, too," she retorted. "I'm not your maid."

"You wouldn't make a very good one. I suppose your rich husband let you have dozens of maids. My parents couldn't keep food on our table."

After her years in a household of strife and quarrels, Hedy had no patience to spare. She demanded that the studio find her somewhere else to live.

In early December, she moved into a six-room bungalow, minimally furnished, in tree-clad Benedict Canyon. She was comfortable there, delighted to be surrounded by green hills. Ericka Manthey, an older Frenchwoman, provided companionship and served as both housekeeper and secretary. And it was a place where Hedy and her new boyfriend were assured of privacy.

With relief, she removed all clothing from her trunks and filled her closets and emptied her vanity case of cosmetics and face creams, arranging them on a bathroom shelf. She'd received them from Jack Dawn, MGM's chief makeup man, who vowed to transform her from a European frau into a screen siren.

As she plucked glittering brooches from the satin lining, she could feel the folded papers tucked behind the fabric. Bartering her secret knowledge to free herself from Fritz hadn't been necessary. But legally he was still her spouse, and there was always a chance he might balk at the divorce action. The preservation of her torpedo drawings and notes on other German weaponry was a form of insurance.

With Reggie, she attended a preview screening of *Rosalie*. Ilona Massey's English was no worse—and no better—than Hedy's. She photographed well, despite lacking Dietrich's elegant mystique. Her important singing number was overshadowed by Eleanor Powell's tap dance, staged on a giant drum surrounded by hundreds of cast members. Afterwards, at a drive-in, Hedy and Reggie ate hot dogs and ice cream and picked apart the plot.

"That picture is foolish, but I daresay it will be popular," she conceded. "I want my first role to be more intelligent."

———◦•◆•◦———

In a gesture of seasonal goodwill, Hedy sent Fritz a Christmas card and a brief note. Before sealing the envelope, she inserted a newspaper photograph taken of her with other European actresses at Mrs. Ruth Roberts's English language class. Writing out her former address, she experienced a surge of longing for Vienna—though not for the Ofenheim Palace, or its owner.

On Christmas Eve he telephoned her.

"It hardly seems like *Heilege Abend*," Hedy told him. "The air here is warm and the skies always bright. We're surrounded by palm trees and tropical flowers."

"When will your studio put you in a picture?"

His interest in her professional life pleased her as much as his cordiality. "No one tells me."

"Trude misses you but is so proud. On St. Stephen's Day, I shall visit her." He told her about his Argentine trip, expressing admiration of the landscape but, typically, revealing nothing specific about his activities. Apologetically he said, "I must put down the phone now. Renée and my father have just arrived for dinner and the exchange of gifts."

Their brief dialogue ended without either of them mentioning divorce, or their current romances.

On Christmas Day, Reggie came to her house and commandeered her kitchen. A skilled cook, he devised a seasonal feast combining elements of British and Austrian cuisine. He insisted on listening to his King's speech, so after the meal they went into the sitting room. He adjusted the shortwave band, and soon the new monarch's voice emerged, faintly, haltingly, saying "We have promised to try to be worthy of your trust, and this is a pledge we will always keep."

When the address ended, Reggie said, "I wonder what his brother is doing. And whether he harbors regret about what he sacrificed."

Hedy commented, "Never did I see a man so . . . what is the word? Like a spell is cast over him."

"Enchanted," he supplied. "I know the feeling."

"But he and his American wife should have stayed out of Germany."

"Going there was a grave mistake," he agreed. "Being feted by Adolf Hitler did him great discredit."

Hedy's gift to him was an antique English tea caddy she'd unearthed in one of the re-sale shops she and Greer frequented.

He gave her an envelope. It contained two sketches—one of a tall, box-like cage with a pitched roof, surrounded by chickens, and another smaller enclosure that contained rabbits.

"Promissory notes. I'm going to build a henhouse and a rabbit hutch for you, and help you stock them."

She responded with a heated kiss. When she murmured her thanks, his narrow moustache lightly grazed her upper lip.

Gently taking her by the arm, he said, "That's not all. I'm no millionaire, who can shower you with jewels like your husband did. But a shiny bauble is the established way to express one's sentiments." He bound her wrist with a ruby bracelet and fastened its clasp. "Wear it to the Warners' tonight."

The guest of honor was one of his titled friends, the international socialite and Hollywood hostess Countess Dorothy di Frasso. Her storied affair with Gary Cooper prompted her transfer from her husband's villa in Rome to a Spanish Revival mansion in Beverly Hills. Her current flame, mobster Bugsy Siegel, hadn't been invited.

Hedy was pleased to see a familiar face in the crowd. Michael Brooke, by birth the Earl of Warwick, was a theatre-mad English aristocrat contracted to Paramount, after a brief stint at MGM.

"What a lucky chap you are, Reggie," he declared. "I first knew Hedy when I was vagabonding round Europe, before she married Herr Mandl. If she'd stuck with me, she could've been my countess."

"You never asked me to be," she replied. "Not before *Ecstasy*—and certainly not after."

Their hostess's close friend Marlene Dietrich was obviously on intimate terms with Brooke. Hedy, still resentful about Erich Remarque's desertion, wanted to dislike her. But the German star poured on the charm, complimenting her performance in *Ecstasy* and giving advice on how best to deal with Mr. Mayer.

"Sweetheart," she said to Dolores del Rio in her smoky voice, "just look at this child. She could be your twin."

On Boxing Day, Hedy and Reggie dined on traditional British fare served by Greer and her mother Nina. Mr. Mayer hadn't yet provided his favorite with a leading role, but he'd sent her a fully decorated tree and invited her to spend Christmas Day at his beach house.

"Mrs. Mayer was very gracious," Greer reported. "Their daughter Irene was there, with her husband Mr. Selznick, and their children.

The chief topic of conversation was the casting for *Gone with the Wind*. I wonder who'll play Scarlett."

"Neither of us," Hedy predicted. "You're English. I barely speak English."

"I had my heart set on being cast as Rhett Butler." Reggie made a comical face, and everyone laughed.

How comfortable she felt with these friends, whose clear, clipped voices were easy to understand. Too many American spoke in a rush, chewing or slurring their words. They often talked over one another and used their incomprehensible and confusing slang.

Hedy was initiated in the unfamiliar custom of Christmas crackers. Reggie showed her how to pop hers and placed the paper crown on her head. Nina called to him for help in the kitchen. Minutes later he reappeared holding aloft a Christmas pudding topped with a holly sprig and ringed with blue flame.

Nina followed him with a bowl. "The brandy butter."

"Just like home," he said gleefully.

It was dark when Reggie returned Hedy to her bungalow. The air in the canyon was chilly, and she shivered as they faced each other on her doorstep.

When he pulled her close, she said, "You want to come to my bedroom, I know. Not yet."

His finger stroked her cheek. "One more present." He held out a folded piece of paper.

She opened it and held it close to her eyes to make out the words. "Arthur Lyons. Who is he?"

"Judy Garland's agent. Joan Crawford's, too. He'll represent you, if you ask. To get on in this town, you need someone like him."

Her grateful kiss carried the promise of more.

She wasn't as much in love with Reggie as he was with her, but she sensed that she could be.

Past disappointments and lingering regret were responsible for her extreme cautiousness. Youthful inexperience and idealism, combined with her parents' persuasions, had made her susceptible to Fritz's intense courtship. Fondness for Ferdi von Starhemberg never ripened into something more. With Erich Remarque she'd found a true and mutual passion, until Marlene Dietrich seduced him away.

She and Reggie celebrated New Year's Eve at a Sunset Boulevard nightclub. During a slow dance, the press of his body against hers roused a physical response that she felt ready to indulge. She drew his head down and whispered her request that they leave the party at once.

"I thought you'd never ask," he replied, his voice low and intimate.

When she took him to bed, she gloried in revealing her body. He traced her torso with his hands and slid them over the swell of her hips. She was pleased to discover that Reggie the actor and artist was very much a sensualist, just as she was.

"Someday I'll paint you. Exactly like this."

He brought her to climax three times before his final, finishing surge. Lying next to him in the darkness, she reflected that this was a satisfying way to see out the most momentous year of her life and to begin the next one.

Chapter 16

When Reggie completed the Judy Garland musical, he moved immediately onto the set of the long-delayed drama featuring Norma Shearer as Marie Antoinette. Every Sunday he came to Hedy's house to play handyman and carpenter. He constructed an artist's easel for her and stretched canvases. He built bookcases. He drove her to Pomona to acquire the residents of her henhouse and rabbit hutch.

They attended the preview screening of *Everybody Sing* in Westwood. As Gerald, a self-important actor, Reggie effectively exaggerated his natural comic abilities.

"I liked best the part on the bus," she said afterwards, "when everybody sang. You looked so handsome in your evening clothes and top hat. I disliked the man knocking you to the floor. Did it hurt?"

"Not at all. In vaudeville, one learns to fall safely. And get the laugh."

"The young girl's voice is delightful. Sometimes she's in my exercise class. We're the shy ones."

"Judy Garland is a huge talent. Yet Ida Koverman had to persuade L.B. to sign her."

From Reggie, Hedy learned she was scheduled for a screen test. He spotted the item in a newspaper, whose columnist also predicted that she would be loaned to Paramount Pictures.

"That was the first studio to offer me a contract," she told him. "After *Ecstasy* and before I ever met Mr. Mayer."

On the day of her test, she reported first to the make-up department. Wardrobe had provided a clinging white sequined gown, previously worn by the late Jean Harlow in her final film.

"Lucky for you," said Jack Dawn, who had glamorized her for publicity photographs. "She was a great star, and one of the most popular girls on the lot."

"But she died. Which is very unlucky."

He sat her down in front of the mirror and draped a cloth over her shoulders and chest. With a miniature sponge, he applied a thick layer of foundation. He brushed rouge beneath her cheekbones and used a tweezer and a dark pencil to shape her brows.

"Your lips are perfection," he told her. "The other women who sit here would surrender their salaries for a mouth like yours."

Chief hair stylist Sydney Guilaroff abandoned wig-making for the *Marie Antoinette* cast to arrange her hair. Smiling all the while, he brushed the thick mass till it gleamed. When she fidgeted, he said soothingly, "Don't be anxious."

"Reggie says the test means there's a part for me. Is that true?"

"Usually," he replied, lisping through bobby pins held between his teeth.

Her heartbeat quickened when she found Mr. Mayer waiting for her on the set.

"Now that we've slimmed you down and taught you to speak English," Mayer said, "we'll see how you photograph. Soon as your test is edited, Howard and Benny and Ida and I will review it."

"And you'll cast me in a picture?"

"All in good time." He reached up to pat her shoulder. His hand lingered there, stroking the silk—or the skin it barely covered.

The director spoke to her briefly while the camera operator, lighting technician, and sound man carried out their duties. She would perform two scenes, a dramatic, emotional one, and a contrasting quiet one. Her partner was Henry Daniell, an Englishman who, like Reggie, was cast in *Marie Antoinette*. His mesmerizing stare intimidated her during the brief time they were given to run through their dialogue.

Counting the years that had passed since her last appearance before the camera, Hedy hoped she hadn't forgotten how to perform. *Ecstasy* had been a minor production, small in scale, and none of the Austrian or German studio facilities could compare with an MGM soundstage. But when the spectators disappeared behind the brightness of the lights and the bulk of the camera, nervousness faded. She enunciated her words, striving to invest them with feeling and nuance.

Later, in the commissary, Reggie asked, "How was it?"

"Mr. Mayer seemed pleased."

"L.B. was there? That's a promising sign. He doesn't make a habit of attending screen tests."

A week went by, then another, and no word from the executive offices. Greer attempted to console her with self-deprecating stories about her disastrous tests, which failed to lift the cloud of despondency.

"My contract lasts six months. There aren't many more left."

"I'm in the same situation," Greer reminded her.

"But you came here after a successful stage career in London. You could go home. I can't."

"MGM isn't the only studio in town."

Her hopes of remaining there were fading when Ida Koverman phoned.

"Did Mr. Mayer like my test?"

"We all did. You were lovely. Luminous, as Benny Thau said. You're being assigned to acting coach, an Englishwoman who's married to one of our screenwriters. Phyllis Loughton excels at making actresses feel at ease. We're confident she'll loosen you up and make you more comfortable with camera work."

Consumed with dread, Hedy fretted over what was omitted from the assessment. Ida had complimented her looks, not her acting. Unfair, she fumed, for Mayer to judge her abilities based on two brief scenes with a stranger in a contrived setting.

The gray sky and whipping wind sent her outside to chase her hens into their coop before the approaching storm struck. Her mood was as dark as the clouds overhead.

It was time, she decided, to make use of her easel.

She slashed her wet paintbrush across the pristine white canvas, leaving bold streaks of charcoal and midnight. Fully absorbed in developing her stark, abstract image, she was slow to hear the knock at her door.

Reggie stood on the front step, gripping an umbrella.

"I'm on my way home to change, after a very full day pretending to be an eighteenth century French fop. I almost forgot I was invited to a party tonight. My friends will expect me to turn up with my favorite date, but Judy Garland wasn't available."

His quip failed to amuse. "Neither am I. You and your parties," she fumed, venting her anger. "And all the Hollywood people, so false and shallow. They make empty promises and trample on other people's dreams."

"What's the matter with you?"

"I traveled across half the world to be a movie actress. But nothing has gone right since I came here."

"You met me," he said quietly.

"When the studio lets me go, they'll make you drop me, too. Go away, right now, and save them the trouble."

He spun around and marched off to his car.

Returning to her painting, she discovered that inspiration had died. Dismal dark grays and stark black, originally intended as an expression of rage and frustration, equally represented failure and regret.

Ashamed of herself for treating Reggie badly, she dialed his number.

"I'm sorry," she told him brokenly. "Don't be angry. I'll go to your party. If you still want me to."

"My darling, of course I do. It'll cheer you up."

A night of listening to the stars boast about leading roles was more likely to deepen her depression.

—⊃·◆·⊂—

After a mere two years in Hollywood, Reginald Gardiner's reputation as a *bon vivant* and raconteur had ensured his popularity within the film community. The partygoers greeted him warmly, and he was immediately surrounded by an appreciative audience. Hedy, self-conscious about her language deficiencies, intended to find a quiet corner where she could sip her soft drink and monitor the movements and conversations from a safe distance. Charles Boyer prevented her from carrying out her plan.

The romantic idol had starred with Danielle Darrieux in *Mayerling,* one of her favorite films, and opposite Marlene Dietrich in *Garden of Allah.*

"You are exquisite," he said in silky French. "May you find happiness in your new life, as I have done. Allow me to make you known to my wife Pat. Ours was a romance that Hollywood could have devised."

The pretty blonde, an Englishwoman, complimented Hedy's dress.

"Are you working?" the actor asked.

It was the question she encountered most frequently, and her answer was always the same. "I'm contracted to Mr. Mayer, but he does nothing with me." In a matter of weeks, he would decide whether to keep her or, as she expected, to release her.

"You know the French film, *Pépé le Moko?*" Boyer asked.

She placed a hand on her chest. "Jean Gabin broke my heart."

"Walter Wanger is re-making it. In English."

"Charles will be superb as Pépé," his wife said.

Boyer's dark, hooded eyes remained focused on Hedy. "Would you consider playing one of the female characters?"

His question, she assumed, was an idle one, nothing more than *politesse.* "They let you give out parts?"

"Not I. Come, I want our producer to see you."

If he wished, Walter Wanger could have had a career as a movie hero, for he was darkly handsome, with a penetrating gaze and a cultured voice. When Boyer introduced her as Hedy Kiesler, she corrected him.

"I am Hedy Lamarr now."

"L.B.'s idea, I bet," said Wanger. "He never got over her." Responding to Hedy's confused look, he added, "Barbara LaMarr. The world's most beautiful woman, that's how the studio billed her. A real wildcat. She gave birth to an illegitimate child. She committed bigamy. Depending how you count the husbands, she was married five times. Booze and drugs destroyed her. I guess he never told you any of that."

"No." Her situation, already dire, was worse than she knew. Mayer had cursed her with the surname of a doomed, self-destructive actress.

"You're MGM's mystery woman. Every day I see your name in the papers, but they only tell me that you dine out with Reggie Gardiner at Café La Maze. Tell me about yourself."

"I am bad at what you call the small talk. In Austria, I was a popular actress. I traveled to America on the ship with Mr. Mayer. He gave me a contract and my new name and a screen test—but no movie. I haven't any lines to study, and I spend many nights at home. So, I let Reggie bring me to this party." She fidgeted with the ruby bracelet he'd given her.

"You yearn for better things?"

"I want to act."

Boyer intervened, saying, "Look at her, Walter."

"Oh, I'm looking. How do we convince L.B. to let us have her?"

"For what?" she wondered.

"*Algiers*. My version of *Pépé le Moko*. Boyer is the jewel thief. Gaby and Ines are seductresses. Kept women."

"I can't play a scandalous role again. I don't like being the *Ecstasy Girl*."

"Your boss," Wanger continued, "paid a fortune for the rights to remake *Pépé*. But Gabin foiled his plan by refusing to reprise his role in an altered Hollywood version. Certain elements of the story weren't, um, uplifting enough for L.B., so he sold the rights to me.

We're rewriting the script to overcome the censors' objections. Tomorrow I'll ask MGM to send me your test."

Within a week Mayer summoned her to the Thalberg Building.

Ida Koverman greeted her with a tight smile. "I'm pleased for you, Hedy, though it's a shame we won't be the first studio to put you on the screen. You may go right in."

She joined the occupant of the all-white office, not entirely sure what was happening.

Without preamble he announced, "I'm loaning you out to Walter Wanger, an independent producer."

"He is now my boss?" She liked him better than she did Mayer. "What means to loan? Why not sell?"

"Because I make more money. You'll receive your regular salary of five-hundred fifty a week. Wanger pays me fifteen hundred a week while you work for him. The production period will be at least three months. At a minimum, MGM takes in eleven thousand from the deal. And Wanger bears the cost of promoting you and building you into the star I'm sure you'll become. The risk is all his, and the profit mostly mine. Plus, he'll let me have Boyer for one picture. Sharp bargaining on my part."

"There are two female roles, he told me. Which am I to have?"

"The beautiful temptress. John Cromwell is a women's director, he'll be good for you. I couldn't hand you over to just anybody, you know. When Paramount and Fox wanted you, I turned them down flat. Wanger says his new script will pass muster with the Hays Office, and for your sake, I hope so. It was a dodgy property when I got my hands on it. A criminal as a hero? A high-class slut as his love interest? Disgraceful."

He stepped down from behind the curved desk and approached her chair. "*Garden of Allah* proved that audiences will eat up a film about North Africa. Especially if Boyer is featured. You're getting a Dietrich type of role. Selznick, my schmuck of a son-in-law, hoped Wanger would cast his Swedish broad, Ingrid Bergman, as Gaby. I outplayed him. And I will again."

Mayer in a gleeful mood was only slightly less alarming than when venting his rage.

"Can I stop my lessons?"

"Not till you start shooting *Algiers*," he said. "You represent our studio, and we want you to impress Wanger. Go and find Howard Strickling. He'll want a quote from you for our press release."

———◦•◆•◦———

Hedy was included in Reggie's invitation to spend a weekend at Countess Dorothy di Frasso's Palm Springs residence. Hardly a year old, it lacked the mirrored walls and Elsie de Wolfe décor of the eccentric noblewoman's Hollywood house, but it was a comfortable retreat. They were given the rooms in the two-story guest house with a view of the mesa and towering palm trees.

Late on Saturday afternoon, the guests gathered at the pool for swimming and pre-dinner cocktails. When Hedy returned to the cabana to change out of her damp suit, she felt something underfoot.

She shrieked. A sudden, searing sting brought her to a standstill. Her heel was on fire.

She limped to the nearest chair.

Everyone crowded around her.

"Scorpion," Reggie announced, smashing it with a stone. He plucked an ice cube from his drink and gave it to Hedy. "Place this on your wound to numb the pain."

"It feels numb already."

"How dreadful!" their hostess cried. "The poor dear! Whatever shall we do?"

At his most dry, Reggie suggested, "Ring for a medic. Darling, let me help you to your room so you can change out of that damp suit. You don't want to take a chill."

The doctor who examined her detected none of the more serious symptoms of a scorpion sting.

"Your pain will fade. Keep the cold compress on to reduce the swelling."

"There will be no lasting effects?" When he shook his head, she said in relief, "I'm glad, because soon I begin working. In Austria I had a career, but this will be my first Hollywood role."

Securing the clasp of his medical case, he said sympathetically, "You must be distressed about what's going on there, in your native country."

"Another uprising?"

"An invasion—by the Germans."

She sat up, releasing her heel, and the damp cloth fell to the floor. "It could be a rumor."

"I'm afraid not." He retrieved the compress and returned it to her. "This morning's paper contained a well-sourced report. Chancellor Schuschnigg stepped down yesterday."

Her gaze darted to Reggie. "Help me to the main house. Countess Dorothy must have a radio."

The guests, some still clutching their dinner napkins, had already crowded around the gleaming wooden console to listen to the latest bulletin from Europe. Hedy sat with her foot propped on a leather hassock. As she wept into his handkerchief, Reggie squeezed her hand.

The *Anschluss,* that long-dreaded annexation, had come to pass. Inexplicably, the Viennese were celebrating in the streets as they awaited Hitler's expected arrival. The Nazis had already re-named Dollfuss Square for their leader.

Her anguish, deep and harrowing, hollowed her out. Her country was lost. Her mother was stuck in a city under German control, potentially a target of anti-Semitic harassment. Or worse.

What would become of Fritz? If Hitler's Reich disregarded his honorary Aryan status, he'd be treated as harshly as any other Jewish-born Austrian.

Throughout the night she tossed and turned, partly from the discomfort of a throbbing heel, but mainly from heartbreak. After a late breakfast, for which she had no appetite, she and Reggie offered their excuses and began the long drive to her house in Benedict Canyon. For supper, he made cheese toast and insisted that she eat it. The radio droned in the background, repeating what she already knew and hated to hear.

"Why does America care nothing about Austria? Hitler won't stop at German-speaking lands. Every country bordering Germany will be lost to the Fascists. And probably more."

In the morning, a bold black headline was emblazoned on the front page of her newspaper: HITLER SEIZES CONTROL OF AUSTRIA. Her supply of tears wasn't yet drained, she discovered, as Reggie read out quotes from Hitler's speech in Linz. Opponents of the new regime, fearing arrest, were fleeing to Hungary or Czechoslovakia. Jewish shops, closed for the Sabbath, were vandalized. Jews remained in their homes.

Schuschnigg, the deposed Chancellor, was held prisoner in the Belvedere Palace, surrounded by Nazi guards. She hoped young Kurti was at his boarding school. Poor boy, he'd lost his mother in that motorcar crash, and now his father was in grave peril. How would he fare in the future without a parent to look after him?

The von Starhembergs—Nora, Ernst, and their son—had passed the winter in Switzerland, and Hedy prayed they were still there. Ernst would be devastated by the government's failure to rebuff Hitler. Princess Fanny, his formidable mother, shared his devout Catholicism but not his Austrofascist politics. She, along with Ferdi, must be in Austria, now a German territory.

The next day, when American networks broadcast direct transmissions from Vienna, Hedy heard the Führer's shrill, excited voice crackling through the radio speaker. The *Los Angeles Times* ran a description of his triumphant entry into Vienna and the enthusiastic crowds that hailed him. Even more shocking was Mussolini's acceptance of the incursion he'd tried so forcefully to deter.

Rising anger melded with grief. As the Führer continued his high-pitched rant, her fury flared higher and hotter. With vicious fingers, she shredded the newspaper until dozens of tiny scraps littered the floor.

Disregarding the expense of an overseas call, she telephoned her mother.

"All is quiet here," Mutti reported. "But people are so anxious."

"So am I. Please tell me you're making arrangements to leave. If you don't, the Nazis will make you register as Jewish, just like they do in Germany."

"When I can, I'll go to our friends in London. The border is closed now. Your father-in-law, Alexander Mandl, was seized before he could get through. Either he's being held under house arrest, or he's in prison."

"And Fritz?"

"I know nothing. I haven't seen or heard from him since the day after Christmas."

"Last month he contacted me about our divorce. He wants to provide me with an allowance, or a lump sum, even though I've never asked him to. Or expected it. I can't help worrying about him. And what might happen to him."

"Perhaps he received warning and got away before the Germans came. Tomorrow at Mass I'll light a candle for him. And for you, Hedl. Promise to do the same for me."

"I will."

She hadn't attended a church service for many weeks. Perhaps their religion's familiar rituals could provide much needed comfort in this desperate and uncertain time.

Chapter 17

Mindful of Laszlo Willinger's request to bring a selection of her jewelry to his photography studio, Hedy tossed her necklaces, bracelets, and earrings into a plain paper sack. No time to pick and choose when she was running late. Ericka had already started the car.

Uneasy about carrying her valuables to acting class, or to the commissary, she handed the brown bag to the security guard who greeted her at the gate.

"Take care of this for me, please," she said.

"I'll keep it in the office. Have a nice day, Miss Lamarr."

For her final coaching session with Phyllis Loughton, she'd brought the shooting script for *Algiers*. After an hour of scene study, in which she played Gaby and her acting instructor pretended to be Charles Boyer, she joined Greer in the commissary.

"No chicken soup?" Hedy teased.

"Chicken salad, for my daily quota of cluck. If you get finer fare at Warner Brothers, I don't want to hear about it. Over there you'll probably be best friends with Bette Davis and forget all about poor me."

After a firm denial, she said, "*Jezebel*, her new picture, opens this week. Shall we go?"

"Too many Civil War pictures in production while we await

Gone with the Wind. Are you sorry we missed our chance to wear hoopskirts?"

"When they tested me for Frou Frou, I wore one of Garbo's white flouncy ballgowns from *Camille,* and a wig of ringlets. I lost the part to Luise Rainer, a serious actress with two Oscars. She deserves a much better role than that one." She gathered up her purse and her script. "Mr. Willinger postponed my portrait session. I'm going home to memorize lines."

"Fortunate creature. I'm the last of the Neglected Imports, and I can only dream of getting a part to study."

Hedy was in the garden feeding her rabbits when Ericka called her to the telephone.

"Miss Lamarr," said an unfamiliar male voice, "I'm the director of the MGM police department. We've got your jewelry."

She was slow to realize what he was telling her. "I forgot it!"

"One of our guards opened that paper sack, expecting to find his lunch sandwich. Did he ever get a shock! Our detective thinks those stones could be worth as much as a hundred thousand. You better be more careful with your valuables, ma'am."

The incident surfaced in a gossip column, prompting a tirade from Howard Strickling, whose stutter was most noticeable in moments of high emotion.

"We're working our asses off to p-p-promote you. Leaving a fortune in jewelry in a p-p-paper bag, lying around for anybody to find isn't just foolish, it could wreck the p-positive image we work so hard to create for you. How could you be so irresponsible?"

"I gave them to a policeman," she defended herself. "I trusted him to keep them safe. How did the press find out?"

"One of our security guys b-blabbed to a columnist. I threatened to fire him but let him off with a warning."

"I'm sorry, Howard."

"Next time, either wear your diamonds to the studio or leave them at home. Okay?"

"Okay."

———⬦———

The bedside telephone shattered Hedy's slumber. She thought it must be quite early in the morning, otherwise Ericka would answer. Before the fifth ring, she reached for the receiver.

A torrent of German filled her ear. The Mandl butler was calling from the Ofenheim Palace.

"A mob broke through the door," he informed her dolefully. "Young thugs in their brown shirts. They tore through every room, stealing so many things. All the golden plates and the silver cutlery. They smashed porcelain. They took away paintings. Pulled clothes from the wardrobes and scattered them across the floor."

"Did they find the wall safe in Herr Mandl's study?" No telling what sort of incriminating documents were hidden there.

"He emptied it before leaving the country."

"He left? Where did he go?"

"As soon as he heard the German army was invading, he traveled to Switzerland with . . . with someone."

With his blonde baroness, she surmised. "Did his family get away, too?"

"His father was placed in a camp. His sister remains in Italy."

Fritz had outwitted the Nazis, escaping to the neutral nation where he'd deposited a large part of his fortune. Possibly he and his aristocratic mistress had joined Ernst and Nora. It was unlikely that any of them would be able to return to Austria.

Exiles, all of us.

She regarded movie-making as a timely distraction from the barrage of unsettling news. It was equally a source of anxiety. A Hollywood production depended on numerous professionals, organized in a hierarchy that was difficult for a neophyte to discern. The sound men and camera operators and light technicians, union members all, firmly rebuffed her curiosity about their tasks and their equipment.

Warner Brothers produced gangster pictures and intense dramas about modern characters who struggled against temptation. Costs were kept as low as possible, resulting in cheap sets and less than luxurious facilities. L.B. Mayer's dictatorial ways might grate, but he supported and coddled his powerful and promising actors, carefully selecting the director for each project. His films were lushly and lavishly produced, whether a comedy of manners or a historical epic or a musical.

To ensure acceptance by the censorious Hays Office, the revised script for *Algiers* provided Hedy's character Gaby with a fiancé and a female chaperone. Novelist and screenwriter James M. Cain had added spice to the dialogue. An experienced director, John Cromwell gave straightforward instructions in a measured, Midwestern voice. Cinematographer James Wong Howe took his inspiration from the French film, going so far as to directly copy certain shots. In Warner's largest soundstage, carpenters and prop masters had faithfully rendered the Casbah's steep and narrow streets and crowded bazaars. A monorail track erected above the multi-tiered set enabled Howe and his camera to shoot from a lofty position.

Many extras were natives of exotic North African lands—Algeria, Syria, and Libya. Men wore a fez or turban and burnoose with a cloak, and women dressed in loose blouses and skirts with fringed shawls and jewelry. In the background, whether within range of the microphone or not, they spoke Arabic.

The couturier Irene Kalloch created frocks in solid colors to flatter Hedy's white skin, and their elegance was enhanced by the opulent jewelry that Gaby craved. To ensure that her forehead wasn't hidden or her face shadowed, the designer experimented with various hat styles.

"A turban?" Hedy suggested. Reaching for a short piece of white fabric, she wound it around her head to demonstrate.

"The very thing," Irene approved. "We'll make up several, in light and dark colors."

Sometimes before filming, Cromwell projected original footage for his cast and crew to study. Boyer, working hard to present his own version of Pépé, refused to copy Jean Gabin's mannerisms.

As Europeans and French speakers, Hedy and her co-star developed a rapport. Like her, he was appalled by developments in Austria and what they portended for the rest of the Continent. He was her on-set comrade, a calming presence when the pressure of high expectations overwhelmed her. In discussing their characters' relationship, he identified all that Gaby represented to Pépé. She was a beautiful object of desire, a connection to his beloved Paris, a dream personified. And tragically for them both, unobtainable.

"To be an object is uninteresting," she maintained. "A female character should have depth."

"Isn't there a similarity between Gaby and you? She belongs to the older man, very rich, who gives her expensive jewelry. You know what it means to be trapped in a cage of luxury."

"Acting is performance. Not re-living a memory."

"If the memory evokes emotion, and you recreate those feelings for the camera, it is acting. Didn't Max Reinhardt teach you that? And your coach at MGM? Bring the lessons learned, as well as your past life, onto the sound stage." He crushed his ever-present cigarette into the ashtray.

The complexities of blocking occasionally confused her. While her brain was busy remembering her lines, in English, she was supposed to react to the other actors and hit her mark. In Ecstasy she'd rarely spoken, and her slight roles in earlier films were poor preparation for the challenges she faced on this film. She soldiered on, operating on the belief that if she displeased Cromwell he'd correct her, or else Boyer would set her straight in his diplomatic fashion.

The other actress, Sigrid Gurie, was also borrowed talent. They shared a fondness for drawing and passed the time between scenes in Hedy's dressing room, chatting and sketching.

Dining in the commissary, among so many strangers, was an ordeal if Boyer or Sigrid was absent. One day, Bette Davis smiled when stalking past on her high heels, but Hedy was too shy to express how much she'd enjoyed the star's powerful performance in Jezebel.

———◦•◆•◦———

The mystery of Fritz Mandl's whereabouts deepened when newspapers reported that Austria's new government had confiscated his properties and financial holdings. Some journalists speculated that he had fled to Brazil. Hedy assumed he was in Zurich or perhaps Geneva, reunited with the millions he'd deposited in Swiss banks.

Her broadening experience of American journalism had taught her not to believe everything that was printed. One Hollywood gossip insisted that she and Paulette Goddard were engaged in a bitter feud. About what, Hedy had no idea. As far as she knew, all they had in common was an English lover. Because Reggie and Charlie Chaplin were firm friends who enjoyed each other's company, avoiding Paulette was impossible.

With the surge of public and press interest, Howard Strickling received a flood of interview requests. After extensive preparation, he let Hedy talk to English-born columnist Sheilah Graham. During the interview she obediently spouted the studio-approved explanation about *Ecstasy* and her nude scene: youthful naivete.

"When you're young and ambitious," she pointed out, "you are tempted to do practically anything to get famous."

Her estranged husband's notoriety, past and present, was another subject her questioner explored.

"He was so jealous. He made his servants spy on me, and report to him what I did while he was on his travels. Whenever I threatened to leave him, he locked me in my room. I was his prisoner. But now we can wish each other well. Before the *Anschluss*, we sometimes spoke by long distance telephone."

"European actresses complain that Hollywood hasn't accepted them," Miss Graham said, raising a topic Hedy hadn't expected. "Do you agree with them?"

"If an actress gives a good performance, does it matter where she came from? If she's lousy," she added, showing off her American slang, "then she'll fail and have to find other work. Or return home. For my picture, they make me up to be glamorous, but I care most for parts with real character. I want to be a success in *Algiers* so I can send for my mother. And I'll take out citizenship papers, because now I like this country the best. In Hollywood, you're either very unhappy or very happy. There's no in between. At first, I was very unhappy. Now I'm very happy."

Asked if she intended to marry Reggie, she replied that she wasn't sure.

His latest present was a diamond-encrusted bracelet, duly noted by the press. The gossip columnists' frequent coupling of their names resulted in studio pressure to make her mythical divorce a reality.

Ensenada, a picture-postcard beach resort, provided a brief escape from intrusive reporters and distressing news from her homeland. She hoped to relax by the seaside and shop in the street markets, but the process of obtaining her U.S. visa limited her leisure time.

Obtaining her freedom was a simple matter. For a small fee, she employed a local lawyer for herself, and his associate represented Fritz in the court. He presented her case to the presiding judge. Later that day he handed her a document declaring that the marriage was legally dissolved.

When she telephoned Howard with the good news, he warned her to keep quiet about the transaction.

"You're supposed to be divorced already. And your former husband could repudiate the Mexican judgment or otherwise make trouble."

"He won't," she insisted. "He'll be relieved."

"Tell the columnists that you're seeking an annulment from the Vatican. That's more respectable than divorce, which p-plenty of movie fans regard as sordid."

Her return to Hollywood with a new visa was noted by the press. But who was responsible for the item declaring she wanted to lose eight pounds? And the report about her once-a-week fasting regimen of tomato juice and skimmed milk?

Walter Wanger, pleased with his print of *Algiers,* wanted to cast her in his next picture. She'd enjoyed her time at Warner Brothers and would willingly work with him again. But Mr. Mayer, belatedly realizing her value to MGM, refused to release her a second time.

Chapter 18

When a preview of the edited print of *Algiers* was screened at the Fox Wilshire Theatre, Hedy was dismayed to find that Sigrid Gurie had the meatier role. However, hers had the greater visual impact, thanks to James Wong Howe's artistry with the camera and Irene's costuming.

Reggie invited several English friends to join them for an impromptu celebration at the Trocadero. Included in the group were Douglas Fairbanks, Hedy's fellow passenger on the *Normandie,* and her long-ago flirt Michael Brooke.

Fairbanks wanted to know which of her scenes was the most difficult.

"The one that reminded me of my worst times with my husband. Gaby's rich fiancé threatened to lock her up to keep her from meeting Pépé in the Casbah. But she wasn't yet a wife and was free to go."

"And your favorite?" Michael Brooke inquired.

"When Boyer sings 'C'est la vie,' and all the street people are cheerful and dancing."

"But you weren't in that scene."

"That's why I like it."

She was Reggie's date for the *Marie Antoinette* premiere, expected

to eclipse the grandest of all previous Hollywood openings. Search-
lights pointed skyward from Carthay Circle. Spectators crammed into
the grandstands erected near the cinema, and the crowd spilled onto
the sidewalks and street. A deafening roar greeted fan favorite Norma
Shearer and her co-star, Tyrone Power.

The cast members' entrances were carefully staged. Hedy and
Reggie joined the line waiting to pass through a tunnel-like canopy
carpeted in royal blue. When they emerged at the opposite end, they
were instructed to halt so the master of ceremonies, his voice amplified by loudspeakers, could announce them for the benefit of the
distant crowd and the radio audience. Even though neither of them
was a household name, they were greeted by applause. Behind them
came Hollywood's most famous sweethearts, Clark Gable and Carole
Lombard, who received enthusiastic cheers.

Massive floral displays and a flowery arch decorated the theatre
entrance. Despite Mr. Mayer's complaints about the lavish historical
project inherited from Thalberg, he'd spared no expense in recreating
eighteenth century France and replicating the gardens at Versailles.
To Hedy, the formal shaved hedges, classical statues and urns, and
groves of trees resembled a movie set rather than the baroque landscape they represented. Flashbulbs popped as she and Reggie signed
the guest book.

Ida Koverman had shed her office attire for a white gown and white
fox jacket. Merle Oberon carried an oversized muff. Seeing so many
furs, Hedy was glad she'd worn the chinchilla cape over her purple
chiffon gown.

The Countess di Frasso was accompanied by her Count, who had
come over from Italy. Robert Taylor escorted Barbara Stanwyck,
demonstrating that their romance was intact. Freddie Bartholomew, at
fourteen the youngest member of the British contingent, confided to
Reggie and Hedy he was having his very first date—with Judy Garland,
recently cast as Dorothy in a musical version of *The Wizard of Oz*.

"They should leave their mothers at home," Hedy whispered to
Reggie.

The cover of the souvenir program was illustrated with a sketch of the French queen, but Hedy had no time to read it. The lights were dimming.

Cost overruns prohibited the use of the Technicolor process, a sore point with Reggie. He'd often described the richness of the court costumes and the splendor of the scenery, but stark black and white film couldn't detract from their magnificence.

By the time the brave, heartbroken Queen climbed into the tumbril for her journey from prison to guillotine, the audience was reduced to tears.

Mr. Mayer had invited six hundred people to his celebratory party at the Trocadero. Table-hopping with Reggie, Hedy was gratified by warm greetings from colleagues and acquaintances. Those who had attended last month's *Algiers* preview complimented her performance, and the ones who hadn't said they looked forward to its premiere. Charles Boyer and his wife invited her to sit with them.

I'm making friends, she realized.

In the days before her film's premiere, she posed for stills to accompany scheduled interviews with Hollywood's rival columnists.

"Hedda Hopper will come to your house on Sunday," Howard told her. "We can't hold her off any longer. Louella P-parsons of the Hearst newspaper group won't like getting second place, but we hope she'll blame us, not you."

On Saturday night, Hedy sent Reggie away at an early hour and carefully eradicated signs of his frequent presence. The next morning her personal publicity representative arrived with the stylish Hedda in tow.

"About time Mayer let me talk to you. I've waited for months," the powerful columnist huffed, glaring at Don.

"So have I," Hedy replied. "In Vienna I talked to reporters often, before and after the release of *Ecstasy*. There was much interest, for reasons that you know. Shall we go outside? The patio has shade."

As soon as she was seated, Hedda began flinging questions as sharp as darts, impossible to deflect. Hedy launched into her revised recollections of her nude scenes and how ignorant she'd been, too eager to please. She gave a factual description of Fritz's courtship and their married life. As usual, she expressed her desire to bring Mutti to America. Her best defense against discomfiting topics, she found, was to pose questions of her own—about Hollywood, and the stars that her visitor claimed as friends.

Hedda's beady eyes swept across the ledge that separated the patio from the lawn. "Your petunias look so much better than mine. And I like those colorful plant pots."

"They used to be plain, before I painted them."

As the hens trilled softly from their coop, the conversation shifted to Hedy's journey across the Atlantic and the MGM contract and her hopes for the future. Hedda congratulated her on her proficiency in English after less than a year in America.

"You must've studied very hard to make such progress."

"I go to many movies," she said brightly. "And listen to radio broadcasts. They are the best way of learning!"

———◦•◆•◦———

On her premiere night, Hedy selected a new gown of shimmering violet jacquard, printed all over with tiny orchids. Once more she brought out the chinchilla wrap. Even in the middle of a California summer, a Hollywood actress was supposed to wear fur.

A studio limousine carried her and her date to the Four Star Theatre. She clutched Reggie's arm in excitement when she spotted lightbulbs spelling out her name. This was her teenage dream made real.

"I wish Mutti could see."

"An MGM photographer will get a photo," he assured her.

Not as many fans crowded Wilshire Boulevard as had gathered for *Marie Antoinette,* but for the film colony the *Algiers* premiere was noteworthy as the final gala of the summer. Because of the foreign setting and international cast, invitations had been extended to consuls from overseas countries and government attachés posted to the region.

Before entering the theatre, Hedy answered a radio interviewer's questions and read a brief written address. She was the primary focus of attention. Charles Boyer and his wife had retreated to Pebble Beach, and Sigrid Gurie was unwell.

Walter Wanger's date was Joan Bennett, recently divorced from her producer husband. Norma Shearer, basking in her triumph as the martyred French Queen, had come with a mystery man. Bette Davis darted through the foyer, husband Harmon Nelson in tow, greeting friends in her inimitable voice and cackling with laughter.

A humorous Robert Benchley live-action short and a cartoon starring Donald Duck and Goofy preceded Hedy's intensely dramatic picture. From the moment her image appeared on the screen, Hedy took hold of Reggie's hand, holding it so tight that her fingernails scored his palm. He bore it stoically.

As the final credits rolled, the audience responded with deafening applause. Walter Wanger rose and bowed, gesturing for Hedy to do the same.

How different from that Vienna screening of *Ecstasy,* she reflected, when Mutti and Papa and other affronted patrons fled the cinema.

On her way out of the auditorium, men and women whose performances she'd admired gathered around to praise hers. She and Reggie traveled by limousine to a late-night party where she received additional acclaim. It was nearly morning when they were delivered to her bungalow.

"What now?" She tossed her handbag onto the sofa and sat down to remove her shoes.

"A drink," he suggested.

"I mean, what will happen next? Even though people said I was a success, Mr. Mayer didn't come near me all night."

"He was awfully tipsy. On the verge of drunk."

"If he won't loan me to another studio, he should give me a script. A good one."

"Never fear, you'll be summoned to his office soon enough. He's always got his eye on the main chance."

She regarded him through narrowed eyes. "I won't sit around until he sends for me. He can be the one to wait. Everybody else is leaving the city. Couldn't we go to your place in Malibu? Now?"

"There's no food, and the shops won't open till morning. If you want breakfast, I'll have to raid your fridge."

While he gathered up necessities, she changed into blouse and slacks and stuffed some casual clothing into a small suitcase. Despite her preference for sleeping in the nude, she added a silk negligee. Reggie enjoyed the ritual of undressing her before taking her to bed.

Throughout their hour-long drive to the coast, her gaze often returned to the full, white moon. It seemed to smile down at her.

At an early hour of the new day, they reached his rustic cabin near Vaquero Hill, adjacent to the Rindge family property and mansion. They sat together on the front steps, sipping sherry and admiring the moonlit sky and the distant sea.

Late the next morning, Reggie drove down to the village for supplies and a newspaper. Hedy brewed coffee and cracked eggs and sliced bread and pondered last night's events. Perhaps the movie people had said nice things to spare her feelings. Critics, frank to a fault and lacking sensitivity, might not be so generous. She wanted to live up to Mayer's high expectations, and his failure to comment on her performance revived her insecurities.

Hollywood success depended on more than being under contract with a studio. In a community overflowing with talent and beauty, her looks could carry her only so far.

The rumpled state of the paper Reggie brought back indicated he'd already paged through it.

"There's a review," he announced.

"Read it to me." She perched on the chair edge, hands tightly folded.

"*The Los Angeles Times* says, 'Boyer brings a genuine fervor to his portrayal that is far-reaching and Miss Lamarr's consummate loveliness may entitle her to stardom.'"

"That's all? Nothing about my acting?"

"Darling, your movie will be seen all across the country, by plenty of reviewers and thousands upon thousands of people. You can count on many more accolades."

She returned home to find a stack of congratulatory messages from her small cadre of close friends—the Reischs and other Austrian emigres, Greer and Nina Garson, Benny Thau. Howard Strickling had sent flowers.

A horseracing enthusiast, Reggie took her to the Saturday races at Hollywood Park, the new track in Inglewood. Because so many studio moguls invested in thoroughbreds, or served on the Turf Club board, box seats in the grandstand were populated with the famous. The men were dressed in fine suits, and the ladies wore hats and gloves.

"It's like a church service," Hedy murmured.

"For most of the men here, this *is* their religion. Dearly beloved, let us pray that Seabiscuit wins."

"Amen," she responded fervently. She'd bet heavily on the favorite.

She shared the crowd's elation when America's most famous horse achieved an impressive come-from-behind finish. This was, she declared, the most exciting feat she'd ever witnessed.

Her tear-misted eyes landed on a gentleman in a nearby row, grinning as he ripped up his betting tickets.

"I've seen that man before," she said to Reggie, "at almost every party we've attended. Who is he?"

"Gene Markey. Joan Bennett left him to take up with Walter Wanger. Unlucky in love—unlucky at the track."

Glancing again at Markey, she received a wink and a nod.

She turned her attention back to the course, where the Hollywood Gold Cup and a fifty-thousand-dollar prize were being presented to the jockey and the owner.

"Here's a chance to test the value of your new-found fame," Reggie said. "Try and get your picture taken with Seabiscuit."

Reggie, a firm supporter of his British friends, dutifully attended their film previews. He accepted Richard Greene's invitation to see an advance print of *Submarine Patrol,* directed by John Ford. Hedy, intrigued by the title, went with him. Despite her interest in the subject and the leading actor's good looks, boredom set in. The screening room was stale and uncomfortably smoky from all the cigarettes.

In a whisper, she told Reggie she was stepping outside for a breath of fresh air.

Another deserter, a heavyset man, leaned against the wall of the building, puffing away. He waved at her. "Terrible picture, isn't it?"

"A disaster."

"I'm the scriptwriter." He shrugged. "One of them."

Regretting her candor, she said apologetically, "I didn't know. I wasn't being rude on purpose."

"I'm not offended. Your blunt assessment is all too accurate. I'll make Darryl Zanuck excise my name from the credits. William Faulkner can take the blame for this stinker."

"Next time you script a submarine picture, I can help. I know a great deal about them. Underwater torpedoes, too."

"Really? I find that hard to believe." He lodged his cigarette in his mouth and held out his hand. "Gene Markey. A pleasure to meet you, Miss Lamarr. Our paths crossed at some party or other, when I was married to Joan Bennett. Actresses are one of my many weaknesses. So are racehorses. How much money did you win on Seabiscuit?"

"I shouldn't boast," she replied demurely, "but it's a good thing I placed a large bet. If Mr. Mayer doesn't extend my contract, I'll need the money!"

He laughed. "Take me to Chasen's to drown my sorrows over that disastrous *Submarine Patrol*. One cocktail, that's all you have to buy. I'll need my wits about me when I meet with Darryl tomorrow morning."

"I would be glad to, but I can't. I have a boyfriend."

He let the smoking remnant of his cigarette fall to the ground and crushed it under his heel. "If you ever want another one, Miss Hedy Lamarr, get in touch."

⊙·◆·⊙

With Hedy's sudden prominence, press attention escalated. Howard Strickling was infuriated by newspaper articles delving into unsavory details of her past. One focused on Fritz's arms sale to the Nazi regime and the recent seizure of his property, with accompanying photo of Fritz and Ernst von Starhemberg and a line drawing of a naked Hedy. Another piece, riddled with inaccuracies, correctly identified him as the "Munitions King." And it faithfully recounted her escape to Budapest with Ferdi, and the railway station encounter with her outraged spouse. The author predicted that Hedy and Reggie would marry as soon as their respective divorces were final.

"I wasn't the source," she defended herself. "Fritz and his German dealings are widely known. In the months before I left him, people in Vienna spread many rumors about me and . . . and other men."

"Are you engaged to Reginald Gardiner?"

"We're friends."

"Very intimate friends, by all appearances. If you mean to marry him, or anybody else, you'd better tell L.B. beforehand. He expects to be fully informed about our stars' p-personal lives."

"I'm not a star."

"Not yet. We think you will be. How many times do I have to tell you, Hedy? Avoid journalists, unless Don or someone else from my office is p-present. Deflect any questions about *Ecstasy*. Don't discuss your ex-husband. Downplay your romance with Gardiner. Concentrate on your domestic life. Your daily routine, beauty secrets, favorite foods. Get a dog."

"Are you going to tell me what kind of dog?"

Laughing, he replied, "A photogenic one. Without a scandalous backstory. Bette Davis can help. She's the p-president of Tailwaggers, that canine charity."

Why, she wondered, should she inform Mr. Mayer about her plans, when he hadn't revealed his plans for her?

Determined to find out what they might be, she left Howard's domain for the chief executive's suite.

Down the corridor, Greer Garson and Benny Thau were leaving

his office. As he reached out to button her cardigan—the Thalberg Building's powerful air conditioning made it unbearably cold—they exchanged a tender glance.

Accompanying her friend to the elevator, Hedy observed, "You look like you've had good news."

"I've been given the leading role in *Dramatic School*. Mervyn Le Roy is producing, and Robert Sinclair will direct. You've had a run of good luck yourself," Greer added with a smile. "How does it feel to be famous?"

"Nothing's changed, except I'm supposed to talk about myself too much, and I receive lots of invitations. I still prefer spending nights at home with Reggie. If you come over Saturday, I'll show you his latest masterpiece. A watercolor portrait of me, lying on black silk sheets. In the nude."

"How very *Ecstasy* of you. The viewing will have to wait for another time. I've been invited on a riding excursion this weekend, by some of my polo player friends. Are you free for lunch? Mother's meeting me in the commissary."

"I'll join you after I've seen Mr. Mayer."

"Better not mention Reggie's handiwork. You know what a Puritan he is."

"About other people's private lives. Not his own."

She swept past the busy typing pool. The two secretaries stationed near Ida Koverman's office eyed her curiously. Ignoring them, she rapped on Mr. Mayer's door.

"What is it?"

Without announcing herself, Hedy crossed the threshold.

He bounced out of his chair and came to meet her, an unprecedented occurrence. "Sit down, make yourself comfortable." He returned to his place behind the great white desk. "You're a Hollywood sensation, and Walter Wanger's getting too much credit for it. I've spent forty-thousand dollars on your English and acting and other lessons, plus make up and photography and your screen test. I ordered Howard to create a press release about our investment in Miss Hedy Lamarr."

"I've read that many studios are wanting me," she said. "But always you say no. And you haven't asked what I wish to do next."

"You'll do whatever I tell you to do," he replied smoothly. "In order to capitalize on your sudden success, I've got to keep you at Metro. Don't worry, I'll make sure your first picture for us is much, much better than *Algiers*. I've lined up Charlie MacArthur, Mr. Helen Hayes, to improve the screenplay for *A New York Cinderella*. Spencer Tracy plays your love interest. He's an Oscar winner! Josef von Sternberg, who's done terrific things with Dietrich, will direct. After that production wraps, I'm putting you in an epic period piece about Lola Montez, and we'll spare no expense. She was a very sexy beauty who danced her way into the heart of the emperor of Germany."

"King Ludwig," she corrected him. "He ruled Bavaria before unification."

"We're going to work you hard, my dear. And at the end of the year, when we renew your next six-month option, your salary will increase."

"There's something else I need. More important than money."

He spread his arms wide. "Anything."

"Since the *Anschluss* I've had no letters from Mutti, even though I've often been writing to her. Her parents were Jews, and she's mother-in-law to Fritz Mandl. I fear for her safety. She wants to go to London, where she has friends."

"I'll cable Bob Ritchie. He might be able to arrange things through our Vienna office."

"Thank you." She gestured towards his mother's photograph. "You know what it means to have a caring parent. When I was so desperate to run away from my husband, Mutti didn't stop me from leaving Austria. Even though she would be all alone."

He wiped a tear from the corner of his eye. "We'll find a way to get to her America, so she can see what a good father I am to you."

Chapter 19

Raised in a genteel household, schooled in polite behavior, Hedy had difficulty refusing interview requests. Disregarding her publicist's edicts, she answered reporters' questions about *Ecstasy* and her life as Frau Mandl, and flashed her eleven-carat diamond ring from Cartier in Paris.

But when a newspaperman expressed sympathy for her head cold, she didn't admit she'd caught it posing naked for Reggie's current painting. She liked Howard Strickling too much to cause a heart attack, and she was too dependent on Mayer's goodwill to risk giving him a stroke.

Her spectacular screen debut wasn't the only big story to capture the attention of the film community at mid-summer. Over a three-day period, millionaire and sometime producer Howard Hughes had completed an around-the-world airplane flight. Hedy followed each stage of his journey with fascination and frequently expressed admiration of the aviator, risking the wrath of his spirited girlfriend, Katharine Hepburn.

Shy and star-struck, not entirely comfortable as the newest member of the Hollywood elite, she was startled to receive a telephone call from the queen of Warner Brothers.

"*Dar*-ling," Bette Davis drawled, "I'm giving a sit-down dinner and a ball to raise money for the Tailwaggers Fund, so we can build a dog hospital and train more seeing-eye dogs for the blind. *Ev*-erybody's coming. We'll have raffles and games. Bring your checkbook, because Edgar Bergen, or maybe Charlie McCarthy, will auction off a cocker spaniel. I'm so *very* keen to entice you that I've set you up with a special date. I heard that you want to meet Howard Hughes."

Out of loyalty to Reggie, she hesitated. "I've got a boyfriend." It was a frequent refrain.

"Yes, yes, I know. Dear Reggie, he won't mind a bit. It's all about publicity, for Howard Hughes and for you and for this wonderful cause that's so dear to my heart. *Life* magazine will cover the event. You simply *can't* refuse. I'd be disappointed, and so will Howard. He looks forward to escorting you."

From Hedy's perspective, the evening got off to a bad start. Hughes, gangly and awkward in his creased tuxedo, was late picking her up. He didn't apologize but merely announced that he'd been busy at his aircraft factory. During the drive to the Beverly Hills Hotel he gazed at her intently but addressed only a few words in a high, faint voice with an underlying Western twang. His wealth, ambition, and achievements matched Fritz Mandl's, but he lacked her former husband's social skills.

"You're more exquisite in the flesh than on the screen. Just like everyone says." He shrugged his bony shoulder. "You hear that a lot, I bet."

She had no patience for platitudes. "I'd like to know more about your flight around the world."

"You and everyone else. I'm tired of discussing it."

His lack of charm and dash contrasted with his reputation as Hollywood's great lothario, the fickle lover of countless screen beauties. After a few minutes in his company, she had no wish to be another of his many conquests. Wistfully, she thought of Reggie, his wit and his *joie de vivre* and his elegance. He would have entered into Bette's planned activities with relish, whereas Howard Hughes wore the expression of a man bound for a funeral instead of a frolic.

A lively game of musical chairs was already in progress when they reached the Beverly Hills Hotel. Bette, wearing a pink Antebellum gown, fluttered up to greet them.

"What a pity you missed our *mar*-velous dinner," she said to Hedy, while Hughes glared at the *Life* magazine photographer. "After this nice man shoots some pictures, we'll see about getting you some food. Look, here's Lord Buffington, our other guest of honor! Isn't he a-*dor*-able? Hedy, wouldn't you like to hold him?"

Edgar Bergen handed her a squirming spaniel pup. Cradling it, Hedy watched her hostess abscond with her date. After briefly posing together for the cameraman, they vanished through a door at the back of the ballroom.

"What a schemer," Norma Shearer muttered. "Parading herself in front of Selznick in that Southern belle gown, trying to convince him she should play Scarlett O'Hara. Can you imagine? Now, don't be cross that she stole Howard away. You're far better off with Reggie, he's such a love. His jokes kept up our spirits when we were shooting *Marie Antoinette*."

"I'm not interested in Mr. Hughes," Hedy said truthfully. "Miss Davis is welcome to him."

"Kate Hepburn might have something to say about that. Not to mention Bette's husband. Come and meet my friend Jimmy Stewart, I'm sure he's dying to know you."

They dodged the balloons littering the dance floor. When the skinny young actor found out that Hedy hadn't eaten, he gallantly rose from the table and offered to get something from the kitchen. He returned with a bowl containing three mounds of ice cream—vanilla, chocolate, and strawberry.

"Best I could do," he said apologetically. "Miss Davis is serving the remains of the banquet to Mr. Hughes, and I didn't like to interrupt. I heard him promise her that he'd buy every single raffle ticket if she'd go out with him just once."

"Ice cream is my favorite thing," Hedy assured him. "But please don't let that magazine man photograph me eating it. Mr. Mayer doesn't want me anywhere near food."

Within days, the tycoon contacted her. He wanted a second date.

"Is Miss Davis too busy for you? How unfortunate, after all the money you spent on her charity. Sorry, Mr. Hughes, I'm not available."

"Tonight? Or never?" He didn't wait for an answer. "Why?"

She wouldn't dissemble. "I'm attached to someone. And because you remind me of my former husband."

"You must've liked something about him. After all, you married him."

"His intelligence and his sophistication were attractive. It was after our wedding that I found out he could be selfish and controlling and deceitful."

"Boy, you've got me pegged. It's a damn shame, but I applaud your perception."

She returned to her easel and the Alpine landscape inspired by a bout of homesickness. As she painted, she thought about Fritz.

Exile from Austria and the Nazi sequestration of his properties had no discernible impact on his habits. He'd left Switzerland to spend the remainder of the summer on the Riviera, where he'd recently purchased a mansion. His Vienna lawyer had received a copy of her Mexican divorce decree but advised him to obtain a divorce in an American jurisdiction to ensure legality. A Texas law firm was taking care of it, with no cost to Hedy, and the matter would be kept confidential.

During one of his occasional telephone calls, he told her, "I want to provide a financial settlement. My former wife shouldn't have to occupy a rented property. Give me your bank account number, and I will wire a deposit of ten thousand dollars."

"Fritz," she breathed into the phone. "That's a lot of money."

"Buy a nice house, Hasi. And if you need more, let me know. All I ask in return is that you remain friendly, and don't condemn me when speaking to the press. My reputation has suffered enough. We'll . . . I'll stay in France until I can secure Father's release from the internment camp. I mean to take him and Renée with me to Buenos Aires, as well as my secretary and others. I invested in Argentine businesses, you know, which are likely to deliver substantial profits."

Fritz was as good as his word, and within days her bank informed her that the promised funds were deposited. Eager to put them to the specified use, she looked forward to house-hunting expeditions with Greer. But when she called the Garson residence, Nina reported that her daughter had suffered a riding accident so severe that spinal surgery was required.

Making a pilgrimage to Good Samaritan Hospital, Hedy found Greer in a private flower-filled room, wearing an elegant bed jacket and deep in conversation with Benny Thau. He made space on the windowsill for the bouquet she'd brought and promptly departed.

"Are the two of you having an affair?" she asked, taking the bedside chair he'd vacated.

"We're dating. Rather, we were. Before I tumbled off my horse."

"Does Mr. Mayer know? He's in love with you. It's no secret—everybody knows."

"That may be, but he ordered Benny to take me out. Show Miss Garson a good time, he said. He felt sorry for me because I spent so many nights at home with Mother."

"If he discovers your romance, he'll be furious."

"What difference will it make? He can't ruin my career. I haven't got one." With a brave attempt at a smile, Greer added, "My first Hollywood picture was that x-ray of my backbone. The studio cast Ilona in a musical straightaway. You were loaned to Wanger and became a star. I'm forever a Neglected Import."

"Mr. Mayer believes in you."

"Much good it's done. An actress who isn't allowed to act is a nonentity. A nothing. A nobody. Whatever MGM demanded, I did it. To get slimmer, I starved myself into anemia. I've worked with a performance coach. I hired a brilliant talent agent. Frankly, I don't care if Mayer gives up on me."

"You say that because you feel poorly. You should do battle with him. Fight!"

"That's rather difficult to do from this position, dearie. Honestly, I'd be relieved to return home to England. I dream of it as I lie here, facing heaven knows how many weeks in a wheelchair. Now, be a friend and cheer me up with your news."

This wasn't the best moment to mention *A New York Cinderella* and Mayer's Lola Montez project. "I'm buying a house. And I plan to get a dog. Reggie's painting me again, this time in oils, on canvas. A life-sized portrait."

"With or without clothes?"

"With."

"And you'll be co-starring with Spencer Tracy."

"Who told you?"

"Your next director, Josef von Sternberg. He sends the orchids, every day. Aren't you rather young to be Tracy's love interest?"

"Mr. Mayer doesn't think so," Hedy answered. "And I do prefer older men."

<hr>

"A highly unlikely scenario," Reggie responded after Hedy described her role in *A New York Cinderella*. "Naturally you play a beautiful foreigner, that's typecasting. But no one will believe that a man in his right senses would abandon you for someone else."

"For his wife. But Georgi's lover does return. He comes for her after she marries the humble but brilliant doctor who saved her from jumping off the ship when she was heartbroken."

Picking up his hammer, Reggie pounded the air. "They all need a good bash in the head."

His apartment was ten minutes away by foot, and he routinely turned up at her newly purchased Camden Drive house in his work clothes, toolbox in hand. He'd recreated the outdoor rabbit hutch and chicken coop and was converting a back room into a lounge for entertaining. He also intended to build a backyard swimming pool.

"It's such a dilemma. I must decide which man I truly love."

"You choose humble Spencer Tracy over handsome Walter Pidgeon, of course."

"How did you guess?"

"Because I know which actor earns the bigger salary. Pass that short section of plywood, please."

When their paths crossed at parties and premieres, Spencer Tracy was genial and polite. On the set, he seemed much less friendly. Hedy couldn't shake her suspicion that he disapproved of her performance, and she dreaded every scene they had together. This was a contrast to her liking for Walter Pidgeon, Greer Garson's near neighbor.

Reggie, on a break from his own film, visited Stage 14 to discover them locked in an embrace during a kissing scene. After observing several retakes, he muttered to von Sternberg that it was most unfair for his friend to be paid money for such pleasant work.

"Mr. Pidgeon," the director called out, "don't put quite so much feeling into your performance. Mr. Gardiner prefers more restraint."

When the columnists seized on this as proof of Reggie's jealousy, Hedy laughed it off. "They should know better than to take a comedian seriously."

At this crucial point in her career, when confidence often wavered, the studio abruptly dismissed her acting coach. On a bright Sunday she arrived at the Garson home to pour out her feelings. Greer, whose coach was both ally and confidante, would understand how unsettling this loss was.

"Mr. Mayer spends more than one million dollars to make this picture. To save money, he fires Phyllis. The person who helps me give a good performance. What should I do?"

"March into his monstrosity of an office and demand that he reverse his decision. How do you suppose I stopped him canceling my contract? I followed the advice you gave me when I was in hospital. I climbed out of my wheelchair and tottered into the lion's den, and I roared at him. As a result, I got a screen test for *Goodbye Mr. Chips,* and I was cast in the wife role. The picture's being shot in England. I've got my ticket home, and Mayer is paying for it. Vindication!"

"You're leaving for London, where my mother is escaping to from Vienna. And I'll be here in California with yours. While you're away, who will listen to my troubles and comfort me?"

"Reggie, I should think. Don't give way about Phyllis, dearie. Be as firm with the boss as you told me to be."

"I will," she decided.

Mayer, increasingly horse-mad, maintained a large stable on the MGM property and went riding every morning with Howard Strickling. At an early hour, Hedy stationed herself at his private entrance to the Thalberg building to waylay him. When he arrived, his reddened face glistened with perspiration. In jacket and jodhpurs, his figure looked especially rotund and tubby.

"Mr. Mayer, I'm begging you to let me continue working with Phyllis Loughton. She's taught me so much, and I really need her if I'm to be a success in this role."

"Your picture is already costing me a bundle, and I have to trim expenses. For the past year we've given you all kinds of private instruction, and it didn't come cheap. We've got other coaches on our roster, you know. You can work with any of them."

She stared him down. "You've seen the *Algiers* reviews. My looks and my costumes received more comments than my acting. If I wanted to be a fashion *mannequin,* I'd have stayed in Paris. I know I can improve, with guidance from Phyllis."

He reached up to pat her shoulder. "You'll do fine. Run along, now. Ida and the rest of them will wonder why I'm so late. I've got to shower and change. Lots of work today. Running the best and most profitable studio in the world is no picnic, you know."

⸺◦•◆•◦⸺

After two weeks' work on his latest film, Reggie tumbled down a flight of stairs and broke his arm in three places. During his lengthy hospital stay, Hedy wore herself out careening from her house to the studio to his room at Cedars of Lebanon.

"Good thing I finished building your cocktail bar," he said, "and hanged my photograph beside it. Your party guests can toast me in absentia."

"I won't be entertaining while you lie here in pain," she assured him. "Or going out at night until you've recovered enough to go with me. Even if I have to take you in an ambulance."

"I'll only feel worse if you sit home alone. Just promise me you won't accept a date with David Niven. Or anybody else who went to Sandhurst. Or served in the British military. They can't be trusted. Unlike those of us who attended the Royal Academy of Dramatic Arts." He raised his good arm and stroked his moustache.

"I've got Toni for company." She'd adopted her dog from the Tailwaggers' kennel and named it for the one in *Storm in a Water Glass*, her early Sascha Studios film. "I can use my nights at home to study my part—although I don't know why I bother. The director changes it every day."

Von Sternberg was constantly revising the shooting script of *A New York Cinderella,* and Hedy often received new material shortly before the cameras rolled. Because he demanded complete silence on the set, she was unable to request clarifications when confused. Adding to her dismay, Mayer had taken on the responsibilities of producer, and his presence was as unwelcome as it was unsettling. And she had to contend with a co-star whose biting criticisms ventured into rudeness.

"Could you maybe *perform* your part?" Spencer Tracy said one day. "Instead of simply reciting the lines from memory."

"I'd do better if our dialogue didn't change every five minutes," she retorted. "If you dislike my acting, tell Mr. Mayer to let me work with Phyllis Loughton. At least I'd have a chance of doing something more with this terrible role."

His annoyed expression gave way to one resembling pity. Instead of pursuing the quarrel, he shook his head regretfully and moved away.

The scheduled shower scene was another source of frustration, an unwelcome and inconvenient reminder of *Ecstasy*—which Mr. Mayer and Howard constantly warned her not to mention. But audiences were sure to make the connection with that movie when they saw this one. Should she express her reluctance to remove her clothes? Would it make any difference if she did?

Resigned, she put on the flesh-colored undergarments she was given and covered them with a blue terry cloth bathrobe. When she left her dressing room, she found a male reporter lurking at the door.

"Didn't you give up making nudie movies?" he asked as she strode past. "One of the grips told me you're going to strip down to nothing."

"Not until I'm behind the shower curtain. And even then, I won't be completely unclothed."

After Von Sternberg and the cameraman examined the shower unit, Hedy's stand-in turned on the water and the sound man shoved his microphone inside. When the girl stepped out, dripping, a crew member wiped up the puddle she left on the floor.

Hedy climbed into the cubicle and pulled the curtain all the way across, making sure there was no gap. She slipped off her robe and tossed it over the rail.

"Action!"

She gripped the taps and twisted them. Lukewarm water poured from the shower head, and she backed away to avoid a drenching. Closing her eyes against the spray, she began to sing.

Responding to her cue, a knock on the door, she called, "Who's there?"

"Karl," Spencer replied.

"Just a minute," she caroled.

"Cut! That's a wrap."

A disembodied arm returned her robe and she put it on again, pulling the belt tight.

A harmless scene in a romantic comedy. Claudette Colbert or Bette Davis wouldn't think anything of it, because their reputations hadn't been darkened by a notorious film.

Her sense of ill-usage was compounded when she learned that Mayer had shelved the enticing Lola Montez project.

After an especially vitriolic argument with the studio boss, Von

Sternberg declared he was quitting the picture and stormed off the set.

"We're on a two-week break," she told Reggie during a hospital visit, "while they look for a new director and fix that stupid script."

Cast and crew reassembled with Frank Borgaze, an Academy Award recipient, in charge. Mayer observed the first few hours of shooting, and his dissatisfaction was proved at day's end, when he shut down production for a second time. A week later, after further rewrites, filming resumed. During the hiatus, *A New York Cinderella* acquired a new title: *I Take This Woman*.

"Reggie says it should be called *I Re-Take This Woman*," Hedy told her co-star.

"Everyone else in Hollywood refers to it as *Mayer's Folly*," Spencer replied gloomily.

With a competent, businesslike director at the helm, his mood improved. Like battle-tested veterans, he and Hedy settled into an easier working relationship. Sometimes he flirted with her, and she responded in kind. He admitted he was impatient to be cut loose and head over to Twentieth Century Fox for *Stanley and Livingston*, a project of far greater significance.

Hedy shared his eagerness to complete a picture that seemed destined to fail—and deserved to, in her opinion. Surely a better role would be forthcoming. Her performance in *Algiers* combined with Howard Strickling's diligent placement of publicity stills had transformed her from a foreign-born neophyte into an international icon of beauty and glamour.

Dining at the Brown Derby with Reggie, still recuperating from his broken arm, she commented, "Our crew and cast members act surprised whenever I do something friendly or nice. They expect me to be aloof and arrogant. First, the publicists kept me away from reporters, and made me a lady of mystery. Now I'm the rich girl from Vienna, the unhappy wife who ran away from the bad millionaire." She sliced his meat in small pieces and fed them to him. "It's no wonder people think I'm odd. But really, I'm just an ordinary person."

"Not exactly," he demurred. He put a cigarette between his lips and handed her his lighter. "I'm one of the blessed few to whom you reveal all of your many attributes. And I refer to the creative and intellectual ones—not merely the physical."

News from Europe added to her pessimism. Hitler, unchecked, had overrun Czechoslovakia. German and Austrian Jews suffered extreme acts of violence, their homes and businesses invaded and destroyed. American leaders uttered disapproving statements and expressed sympathy but wouldn't commit to receiving refugees. With every headline and radio bulletin, Hedy's hatred of the Nazi regime intensified. As did her disgust at the inability or unwillingness of democratic governments to take action and offer relief.

Her final scene before the Christmas break took place on the New York subway platform recreated by MGM's construction crew and set dressers. She joined a large group of burly extras who were instructed to block her path to the turnstiles.

"Shove her. Push her!" Frank Borzage commanded as she fought her way through the crowd.

Twelve takes later, he ordered everyone back to their places. During a quick make-up check, Hedy prayed that the next round of mayhem would be the last.

"Let her have it!" the director yelled at the men. "Poke her with your elbows. Step on her feet. Forget she's Hedy Lamarr! She's just a broad getting in your way."

Without complaint, she endured the constant and repeated pummeling, but by lunchtime she was feeling dizzy.

"No, that's not right. Let's try one more time."

She focused on Spencer's face as he frantically tried to break through the crowd to reach her. With unfeigned relief, she fell into his embrace and kissed him.

"Cut. Good job, people."

She limped over to a stool and sat down to rub her feet.

"You're a real trouper," Borzage told her.

"Ignoring bruised shins and trampled toes might be the best acting

I've ever done," she replied unsteadily, pulling a handkerchief from her skirt pocket.

"Hey," said Spencer, coming over, "are you crying? You performed the hell out of that scene. Every time."

"Thanks for noticing." She heaved a sigh. "Not so long ago, I thought making a movie, any movie, was better than sitting around waiting for another part. I've changed my mind."

"Yeah, this picture's a stinker. They don't all turn out well. You'll learn that the really good ones are the exception. Let's hope that the next time we work together, we'll get a decent script. And a director who knows his ass from his elbow."

"You'd work with me again?"

"Hell, yeah! You're a hot property, and *Mayer's Folly* won't change that. Dry your eyes, kid, and come to my dressing room. I'm on the wagon, so I can't offer you a whisky. But I've got a box of chocolates I don't mind sharing. You look like you need 'em bad."

Chapter 20

Designated by the press as Glamour Girl of 1938, Hedy began the next year as Hollywood's most storied and sought-after actress. But no other director could have her yet, because she must resume the never-ending chore of making *I Take This Woman*.

Reluctantly, she joined the line of performers and crew members clutching their time cards. When she'd clocked in, she made her way to her dressing room. Mr. Mayer sat in a chintz-covered chair, clutching the armrests.

"You're getting your acting coach."

"Phyllis?"

"Glesca Marshall. She's on her way over." He cleared his throat. "You should know that she's, ah, what you might call mannish. But don't worry, she won't try and hook you. She's Alla Nazimova's, um, secretary. They're very, uh, intimate. I'm sure you get my drift. Oh, and we've recast the Walter Pidgeon role. With an actor called Taylor."

"Robert Taylor?"

"Kent Taylor. No relation, but almost as handsome. Come to think of it, you and Bob Taylor together would set the screen on fire. Ben Hecht was working up a script that might do the trick. *Lady of the Tropics*, I think it's called."

She was tempted to tell him she'd agree to do the tropical picture on the condition that its script was a thousand times better than *I Take This Woman*. But because he was being nice to her, she withheld the retort.

"We've hired the instructor from the La Conga club to teach you and Spence to dance the rumba. My favorite," he added, unnecessarily. She'd witnessed his gyrations at numerous private parties and in all the popular nightclubs.

Glesca Marshall's first task was preparing Hedy for the opening scene, in which she attempted to leap to her death from a ship's deck.

"You see the silliness of it," she said. "If I'm committing suicide, why do I put the fur coat over my evening gown? I want to drown in the ocean, so it makes no difference if I get cold."

"Have you shared your concerns with the director?"

"Not often. Complaining makes actresses unpopular. But I told him Georgi shouldn't only be the assistant in her husband's medical office. She's wanting to help his patients, who are all foreigners and poor people. She's an *emigrée* herself. If she is fluent in all the languages I speak, she can translate for the Germans and the French and the Italians and the Russians and the Hungarians."

"Did Mr. Borzage accept your suggestion?"

"Yes." Crossing her legs, Hedy said, "When I studied with Reinhardt, there was much emphasis on acting with the whole body, to make the character a physical being. But for the camera, I have to . . . to pose. 'Stand still!' this director tells me, so the cameraman can get close-ups of my face. Adrian designs lovely costumes for me to wear, but I can't move about easily. No one seems to care."

Secure in her athleticism and determined to further prove her mettle to the production team, she refused the offer of a stunt double for her leap into the ocean. The publicity department leaked this information beforehand, drawing a number of spectators.

From her perch at the ship's railing there was an eight-foot drop to the stack of mattresses down below. Wishing her luck, her stand-in moved out of the way.

Let me do this right the first time, Hedy prayed as she prepared to jump.

The instant she landed, the director shouted, "Cut!"

Everyone rushed over to make sure she was unhurt. Rising without assistance, she laughed off their concern and readied herself for a second take. It wasn't necessary.

Moviemaking was good fun, when it involved flying through the air. And dancing the rumba.

As her self-assurance at the studio increased, contentment with her love life had waned. Reggie's shattered arm wasn't healing properly, magnifying her guilt about the way her feelings had changed and her reluctance to communicate that to him. To refute columnists' predictions that wedding bells would ring as soon as his divorce was final, she accepted dinner invitations from other men. Bob Ritchie, recently arrived from London, gradually replaced Reggie as her regular escort for public events.

Swayed by an attack of remorse and the need to explain her behavior, she invited Reggie to dinner. During his protracted convalescence he'd lost a great deal of weight, so she served him the richest Austrian dishes in her limited repertoire.

"I suppose you'll say you're just friends with Ritchie," he commented. "With greater truth, I hope, than you've been saying about us."

Removing his empty plate, she replied, "I never went out such a long time with any man as I have with you. More than a year."

"This sounds most unpromising."

"I love you. I will always. But if we aren't going to marry, we shouldn't see only each other. It gives a wrong impression."

"You seem quite sure about not marrying me. Is it the studio? I suppose the all-powerful L.B. and his minion Howard Strickling object because I'm not MGM's biggest star. I've had a good innings— six pictures in three years. I'm the town's most reliable and reputable British character actor."

She shook her head. "I won't allow them to interfere in my private life. They do enough as it is, feeding the papers information about me, telling me whether I can or can't be interviewed. Too much has happened to me in the past year, good and bad. How can I make another person happy when I'm sometimes so unhappy myself?"

"I believed I was able to make you happy. God knows I've tried."

"You have. You do. I depend on your friendship. Your jokes. And your art. We can still see each other often, and talk about books, and paint together."

"You tell me this now when Wynn, at long last, has filed the papers for our divorce. Her lawyer recently posted the documents from London. As soon as they arrive, I'll sign and return them." His expressive face was unusually still.

"I'm glad for you. But your freedom comes too late for us." Gazing into his dark eyes, she could see she was inflicting great pain. "We've grown so comfortable with each other. And that's why we're much better as friends than lovers. Or husband and wife."

"It won't be easy," he muttered, "watching all the other chaps giving you the rush. I hope they compare so unfavorably with me that I get another chance. Hollywood isn't exactly overrun with true gentlemen, Hedy. Keep clear of those who won't cherish you as I've done. And always will."

He left without kissing her goodnight.

Later that week, to the relief of all involved, the cameras on the set of *I Take This Woman* were shuttered and the lights dimmed. There was no wrap party like the one Walter Wanger had provided for his *Algiers* cast and crew, no champagne toasts. At two o'clock in the morning, Hedy stepped out of Stage 14 and into the darkness and made her weary way to the East Gate. She was untangled from her second Hollywood production, just as she was from Reggie Gardiner.

———◦•◆•◦———

More than a year had passed since Hedy refused a second date with millionaire Howard Hughes. Since then, the list of his conquests had lengthened. After discarding Katharine Hepburn for Bette Davis, whose marriage didn't survive their affair, he was briefly engaged to Ginger Rogers. She was succeeded by the young debutante Brenda Frazier. After romancing Olivia de Haviland, he dated her sister, Joan Fontaine. The gossip columnists extensively documented his relationships with women. Speculation about his intimate connections with some the film colony's handsomest actors was conducted in furtive whispers.

Wary of her admirer's ulterior motive for inviting her to his house but curious to see it, Hedy agreed to go. Better to meet the wolf in his den, she concluded, than to appear with him in public and ignite a firestorm of rumors. When not setting aviation records in one of his airplanes, Hughes produced movies and he never counted the cost—unlike Mr. Mayer. She could at least find out whether he wanted to cast her in one of his upcoming projects.

A chauffeur-driven Rolls Royce delivered her to Muirfield, a Spanish-style mansion near the Wilshire golf course. Its interior was a contrast to the owner's casual and sometimes sloppy attire. The rooms were substantial in size, handsomely and richly appointed. A butler ushered her into one with full-length windows and French doors that revealed gardens and grass. It was spacious enough to hold an enormous bookcase, many chairs, a sofa upholstered in floral fabric, a round table with two place settings, and the desk where Howard Hughes was seated.

"You'd probably prefer the Trocadero," he said, his peculiar treble voice pitched loud enough to carry over the voices issuing from the radio. His white shirt was open at the collar and his cuffs were rolled up to his elbows. He wore baggy brown trousers and sneakers, without any socks.

"If you'd taken me there, I wouldn't feel overdressed." She indicated the long velvet dirndl she sometimes wore to evening parties. "I like the way you've decorated your rooms."

"None of my doing. The place looked like this when I bought it. I don't drink liquor, but you can have anything you want."

"Whatever you choose will suit me."

He poured two glasses of water from a carafe on the table. "Not much longer till dinner arrives. You like steak?"

"Very much."

She appreciated his height and his dark good looks, and his shy smile was boyishly attractive. His neck appeared too thin to support his head, and the lower part of his face formed a sharp triangle point.

She wandered over to the antique globe and gave it a spin. "On the night of the Tailwaggers Ball, you wouldn't speak of your great adventure. Won't you please tell me what it was like, flying around the entire world in only three days?"

"Exciting. Terrifying. I used up enough adrenalin for several lifetimes. Each stage was different. At Paris, I made repairs and took on provisions for the crew and me. The takeoff was a nightmare because of the crosswinds. Over Germany, I had to fly at an extremely high altitude because Hitler didn't want us to see his military installations. Siberia was challenging. Mountainous terrain, and my wings iced up from the cold. But the worst part of my journey came at the end. Facing the crowd, trying to make coherent speeches. All the press conferences and parades."

She leaned against the bookcase. "People wonder what your next feat will be." Besides seducing actresses, she almost said, but didn't.

"I'm open to ideas. For now, I want to build new types of airplanes for wartime use. And purchase a commercial airline. I'm buying up stock in TWA as fast as I can."

"You remind me of my ex-husband."

"You've said that before. It's no compliment, I know."

"Fritz takes risks, in business and in life. He's ambitious. Like you, he's a millionaire who manages a family enterprise. Or did, before the Nazis ran him out of Austria. Unlike you, he's secretive about his dealings."

"Were you a virgin when you married him?"

Offended by the question, she stared up at him. "That's no business of yours, Mr. Hughes. If you can't behave like a gentleman, I will leave."

"Call me Howard. You can't go without eating. At that dog party you missed a meal because of me. I must make amends."

She was still nursing her grievance when two servants brought their food. Hedy received a salad, and they were both served steak, lean and lightly marbled. A bowl of peas, not fresh but canned, was placed in front of her host. With great concentration, he spooned out a small number of them. He was willing to share, but they looked most unappetizing. For dessert, they had plain vanilla ice cream with caramel sauce. Without a doubt, this was worst meal she'd been served in a private home since arriving in Hollywood.

Not so much like Fritz after all, she realized, poised between amusement and resentment. Howard Hughes is no epicure.

In an effort to prevent any more deeply personal questions, she expressed interest in his oil drilling business. The topic failed to rouse his enthusiasm.

"I'm not much involved with Hughes Tool. Aviation is my primary focus. And to a lesser extent, filmmaking."

He got up and left the table, moving to an armchair. She sat on the sofa.

"I imagine L.B. treats you pretty well. He's a fool if he doesn't."

She had no intention of airing all of her many complaints to a man she hardly knew and didn't trust. "I'm getting used to his ways. At the moment I'm happy, because he gave me a new acting coach. Glesca Marshall."

"The bulldyker? I'll bet you had to fight her off. Or maybe you didn't try."

"Your mind is dirty," she said primly. His excursions into her sexuality were disturbing.

"Sorry. Most Hollywood broads aren't so classy. Or touchy. And so many of you Germans have Sapphic tendencies. Dietrich sure does."

"I'm Austrian," she reminded him. "Is it true that you had a fling with Randolph Scott?"

He chewed his lower lip. "People will say anything." Leaving his chair, he came to sit beside her. "You broke up with your boyfriend.

The English fellow, Gardiner." As he nudged even closer, he murmured, "Didn't you come to me for consolation? And a little of what you've been missing."

"I wanted interesting conversation with an intelligent man. An inventor. What you do interests me. I enjoy drawing up plans and designing and making things. Mechanical objects, sometimes."

He drew back, and his bushy eyebrows jutted downward. "No kidding? Well, that's unexpected. Nobody warned me that world's most beautiful woman has smarts to match her looks."

"Because they don't care. And they wouldn't believe it. People define me by what they read in publications that never give the whole story, or the full truth. They don't even realize that Hedy Lamarr is an invention."

Moving closer, he murmured, "Can I kiss you?"

Giving her no chance to respond, he placed one long arm around her shoulders and pulled her against his chest. He clamped his mouth on hers.

She felt nothing. Not the slightest hint of a spark.

"How about some mood music?"

He reached across her to pick up an object on the side table. With his forefinger he spun a central dial, similar to the one on a telephone, set into the wooden box. The actors' voices in the melodrama were suddenly, magically replaced by a Stravinsky orchestral piece.

"What's this?" She took the box from him. Embedded in the veneer were the call numbers of all the Los Angeles radio stations.

"Philco's Mystery Control. They're releasing it to the public sometime this year. I saw the prototype, and the company gave me this one right off the assembly line."

"This dial changes the station?"

"Exactly. It's a type of wireless device, same as a radio. Inside there's a battery and a tube and an antenna. The volume can be adjusted, as well as the frequency." He demonstrated.

"A remote control for a household radio. What will they think of next?" When he handed the unit back to her, she manipulated the dial. "How wonderful it must be to develop something so useful and convenient."

He rummaged in the drawer of the side table and handed her the instruction booklet. Lounging against the pillow, he watched her study it. "You're no ordinary wet deck," he murmured.

She glanced over at him. "A what?"

"Well-used female. Experienced."

Ordinarily, the comparison with a prostitute would send her charging off in a rage. Utterly absorbed by the intricacies of his Mystery Control, she let it pass without remark or rebuke.

<hr />

The next day, Hedy used her free time to rearrange her closets and sort her growing collection of shoes and handbags. When the phone rang she considered not answering. But it might be Reggie. Or her date for that evening. Or someone from the studio could be trying to reach her.

"Good morning, Miss Hedy Lamarr." An American voice, smooth and confident, but unfamiliar.

"Good morning. Who is speaking?"

"Gene. Gene Markey. Formerly Mr. Joan Bennett. Hedda Hopper told me you're playing the field. Care to play it with me tonight?"

Intrigued, she answered, "Possibly."

"Well, will you?"

"If Howard Hughes can bear being stood up." She hadn't absolutely committed to going out with the eccentric millionaire. "Where will we go?"

"Earl Carroll's supper club. Beryl Wallace is dancing and singing tonight. Does that appeal to you?"

In that setting, she would be spared the necessity of maintaining a dialogue with her escort, practically a stranger.

She was pleased and surprised to discover that Gene Markey was the type of man she most appreciated. He was older, brilliant and articulate and cultured, with a wide range of interests and abilities. Educated at an Ivy League college, he'd served as an infantryman in the war. After his discharge, he studied at the Chicago Institute of Art, and had published a book of caricatures of notable literary figures. His career as a journalist and novelist ended a decade ago, when he'd put his talents to good use scripting and producing Hollywood films.

His charm and charisma were belied by his unassuming appearance and bulk. Enthralled by his vibrant personality, Hedy didn't mind that he wasn't movie-star handsome. A tall man, he had a thick neck and broad shoulders. His clean-shaven face was full and fleshy, and he combed his thinning hair back to expose a broad forehead. Black, sharply angled brows gave him a permanent expression of inquiry.

A loud blast of music from the orchestra curtailed their conversation. For the duration of the lavish floor show that took place on the huge revolving stage, Hedy was impatient for it to end. When it did, Gene ordered a sherry for her and they chatted until closing time.

She hoped he didn't consider her dull or uninteresting, or worse, vapid. Important and driven men too often discounted an attractive female's intelligence. Fritz never realized how much knowledge of weaponry she'd absorbed during his dinner party conversations and meetings. Or how much she'd learned—and understood—about torpedo guidance. Her technical questions about the Philco Mystery Control had startled Howard Hughes.

The next morning, she washed and dried her hair and gave it one hundred strokes with the hairbrush. She was primping for Gene, in case he wanted to see her again. She hoped he did.

The doorbell rang. Twice.

By the time she reached her bedroom window, the florist's delivery van was backing away from the house.

Because it had been Reggie's habit to send her tuberoses, Hedy assumed he was the source of the large bouquet her housekeeper had set in a vase of water. When she remembered to open the tiny envelope tucked in among the fronds, she discovered that it came from Gene Markey. She didn't have his telephone number, so she couldn't thank him, or ask how he knew exactly what she liked. It didn't matter. A man interested enough to discover her favorite flower was bound to contact her again.

"Somebody told you I like tuberoses," she said when he phoned.

"Remember our little chat when we met last summer?"

"Yes. At that screening of the very bad submarine picture you wrote."

"Ever since, I've paid close attention whenever your name pops up in a column. That's how I learned what sort of bouquet Reggie Gardiner always ordered for you. I phoned around to florists' shops till I got the same one he used."

"It's very sweet of you."

"And unoriginal. I'll do better in future," he said, vanquishing her concern that this would be a casual flirtation.

That evening he took her to Marcel La Maze's new bistro.

"Are you a member at his Clover Club?" she asked during the drive.

"I am, and I spotted you there plenty of times. You never noticed me."

"Probably because you were with your wife."

"Ex-wife, now," he reminded her with a smile. "Marcel has the best wine palate on the West Coast. And his bartender knows how to mix a Melinda."

"What's that?"

"The cocktail I created and named after my daughter. Two thirds scotch, one third Italian vermouth, and a dash of angostura bitters. It'll be years before she can enjoy one herself. She turns five next month."

Every morning, he explained, he returned to his former marital home to eat breakfast with little Melinda and Joan Bennet's daughter from her first marriage. His fondness for children and his rapport with them was evident when he referred to Shirley Temple, whose movies he produced. Her next feature, *The Little Princess,* would be released in a few weeks. He was giving Melinda a copy of the book for her birthday, so he could read a chapter to her and her ten-year-old half-sister when he visited them at weekends.

Hedy was conscious of a curious and unaccountable yearning for motherhood. Although she'd mentioned it to interviewers, in a vague and abstract fashion, until this moment she hadn't regarded any particular man as a potential father of her children. The intensity of her response to this one was exhilarating and more than a little alarming.

As they approached the restaurant entrance, he said, "Are you really furious with Joan for dyeing her hair black?"

"You should know better than to believe those ridiculous items in the gossip columns. I don't care whether she and Joan Crawford changed their hair. Were they copying me? Or did they do it because Scarlett O'Hara is a brunette?"

"Every actress in town went crazy for that part. Goodness knows what the dears will do now that Selznick has chosen Vivien Leigh."

"Whose hair is naturally dark. Like mine."

"She's a lovely little thing, to be sure. But you're the most beautiful girl in the world."

A timeworn description, yet her pulses fluttered when he uttered it.

Every night afterwards they went out, to one or more or the clubs and restaurants lining Sunset Boulevard. In her state of euphoria, she hardly cared that MGM wasn't releasing *I Take This Woman*.

"Shelved indefinitely. That's what they told me."

"All that effort to make you a star," Gene said, wagging his large head, "and then sticking you in the wrong kind of picture. It's worse than mismanagement, it's positively criminal. I thought L.B. was smarter than that."

She sighed. "He'd pay more attention if I had a mane and a tail and four long legs."

His laugh was loud enough to draw stares from La Maze's other customers. "How idiotic of him. Though I admit, I share his passion for thoroughbreds. I'd like to own a racing stable someday."

After a week of dinner dates, he escorted her to a performance of *Giselle* by the Ballet Russe de Monte Carlo, their first appearance at an important social event. Every entertainment reporter in town avidly followed and chronicled their sudden and unexpected romance. If he gazed adoringly across their favorite table at La Maze's, hanging on her every word, she read about it the next morning while eating breakfast.

She filled her letters to Mutti with descriptions of Gene's brilliance, his kindness, his attentiveness, his concern for her career. After two weeks, she was positive she'd marry him. If he proposed.

When she ran into Reggie at the studio, he commented wryly, "You and Markey got serious awfully fast."

To avoid his probing eyes, she stared at the toes of her shoes. "I've just been scolded about it. First by Howard. Then by Mr. Mayer."

"Look at me." His smile was wistful. "If Gene makes you happy, and he'd better, I wish only the best for both of you."

"That's nice to hear from anyone, but from you most of all." She shook her head in frustration. "I'm getting the same advice and complaints as when you and I were dating. Don't be exclusive. Go out with the starriest actors and get your picture in the papers, it's good for your image. Howard Strickling wants a whole universe of strangers, all the men who fell in love with Gaby in *Algiers,* to think I'm available and unattached. It's bad enough that Mr. Mayer put me in a terrible movie and then hid it away in a vault. For four years Fritz controlled my existence, every part of it. And now that I'm supposed to have my independence, I'm being treated like an unsatisfactory child, told what to do and where to go and who to go with and how to behave." With a conspiratorial grin, she added, "Gene and I could fight back if we double-dated with you and your current girl. Are you still together?"

"Adrienne invited me to go with her to New York, but I've been advised not to travel. This broken wing of mine isn't healing properly, and I'm in constant pain. The doctors are threatening to smash it again in order to re-set it."

"Oh, darling, that's too cruel. You've suffered so much already."

"Other places hurt even worse." He placed a hand over his heart. "This year, young as it is, has eaten up nearly all my British stoicism. I had to endure an extended stay in hospital. My girl cast me aside and is enamored of someone else. Now my career at MGM is in peril."

"What do you mean?"

"I won't be a contract player here for much longer. However, my agent assures me after L.B. releases me from my bond, I'll be cast in a Laurel and Hardy aviator film. Working with that pair is bound to cheer me up."

Realizing how much she'd missed him, she said, "Come along to Nina Saemundsson's sculpture studio. She wants to photograph me posing with my own statue before she ships it to New York. It's being exhibited at the World's Fair."

"Your new boyfriend won't mind?"

"I don't make a fuss over Gene's visits to Joan and their daughters. He has no reason to complain if I take my favorite painter to meet a sculptress."

"Is it a life-sized statue?"

"A bust."

"How can I refuse? I've always held your bust in high regard."

His quip reminded her of a grievance. "Mr. Mayer certainly doesn't. He's all the time telling me that my breasts are too small."

Hedy's bouquet of purple flowers was rapidly wilting in the Mexicali heat, and so was she. Despite her discomfort in her fur coat, she beamed for the photographers gathered outside the pale pink Governor's palace.

She and Gene had spent last night in separate rooms at the Grant Hotel in San Diego. This morning they'd crossed the border to exchange their marriage vows before a Mexican magistrate, with the American consul serving as translator. Gene had taken her to a jai alai game, and now he wanted to go to the Golden Lion café for a celebratory lunch. Afterwards, his Filipino chauffeur would drive them back to Los Angeles.

As they sped away from Mexicali, Hedy's damp palm curled over her husband's hand. This union was more than act of love and commitment, it was her rebellion against Mayer's interference in her personal life. Whatever the repercussions, matrimony ensured the stability and domesticity she craved. Gene was a source of professional advice, and she trusted him to protect her interests. Theirs was a match made in heaven, even if it took place less than month after their first date. The honeymoon would come later, because they both had to report for work on Monday morning.

She appreciated the fact that Gene was a producer and not an actor. Most of the time he worked in an office at Twentieth Century Fox. He wouldn't spend all hours of the day and night in a soundstage wooing a fellow performer, in or out of character. And she was untroubled by his devotion to his darling daughter, to the yacht that bore her name, and to all those four-legged fillies who galloped across Southern California racecourses.

"When will I meet Melinda and Diana?" she asked.

"Not until Joan and I prepare them. They're young, and need time to adjust to the concept of a stepmother. Can you be patient?"

"I can be whatever you need me to be," she assured him. She was eager to give him another child—a son, since he already had two little girls. "I've told interviewers that I want ten children. But if I had just one baby boy, I'd be the happiest woman in the world."

"Let's make a home for ourselves before we begin to populate it."

They had already acquired a sprawling single-story farmhouse on four acres in Benedict Canyon. Hedgerow Farm offered ample space for children and animals and was equipped with swimming pool and pool house. Margaret Wood, Hedy's friend from the MGM wardrobe department, would occupy the North Camden Drive property it until it sold. The likeliest buyer was English actor Leslie Howard, working on David Selznick's *Gone with the Wind,* who would share the place with his friend Laurence Olivier, Heathcliff in *Wuthering Heights.* Hedy suspected Howard's co-star and Olivier's mistress, the exquisite Vivien Leigh, would join them whenever she was free of Scarlett O'Hara's corset and hoopskirt.

Several of the British actors and actresses had been cool towards Hedy ever since her break-up with Reggie, a popular member of their tight-knit community. Her elopement was no surprise to him—before rushing off to Mexico she'd contacted him by phone to share her news. When he repeated his assertion that her happiness was of primary importance, he sounded sincere.

Hours after their matrimonial adventure, she and Gene had to cope with an unexpected publicity crisis. With a clear understanding of the columnists' power to roughen or smooth a celebrity's life, he chose to inform Louella Parsons and Hedda Hopper of their plans in advance. Because of his closer friendship with Louella, he'd issued her telegram from San Diego on the eve of the wedding. Hedy, grateful for Hedda's favorable treatment, sent the other one—disastrously, it was never delivered. Gene took immediate steps to soothe Hedda's outrage over losing the season's biggest celebrity scoop to her hated rival. He wrote a lengthy note of apology and enclosed a copy of Hedy's cable as proof of good intentions.

Hedy returned to MGM to face Mr. Mayer.

Red-faced and sputtering with rage, he accused her of treachery and lectured her about the studio's responsibilities when one of their stars contemplated marriage.

"Running off to Mexico is an affront to decency," he stormed. "It should've been a proper ceremony in a church filled with flowers, and you wearing a suit that Adrian designed for the occasion, and a stylish hat. Or one of those little veils you Catholics wear."

"A church wedding wasn't possible," she protested. "The Vatican hasn't annulled my marriage to Fritz Mandl. Getting married in a Catholic country was the best I could do."

"I could've given you away. Such a beautiful celebration I'd have thrown. The world's best singers are under contract to me, you could've had any one of them. Nelson Eddy. Jeannette MacDonald. Judy Garland. Instead, you chose a cheap mariachi band."

"There was no music."

"Markey's too old for you," he complained. "And he's divorced."

"So am I," she reminded him.

"We're promoting you as the greatest screen beauty since Garbo. If you turn into a Beverly Hills housewife, our efforts will be wasted."

Bobbing up from the chair, she drew herself to her full height and glared back at him. "Mr. Mayer, I am grateful to you for so much. But nearly a year has passed since *Algiers* was released. You discarded the only picture I've made for MGM. You haven't yet cast me in another."

"Ben Hecht is still working on the script for *Lady of the Tropics.* It's a terrific story. Manon, a half-Asian broad, wants to escape Saigon and go to Paris with a handsome fellow who's already engaged to an heiress. He marries the exotic girl and plans to take her away, but he has difficulty arranging her passport. She gives herself to a powerful man who can solve the problem, the villain of the piece. And then she plugs him and runs away. Just when her husband finds her again, she shoots herself."

Conflict and drama. With a death scene! "When does production begin?"

"Can't say for sure. If we're able to use you sooner, in something else, we will. Perhaps it'll be *The Women.* Joan Crawford will be furious if she doesn't get to play the husband-stealing bad girl. But what man wouldn't leave his wife if you crooked your finger at him?"

"Unless you give me work, I'll stay at home and decorate my new house. And wait for the stork to arrive."

He stood up, his face contorted with outrage. "You'd better not be pregnant. You've only been married a few days!"

"I'm not. But I intend to be. Very soon!"

She'd shocked him into speechlessness. It was time to leave.

Before she crossed the threshold, he shouted, "At least when you've had a baby, your tits will get bigger!"

Horrid man, she fumed, flouncing past his secretaries.

The weekend after the wedding, Gene courted additional retribution from Hedda by accepting an invitation to join Louella and Harry Parsons at Marsons Farm, their San Fernando Valley getaway. Robert Taylor was there with Barbara Stanwyck.

Walking up to Hedy, he beamed at her. "Soon we'll be working together."

"How soon? In what?"

"*Lady of the Tropics.* My agent says we start shooting next month."

Well, well. The threat of a pregnancy had horrified her employer so much, he was putting her back to work immediately.

Chapter 21

Hedy's working relationship with Metro's celebrated costume creator had developed into a close friendship. She and Reggie had frequently double-dated with Adrian and Janet Gaynor. The designer's well-known preference for men hadn't precluded romance with the popular actress, and throughout Hedy's wardrobe appointments he gushed about Janet. His *Marie Antoinette* costumes were universally admired, and he'd just finished dressing witches, munchkins, and more in *The Wizard of Oz*, awaiting release. His excitement about producing Asian-influenced gowns for Hedy to wear in *Lady of the Tropics* was endearing.

When he showed her his latest sketches for *The Women*, she confided, "I'm hoping to play one of them."

"But you aren't on the cast list I received. Both pictures will start production at almost the same time. Didn't anybody tell you that?"

Her heart sank. *The Women* was a far better script, its characters were livelier and more interesting than Manon. "All too often I'm the last person to hear important news, even when it's about me. Can you please make my breasts look larger? Mr. Mayer says they're small." She unbuttoned her blouse, revealing her brassiere.

"His son-in-law made a similar comment about Vivien Leigh's.

You slender ladies would look top-heavy with larger busts. Proportion is essential to elegance. Stylish clothes will always hang better on you than on, say, Mae West."

Laughing, she said, "That's comforting. I suppose."

For several reasons, the onset of her monthly period was disappointing. Pregnancy would have ensured a speedy production for *Lady of the Tropics*—the director would want to finish it quickly, before she started showing. The baby she desperately wanted would enhance her domestic life, and shared parenthood would reinforce the commitment she and Gene had entered into with such haste. An experienced father, he enjoyed the company of children. With a son to raise, he might not be as eager to dine out every night of the week and go nightclub-hopping. On weekends he visited the racetracks at Hollywood Park or Santa Anita, and sometimes he went to director King Vidor's Beverly Hills estate for skeet-shooting.

To raise Hedy's spirits, Gene gave her a Great Dane. The dog's tread was so loud that she named him Donner, the German word for thunder. Toni, her spaniel, was visibly awed by the size of this new companion, and her cat Mitzi avoided him altogether.

Within a few weeks of their wedding, Hedy became the comforter when Gene's mother suffered a heart attack and was admitted to Good Samaritan Hospital. Hedy was relegated to outsider status as her husband, his former wife, and their daughters joined Colonel Markey at the patient's bedside. During the final vigil, out of respect for their family bond, she remained outside in the corridor.

Hedy's relationship with Joan Bennett had always been amicable and continued to be, except with regard to Melinda. A perfectly reasonable request that the child occasionally come to Benedict Canyon to have breakfast with her father was rebuffed, and he continued to visit his ex-wife's home each morning. The little girl shunned Hedy on the rare occasions when they did meet, despite her every effort to bridge the gap between them. A period of intense grief was no time to make the attempt, so she resolved to be patient—excellent preparation for motherhood.

The funeral was held at Good Shepherd Church. Hedy sat between Gene and his daughter, whose tearful little face tore at her heart. When she used her handkerchief to dry the wet cheeks, Melinda's tiny clenched fist batted it away. Her half-sister Diana stared straight ahead, refusing to acknowledge Hedy's presence.

She received better treatment from Gene's third little girl, the one he hadn't fathered, when he invited her to the *Susannah of the Mounties* set. Chatting with Shirley Temple, Hedy envied her aplomb and her moviemaking experience.

"She looks like a child and talks like an adult. There's more worldly wisdom beneath that curly mop than I imagined," she commented to Gene during their homeward drive.

"In that respect, you two are similar. None of your admirers would guess that you're a whiz at bridge and a demon at chess. Or that you speak as many foreign languages as I've got fingers on this hand."

In contrast to Fritz, he was unperturbed by regular encounters with her former lovers. Reggie was too fond of her and too gentlemanly to let awkwardness mar their friendship, and he got on well with her husband. Erich Remarque, who had followed Marlene Dietrich to California, looked so lonely and mournful and out of place at parties that her husband pitied him. By now, Gene said, he'd discovered what everyone in town knew, that Marlene was incapable of being faithful to anyone, man or woman.

Said Hedy, "He appears to be burdened by all the pain of Europe."

Erich sought her out one night to tell her that the Germans had seized control of Czechoslovakia.

"England and France failed to step in. Like your Vienna, Prague has been overrun by Nazis. There will be a war on the Continent, more devastating than the last one. The Reich seized your former husband's factories and uses them to churn out weapons by the hundreds of thousands. Yet when I saw him in Cap d'Antibes, Mandl looked like he hadn't a care in the world."

"Probably he hasn't. He took out citizenship in Argentina and owns a great deal of property there, farms and factories. What of you, Erich?

Will you remain in Hollywood?"

His eyes scanned the room until they landed on Marlene, whispering intimately to her great love Douglas Fairbanks. "I go where she goes. Yearning for happiness. Being denied it."

Taking Glesca Marshall's advice to observe and study talented colleagues, Hedy visited the *Stanley and Livingston* set. Actress Nancy Kelly's absence had forced a halt, and the production team scrambled to locate a stand-in for a shot that included Stanley's love interest.

"Let Hedy do it," Spencer shouted to the producer from his perch high on the ship's deck. "You're shooting from behind, nobody will be able to tell it's her."

"Would you?" Darryl Zanuck asked her.

"I don't object to a scene with Spencer." Wrinkling her nose, she added, "As long as it isn't for *I Take This Woman*."

Everyone within earshot laughed.

"Take Miss Lamarr to Miss Kelly's dressing room right away and put her into costume."

Hedy returned to the set in a Victorian walking dress, and briefly stood on the ship's dock while the camera rolled.

"Will Gene make a stink if we don't pay you a day rate?" Zanuck was a close friend of her husband's.

"Consider it a favor," she replied. "Always I find myself near ships," she added. "*Normandie* brought me to America. In *Algiers*, a French Line vessel took me away from Charles Boyer. I almost throw myself over the rail in *I Take This Woman*. For *Lady of the Tropics*, I commit suicide with a pistol as I gaze at a boat in the harbor. And now I'm married to a man who owns a yacht."

⟨◆⟩

Lady of the Tropics was a refreshing contrast to the turmoil that had plagued *I Take This Woman*. She enjoyed the camaraderie on the set and made a concerted effort to counter her reputation for aloofness. Filming progressed seamlessly, with a short break immediately after

Robert Taylor's midnight marriage to Barbara Stanwyck. On his return, he repeated the rite in a wedding scene with Hedy.

Each time she completed a take, she pondered her peculiarly impersonal relationship with her colleagues. The director observed all aspects of a scene but mainly focused on her interactions with her fellow actors. The cameraman meticulously framed his shots, insisting that her face be lit to perfection. The sound technician manipulated the overhead microphone boom, and the man wearing headphones monitored sound levels when she spoke. The script girl made sure she recited her lines correctly. To the girl from Wardrobe, she was a dress dummy with the ability to breathe and move and speak.

As usual, Adrian had provided Hedy with an array of exquisite garments, every one designed to convey an exotic, Asiatic flair. She wore several distinctive hats and turbans, and in one scene had to contend with a towering jewel-studded headdress.

To her considerable relief, Mr. Mayer reinstated Phyllis Loughton. Hedy was interested to hear that her acting coach's past successes directing plays in New York and Los Angeles had given rise to a desire to direct pictures.

"Right now, Dorothy Arzner is Hollywood's only female director," Phyllis said with perceptible envy. "She worked her way up from stenographer to a big contract here at MGM. And there was Lois Weber, but that was back in the days of silent pictures."

"I'd like it if you could direct me," Hedy told her. "I'll ask Mr. Mayer."

"Please don't! He'd be appalled, especially now that I have a baby on the way. His view of women is terribly old-fashioned."

Their sessions together often shifted from character development and dialogue rehearsal to pregnancy and setting up a nursery. At the wrap party Hedy presented Phyllis with an English pram that Nina Garson had helped her choose.

"You can borrow it," Phyllis promised.

"You'll probably still be using this one when my baby arrives," she said brightly.

"Are you expecting?"

"Not yet," she admitted. "But I'm hopeful."

Greer had returned to California after completing work on *Goodbye, Mr. Chips.* She'd been tempted to remain in England, she confessed to Hedy, but Mr. Mayer had lured her back with familiar promises of wonderful scripts and a brilliant future.

On Greer's premiere night at the Four Star Theatre, Hedy was one of the few attendees aware that the statuesque redhead climbing out of a limousine was the actress on whom L.B. Mayer pinned enormous hopes.

When her friend entered the lobby, Hedy embraced her, saying, "I'm so very happy for you."

"And I for you. No longer Mayer's Neglected Imports, are we?"

"Hard-working imports, now. Bob Taylor says he'll be your co-star, after we wrap *Lady of the Tropics.*"

"What's next for you, dearie?"

"Motherhood. After four months of wedlock and plenty of sex with my husband, I haven't conceived. I'm considering an adoption. If Gene agrees."

Cocking her head in his direction, Greer said, "He adores you, and so he should. But I do feel sorry for Reggie. He must be awfully cut up."

"We're still great chums. And Gene doesn't mind." Aware of Benny Thau's hovering presence, Hedy whispered, "Are you two still an item?"

"It seems so. He's very attentive. I rather enjoy his attentions."

Because her marriage had taken place in a civil court in Mexico, Hedy had never uttered the religious vows that covered the "in sickness and in health" contingency. But she fulfilled that unspoken promise when Gene landed in Good Samaritan with an attack of bronchitis followed by pneumonia. She moved into an adjacent hospital room until he was discharged, and nursed him herself when he was home again. His doctors insisted on complete rest, so she went unescorted to her *Lady of the Tropics* premiere.

Seated at her husband's bedside the next morning, Hedy turned the pages of the *Los Angeles Times,* eager to learn what Hedda Hopper thought of her performance.

"Well?" Gene prompted.

"'A yardage of tripe,'" she read, "'from the moment Hedy made her Mona Lisa entrance to her final fadeout in her death scene, which incidentally, she did darned well.'" Lowering the paper, she said, "That's the kindest she's been to me since we married. I'll send her a note of thanks. She certainly won't receive one from poor Bob Taylor—she savaged him!"

"Can I see the racing reports?"

She hunted for that section and handed it to him. Cradling her cat Mitzi, she announced, "The studio has decided my next picture. It's a musical!"

Her husband lifted a skeptical eyebrow. "Hedy Lamarr, singing and dancing?"

"It's called *Ziegfeld Girl*. There are three of us. Lana Turner plays the baddie. And maybe I'll have scenes with that nice Jimmy Stewart."

"He plays a showgirl? The Hays Office won't like that."

"Of course not. I have more news, and you'll never guess what it is."

"The *Ecstasy* sequel?"

"Machatý refuses to do it. And if he hadn't, I would. No, it's worse. Much worse."

He groaned. "L.B. can't be resurrecting his folly. Is he?"

She nodded. "*I Take This Woman* resumes production after Spencer finishes *Northwest Passage*. If I can get pregnant in a hurry, Mr. Mayer might put it back on the shelf. Maybe forever." She stroked the cat's furry head. "I want a baby."

"Yes, darling, I know. A boy."

"The nursery has been ready for months. Last week, when I consulted my contract attorney about getting divorced from MGM, I asked him about adoption agencies. He recommended the California's Children's Society."

Slowly Gene replied, "I could use a little more time to accustom myself. But I'm not opposed, if that's what you really want to do."

"More than anything in the world!"

On Labor Day weekend, Germany invaded Poland. Britain and France declared war against Germany. These hostilities, Hedy feared, would prevent Mutti from leaving London, the inevitable target of enemy bombers. She'd received a letter from Nora, now Princess von Starhemberg, occupying Fritz's Château des Pins in Cap D'Antibes. The Riviera, her friend wrote, was no longer Europe's carefree playground. Working as a volunteer, Nora managed relief efforts for exiled Austrians. Ernst, veteran of the Great War and former commander of the *Heimwehr*, sought permission from the French government to create a regiment of displaced Austrians eager to fight Hitler

In a season of dread and dismay, the arrival of James Lamarr Markey brightened Hedy's mood and enlivened her home. She and Gene bestowed his grandfather's name upon their blue-eyed orphan, but from the moment she took him into her arms he was Jamesie. Cooing over her infant, spooning mashed fruit into his cherubic mouth, putting him down for the night, her only sorrow was that he'd been born into a warring world.

All too familiar with the perils posed by Nazi aggression, and Hitler's clear intent for world domination, she deplored her adopted country's unwillingness to enter the fray. Neutrality, she knew, had prolonged the Great War, until America's belated participation ensured its conclusion.

Treasuring every moment with her son, she was reluctant to resume work. Conveniently, her lawyer and agent pointed out that MGM hadn't paid her salary in full, enabling her to declare her studio contract null and void. To underscore her case, she entered negotiations with a Broadway producer preparing a new play, *Salome,* to be directed by Otto Preminger—a friend and sometime lover from her student days with Max Reinhardt. MGM countered, seeking an injunction to prevent her employment in the theatre. A Superior Court responded with a restraining order against her.

Although she avoided Mr. Mayer, she didn't let their intensifying legal dispute impair her relationships with his employees. She took Jamesie to visit Margaret Wood and her baby. She invited Ida Koverman to a poolside lunch, hoping the older woman might support her cause.

Holding the boy on her lap, she asked, "Why does Mr. Mayer still want me? He seems unhappy about *Lady of the Tropics. I Take This Woman* is beyond repair, everyone says so. He agreed to release Luise Rainer, who won two Oscars. To him, I'm just another glamor girl in Adrian frocks. But he won't let me go."

"From the very beginning, you've been a problem for L.B. Because of *Ecstasy,* as you know. When he loaned you to Wanger, he didn't expect *Algiers* to be so successful. You disappointed him by getting involved with Reggie Gardiner, a minor player, instead of dating any of our major stars. And without telling him beforehand, you ran off and married Gene Markey."

"Mr. Mayer claims to be a father to me. Above all else, my Papa wanted me to be happy. To follow my heart."

"What does your husband say about this contract mess?"

"You know producers," Hedy hedged, "always so busy. All day he is working hard. When we go out at night, people are talking business to him. When we're on the train to New York, we'll have plenty of time to discuss my future."

"L.B. sees your pursuit of a Broadway role as a ploy to get a pay increase."

"He's wrong. Of course I'd be glad of more money, but I really do want to play Salome. Instead of making a movie about her, he cast me in a tropical melodrama that did me no good and turned Bob Taylor into a joke. Did you read Jimmy Fidler's column? I am so good a shot, he wrote, I should've turned my pistol on the scriptwriter instead of the villain." She lifted the child to press a hearty kiss on each plump cheek. "We've approved our architect's plans for an extension, so we can have a larger nursery and a room for the nanny. I want Jamesie to have someone like dear Nixy, who looked after me."

Ida said gravely, "My dear, I've never been married or had a child, so my advice on both subjects may seem worthless. But I'll give it anyway. Your delightful little boy is a real person. Not another doll that you've added to that collection you showed me. Or a timely distraction from problems that need to be resolved. Whatever difficulties you and Gene might be facing, little Jamesie can't cure them."

"He doesn't have to. We're a perfect family. Gene is a wonderful husband. He gave me a birthday party at the Beverly Wilshire. Louella Parsons came, and Norma Shearer, Myrna and Arthur Hornblow, and so many friends. Gene wore his naval dress uniform. We're living the American dream that Mr. Mayer wants in his pictures. The pretty white house. The beautiful baby. The successful husband. The devoted wife and mother."

"Every story contains conflict," Ida pointed out, collecting her purse. "When it arises, you discover who your real friends are. Don't be so hard on L.B. He'll stand by you, through thick and thin."

⊂•◆•⊃

Surrendering her dream of playing Salome and accepting defeat in her battle for a higher salary, Hedy reported to the set for the next—surely the final—iteration of *I Take This Woman*. Listlessly she studied the drab, brush-covered western hills and the Hollywoodland sign as the Filipino chauffeur drove her to Culver City. Her feelings were akin those Marie Antoinette must have experienced riding in the tumbril to her execution.

Mayer had assigned a third director, "One Take" Woody Van Dyke, who disposed of every reel of film that had been canned prior to his arrival. Under duress, Spencer Tracy returned to the set. So many of the original players were unavailable that roles were re-cast. Mayer no longer cared enough about the production to interfere, and after spending a million dollars on it he had no expectation of earning back a fraction of the sum.

Miraculously, Van Dyke injected a new energy and optimism into

Hedy and her co-workers. He predicted they would finish by Christmas, and as the days sped past she and the others began to believe him. Despite his reputation for swift efficiency, he took the time to work with her, winning her trust while improving her performance.

"You're an intuitive actress, very natural, and that's all to the good. But a certain amount artifice is required for camera work. Georgi's a lot like you, there's much more to depth to her than appears on the page. Remember that, and you'll do just fine. Get some rest over Thanksgiving. Afterwards I'm going to push on quickly to wrap this picture."

President Roosevelt had thrown the nation into confusion by decreeing that the holiday would be the next to last Thursday in November instead of the last one. Hedy hadn't lived in America long enough for this change to matter.

She was attempting to stuff and truss a turkey when Gene carried a telegram into the kitchen.

"For you. From Fritz Mandl."

Holding up wet hands, she asked him to read it to her.

"'My dear Hasi. Stop. Yesterday I married Baroness Herthe Schneider in Maryland. Stop. At a later date I will make a public announcement. Stop. Fritz.'" Frowning, Gene looked up. "You said he was in Argentina."

"He never stays in one place for very long," she replied, plunging her fingers into the mixture of bread crumbs and beaten egg. "Hella. Hedy. Herthe. Does he choose his wives by the first letter of their names?"

She put Fritz out of her mind, until a New York-based publicist informed her that he'd been admitted to the LeRoy Sanitarium with an unspecified illness. Concerned, Hedy directed the long-distance operator to place a call. After being passed to successive members of medical staff, she reached him.

"Hasi, so kind of you to ring. I've longed to hear your sweet, soothing voice."

"Shouldn't your bride be soothing you?"

"Poor lamb, she went through quite an ordeal to give me a daughter. To spare her embarrassment about becoming a mother so soon after our wedding, I told the press we came to the hospital because I was sick. All will be revealed after she recovers, at the big New Year's party I'm planning."

Why had he waited so long to wed his pregnant mistress? Hedy pitied the woman who had carried his child for nearly nine months without the security of marriage.

"I have noticed that my name never appears in print without yours attached to it," he went on. "As long as newspapers exist, we will be connected."

Better for him than for her, she reflected.

Shortly after this conversation, Hedy spotted a newspaper photo of Fritz and his blonde, dubbed "Hedy's Successor." In a subsequent interview he stated his desire to visit Hollywood in order to introduce the third Frau Mandl to the second one. She used that section to feed the flames in her fireplace.

"I hope he doesn't mean it," Hedy said worriedly, during breakfast. "Maybe he's just saying that to make headlines. He used to avoid press attention, and now he seeks it."

"Let them come," Gene said, lifting a forkful of eggs. "We'll be in New York with the Zanucks, to premiere *The Blue Bird* and *The Grapes of Wrath*. Our timing couldn't be better. We escape the furor over my ex-wife's marriage to Walter Wanger, and we avoid the Mandls."

Their stay in New York instilled in Hedy a fresh awareness of the inconveniences of fame. Wherever she and Gene went—to a restaurant, a theatre, a nightclub—she was recognized and mobbed. Flashing cameras and shouting reporters and eager autograph seekers followed her day and night. The newspapers described her clothing in detail. Dark glasses failed to conceal her identity. She gave up wearing her fur coat and instead left the hotel in a plain woolen one, to no avail. Her husband laughed to see her tie a scarf over her hair and put on a pair of black-rimmed spectacles. Thus disguised, she succeeded in moving about the city undetected.

Wire reports delivered the latest Hollywood news to the metropolitan press. Hedy was pleased to read a prediction that she would portray the eccentric novelist George Sand in a biographical film about Chopin, one of her favorite composers. She would happily fling off her glamor queen trappings to wear a gentleman's waistcoat and trousers, and smoke a cigar. It was time to prove her merits in a role with substance and complexity.

Chapter 22

For the first time the annual Academy Awards banquet and its Oscar presentations were being recorded on film. Gene, in one of his glum moods, annoyed Hedy by refusing to smile for the cameras when they arrived at the Ambassador Hotel's Cocoanut Grove restaurant. His tuxedo lent distinction to his solid figure, but his dour expression spoiled the effect. He left her side to greet Bob Hope, who was making his debut as master of ceremonies.

Greer Garson, swathed in white tulle and wearing white orchids in her red hair, rustled over to give Hedy a cautious embrace that spared their gowns from being crushed. "Gene's new moustache makes him look almost as dashing as Reggie, and you're more beautiful than ever. Show me your dress."

Hedy parted the full-length velvet cloak to reveal peach satin decorated with swirls of black velvet appliqué at the neck. "I hope you win Best Actress." Greer was nominated for *Goodbye, Mr. Chips*.

"Oh, I didn't. The news was leaked to the press in advance, and you can read the list of recipients in the late edition of the newspaper. It's no surprise to me. Catherine Chipping is a small part, and by no means as dramatic or demanding a role as Scarlett O'Hara. Vivien takes home that little golden gentleman, and in the interest of British solidarity, I'm all for it. To be a nominee is more than I ever expected. I tell myself it makes up for my second picture being a sad flop."

"I'll probably never recover from *I Take This Woman*. The reviewers can't decide whether I have talent or whether I don't. All Hollywood wonders why I'm not given better scripts. But I can't afford to turn down anything I'm offered, especially now that—" She glanced around to see who was within earshot. "I have so much to tell you, if we can find time for a private chat."

"I'd love to show you our grand new house on Roxbury Drive. Bring the baby over so Mother and I can dote on him."

"Let's choose a date before I start on *Boom Town*."

"Now there's a sure winner," said Greer encouragingly. "How could it not be, with Clark Gable and Claudette Colbert and Spencer Tracy?"

"Mr. Gable was my secret weapon—he convinced Mr. Mayer to cast me as Karen, the other woman. She's sharp and professional, and I like her, so I fought for that part even though it's not a very big one." With a grin, she said, "When I visit you, I'll bring a cake. I bake one every day, for practice. The bridge club is auctioning movie stars' baked goods to raise money for the Finland Relief Fund. How I wish Austria had stood as firm against Germany as Finland does against Russia."

Although David Selznick was Vivien Leigh's official escort, Larry Olivier maintained a hovering proximity and sat next to her at dinner. Hedda Hopper kept calculating eyes on them. It was no secret that she longed to write about the lovers but didn't quite dare to invoke the wrath of Selznick or of his father-in-law Mayer, to whom Olivier was contracted. Louella Parsons, on the arm of her doctor husband, had stuffed her grandmotherly figure into a bold print gown.

Wary of the rival columnists, Hedy kept her distance. Hedda had veered from champion to critic. Louella's fondness for Gene precluded overt criticism of his wife, but that could change. Both women possessed acute powers of perception, and Hedy understood the necessity of demonstrating marital harmony and happiness.

Though she shrank from revealing the fragility of her marriage, it was increasingly obvious to her. Gene might be a better and kinder man than Fritz, but there were similarities. Like her first husband, he had convinced her that he'd fallen deeply in love, but in retrospect she understood that his courtship had been partly motivated by the luster of her sudden fame and his masculine need to impress other men. Flattered by attentions from an older, sophisticated suitor, for a second time she'd let infatuation overcome pragmatism. Their hasty elopement took place before she learned the extent to which Gene's preference for the night life and the demands of his studio job could be barriers to the intimacy and support she craved. He was incommunicative, wholly absorbed in a variety of pursuits that drew him away from hearth and home. A man with his literary gifts should devote more time to his writing. Instead, he was always rushing off to another social event, with or without his wife. He was fond of Jamesie but bestowed a far greater degree of paternal attention on his daughter Melinda.

This sense of entrapment was familiar from her years with Fritz, but she was unsure how to resolve an untenable situation. She wasn't concerned solely for herself—she must also consider her son's welfare. The California Children's Society had strict regulations, it required an adopting couple to stay together for a full year before granting legal custody. If she initiated a separation, or a divorce, before the completion of the crucial twelve months, they would take Jamesie away.

Loud and sustained applause drew her attention away from her dilemma. She realized that everyone in the dining room had turned towards an occupant of a table far at the back. Hattie McDaniel, the first of her race to be honored with a nomination, was seated far apart from her *Gone with The Wind* castmates.

"The Grove doesn't serve blacks," Gene whispered. "Selznick forced them to let her attend the ceremony."

"That was the decent thing to do," she replied, wondering whether Mr. Mayer, his arch-conservative father-in-law, would have demonstrated such liberality.

Hattie had a long walk to receive her Oscar for Best Supporting Actress. Standing at the microphone, she calmly launched into her acceptance speech, expressing her gratitude. "It is a tribute to a country where people are free to honor noteworthy achievements, regardless of creed, or race, or color. My heart is too full to tell you just how I feel," she concluded, her voice breaking with emotion, "and may I say thank you. And God bless you."

Sometimes, Hedy thought, unable to hold back her own tears, the movie business can be perfectly wonderful.

Although two months separated the Markeys' first wedding anniversary and Jamesie's first birthday, Hedy devised a double celebration. Her guest list included the two most significant couples in their social circle—Myrna Loy and Arthur Hornblow, and Adrian and a joyfully expectant Janet Gaynor. The day before, at the Bel Air Country Club cake auction, Hedy's high bidding won Myrna's and Janet's cakes, displayed side by side on a table decorated with a miniature train set and other toys. Worth Hollings, Jamesie's nanny, put him down for his nap earlier than usual to ensure that he would be bright and happy when he made his appearance.

Gene planned to collect Melinda after work. Until now his ex-wife prevented their daughter's visits to Hedgerow Farm, citing unwillingness to disrupt the child's routine. Hedy, pleased that Joan had relented, didn't want her stepdaughter to feel left out when Jamesie received his gifts. She had wrapped a miniature trunk containing an extensive wardrobe for the Shirley Temple doll she'd given Melinda on her birthday.

The houseboy mixed drinks. The cook was stationed at the punch-bowl. Nearly all the guests had assembled by the time Gene returned. Alone.

"Where's Melinda?"

"She's not coming."

"Why?" His hesitation told her he was forming a plausible excuse.

"It doesn't matter. Jamesie is too young to care that she's not here.

He doesn't even know her."

"I care," she retorted, her voice pitched high from emotion. "Is that what Joan wants, to upset me on our important day?"

"Calm down," he pleaded. "Don't make a fuss in front of everyone. This birthday party would be confusing for Melinda, Joan says, because she so recently had her own."

"But I've bought clothes for her new doll. I'm serving her favorite ice cream flavor."

When he reached out to place a consoling hand on her shoulder, she turned on him and retreated to the empty kitchen.

Janet Gaynor followed her. "Hedy, don't fret about Joan's interference. She's no threat. She left Gene for Walter Wanger, and now she's married to him."

Hedy's smile was wobbly. "I'll be better. After I've had a piece of your lovely coconut cake."

"It might not be any good. Better cut Myrna's first."

Hedy pulled out a chair for her friend. "How do you feel about not being an actress? Do you miss it?"

"At times. But I've never had a moment's regret. I gave it up because I wanted a more interesting and less restricted life than I found working in pictures all those years." Janet's arms circled her protruding belly. "With baby on the way, I'm even more certain my decision was the right one."

"When Fritz refused to let me work, I was desperate for it. Yet when I'm playing with Jamesie, I sometimes think I could be perfectly happy if I never returned to the studio. I want so much to give him a sister or a brother. Adrian could design pretty maternity frocks for me, like he does for you. But it isn't possible."

"Is Gene so reluctant to have another child?"

Shaking her head, she replied, "There's no point asking him. We're not as compatible as we thought when we began our marriage. And we can't take steps to end it before Jamesie's adoption is final, or the agency will reclaim him. Without a salary, I couldn't support him after I'm divorced. I'd need to keep working. But if I'm on a film set morning, noon, and night, how can I be a good mother to my boy?" She pressed her fist against her forehead. "I hardly know what to do. Lately I've been wishing I'd married Reggie instead of Gene."

"He probably wishes that, too. Reggie, I mean."

"He understands me, much better than either of my husbands. He cares for me, whether I'm feeling vulnerable and full of doubt, or in a bad temper. We had fun together, and we could be serious with each other. And to him I was more than a glamorous prop to show off in public."

Rising, Janet said, "Let's get your birthday boy so he can receive his guests. I'll come with you. I want to see that pillow cover you embroidered on the set of your last picture. Adrian said you drew the pattern yourself, using your animals for models."

Hedy took her to the nursery and showed her the farm scene tapestry. "I put up the baby duck wallpaper, without any help. And sewed the curtains. It kept me occupied on all those nights when Gene had to stay late at work. And during his weekend visits to Melinda," she couldn't help adding, with an edge to her voice.

———◦◆◦———

Called to the studio for a photography session, Hedy found hairdresser Sydney Guilaroff studying a printed sheet. With her forefinger, she circled her head. "Same face. Same hair," she said. "Why do they want new pictures?"

"You know the reason, doll. Our Publicity Department wants to make a big announcement about your next picture. Who's shooting you today?"

"Laszlo Willinger, again. Even in Vienna, when I was Hedy Kiesler, I was posing for him."

"Let's surprise him today. How about I take off four, five inches all around? And I could cut the hair in front and curl it in front to frame your features."

"I'd like that." There wasn't much else she could change about her life. "It suits my character, because she's a chic and sophisticated businesswoman."

Delighted with her altered appearance, Hedy proceeded to Willinger's studio, across the avenue from Joan Crawford's dressing room.

Howard Strickling looked up from the rack of gowns and furs he was inspecting. "What the hell have you d-done?"

"Sydney was feeling inspired. Smart, isn't it?" She stroked the short, soft curls that grazed her temples.

"He's made extra work for me. I've got to write a p-press release, to inform all those women who try so hard to look like you."

Make up man Jack Dawn said in his Kentucky drawl, "You should probably phone the sensational news to Joan Bennett. She dyed her hair black like Hedy's, so she'll surely want to copy this new look."

When Howard's bulletin was printed in the newspaper, Gene showed it to Hedy, wearing his most cynical smile.

Look for a change in hair styles, girls—Hedy Lamarr has trimmed her raven locks. Miss Lamarr, who popularized the shoulder-length bob, had her hair cut four inches shorter for a new film role. It is still parted in the center but the ends, no longer permitted to fly free, are curled and turned under. Hair stylist Sydney Guilaroff predicted that the new hairstyle would quickly replace the long bob.

"In Europe there is a tragic war," she responded. "Fighting in the air and at sea. Soldiers dying. Hundreds of thousands marched into concentration camps. And because women care about how I arrange my hair, it makes news. I love America, but it does perplex me!"

———◁•◆•▷———

"Louella Parsons shouldn't interfere in what doesn't concern her," Hedy told her husband, whose balding head was bent over *The Los Angeles Examiner*.

"At least Lolly scotched that foul rumor Jimmie Fidler was peddling," Gene replied. "As she rightly points out, the faintest suggestion of divorce could obstruct the adoption process. I've posted a letter to Fidler to refute his unfounded assertion and advised him to direct any questions to me. I wish I knew his source. Have you confided in Greer?"

"She hates talking to columnists, and she's no gossip."

"Could it have been Janet Gaynor?"

Hedy shook her head. "She knows how upset I was over Melinda missing Jamesie's party, but I never said we were separating." She cracked one of the eggs she'd gathered from the henhouse. "It could've been Joan, you know. Stirring up trouble again."

He set down his coffee cup so hard that the liquid sloshed over the rim. "Oh, for God's sake, Hedy. Can't you leave her out of it?"

"Why can't Hedda Hopper?" she shot back. "From the day we eloped, she's been mixing me and you and Joan all together in the same paragraph." She picked up his plate of uneaten toast.

"I wanted another piece."

"We should both stick to our diets. The studio insists on my staying slim, and your doctor advises you to take off some weight. Maybe your third wife will let you have seconds."

Determined to look her best in Adrian's form-fitting outfits, she kept herself in a constant state of deprivation. Following her regimen wasn't so difficult. The breakdown of her marriage had drastically reduced her appetite.

"When I get this thin," she commented to Adrian, "my breasts are even less full than they were before. Mr. Mayer always notices. I wish I could do something to make them bigger."

"A friend of mine might be able to help."

"No doctors! I don't want an operation."

"I wasn't thinking of that. Anyway, George Antheil is a musician."

She laughed. "He makes ladies' bosoms grow by playing music?"

"If he could, I'm sure he would. He composes film scores, but he's famous for his *avant-garde* masterpiece, *Ballet Mécanique*. Or perhaps I should say, infamous."

"I remember it. Many instruments and player pianos and noise-makers. My father's cousin Friedrich premiered the film version in Vienna. But how can this composer of modern music improve my figure?"

"He's also an expert on human glands and the ways they regulate the female anatomy. Read his articles in *Esquire*. Even better, you could consult him in person. He's an original, just like you, another fish out of water in Hollywood. Don't wriggle, darling, or you'll get a pin in your waist."

"I hate fittings."

"Your measurements have changed so much from dieting that I can't rely on your dressmaker's dummy. You're losing weight as fast as my wife is gaining."

"How is she?"

"Quite well, thanks. Demanding bigger maternity shifts that that won't make her look like a frump. I do my best to comply."

In a strange reversal, MGM had become Hedy's refuge from an unhappy home life, instead of the other way around. Jack Conway, the director responsible for her pleasant experience making *Lady of the Tropics* was assigned to *Boom Town*. Having battled to win the part of Karen Van Meer, she worked diligently with Phyllis Loughton, refining her characterization.

Gable and Tracy played wildcat oil prospectors who were alternately partners or rivals. Hedy and Claudette Colbert were amused by the male competitiveness that broke out whenever the cameras were rolling.

"Spencer drives me crazy," Claudette confided. "He can always steal a scene, usually by underplaying the highly emotional moments."

"I spent two years working with him, off and on," Hedy told her, "and I've never been quite sure whether he likes me or doesn't. It no longer bothers me. The only thing that matters is proving to Mr. Mayer that I deserve more scripts as good as this one. And that I can hold my own against Clark, like you and Vivien Leigh did. Both of you won Oscars playing opposite him."

The subject of their conversation sidled up to her. Clark leaned down, blasting her with his halitosis when he said, "I came over to give you a warning."

"About what? To expect another one of your silly pranks?"

"This is no joke. My wife is on her way to the set. She's going to watch while we shoot our big love scene."

"Why should I mind? Do you?"

Clark's tanned face grew ruddy with embarrassment. "Well, it's like this," he drawled. "Carole's one hell of a jealous broad. You're a sweet kid, I'm always telling her, married to an important producer. But I haven't convinced her you're not a man-slayer, out to seduce every guy in Hollywood."

"No time for that," Hedy replied. "I've got a baby and a husband."

"Right. I get it. And I don't want her putting you off your game."

"I think you're the one worried about that," Claudette said. "Watch out, Hedy, here she comes. I'll do what I can to distract her."

Lombard swept onto the soundstage, looking every inch the movie queen.

"Lovely dress, Carole," Claudette said.

"Irene Kalloch designed it for me." The golden goddess turned to her husband. "Pa, get me a chair."

"You bet, Ma." Thoroughly cowed by his mate, the King of Hollywood hastened to obey.

"Quiet on the set. Places, please."

The clapper loader boomed, "Take One."

For Hedy, professional success was a higher priority than the state of the Gables' marriage. She exerted herself to give a convincing portrayal of the husband-stealing Karen. If Clark paid the price when he got home, so be it.

After a tense weekend yachting expedition to Catalina Island, Gene suggested to Hedy that they write out a list of characteristics they most disliked in each other.

"It might bring about better understanding and help us repair our relationship."

She refused to participate. "We'll only make ourselves angry and start quarreling again. Instead of silly games, let's be completely honest with each other. Most of Hollywood has guessed what we both know to be true. For what reason should we hold onto each other, constantly putting on a charade in front of everybody?"

"Finalizing Jamesie's adoption is reason enough."

"I can't bear to bring up a child in a hurting home. We should separate now and delay the divorce until after the custody hearing. If you explain to the Children's Society that I'm a good mother, and I describe how attentive you are to your daughters, even though you don't live with them, we can convince them not to take Jamesie away from us."

They entered into a sober discussion of the necessary arrangements and logistics. He would move in with his widower father. She'd remain at the Benedict Canyon house with their son and the staff and her menagerie.

"You can be the one to inform the press," he said when he brought his hastily-packed suitcase downstairs. "My doing it would be ungentlemanly."

He was a stickler for proper form, a quality she respected. "But it's the Fourth of July holiday. Howard Strickling is away."

"You don't need a spokesman, you're capable of dealing with the reporters on your own. Be sure to stress that this is a separation, nothing more. Your lawyer will probably advise you to cite incompatibility, which absolves us both of fault. I'd appreciate your giving Lolly an interview as soon as you feel ready. She's been a good friend to me, and to us. You don't owe Hedda anything."

"All right." She also appreciated his sense of loyalty, which boded well for their relationship in future.

He patted the Great Dane's massive head. "Good bye, old fellow." When he picked up his suitcase and moved towards the front door, the dog ambled after him.

"Do you want to take Donner? You gave him to me, I know, but I've got Toni and all the other animals. He's so attached to you."

She slipped the leash from its hook in the kitchen and handed it to him. Surrendering a pet, she realized, was just as wrenching as her husband's departure, but in this difficult moment it was the kindest thing she could do.

Gene reached for the leash, then his hand fell. "I can't cope with a dog. Father's health is declining rapidly, and the doctors doubt he'll last out the month. You keep Donner till I'm settled." He planted a kiss on her cheek. "We'll both get through this, and we can manage it without too much fuss. I hope."

She contacted her attorney and sought solace from her closest female friends. Meeting a flock of reporters at the studio gates on a blazing hot Saturday morning, she recited her explanation, simple and succinct.

The Markeys' split vied with war news for front page coverage in the Sunday paper. Hedy checked to make sure she was quoted accurately before studying the report about Germany's effort to blockade Britain with submarines. Her hopes of getting Mutti out of London were growing dim as the fighting escalated.

In the midst of domestic upheaval and concern for her mother, she started work on *Comrade X*. With Gable as co-star, she could expect an onslaught of practical jokes. The film reunited her with European friends: Walter Reisch's fertile brain had supplied the plot, and Gottfried Reinhardt, Max's son, was the producer. Gable played Mac, a Texas newspaperman covertly spying in Russia, and Hedy was the communist lady streetcar conductor whose father wanted the Yank to take her to America. In a departure for a comedy, the script ventured into current politics, ridiculing Russia's totalitarianism and referencing the Nazi regime in Germany.

"Not the most glamorous costume," Adrian said apologetically, when she paraded before him in her plain uniform and cap.

"The nightgown is all right," she comforted him. "I only wish I filled it out better. At the top."

"Stop complaining about your figure, Hedy."

"I read an *Esquire* article by your friend George Antheil, the glands man. I'd like to meet him. Can you arrange it?"

"Easily," he said, tightening the belt around her waist. "Janet will invite both of you to dinner. Poor man, he needs cheering up. His brother died in a plane crash overseas, and his wife and son are visiting relatives, so he shuts himself away in a miserable hotel room to wrestle with his latest musical score. An evening with Hollywood's greatest beauty will do him a world of good." With a sympathetic smile, he added, "Janet worries that Gene might sue for custody of Jamesie. Do you think he will?"

"He says he won't, and I believe him. He's busy at work and with settling his father's estate. He has a far greater love for his daughter and stepdaughter. That used to pain me, but now I'm relieved. Jamesie's entirely mine, even if I wasn't the one who brought him into the world. You're a father, you must understand how desperate I am to hold onto him."

Adrian's smile was beatific. "Oh, yes! Robin changes every day. At birth he was seven pounds, and he gains weight daily. I do worry he'll grow up to look like me instead of his mother. He's got my dark hair and an unusually narrow and elongated face, for an infant. Our pediatrician assures me that I'm ridiculous to make assumptions when he's only six weeks old."

No longer tied to a highly social spouse who rarely missed a screening, party, or premiere, Hedy spent her evenings at home working on artistic and design projects. Rearranging the smaller sitting room to suit herself, she added a work lamp and drafting table, and filled the bookcase with journals and books on the mechanics of weaponry, her current obsession. After feeding Jamesie and putting him to bed, she spent hours poring over biographies of famous inventors, bridging the centuries from Leonardo da Vinci to Thomas Edison. While dreaming up practical labor-saving devices, she kept her radio on at all times. Whenever the war news penetrated her concentration, her busy pencil paused.

Annoyed by the wasteful disposal of soda pop bottles, she envisioned a home-made beverage made from ingredients concentrated in a solid form that would fizz on contact with tap water.

"Like a bouillon cube," she told Howard Hughes, the one Hollywood resident with whom she felt comfortable discussing her ideas. "I'd like to create several versions. Some could taste similar to Coca-Cola or Dr. Pepper. Others would have fruit flavors. Anybody with access to water could have a fizzy beverage. Soldiers in the field. People who go camping. What do you think?"

Hughes signaled to one of Ciro's waiters. "Bring me a phone." When the instrument was delivered, he dialed a number. "Larry, I'm putting you in charge of Hedy Lamarr's soda pop project. No, this isn't a joke. Find another chemist to help and give her whatever materials she needs. Someone in Legal can advise her about the patent."

After he hung up, she asked whether her idea was workable.

"You bet. When are you coming back to Muirfield House? We didn't get very far the last time, as I recall."

"If I'm supposed to sleep with you to get those chemists, I don't want them," she said firmly. "You have a terrible reputation. I'm trying to show the Children's Society that I'm an excellent mother and a proper guardian. Adopting Jamesie will be difficult enough without being linked up with you in the gossip columns." She spread caviar onto a cracker and put it in her mouth.

"Okay. I can wait." His grin was predatory.

"If my cola drink is profitable, I wouldn't have to make as many movies. And I could do more to support Britain and other countries fighting Hitler."

"In what way?" he asked, holding his unlit cigarette against the candle flame until it the tip glowed red.

"It's complicated to explain."

"Try."

"Several years ago, when I was with my first husband, I discovered a top-secret torpedo that a German engineer was developing. For all I know, it was put into production and is being deployed against the British navy. I learned about the types of weapons Fritz's factories made, which the Nazis are using now. You see, he entertained industrialists and military men, and I listened carefully to their discussions. I made lots of notes. And I've got some drawings. Could you and your company do anything with my information?"

"About munitions? Not interested. Aviation is my passion. I'm building a twin-engine bomber, made of fused wood and plastic, readying it for testing. I'll let the Army decide what ordnance it should carry. If you're so eager to share whatever it is that you found out, you should contact the National Inventors' Council."

Intrigued, she put down her drink. "What does it do?"

"The Council has a mandate from the government to collect and analyze suggestions for weapons that could be patented and put into production for national defense. The head research man at General Motors is involved."

"He'd probably be interested in my design for an automobile." With her finger, she drew an invisible sketch on the tablecloth. "The roof is shaped like this, and here's where I want to position the headlamps and taillights." She looked up at him to say, "But I've set it aside for now, while I study military technology. Would you let me visit your factory to see your new bomber?"

"Sure, if you swear to keep quiet. It's *my* top-secret project."

That night, instead of memorizing her lines for tomorrow's scenes with Clark, she spent a long time in her attic, pointing a flashlight into dark corners. She shoved aside suitcases, sneezing from the dust she raised. She lifted lids and peered inside boxes.

Where was her vanity case? The relic of her many escapes, foiled or successful, had vanished. And with it, the notes and torpedo drawings she'd smuggled out of Austria.

Discouraged, she descended the ladder.

The next morning, she went to the kitchen to enlist her maid in the search.

"Blanche, I've hunted everywhere for my leather vanity case. I looked all over the attic and inside every closet. Do you know where it is?"

"No, ma'am. Last time I seen it, you was movin' from that other house to this one. You made a pile of things you said you didn't need no more. I carried them to the same man as took some of Miss Harlow's belongings after she died."

Hedy had left North Camden Drive over a year ago.

"If you can find out whether he's got that case, I'd be very grateful."

"He don't have it no more, ma'am. He closed his business and moved away. Up to Visalia, his daughter told me. You ready for your breakfast?"

Her hopes shattered, she said dully, "Yes, please."

She'd lost all those painstaking notes and annotated sketches. The case and its hidden contents were probably decaying on a rubbish heap somewhere.

On leaving the breakfast table, she asked Blanche to bring a large pot of coffee to her workroom and sat down at her desk. Mining her memory for concepts she'd carefully recorded years ago, she began to make notes. Visualizing the torpedo, she recreated her drawings.

The National Inventors' Council wanted ideas. She could provide them with facts.

PART 3: 1940–1945

"Hedy is a quite nice, but mad, girl who besides being very beautiful indeed spends most of her spare time inventing things."
—George Antheil

Chapter 23

Resting her hand on the crib rail, Hedy smiled down at the sleeping baby and whispered, "I wish I'd seen Jamesie when he was this tiny."

Janet Gaynor's dimpled face glowed with maternal love. "Hedda and Louella and the other gossip mongers say I quit the movies because I wasn't getting good parts after winning my Oscar, which is ridiculous. I had my best role in *A Star is Born*, and a big success. But more than strong scripts or more awards, I wanted a husband and child and a quiet home life."

As they left the nursery Hedy told her, "I can't do what you've done. I've got to provide for my son, or the Children's Society will take him back."

"No need to worry about that. You're an asset to MGM, and L.B. knows it."

"*Boom Town* is a sure hit," Adrian predicted, handing Hedy a glass of orange soda. "*Comrade X* will be, too."

"Because of Clark, not me." When Janet inquired about their on-set relationship, she replied, "We're having a good time. He teases me, always in a nice way, never mean. To make me relax, he says. Did you ever work with him?"

"Years ago, before the talkies. I was a dancing slave girl in *Ben Hur,* and so was Myrna. Our day rate was only fifteen dollars. Carole, such a pretty teenager, was hired as extra. Clark was a centurion. He'd made a splash as a stage actor, but the studios were slow to recognize his promise."

"And his looks," her husband commented.

"I had comic parts in my early pictures," Hedy told them, "and I prefer them to drama. But Mr. Mayer doesn't care that I'm tired of playing the glamorous and exotic 'other woman' who is bad and dies—or causes her lover's death." With a smile at her host, she said, "Although I do miss the elegant dresses you've designed for me. Maybe in my next picture, they'll let me be amusing in beautiful clothes instead of . . . of plain ones."

Adrian grinned. "You were about to say 'ugly.' Don't deny it."

"You've given Golubka the most attractive ugly clothes ever made," she assured him.

With her eye on the clock, Janet said, "George is late. Boski's not home to remind him of appointments." She rose. "No telling when he'll turn up, so we might as well go into the dining room."

The green marble tabletop was laid with four settings of gold cutlery. Janet and Adrian sat at the head and foot, Hedy across from their tardy guest's empty chair. The doorbell chimed, and everyone bobbed up.

George Antheil's shaggy, brown hair and square, boyish face belied both his age and his achievements as musician and writer. His baggy suit seemed too large for his small frame. He wore a black armband on his jacket's left sleeve.

Jerkily, he moved towards Hedy. "It's really you! I accused Adrian of playing a diabolical joke when he said Hedy Lamarr wanted to meet me."

"I'm so sorry about your loss," she told him.

Janet murmured, "I trust Boski's visit will relieve your parents' grief just a little. A toddler in the house will cheer them."

"They'll enjoy spoiling Peter, no doubt about it," George replied.

"Your music must be a consolation," Hedy said. "For me it is."

"I'm supposed to be composing a movie score, but I've lost my focus. Henry's death is a tragedy to my parents, and it's devastating for his Finnish fiancée. Me, I'm consumed with anger that he fell victim to the fatal fevers raging throughout Europe. Fascism. Communism. Invasions. War."

"Why does America ignore it?" she demanded. "No action, many pitying words. Poor Austria, the people say. Poor Poland. Poor Britain. Poor Finland.'"

His keen eyes locked with hers. "My brother left Estonia to take up a posting in Helsinki when the Soviets shot down his plane. A commercial flight, not a military one. A precursor of more conflict. I've produced a predictive tract, *The Shape of the War to Come,* which I mean to publish anonymously. I can give you a draft."

Alert to Janet's faint frown of dismay over the direction of the conversation, Hedy answered simply, "Please do."

For some time after the butler served the consommé, George left his bowl untouched. He clutched his gold spoon, his gaze fastened on Hedy. "I didn't think it possible, but you're more exquisite in person. Black and white film flatters the features, but yours don't need it. Your coloring is remarkable, and you don't spoil it the way many beauties do by overuse of makeup."

"Lipstick only," she acknowledged. "From the dime store. Very inexpensive. Sometimes a dab of face powder." His assessment echoed what most men said on meeting her, but his artistic perception and matter-of-fact delivery were atypical. She received his stark statement of appreciation in a friendlier spirit than the more effusive compliments she often received. "I pay less attention to my face than other people do, Mr. Antheil."

"George."

"I've read your article about hormones. Now I hope you will help me improve my breasts. How would you describe them?" She indicated her chest.

Flushing, he shifted his glance downward. "Very nice. Perfectly fine."

"What do they reveal about my glands?"

"Oh. Right. Well, I'd say they fit into the postpituitary category." With an air of desperation, he reached for his water glass and drank steadily. When it was empty, he continued, "You're a thymocentric. Of the anterior postpituitary type. What I refer to as prepit-thymus. You'll have seen that term on the charts printed in my *Esquire* piece."

"What can I do about it?"

After brief hesitation, he replied, "They don't have to be bigger, you know. But for breasts where, um, there's a deficiency of postpituitary, an activating substance could, um, be beneficial."

"You're saying they could grow larger?" Arching her back, she thrust out her bosoms. "Like this?"

"Sure."

"Your article doesn't explain how that happens."

"I'm not convinced you need the information, Miss Lamarr."

"You must call me Hedy."

"George," Janet intervened, "potatoes?"

"Sure."

The butler, patiently standing by with the platter, served him.

Discussion turned from Hedy's bodily attributes to George's recent experiences teaching at Stanford. And he described his place of residence, the Hollywood-Franklin hotel.

"We're a motley crew. Bit players. Eager young starlets. Studio musicians. Radio personalities. Little girls with ringlets and piping voices, whose mothers are convinced their darlings are destined to rival Shirley Temple. Some of the guests work shifts at the front desk and at the switchboard. A desirable vantage for the ambitious. They can keep tabs on any incoming phone calls from talent agents and producers."

"No wonder you can't concentrate on your work," Hedy commented. "You should live somewhere else."

"The place suits me. It's cheap. The walls are so thick that the rooms are soundproof. When I'm playing the piano, I can't disturb anybody. Unless the weather's hot, and I keep my windows open."

Captivated by the unusual specimen seated across from her, Hedy considered the nature of the attraction. Not physical, she decided, or a response to his obvious admiration. She perceived that insouciance and bravado overlaid a seriousness that matched her own. Whether or not she could persuade him to help her enlarge her breasts, she genuinely liked him, in large part because he wasn't an actor. She already knew too many of them.

She was the first to leave, citing her need to study her script and check on Jamesie. Pausing at the dilapidated vehicle parked beside her red car, she used her lipstick to scrawl her telephone number on the driver's side of the windshield.

———◆———

Blanche was pouring Hedy's second cup of morning coffee when the phone rang.

"Maybe they don't need you today after all," the maid said before answering. "Miz Lamarr's residence. Yes, sir, she's still here. I'll see can she talk to you." Placing her hand over the mouthpiece, she whispered, "Mr. Ant-hill."

Hedy gestured to her to place the phone on the table. "Good morning, George. I didn't guess you also keep studio hours."

"Too early back East to phone my wife. Thought I'd give you a buzz instead."

"I'm glad you did. I'd like to talk with you again, about many things. Do you have dinner plans?"

"Fancy free, that's me."

"Come at seven o'clock. Blanche will give you the address, and tell you how to find the house. I've got to rush over to Metro. We start shooting my new picture this morning, so I mustn't be late."

Her buoyant mood didn't long survive her passage through the studio gates. She expected to find Jack Dawn in her dressing room, but he'd sent his associate Stan Campbell to apply her make up. One of Sydney Guilaroff's assistants dressed her hair, groaning audibly when she covered his handiwork with her streetcar conductor's cap. Her good friend Margaret Wood from Wardrobe helped her assemble the simple bus conductor's uniform Adrian had designed.

When she stepped onto the set she was welcomed by producer Gottfried Reinhardt and King Vidor, a director of long experience and impressive reputation. Her jitters subsided a little at the sight of her handsome co-star.

"In this movie we marry," she greeted Clark. "Will your jealous wife come to the set every day to intimidate me?"

He grinned. "Not this time. All year long Carole's been working her ass off at RKO. Until she starts her picture for Hitchcock, she'll be chasing chickens and ducks at our Encino farm. And helping her best pal Lucille Ball plan her wedding to that Cubano bandleader." A frown creased his sun-darkened brow, and he patted her shoulder. "I guess marriage isn't the easiest subject right now. Sorry it didn't work out for you and Gene."

"You and Carole eloped a few weeks after we did," she reflected. "But you knew each other for a long time."

"When do you go before the judge?"

"Next month, my lawyer tells me."

"That's tough. We'll have to do what we can to make this a smooth shoot for you."

They sat down together to rehearse their dialogue. He was patient with her mistakes, and his earlier remark made her suspect he deliberately fumbled his own lines to make her feel better. "If you keep being so nice to me," she said, "the press will say we're having an affair."

"Carole would murder us both." He walked away, then turned around to say, "False gossip would be just as fatal as actually having sex. My wife is a terrific shot—she can demolish clay pigeons."

"So can I," Hedy boasted.

Before they started the scene, the make-up man appeared. After applying the powder puff and lip brush, he held up a mirror.

"Forget about your face," Clark called. "Come on, let's do some acting."

His contract with the studio stipulated that his workday ended at six o'clock. At the designated hour, his stand-in Lew Smith held up his hand to signal it was time to halt.

"That's enough for today," the director called out.

Hedy left the soundstage in a more confident frame of mind. King Vidor seemed satisfied, and Clark had praised her comedic timing.

Her houseboy Mark, in uniform, had set the table. In the kitchen, her cook prepared the evening meal. Hedy helped Worth bathe Jamesie, then went to her own bathroom to scrub away the thick coating of cosmetics Stan had so skillfully painted on. After she powdered her face and reapplied her lipstick, she took her soap-scented son onto her lap and read a story. Hearing a knock at the door, she kissed him goodnight and handed him over to his nanny.

Mark ushered George Antheil into the parlor. His appearance was improved from last night. He wore suit and tie, and an inch had been trimmed from his hair.

After sampling the cocktail her servant presented, George told her, "I've never driven through Benedict Canyon. It's nice up here. I like your house."

"Just right for me and for Jamesie," she acknowledged. "Plenty of room for our farm animals and my gardens. There's a small citrus orchard at the back of the property."

He glanced at the Great Dane on the hearth rug. "You need lots of space for that massive beast. Good for you, keeping the dog as well as the kid."

"Eventually Gene will take Donner. Jamesie stays with me." Briefly she explained her situation with respect to the Children's Society. "They haven't yet attempted to take him back, but they won't approve of my getting divorced."

When she led the way to her dining room, he hung back. "You're a painter? And a wood carver, I see. But why the drafting table? Don't tell me you're an architect in your spare time."

"Only of chicken coops," she said with a laugh. "Inventing is a sort of hobby. Sketching my ideas, scribbling notes."

He stared at her. "You're joking."

She pointed at the stack of drawing pads and jumble of pencils on a table. "After dinner I'll show you my projects."

"I wish you better luck with yours than I've had with mine. I created a new and vastly simplified system of musical notation. I even received a French patent, but unfortunately it expired. SEE-Note, I call it."

"How does it work?"

"It's a paper, printed across with black bars corresponding to the keyboard notes one is meant to play, unfurling like a scroll or a player piano roll. To finish developing it, I need more money. And time. But in order to house and feed my family, I'm slaving away as a university instructor and writing background music for films."

As soon as they were seated and their salads were served, Hedy guided him to the topic of greatest interest to her. "Tell me how I can have larger breasts."

His fork speared a tomato wedge. "You need an activating substance."

"Explain, please."

"Ladies seeking to increase the size of their, um, bosoms, consult quacks, who recommend injections of postpituitary extract. That accomplishes nothing. The gland remains lazy and unproductive, because the extract takes over its work. When the injections stop—poof! What was gained is quickly lost."

"I see. Yes, that makes sense."

"Whereas an activating substance gives the gland a good, hard kick to force it into action. And then the breasts will stay, um, full." He paused to chew and swallow. "Listen, Miss Lamarr— "

"Hedy."

"Okay. Hedy, from what I can see, you're perfect as you are. You don't need an inch more, or even half an inch. Forget that I'm an expert on glands. I'm a man capable of assessing—and appreciating—a dame's figure. And I swear, I detect no fault in yours. You're gorgeous, and you're smart enough to invent things, whatever they might be. That's enough to bowl over any fellow worth having."

"But Mr. Mayer wants me to have a bigger chest."

"He's crazy. That's not where they point the camera. Is it?"

She shook her head. "Mostly they focus on my face. Or my profile. And for the papers and movie advertisements, the photographer takes head shots."

"You look perfectly healthy to me. Sure, if you try an activating substance, it'll make you bigger on top. But it might affect some other part in a way you wouldn't like." He put down his utensils. "Have I convinced you yet?"

"I think so."

"That's a nice change. I rarely win my debates with Boski. Her name's Elisabeth. Erzsebet, actually. Her parents named her after the Empress. She was born in Hungary, near Budapest."

"I played Sissi on the stage. In Vienna."

"Boski studied there, before she went to university in Berlin. That's where we met. Despite her reputation as a fierce radical, she hated my modernistic compositions. Probably still does, although she's used to them now." When she asked how long he'd been married, he answered, "We've lived together since '23, and a couple of years later tied the knot in Paris. For a decade we occupied a flat above the Shakespeare and Company bookstore. Made friends with all the great folk who haunted the place. Stravinsky and Ezra Pound and Man Ray."

"At one time you worked with Friedrich Kiesler, my father's cousin. My birth name is Hedwig Eva Maria Kiesler."

He nodded. "We knew him in Paris, and in Vienna. He arranged the screenings of the *Ballet Mécanique* film. The silent version, without the symphony I composed for it." His brows lifted. "Well, well, what a true twig of the Kiesler family tree you are. As an artist, he was highly respected, and as I recall he ventured into architecture. Are your chicken coop designs *avant-garde?*"

"Not at all. Cousin Friedrich would be disappointed. Not that he'll ever travel from New York to see them."

"Wise of him to get away from Europe when he did. In retrospect, all of us were." He struck his head with a balled fist. "What a damned forgetful fool I am. I meant to bring the draft of my war book."

"Next time," she said, certain there would be one.

They returned to her parlor to continue the exchange of thoughts about the European conflict. George, occupying the leather club chair Gene had left behind, declared that Hitler had ambitions beyond seizing a great swathe of the Continent. He was seeding the oceans with explosive mines. His U-boats decimated Allied warships and merchant vessels. His Luftwaffe planes rained missiles on ships in the English Channel, the prelude to a German invasion of Britain.

"We've got another connection, in addition to the Adrians and that murdered Empress and your Kiesler cousin. Your husband, the first one, got rich producing armaments. During the last war, I was an inspector of ordnance at a Pennsylvania arsenal."

She curled up on the sofa. "Did you inspect cartridges? Or torpedoes?"

"Smokeless powder charges for various types of guns, before they were shipped overseas for use in the trenches. I hope they did the job for those poor shell-shocked bastards."

"Fritz would never let me go into any of his factories. I would've liked to examine the machinery and watch the assembly of the products."

"What were they, do you know?"

"The outside parts of tanks. Brass for shell casings and bombs. Finished weapons, too. He sold those to Mussolini. And Franco. And eventually, to Hitler. He also intended to build military aircraft, like my friend Howard Hughes is doing. After Fritz left Austria, the Germans took possession of his factories and sequestered his residential properties." She shuddered. "Bombs from Hirtenberger and the other plants are probably falling on London as we speak. That's where my mother went, after the *Anschluss*."

"I imagine she's having a rough time of it. You should get her out."

"I'm trying. I've been quite a pest to the British and Canadian consulates here. With the U-boats constantly patrolling England's coast, I worry about her traveling by ship."

"It gives me no pleasure to have predicted the extent of German aggression so accurately," George said darkly. "I was drawing on information my brother Henry shared. Russia will be Hitler's next target."

She broke in to say, "My friend Walter Reisch put that in the script for *Comrade X.*"

"This year, fiction. Next year, fact. Mark my words." He fell silent, his attention drawn to the instrument in the corner. "Do you play?"

"Almost daily. It's in tune, if you want to try it."

He needed no urging.

She relaxed against the sofa cushions, listening to her new friend pound the keys. The unfamiliar piece must be one of his compositions. Not the sort of jarring, modernist piece he was known for, but something soft and lyrical. His movie score, she supposed, as her eyelids drooped.

On waking, she immediately sensed his desertion. The lamplight was low, the rooms silent. Placing her hand on the armrest, her fingers grazed a jagged paper scrap torn from her drawing pad. *"Thanks,"* George had scribbled, and below was his hotel's telephone number. Before making her way to her bedroom, she tucked the note beneath the ruler on her drafting board.

Chapter 24

Hedy returned home from a busy workday at the studio, anticipating a simple supper and a quiet night of doodling and drafting. She checked the broadcast schedule in her radio guide and dialed the shortwave frequency to tune in the latest news bulletin from Britain. The whine and crackle subsided, giving way to a clipped voice describing an attack so horrifying that she had to sit down to absorb the blow.

A German submarine had torpedoed a transport ship bound for Canada, exactly the type of vessel that Mutti would board when she left England. Of the thousand persons aboard, a third were child evacuees.

Hedy sucked in a breath, dreading to hear that the liner was lying on the bottom of the sea. To her relief, the presenter declared that all passengers safely boarded lifeboats. The fate of the abandoned ship, part of a large convoy, was not given.

Miraculously, innocent lives had been spared. This time.

With a thankful prayer, she climbed to her feet.

As she usually did between feeding Jamesie his supper and eating her own, she walked her dogs Donner and Toni through her section of Benedict Canyon. Her thoughts were chaotic, her mind filled with images of German subs and Hellmuth Walter's torpedo and the belching smokestacks of Hirtenberger Patronen-fabrik, where so many deadly devices of war were manufactured.

She reviewed her conversation with her peculiar new friend George, wondering whether she should reveal her plan to him.

Howard Hughes had advised her to offer her notes to the National Inventors' Council. Ever since, she'd pondered whether she might be able to develop a torpedo similar to the one Hellmuth Walter had described, capable of reaching its target without being traced or intercepted.

George had worked in an armory. Even better, he was an inventor who had successfully obtained a patent for his See-Note. He might have useful suggestions.

But what if he ridiculed her burning ambition to turn her knowledge against Hitler? Or revealed her intent to members of the film community? Many people regarded her as eccentric, and the columnists relished tales of her odd behavior and whimsy. She could well imagine Hedda Hopper's jibes and ridicule. Louella Parsons had professed sympathy in the aftermath of her separation from Gene, but she'd seize a scoop as avidly as Toni would a bone—and run with it.

No, her project had to remain a secret.

After supper she switched on her workroom radio. An updated report about the transport ship, identified as the Holland-America liner S.S. *Volendam,* was encouraging. The rescued passengers, taken aboard other vessels in the area, disembarked in the place where they had begun their journey. The intact transport was being towed back to its Scottish port for repairs. All three hundred and twenty-one evacuees traveling under the auspices of the Children Overseas Reception Board had survived their ordeal. Whether or not they would ever again risk an Atlantic crossing was unknown. Hedy pitied the parents weighing that hard decision.

As a daughter increasingly desperate to remove her mother from a city bombarded by warplanes, she felt similarly torn.

Motivated by her need to speed up the emigration process for

Mutti, she accepted a date with a British consular officer. Over dinner he pointed out that air raid signals gave Londoners the opportunity to take shelter before a strike. No such advance warning system existed for the ships at sea, they had no means of evading the enemy submarines. All passenger vessels entering the North Atlantic were vulnerable to attack.

Even at the studio, immersed in an imaginary world, she couldn't escape harsh reality. Walter Reisch mined communist ideology for laughs, but he also depicted Russia's capitulation to a Nazi incursion. Which, according to George Antheil, would eventually take place.

I really should speak with him again, she decided.

Picking up on the first ring, he announced, "I've been watching you on the big screen."

"In what?"

"*Boom Town.* Janet and Adrian took me to the cinema in Carthay Circle. Halfway through, your mammary region appeared. It was quite noticeable."

His singular review prompted a chuckle. "Thank you for that piece of good news. I needed some today."

"What's wrong?"

"Tomorrow my lawyer files my divorce petition with the court."

"That's what you want him to do, isn't it?"

"Even so, it makes me sad. I dislike failure. And confronting the past. I'm thinking I should move away, find a house down in Beverly Hills. I'll be at the studio all the time and getting there would be so much easier if I lived closer to Culver City." Remembering the purpose of her call, she said, "I need to share something with you. It's important. Not only to me, but possibly for the entire world. That sounds mad, I know, but I'll explain. I won't try to do it over the phone. When can I see you?"

"Not for a few days, I'm afraid. This weekend?"

"Come to lunch on Sunday."

On the eve of their meeting, the radio blared news of a savage bombing raid over London. For eight hours, from afternoon throughout the night, thousands of warplanes had dropped their ordnance onto Britain's capital. The Sunday paper contained an eyewitness account of the devastation. After reading every word, Hedy took the dogs out into the morning fog for a long stroll. As they followed the familiar stretch of road, her spirits were low and her heart heavy.

Because it was her cook's day off and Mark Manuel was visiting his parents, Hedy was responsible for lunch preparations. With unsteady hands she made sandwiches and tossed a simple salad, too consumed by grief to be creative. George arrived while she was setting the table.

"Did the court petition go badly?"

"What? Oh. No. I haven't been thinking about the divorce, I've been too worried about Mutti. That air attack must've seemed like the end of the world."

"In coming days and weeks, London and all of Britain's major industrial cities will be targeted. The Germans are retaliating for the Royal Air Force's bombing runs over Berlin."

"You've said the war will get worse before it gets better. I'm sure it's true, but I can't bear to hear that right now."

When she apologized for the plainness of their meal, he declared that any homemade food was an improvement on he'd been eating since his wife's departure.

"One day I'll serve my wiener schnitzel to your family," she promised.

"That sounds terrific. But don't ever offer me *blutwurst*," he warned. "I went off it in boyhood. My Prussian relatives gave me a ghastly tour of a slaughterhouse near Marienberg." He shuddered dramatically.

She removed their empty plates to the sink and led him outdoors to the stretch of lawn that bordered her swimming pool. The fog had lifted, and the early afternoon sunshine required the unfurling of the large umbrella.

"Another perfect California day," Hedy observed. "And far away in England, people are sifting through wreckage and gathering up their dead. If I were there, I'd help them. And curse the Germans."

"We can do that here." He stood up and raised two fists, shouting,

"Damn the murdering Krauts! To hell with every Nazi! As for you, Herr Hitler, may the devil himself fuck you in the ass!" With a twisted grin, he said, "Sorry if that offended you. I got carried away."

She waved off his apology. "Here I am living in this Hollywood paradise, doing Mr. Mayer's bidding and making lots of money, while there's such terrible suffering all over Europe. I want to do more than bake cakes for charities and subscribe to relief funds and knit socks for foreign soldiers. I'm determined to do something really important. You've heard about the National Inventors' Council? Howard Hughes told me about it."

"You know him?"

"He assigned two of his chemists to help with one of my projects." George's eyes opened wide when she described her cube of concentrated soda pop ingredients. "They're calculating the correct amounts to create each of the flavors and deciding exactly how much water should be added. A lawyer form the Hughes company is supposed to help me apply for a patent."

"I doubt the Inventors' Council will be interested in your fizzy drink. But I'd use it."

"That isn't my important thing," she told him severely. "The Council was started by the Commerce Department to collect ideas and projects from inventors and scientists, and even ordinary citizens. They'll deliver the best ones to the Army and the Navy."

He interrupted to say, "I wouldn't call you an ordinary citizen. Nor do I understand what exactly you propose to do."

"Travel to Washington and talk with the Council. They could ask me questions. I would share my notes and sketches with them."

"I'm still confused."

"I have information about weapons. Aircraft. Submarines. Torpedoes. I heard about them during my husband's dinner parties, from military men and engineers who visited us in Vienna or at the country estate. And I met another man who was working on a new type of torpedo. I saw a copy of his secret plans, which Fritz kept hidden away. He didn't know I found them and probably wouldn't believe I could comprehend them. But I did. Now Hitler controls the Hirtenberger factories and the one at Enzesfield, and his warplanes or U-boats might be using that special torpedo. I could write to Dr. Kettering, the chairman of the Inventors' Council, and offer to share with them everything I know."

George was shaking his head. "You're a movie star, Hedy. A glamor girl. He won't take you seriously."

"Mata Hari was a dancer and wore hardly any clothing. She was a double agent."

"It didn't end well for her," he pointed out.

"You're not being helpful."

"Even if Kettering and the Council agreed to meet with you, which is by no means certain, your information isn't current. It's several years out of date."

She stared at the pool water, rippled by the breeze. "I wanted to give it to somebody with the ability to design a weapon for the Allies to use against Germany. But Howard Hughes is only interested in aviation technology. I might work on the torpedo on my own. Or you and I could do it together."

"Why me?"

"Because you're a real inventor. You've got a patent."

"A French one. And as I told you, it expired," he reminded her. "I'm supposed to be composing title music. When Boski and Peter get home, we'll start looking for a rental house. I haven't had time."

"While we design a torpedo, your wife and son can be swimming in my pool. And playing with my animals."

"I'll think about it."

"Remember those Nazis you were damning to hell a few minutes ago? Any day, one of their missiles could land on my mother. We're both capable, and we're clever. And we're angry about the destruction of Europe. Don't you see? It's our duty to do everything we possibly can to stop it."

⊃•◆•⊂

German attacks on London intensified, and for two weeks the bombs descended by day and by night. When Hedy succeeded in reaching her mother by telephone, she learned that the end of her street was reduced to rubble.

"I could apply to serve as chaperone on a children's transport," Mutti said, her voice muted and faint. "Or travel to Canada on a regular passenger service. With the bombings so bad here and at the seacoast, people want to leave. Especially those of us who have cause to fear the Germans, if they invade. It might be difficult getting a berth, but I'll try."

Hedy resumed work in the morning, and returned home in a state of exhaustion. For hours on end she'd pummeled another actress in a long and physically demanding fight scene, then did battle with Clark Gable as he tried to separate her from her foe. Her hair was a tangled mess, she'd broken a fingernail, and her forearm was bruised.

She opened the wooden door panel in the wall, concealing a newly installed radio tuner and her Victrola. She pressed the button of the station that broadcast an 8:30 report from London.

The cook had left a bowl of chicken salad in the refrigerator, and a still-warm blackberry pie was waiting on the counter. Too tired to notice what she ate, Hedy tucked a napkin into her collar and sat down at the kitchen table. Apart from the radio's drone, the house was quiet. Her servants had Saturday evening off, and all of Sunday. By this time Worth would have fed Jamesie and put him to bed, winding up the clown music box that soothed him to sleep each night.

When the announcer began the news report, Hedy moved to the hallway to listen.

London and Liverpool had been bombed overnight. British planes successfully deflected a daytime Luftwaffe raid. The RAF had launched an attack on German warships in the English Channel. Artifacts from the British Museum were being moved to an Underground tunnel on the Piccadilly Line.

She spent the next day completing tasks left unfinished during her busy week. Greer, enjoying another enormous success as Elizabeth

Bennet in *Pride and Prejudice,* stopped by to purchase fresh Hedge-row Farm eggs and discuss her next role.

"My character in *Blossoms in the Dust* is the founder of the Texas Children's Society. It's exactly like the one that took Jamesie in when he was orphaned. The Jane Austen picture was a marvelous romp, and I'd welcome another, but Mr. Mayer prefers me as a dignified, serious, virtuous woman. This time she's a real person, and terribly keen that I personify her. Knowing next to nothing about children, I've been reluctant to take on Mrs. Gladney, the 'Lullaby Lady.' Most daunting of all, I'm supposed to meet her."

"Will you do a Texas accent?"

"Perish the thought! Imagine me surrounded by dozens of fussy babies with full nappies. How I'll hold onto my temper through it all, I can't imagine. If you want to put your boy in pictures, this would be the one."

"Never! The California Children's Society would take him away at once. And I wouldn't blame them."

"You'll let me practice with him, won't you? I must learn how to hold a little one, and feed it, and stop it crying. Being motherly will require my very best acting."

Laughing, Hedy assured her, "When he's at his squirmiest, I'll bring him to Roxbury Drive."

"While Reggie and I were performing our play for British War Relief, he complained to me about your preference for American millionaires. Howard Hughes. The Woolworth heir."

"A few casual dates, that's all. I haven't time for a steady boyfriend. The minute I finish my current picture, I start a new one with Jimmy Stewart. And immediately after that, production begins on *Ziegfeld Girl.* With Jimmy again, and Judy Garland. It's a musical. Adrian says the costumes are the most elaborate he's ever done."

As inevitably happened when Europeans were together, the talk turned to war. Unless America joined the Allied fight, they agreed, half the world would be lost to fascism.

Greer reached for her basket of eggs. "Must be going. Mother expects me home for tea. Nowadays we take it during the 4:30 broad-cast from London. So disheartening."

Going to the nursery, Hedy found Jamesie awake but drowsy from his afternoon nap. She lifted him from the crib and carried him to her workroom. While he amused himself with a stuffed piglet, she searched her bookshelves for the latest edition of *Mellor's Modern Inorganic Chemistry*. Her hand closed on the spine as the London bulletin began. The lead report carried the news she dreaded most.

Not again.

Another German U-boat had torpedoed another British transport bound for Montreal. A Royal Navy destroyer in the vicinity was able to rescue the survivors who had boarded lifeboats. The crew and an unknown number of the passengers—evacuees, mostly children—had gone down with the ship.

Rage and wretchedness consumed Hedy as she gazed at her son, unaffected by the inhumanity of war. Motivated by love and desper-ation, mothers and fathers had unselfishly placed their sons and daughters on that unnamed vessel, believing it would carry them to safety, far away from the Nazi menace. Their present agony was beyond imagining. Their losses shredded her heart.

The remainder of the broadcast was devoted to the usual recount-ing of bombing sorties over Britain.

She stared at the papers spread across her desk. Her eyes were riveted to a summary of that long-ago conversation with the German propul-sion engineer. Had one of Hellmuth Walter's wire-guided torpedoes blasted the British ship into bits? He'd been trying to perfect an alter-native method of directing the weapon to its target. Aircraft missiles, he'd told her, could be controlled remotely, by a specific and unique radio frequency that couldn't be blocked by an adversary. Jamming, he'd called it.

The Allies would gain a much-needed advantage in naval combat, if they possessed an underwater torpedo that was impervious to signal interception. And when the United States entered the war—it was essential, for the future of mankind—the military would require significant technological innovation to prevail. For that very reason, the government had convened the National Inventors' Council.

It was Jamesie's suppertime, so Hedy couldn't pursue this train of thought. He was more interested in rolling his meatballs across the plate with his plump forefinger than in eating them, but she couldn't bring herself to discipline him tonight. On the other side of the world, grieving mothers of drowned children were remembering moments like this one.

"One more tiny bite of meat, and you may have your banana," she encouraged him.

After he finished, she wiped his rosy mouth and led him to the bathroom. She turned on the taps and tested the water temperature. Into the tub he went, naked and laughing. Hedy ran a damp washcloth over his front and back and each limb as he wriggled about, trying to reach his rubber duck.

Her fingers gently circled a chubby forearm. Images of small, pale bodies floating in the cold, dark ocean filled her mind. Her tears slid down her cheeks and dropped into the water.

She lifted Jamesie from the tub and wrapped a towel around him. Getting him into his pajamas was always a challenge, but she didn't scold when he resisted. She tucked him into bed with his beloved piglet and read a cheerful story about a wise little hen, a present from Walt Disney. He fell asleep before she finished. After switching off the light, she crept out of the nursery.

Her brain afire with questions, she paused on the threshold of her study. Which of the many technical volumes in her bookcase contained the solution to the problem of signal jamming? Where in her recon-structed notes about torpedo guidance could she find inspiration?

The jazzy brass tune flowing from her radio speaker did not suit her somber mood. She envied Howard Hughes the convenient device he used to change the frequency without getting up.

Suddenly and vividly conscious of the potential contained in that fascinating wooden box, she rushed back to the study for paper and pencil. She sketched out a square, and added a dial with finger holes similar to those of a telephone. The Philco Mystery Control tuned in the frequency, sending it to the console through a direct connection that could conceivably be blocked.

There must be a way to create confusion. Not in the receiver itself, but for anyone trying to intercept and impede the connection. She drew squiggly lines to represent radio waves, then slashed a dark black line through every other one to represent signal jamming.

Staring at her rough sketch, she remembered an image she'd seen in magazine article.

She sifted through a stack of periodicals until she found a recent issue of *Electronics,* thumbing through until she found the photograph of a model yacht, a replica of the *North Star.* The vessel was five feet long, a quarter the size of a German torpedo. Its radio control system was described in detail, and the article was well-illustrated.

A circuitry diagram for the transmitter depicted a telephone-like dial with nine holes. The first was labelled "blank." The succeeding eight directed the various operations: forward and reverse, the rudder's side-to-side motion, and the speed of the boat.

She re-drew her dial, adding a blank hole in every other space to indicate the break in the sequence. But her pattern was consistent, and therefore discernible. Somehow, she must interrupt the frequency but without preventing signal reception.

I can do it. I know I can. But I'm going to need help.

From George.

The 8:30 London report had begun. It offered no update about the torpedoed transport ship, only a repetition of what she'd heard four hours earlier.

The morning newspaper presented an unbearable amount of detail. The human losses were greater than radio bulletins indicated, as many as three hundred were missing from a passenger list of four hundred. Some had been instantly killed by the explosion, or died slowly from devastating injuries. Drowning or exposure to freezing water further reduced survivor numbers.

Children had climbed into the lifeboats as instructed, only to be lashed by wind and hail or tipped overboard by the fierce waves. Eighty-three of them perished.

And London's skies were dark with Luftwaffe planes, releasing their incendiary cargo over neighborhoods like the one where her mother had taken refuge.

Hedy set aside her nascent plans for an undetectable submarine torpedo. Reaching for her sketchpad, she considered the necessary features of an anti-aircraft weapon.

Chapter 25

"What do you think?"

George didn't look up from the sheaf of descriptions and drawings she'd handed him. "I'm not sure. I can't make out you've written here. Is this scrawl written in English or German?"

"Never mind about the language. Look at my diagrams." Hedy plopped down beside him on the sofa and pointed to an illustration. "Here's the anti-aircraft device. In Vienna, we dined with a man who boasted to Fritz about a shell casing that was magnetized to pull a missile towards an airborne target. I'm not sure whether the Germans developed it. But I will. For the Allies."

"Your design for a telephone dial?" He held up a page.

"That's the directional system for my torpedo. The holes represent radio frequencies. Each one is separated by blank space, representing a break in the signal transmission. I'm trying to work out how it can be done sequentially, so sender and receiver can communicate without the frequency being detected. To prevent jamming."

"Is it to be used in the sky or underwater?"

"I haven't decided. The Germans wanted to use remote control for submarine torpedoes, to replace wire guidance. I never found out if they succeeded."

He scratched his head with a bandaged index finger. "Glide bombs that drop from airplanes are controlled with radio frequencies."

"How did you injure yourself?"

"Stupidly. I was sharpening my pencil with a knife and it slipped. Dr. Eshman fixed me up, but I've had to use four fingers to play the piano. Damned inconvenient." He lowered the papers and his keen eyes locked with hers. "A theory or an idea is just the beginning. An inventor must render a new concept with perfect clarity, and extensive documentation. And then comes the difficult work of determining the practical application."

"I doubt I could expand these plans by myself. Or obtain patents for them. That's why you'll be helping me. Also, I need a man with me when I appear before the Inventors' Council. As you've said, they won't take me seriously. Not at first. If they dismiss me as a silly actress, I can't help Britain and her allies beat Hitler and send him to the devil who is going to fuck him."

"In the ass. Okay. Tell me more."

She handed over *Electronics* magazine and showed him the article on the remote-controlled model yacht. She described the Philco Mystery Control she'd seen at Muirfield.

"Howard Hughes would be a better choice as co-inventor."

"He's only interested in aircraft. And he's a very strange person."

"So am I," George declared, as though it was a point of pride.

"I'd have to put up with his pawing me and trying to seduce me. It will be easier, working with a married man."

He cocked his head. "You think I'm a saint? My wife knows better."

With a shrug she replied, "That's none of my concern."

"I sure hope you've got a boyfriend. Otherwise, Boski's going to grow suspicious about my coming over here."

"Tell her I'm seeing John Howard, from the *Bulldog Drummond* movies. He made an important picture with Katharine Hepburn and Cary Grant and Jimmy Stewart, and Universal signed him to a seven-year contract. We had a date last night."

"Let me guess. Tall, dark, and handsome."

"Extremely. He's also perfectly nice. An artist as well as an actor. But not interested in inventing."

"You truly prefer spending your spare time working on military technology, with me, when you could be romancing the man of your dreams?"

"I'll do both," she said firmly. "And act in my movies. And raise my son in a world without any wars. Don't you want the same for your Peter?"

"Of course. Equal partners?"

"Naturally. If there's any profit to be made, we'll divide it fifty-fifty." After a brisk handshake, she collected her scattered papers. "Go back to your hotel and your composing. I must be in bed soon. Very early in the morning, before I report to the studio, I'm going to court."

"What for?"

"To tell the judge all the reasons my marriage to Gene broke down. He arranged the hearing so it wouldn't interfere with my shooting schedule."

"Better write down your explanation and memorize it, like you would your dialogue."

She beamed at him. "See, already you are a helpful partner!"

As usual, in the morning there was a folded newspaper on the breakfast tray her maid Blanche carried to her bedroom. Hedy had no time to read, but one headline captured her attention.

After more than a week at sea, with limited provisions and waning hopes of salvation, the last survivors from the torpedoed transport ship had been rescued. Forty adults and six children had struggled valiantly, clinging to their lifeboat as wind and waves battered it. Throughout their ordeal, the lone female told stories and kept up youngest passengers' spirits with games and songs. Reunited with their families, they were recuperating in hospital.

Buoyed by this account, she ate quickly and put on a cheerful pink and white dress.

Every reporter in town had spotted her name on Judge Baird's docket, and they packed his courtroom. Hedy's nerves were aflutter as she took the stand. In response to her attorney's calm, probing questions, she gave a faithful account of her life with Gene.

"When we were first married, I would tell him all the little events of my day, thinking he'd like to know. I expected he would do the same and share what he'd been doing when we were apart. But he never did. At night he preferred dining in restaurants and going to parties and attending film screenings. Because of my schedule at the studio, I couldn't stay out late. Often, he went places without me. On weekends, when I could, I'd go with him to Hollywood Park to watch the races, or for an excursion on his yacht."

"You and Mr. Markey lived together as husband and wife for fifteen months," the lawyer stated. "During that period, how many evenings would you say you spent together at home?"

"I remember very few. No more than four, I think. Over time we became strangers to each other. I lost weight from all my worrying about that." She wouldn't mention her difficulties with Melinda, or the rupture Joan Bennett had created by keeping Gene's daughter away from Hedgerow Farm. "One day in the summer, we realized that our marriage wasn't going to improve. He walked out of the house with his suitcase."

The judge posed a question of his own. "How long were you and Mr. Markey acquainted before your wedding in Mexico?"

"About four weeks."

"There's the cause of your troubles," he said before referring to the documents that had been presented at the start of the hearing.

She was tempted to say that when she eloped with Gene, she'd been thinking with her heart—which Papa had so often encouraged her to do. But her lawyer had warned her not to volunteer any information, only to respond to the questions she was asked. She therefore sat quietly until dismissed.

In stating his decision, Judge Baird awarded Hedy the Benedict Canyon property and its contents, except for any furnishings that were Gene's prior to their union. Final dissolution of their marriage would take place at a later date.

Outside the courthouse, she had to pass through a barrier of photographers to reach the car that would carry her to Culver City.

Now she needed to convince the California Children's Society that a twice-divorced film star noted for her sexual allure, and whose every move was tracked by the press, should retain custody of Jamesie.

Resolved to make changes, Hedy entrusted Hedgerow Farm to her servant Mark Manuel and rented a house in Bel Air. Painted white, it had many gables and a windowless façade that prevented passers-by from seeing inside. Although the property lacked a swimming pool, there was a room over the garage for the nanny, a well-equipped kitchen for the cook, and a fenced backyard where Jamesie and the animals could play.

Her social life was limited and discreet. At the end of her working day, she dined with John Howard at La Maze or Ciro's, or met Reggie for a drink.

George Antheil, glad to be spared the treacherous winding journey up the canyon, visited her almost nightly. He'd moved his family into a compact brick-and-stucco bungalow less than half an hour's drive from her new location. Boyishly eager to introduce her to his wife and son, he enlisted her help in arranging artwork acquired during the couple's years in Europe.

Boski Antheil was even shorter than her husband, an intense little woman with shining black hair. In looks and manner, she resembled a younger version of Mutti. Her greeting was on the chilly side of polite, and she clearly harbored concerns about George's involvement with a famously beautiful actress. She thawed ever so slightly when informed that Hedy was related to the Antheil's friend Friedrich Kiesler, an early supporter of George's *Ballet Mécanique*.

"Your husband's symphony is to him what *Ecstasy* is for me," said Hedy over the din of George's hammer pounding a nail into the plaster. "We each have a shocking thing everybody remembers, no matter what else we accomplish. If you prefer, we can speak in Hungarian. Or German. Or French. That way he won't realize we're discussing him."

"There's nothing you can tell me about George that I don't know," was Boski's frigid response.

"I suppose not," she agreed, resolved to keep the relationship cordial. She couldn't let a jealous wife become an obstacle in the pursuit of torpedo and missile technology. Crossing the room, she studied the framed canvases leaning against the wall. "What a lot of moderns you own. A Braque. And those . . . are they by Picasso?"

"We've been lucky in our friendships."

"The collection is reduced from what it was," George said. "When money's tight, we sell a painting or two."

"Those days are over, I trust." Boski handed him a picture. "Now that you're composing scores. And publishing a book."

"I'd rather work on my next symphony," he grumbled.

"That doesn't pay. Neither will messing about with radio frequencies and missile trajectories."

"Now, now," her husband soothed. "We've been over it a dozen times since you got home. Hedy and I are saving the world from Hitler."

"Better hurry," Boski retorted. "Will Miss Lamarr drink beer with lunch, or does she prefer wine?"

"Dr. Pepper, if you have it," Hedy said. After Boski retreated to the kitchen, she whispered to George, "I like her better than she likes me."

"Give her time. Anyway, I'm the one who made her cross. I've told her I plan to limit my film work to make time for my own compositions."

"Play one of them for me." She gestured at the piano.

He put down his hammer. "How about a duet?"

"As long as it isn't 'Chopsticks.'"

He indicated an impressive stack of music books on a table beside the instrument. "Pick your poison."

"You know I don't read music very well. I play pieces from memory." Sinking onto the bench, she decided, "'Rite of Spring,' by your friend Stravinsky. We've done that one before." During breaks in their inventing sessions, they sometimes played together.

He sat down on her left side, and as she pressed the notes of the treble part, he joined in with the bass.

After they began the second section, she abruptly stopped.

"What's the matter?"

"I thought of something."

His wide eyes returned her gaze, expectantly. "Well?"

"We communicate with each other through the music. It's a type of transmission, controlled by the sequence of notes. Our fingers skip from key to key. Sometimes they land at the same time, and sometimes they don't. Our hands are constantly changing position."

"Yes."

"Think about radio frequencies. Imagine that two simultaneous piano notes represent a signal being received." Her splayed fingers struck a chord. Next, she played an arpeggio by striking one key at a time. "No connection. No signal."

"The blank hole in the dial."

"Exactly!"

"Here we have eighty-eight keys. Any number of possible combinations."

In her excitement, she bounded up and down on the bench. "This keyboard showed us how to jam torpedo guidance signals."

"A player piano roll, something I know a great deal about, is a reliable means of synchronizing notes. Or signals, as you put it. Something to think about. Shall we continue?"

They played on, their hands crossing, their bodies swaying.

"You're supposed to be hanging the pictures," Boski reminded them.

They abandoned the piano and resumed their task.

Handing a Picasso to George, Hedy said, "My portrait is going to be exhibited."

"Who's the artist?"

"Reginald Gardiner. We used to—used to see each other a lot."

"I'll bet," he said, holding a nail between his teeth.

"Saw a lot *of* each other, more likely," Boski muttered.

"Don't listen to her. We lived in sin for quite a long time before I made her an honest woman."

"My boyfriend, John Howard, submitted some of his watercolors to the exhibit." Clarifying her involvement with another man would, she hoped, lessen Boski's hostility.

"Isn't that awkward for you?" the other woman asked.

"Boski," her husband, his voice tinged with displeasure.

"Not at all," Hedy answered blithely. "Reggie's a proper English-man and a true gentleman, and he'll always be my very dear friend."

"That's nice, I'm sure," Bosky said unsmilingly. "Lunch is ready."

The next time George came to Hedy's house, he insisted on intro-ducing a witness to observe their deliberations, in order to attest to the originality of their projects and document their progress. As part of the patent process, he explained, they were required to prove that the initial concept was theirs exclusively.

"Couldn't Boski do it?"

"Even if she were interested in our projects, which she's not, she lacks the necessary objectivity. I've already talked to Louis Eshman, the medic who tended my cut finger. He's on the staff at Cedars Sinai and is highly respected. You'll love his accent. Unmistakably and thoroughly New York."

"We'd best get busy, or we won't have anything to show him."

"This time I'll take notes, otherwise they won't be legible. What's your pleasure tonight, torpedo guidance or the magnetic proximity shell?"

She went to her desk and wrote a single word on a sheet of paper. Handing it to him, she said, "This."

"*Frequenzspringen,*" he read. "Translation, please."

"The hopping of the frequencies."

Adding the doctor to their work sessions proved helpful on two fronts. In addition to monitoring their activities, he diagnosed Hedy's recurrent mouth pain as impacted wisdom teeth. He advised her to have them out as soon as possible, but she was too busy with *Come Live with Me* to have surgery.

When the set decorator showed Hedy the music box Ian Hunter would give her in their first scene together, she complained that it was too ugly to belong to a European.

"Let me bring mine from home," she pleaded. "It was a gift from my Papa. The tune is very pretty, and a ballerina dances in a circle on top."

Jimmy Stewart was the most amiable co-star she'd had thus far at MGM, even nicer than Clark Gable. Between takes they battled one another in friendly games of Chinese Checkers, and he entertained her by banging out boogie-woogie tunes on a soundstage piano. He shared her love of sweets, and they frequently dipped into the big box of chocolates she always kept in her dressing room. An avid pilot, he was desperate to enlist in the Army Air Corps and was despondent over his failure to meet the physical requirements for military service. Determined to gain weight, during lunch breaks he devoured the commissary spaghetti. Hedy, her gums throbbing, swallowed Mama Mayer's chicken soup. For every milk shake she drank, he had two. When he wasn't needed in a scene, he visited the studio gym for muscle-building sessions with trainer Don Lewis.

"What were those gosh-darned writers thinking, giving a man's name to the most feminine creature in Hollywood," Jimmy commented as they recited lines before a take. "You sure don't look like a Johnny to me."

"My last character was called Georgi. At least I'm playing a Viennese instead of a Frenchwoman or a Russian."

By the first week of November, she was working on two inventions and two pictures. *Come Live with Me* hadn't yet wrapped when she reported to the set of *Ziegfeld Girl*. As she bounced between soundstages, changing in and out of Adrian's lovely costumes, she was busily calculating missile trajectories and frequency patterns.

Armed with an outline of their plan for torpedo guidance, George traveled to Washington to share it with the Department of Commerce. While there, he was granted an interview with a member of the National Inventors' Council. Encouraged by his reception, he returned to Los Angeles to brief Hedy and Lou Eshman on his successful meetings.

"Yesterday I sent a follow-up letter to Mr. Reynolds, describing the magnetic anti-aircraft shell. He'll be in touch with me if the Council requires more information."

"Fritz rang me this afternoon," Hedy told them. "He always remembers my birthday. We talked for an hour. I wanted so much to ask him about the maximum thickness of a torpedo casing. He would know, his company manufactured them. But it would make him suspicious."

"What on earth do you have to say to each other?" George wondered.

"I complain to him about my career, and he gives me advice. He always asks if Mutti is all right. He's very fond of her."

"And of you, apparently." George circulated a draft of their proposal for the anti-aircraft technology, already submitted to the National Inventors' Council.

Lou drew out his pen to make notations during the discussion. He excused himself earlier than usual, so he could attend his twin daughters' dance recital.

Hedy sat down on the carpet to show George the refinements she made to the torpedo guidance system. For her simulation, she relied on the nearest available objects. Her gold cigarette case represented a torpedo-bearing ship, with a silver matchbox as a partnering airplane. Between the two she laid out the matches in parallel lines, placeholders for the frequencies, filling the space between each one with a straight pin.

"To guide the torpedo, the operator sends out the directional signal at repeated intervals. Each matchstick is a connection, the successful receiving of the frequency." She pointed to the pins. "These are the blanks. To prevent detection, there is a hopping of the frequency. Either it reaches a receiver or it goes to a blank, with the signal coordinated by the plane and directed down to the ship. Whenever it's necessary to alter the torpedo's movement, the timing of the transmission will be changed."

George was frantically jotting down her explanation and making a rough diagram. "Got it."

"Anyone attempting to intercept the signaling sequence will assume it's random, because it goes out over multiple frequencies. But the alternating radio waves from the sending ship and the receiving torpedo are carefully synchronized." She shoved her hair back from her face. "I wonder how many separate frequencies we ought to include."

He chewed his pencil, studying her handiwork. "Eighty-eight. For the number of keys on a piano. What do you think?"

"I think," she replied with a nod, "we need more matches."

———◦·◆·◦———

Hedy's interest in the works at the "Avocations" art exhibit was intensely personal. Her boyfriend's series of tasteful watercolors included a nude female, discreetly rendered from the neck down to conceal her identity. Because she was publicly known to be dating the artist, everyone would correctly assume that she was his model, and now she regretted letting him display it.

She was more instantly recognizable as the ebony-haired, red-lipped, barefooted subject of "Scorpie." In Reggie's enormous painted canvas, she sat upon a stark black throne wearing a low-cut gown the color of dried blood that clung to her figure. Her right hand clutched a whip, and in the left she held a drooping red rose.

After a close examination, John Howard asked, "Why on earth do you want to buy this from Gardiner? It's so stylized, it hardly counts as portraiture. It doesn't do you justice. Your face lacks expression and your eyes are too cold. Your shoulders aren't that broad. And you don't paint your fingernails."

"Not unless a role requires it. In Vienna, only whores wear red nail varnish." Smiling at the enigmatic version of herself, she added, "Everything about it is meaningful to me. My astrological sign is the Scorpion. Reggie was at my side when a scorpion stung me, and afterwards he said that the venom made me fierce. The whip symbolizes my temper, the sting in the tail. The rose represents tenderness. He sees me as I really am."

"And he's still carrying a torch."

"Only the one he uses for his metal-working projects."

"At your house."

"In my garage, because he can't melt things in his apartment. He took time from his sculpture to make a bootjack out of brass and iron. I watched him solder together the letters of my name, and the year." Troubled by John's expression, she asked, "Are you cross because a columnist spotted us together? We went to a restaurant for dinner. Not really a date."

"Even so, he must've taken it as encouragement. Everyone knows he was much more than a friend to you."

She glared up at him. "You behave like your character in *A Philadelphia Story*. Suspicious. Possessive. It reminds me of my worst times with Fritz, and I dislike it."

She stalked across the room to view a series of caricatures Gene Markey had contributed to the exhibition. How he'd impressed her with his intelligence and his many talents and his ways of charming a woman. Her beauty and her potential for stardom had cast a potent spell. None of it had been enough to sustain their marriage. Her preference for quiet nights at home with Jamesie and her lackluster career decreased her value to him, and his love of the night life had pulled them apart.

John came to stand with her. "Pining for Markey now, are you?"

"I'm wondering why I'm so often cursed with husbands—and lovers—who want me to be someone that I'm not. And will never be."

Her pique lasted all afternoon. When John drove her home, she was still brooding over his burst of jealousy. As soon as he pulled into her tree-shaded driveway, she placed her hand over his to prevent him from switching off the ignition.

"I've decided it would be best to stop seeing each other. I'm not the right sort of girl for you."

"What are you saying? We're going to your premiere tomorrow night."

"I'll send you the ticket. Two of them, so you can invite someone else."

In need of comfort, she sought it from the ever-reliable Reggie, but he didn't answer the telephone. Greer was similarly unavailable. Next, she called Janet Gaynor, who murmured sympathetically and readily volunteered to take Hedy to her own *Comrade X* premiere.

Daringly, she chose to wear velvet trousers instead of an evening gown. At the last minute, to compensate for her lack of formality, she added a red fox coat.

"You won't believe how I spent my day," Janet said as the Adrians' chauffeur sped along Bellagio Road. "I surrendered all my evening gowns to MGM's Wardrobe Department. Because of the war in Europe, my dear husband can't order Belgian sequins to make you Ziegfeld girls sparkle. When you're wearing his creations, I hope you'll appreciate my great sacrifice."

"During the Tony Martin number, Hedy and Lana will steal the picture," Adrian predicted.

"What about Judy Garland?" Hedy asked.

"With that voice, she doesn't need sequined gowns."

"Put me in slacks, in every scene," Hedy pleaded. "And don't give me any silly hats."

Dramatically clutching his chest, the designer moaned, "How you wound me. Just you wait. The headdress I have in mind for you will make you regret mocking my millinery."

Inspired by David Niven's sculptures in the art exhibition, she modeled miniature clay animals as farewell gifts for her *Come Live with Me* castmates. A pig for Jimmy Stewart, a mouse for Donald Meek, and a lion for Ian Hunter.

Impressed by the box office receipts for *Boom Town* and *Comrade X*, and Hedy's positive reviews, Mr. Mayer rewarded her by offering a per picture salary of twenty-five thousand dollars and other perks. If she didn't choose to take lunch in the commissary, she could have it delivered to her dressing room, and she was given a secretary, a script girl, and a personal hairdresser.

Because John Howard had been squiring another actress around town, Hedy was surprised when he stopped by her house shortly before Christmas. She was reluctant to invite him into the living room, where George and Lou Eshman were reviewing final descriptions and blueprints for the radio-controlled torpedo.

She stepped outside to talk to him. The breeze stirred the long glass icicles she'd hung from the eaves. An incongruous holiday decoration—daytime temperatures reached sixty degrees.

"You've got company tonight," he said with a nod at the cars in her driveway. "I should've phoned first."

"Some friends are helping me with a project."

"Your cola cube?"

"More technical that that," she hedged. He was clutching a small box wrapped in white paper and tied with a red bow. "For me?"

"A little something you can open Christmas Day."

She was about to apologize for having no gift for him when she remembered the clay animals. "Stay here. I'll be right back."

She hurried to the living room where her co-inventor and their monitor were waiting for her. Studying her menagerie of miniatures, she decided John should have the sleek, long-backed panther. When she presented it, he responded with a kiss so passionate that she regretted that she wasn't alone. He departed with a lipstick smear beneath his moustache.

"You're a fickle creature," George commented drily before they resumed their discussion. "Last night it was Reggie Gardiner."

"And will be tomorrow." She tugged at the red ribbon and pulled away the wrapping.

"Aren't you going to wait till Christmas?"

"Why should I? John will never know." The box contained a bracelet formed of heart-shaped links sparkling with embedded diamonds. She held it up.

George turned to the doctor. "Are you giving Leah a trinket as fancy as that?"

"She wants a new hairdryer."

"Practical woman. Hedy's distracted, so we might as well call it a night. I'm heading home to my Boski and our bouncing boy."

Lou took a cigarette from the silver box on the table, proof that he was in no hurry to depart.

He waited until George left the house before asking, "When the two of you embarked on this collaboration, did you draw up a document stating the terms of your arrangement?"

"No. We agreed to be equal partners. And we shook hands."

"That makes it easier for him, then. If, as I suspect, he's engaged in double-dealing. How much has George shared with you about his correspondence with the officials in Washington?"

Hedy shrugged. "I know he sent our specs for the anti-aircraft shell. That was a month ago. Or more."

"Plenty of time to receive a response from the Council. Odd that he hasn't said anything about it. Not to either of us. Unless, that is, he assumed full responsibility for the project, cutting you out of the process completely."

"George wouldn't do that."

Or would he?

"The original ideas are yours," Lou went on. "I wouldn't want you to be taken advantage of by an unscrupulous associate. Better find out what George is up to, before it's too late."

"Oh, I will," she vowed. Crossing to the curio shelf, she gathered up several of the animals and offered them to him. "Take this giraffe, and the rabbit, and the dachshund. For your children."

"Thank you. Good Chanukah to you. And Merry Christmas."

She stared at the only creature left, a seated monkey whose creased forehead and broad, flat nose and plump lower lip reminded her of George. Seizing the clay figure, she flung it so hard against the floorboards that it shattered. With the heel of her shoe, she ground the smirking face into dust.

Chapter 26

"You've been avoiding me. Like a guilty person." Arms crossed over her chest, Hedy glared at George.

"You've got it backwards," he replied. "When I phoned you after Christmas, you called me a rat and hung up. Since the first of the year, I've stopped by twice. Both times you refused to see me. I sent a letter. You returned it unopened." He looked from Hedy to Lou. "I deserve to know why I've been frozen out."

"Because we can't trust you. After you tell a lie, nobody will believe you again. Even when you're speaking the truth. That's what my father taught me."

"What lie? Lou, what's she talking about?"

"The magnetic anti-aircraft shell," Hedy answered. "You presented it to the Inventors' Council, and you've been negotiating with them in secret. Without telling me anything. You'd better not take over the radio-control torpedo, because it was *my* idea."

"An amorphous one," he shot back.

"What does that mean?"

"Shapeless," Lou Eshman submitted, breaking his silence. "Without definition."

Incensed, she hopped up from the sofa. "Go away, George, and don't come here again. You stole my plans because you know how valuable they are. Now you insult me with strange words."

"Hedy, you misjudge me. I can prove it. But not till you're ready to listen to reason." George shoved his hat on his head and stalked out of the room.

Seconds later, he was back.

"What do you want?" she asked coldly.

"I need to make something very clear, and I'll use small words. If our work becomes public—and I hope to God it does, because that would mean it's as important as we think it is—will anybody care that George Antheil was involved? Oh, no. It's Hedy Lamarr who will get all the attention. You persuaded me to be your partner. Your *equal* partner. For months I've sacrificed my time and my expertise to our projects, knowing full well I won't receive any credit or a dime in remuneration. Out of patriotism, for the common good, we agreed to give away our inventions. I can derive no material benefit from 'stealing' your ideas, as you put it. Which I would never do. Good night."

Not long after their bitter dispute, Hedy received another letter. She decided to read this one. George reminded her that she'd ceded to him the responsibility of presenting the anti-aircraft shell to the Council, which was the only reason he'd handled the related correspondence. In closing, he described her as "by far one of the most wonderful persons I have ever known."

Unless she accepted his explanation, they couldn't carry on with their endeavors. All along he'd demonstrated faith in her abilities. Without his input and expertise, she'd have no chance of creating useful technologies for the military.

Attached to her gold bracelet was the crystal-faced locket Mutti had sent at Christmas. Inside was a four-leafed clover plucked from a patch of grass near the art gallery in Trafalgar Square. Fingering her good-luck charm, Hedy formulated the apology that would end her quarrel with her co-inventor.

———◦•◆•◦———

For the most spectacular of the Ziegfeld musical numbers, Hedy received a headdress constructed of inwardly curving wires, each studded with spangled stars.

"How do I put it on?"

"You don't." Margaret Wood, her friend from Wardrobe, explained, "I'm attaching it to a supporting rod that we'll strap to your back. These ties go under your bosom and fasten behind."

"This is no costume, it's a torture device. I'm supposed to move up and down that giant staircase. Gracefully."

"You begged L.B. to put you in this picture."

"Because musicals are supposed to be light and fun, not bad melodrama. My character has less personality than a statue."

"Stop fussing, sweetie, and let the torture begin."

A signature Ziegfeld number, "You Stepped Out of a Dream," featured a multitude of chorus girls in elaborate Adrian gowns and outrageous headwear. Hedy, arms extended, maintained an impassive expression as she glided into place beside crooner Tony Martin. Losing her balance and stumbling was a real and very hazardous possibility.

Busby Berkeley, directing from an aerial position, had thrown out the version of the choreography the performers had repeatedly rehearsed. His eleventh-hour alterations compounded the difficulty of shooting the sequence.

After finishing *Ziegfeld Girl,* a case of the flu combined with her tooth ailment put her in the hospital. Throughout her convalescence, she relied on Reggie for companionship and good cheer. Concerned that she was spending too much time cooped up at home, on a bright, mild day he drove her to the beach at Malibu.

"Gene is dating Carole Landis," she told him. "The pretty blonde starlet. John Howard and I ran into them at Ciro's a few weeks ago."

"She's even younger than you are."

"I know." She leaned over and with her forefinger traced a circle in the sand. In the center she added and H and an L. "I've decided to take your advice about legally changing my name. Hedwig Eva Maria

Kiesler no longer exists. As Gene's adopted son, Jamesie remains a Markey. But there's no longer any reason for me to be."

"It makes things simpler. The whole world knows you as Hedy Lamarr."

"Mr. Mayer's creation." After a long sigh, she lay back against her beach chair, peering up at the sky through dark-tinted lenses.

"He works you too hard. And all the while you've been burning the candle at both ends, inventing heaven-knows-what in an effort to save the world. It's no wonder you landed in hospital. Are you and George Antheil good mates again?"

"We forgave each other for the misunderstandings. In the end, the National Inventors' Council didn't care about our anti-aircraft shell."

"Idiots."

"But they are very interested in the radio-directed torpedo. George went to Washington again to meet with Mr. J. Edgar Hoover and other people at the F.B.I. He's trying to convince them that his method of glandular diagnosis can predict war crimes that Hitler and the Nazi leaders might commit in the future."

Reggie groaned. "I should think such predictions are simple enough, based on what they've already done. Bombing Britain to smithereens. Torpedoing ships fill with women and children."

"And the concentration camps," Hedy added darkly. "Mutti fears that's what happened to her Lichtwitz cousins in Hungary. We may never learn their fates."

Gently leading her away from that sad topic, he congratulated her on the positive reception of *Come Live with Me* and the critics' enthusiastic acclaim for her comic turn in *Comrade X*.

But her portrayal of the mannequin-like Sandra, she pointed out with regret, wouldn't impress anybody.

"You need a prestige picture," he told her. "*Ziegfeld Girl* was never going to be that. Not with musical numbers and scanty costumes."

"And headdresses," Hedy muttered.

"Reading doesn't require much stamina. While you recuperate from your flu, do as Greer does. Seek out a critically acclaimed novel or play, with a strong female lead. Contact screenwriters, ask what properties they're working on."

Citing her poor health, Hedy requested medical leave, which she was granted. On learning she would again be paired with Robert Taylor, as another foreign *femme fatale,* she prolonged her layoff. Accusing her of insubordination, the studio broke off contract negotiations. The combination of inactivity, uncertainty about her status, and the failure of her cola cube invention deepened her depression.

When she received a series of letters from an unknown individual who threatened violence against her, she grew fearful and even more reclusive. She changed her phone number and shared the new one with Reggie, Greer, Mutti, and no one else.

The torpedo project had reached a critical stage, and she wanted to re-examine the Philco Mystery Control. Conversing with a fellow inventor, however peculiar, was preferable to another night at home, listening to disturbing news from London.

"Come to Muirfield," Howard Hughes invited her when she telephoned him. "I'll give you a copy of chemists' report on your soda pop."

"I've seen it. Municipal water systems vary, depending on location. My cube requires consistency in the liquid. It's a dud."

If she'd known his mood was amorous, she would have stayed at home. He was more intent on seducing her than discussing inventions.

Prying the remote-control box from her hands, he kissed her, his tongue sliding into her mouth. She didn't object, not even when he pushed up her blouse and inserted his hand under her brassiere to paw at her breasts.

Maybe, she thought, as her body reacted to his touch, sex with this needy man can break my despondency.

She let him unbutton her slacks and helped him by sliding her silk underpants down her thighs, granting him access.

The part of him that had also gone inside Hepburn, Davis, and de Haviland before her was firm enough to belie rumors of impotence. But none of those actresses had taught him about reciprocal pleasure.

As an aviator and inventor, he impressed. As a lover, he was a disaster. While he heaved on top of her, she didn't bother to feign satisfaction.

Afterwards, rearranging her clothes, she regretted their coupling. It had further lowered her spirits.

Sitting up, he placed his head in his hands. "You're too good for me. Too beautiful."

"You only wanted me because I turned you down so many times," she said, without rancor. "Now you can move on to your next conquest without feeling guilty."

"I never feel guilty," he said, placing his Mystery Control in her lap.

⌐◦◆◦⌐

At a dinner party, the hostess seated Hedy beside King Vidor, her *Comrade X* director. When she inquired about his current picture, he said he was casting *H.M. Pulham, Esq.*, based on last year's popular magazine serial. Heeding Reggie's advice, she indicated interest in no uncertain terms.

Bluntly he told her, "You're wrong for the wife."

"I don't play wives. Tell me about the other woman. There must be one."

"She's independent, for her era. Works in advertising. Unconventional. Unforgettable. Her name is Marvin Myles."

"A sure sign that the part should be mine. I often play woman with a man's name."

"But this one's not from a foreign country. She's a New Yorker."

"A city of immigrants," she pointed out. "When people compliment my performance in *Comrade X,* I tell them your direction is responsible. You helped me develop that character and show all sorts of emotions. In my ugly uniform I was able to be a real actress. Not just a face attached to a body wearing an Adrian evening gown."

"Would you really like to look at the script?"

"If there's a real chance of my being cast."

When she finished reading, she was even more eager to take on the role. Exactly the prestige picture Reggie said she needed, in this one she could demonstrate her acting range and dispel her glamor girl image. And it was a period piece, with the primary action taking place some twenty-five years in the past.

While waiting to learn whether she would get the part, she worked feverishly on the torpedo control system. She and George were finalizing the physical mechanics that would render it feasible. On the recommendation of the Inventors' Council, they sought technical assistance from a professor of electrical engineering. Included in their patent application was a reference to the Philco Mystery Control technology, the model for their device's steering signal. A modified version of a player piano roll—George's suggestion—would control and synchronize the alternating frequencies.

"Changing signal frequencies won't prevent detection," Hedy decided. "We need something else to create confusion. Suppose we give the transmitter a different number of tuning condensers than we have on the receiver?"

"All right. How many on which one?"

"A meaningful number." She considered the possibilities. "My birthday is in November, the eleventh month. Seven plus four equals eleven."

"Seven condensers for the transmitter," he said, writing it down. "Four for the receiver. Leaving us with three extra ones to churn out false signals without any corresponding receptors. Which ought to be enough."

Satisfied that they could do no more, they turned over their proposal and diagrams to the firm of patent attorneys Hedy had retained. In June, their final application for the Secret Communication System was filed with the U.S. Patent Office.

"Now we wait," said George.

"I should go to Washington and meet with the Navy men."

"Not until we're able to present them with an approved patent."

Determined to complete his Third Symphony in peace, without the many distractions of Hollywood living, George moved his family to

Manhattan Beach. On a blistering July day, Hedy drove herself to the stucco dwelling they had rented. Perched on the dunes, it overlooked the ocean, its cramped rooms cooled by a constant breeze.

"How happy you must be here. But this is the tiniest house I've ever seen!"

"It suits us. Boski decided that if we're going to starve, we can do it just as easily and more pleasantly away from the city. And all its temptations."

"Do letters reach you?"

"They're forwarded to the village post office. Every day I walk down to collect them." He smiled. "Don't worry, we won't miss any communications from the Patent Office. Your lawyers will inform you when they receive a response."

"It's been over a month since they submitted our application."

"Five weeks. I'm counting, too. A patent review takes a long time. But because the Inventors' Council isn't as hampered by red tape, Kettering could contact us any time."

She brushed back a strand of hair displaced by the wind. "I'll be moving soon myself."

"Back to Hedgerow Farm?"

"Not yet. Franchot Tone will be my tenant until he gets married. I'm looking for another Beverly Hills house. One with a swimming pool."

After her eight-month absence, Hedy was warmly welcomed back by crew members at MGM. She'd always made an effort to keep up with their personal lives, recording birthdays in a little book she kept in her purse so she could hand out cards and homemade presents. Adrian had departed from the studio to set up his own fashion house, and a different designer was responsible for her clothing. Journalists who stopped by the *H.R. Pulham* set were startled to find the famous glamor queen sporting a businesslike bun and wearing simply tailored office attire.

She dined in her dressing room when Margaret Wood from Wardrobe was available to keep her company. Otherwise, she went to the commissary with her friend Ann Sothern, the effervescent blonde star of the popular *Maisie* series. Away from the studio, they played tennis and shopped the stalls at the Farmer's Market. Ann, recently separated from her husband, had designated Hedy as her confidante and chief companion.

"I'm the all-American girlfriend you've always wanted," she declared. "Without me, you'd sound just like those English actors and actresses you hang out with. We're going to work on your slang."

"I'm always messing up," Hedy conceded, "and people mock me. The other day I told a reporter that my dressing room paneling is knotty pine. In her article she spelled it 'naughty pine.'"

Ann let out one of her hearty laughs.

"I'm not on this afternoon's call-sheet. If you're free, we can tour rental houses."

"There's only one you need to look at," Ann stated with conviction. "In the Flats, just around the corner from mine. A pool at the back, and the dearest little playhouse. If you take it, we'd be neighbors!" With a sly grin, she added, "And I'll be able to go swimming every day."

"It sounds perfect."

Arm in arm, they dodged costumed performers and studio workers entering and exiting the commissary. At every soundstage along Main Street, a bright red light glowed to signal that the cameras were rolling inside.

When Gene Markey, dressed in Naval Reserve uniform, visited Hedy on the set, he was offered a chair so he could watch her shoot a scene with Robert Young. As soon as she finished, he asked if they might speak in private. She took him to her dressing room.

"Quite an improvement on the last one," Gene observed, before examining the diagram on her drawing board. "Another project for the National Inventors' Council?"

She laughed. "Hardly so important. It's a floor plan. I'm working out how to arrange my furniture in the new house. If you've got any influence with the powerful Navy people in Washington, do put in a good word for George and me. We haven't had any news since the Council passed our paperwork to them for evaluation."

"I'd gladly help you if I could, but my posting doesn't take me anywhere near the capital. I'm headed to Balboa in the Canal Zone, to serve as a deck officer."

Her worried eyes met his. "Are you going on active duty because America is sending ships into the Pacific? I suppose it has something to do with the Japanese."

"I'm not able to say any more about it," he said apologetically. "I've come to extend an invitation, as well as to ask a favor. Joan and Walter Wanger are throwing a farewell party for me. I'd like for you to attend, and bring Jamesie along. Melinda and Diana will be there."

"Both ex-wives. All your children and stepchildren. And how many girlfriends?" she teased.

"All of them, I hope. You should know, in case the press gets wind of it, I've instructed my lawyer to submit the request for our final divorce decree."

"You must be planning to marry Olivia de Haviland," she guessed.

"No time to arrange a ceremony, even if we felt ready. I'm too busy handing over all my production duties at Twentieth Century and preparing for an absence of uncertain duration. Every other person in town stops by the office to give me presents, or insists on taking me to lunch or dinner, when what I really want is more time and enough organizational help. Which brings me to that favor. Would you be able to take Donner back?"

"If that makes things easier for you."

"Liz Whitney returned him to me. When my orders for Panama came through, I gave him to Olivia. But she's not happy about it, and neither is he. That's why he needs you, only temporarily." He asked for a piece of paper and jotted down a telephone number. "Carole Landis adores Great Danes, and she's willing to take him, but I'm not able to handle the arrangements. She and her mother live right on the beach in Santa Monica, where he'll have plenty of room."

"Your love life is so much more complicated than mine." Her smile faded and she hugged him hard, pressing her cheek against the ribbons pinned to his chest. "Be careful, Gene. For Olivia's sake, or Carole's, keep away from those Panamanian ladies."

"I'll try."

———o·◆·o———

The boldface headline was as startling as it was unexpected.

HEDY LAMARR INVENTION SEEN AS DEFENSE AID.

She read the article twice before telephoning George.

"Why is the Council telling the press about our invention?"

"What?"

"It's right here, in the *Los Angeles Times*. 'Hedy Lamarr—screen siren and inventor,'" she read. "'The film favorite for the first time was portrayed in this dual role. Her invention, held secret by the government, is considered of great potential value in the national defense program.'"

"Who's the source, does it say?"

"Colonel Lent of the National Inventors' Council. Our invention, he says, is in the 'red hot' category, and 'involves the remote control of apparatus used in warfare.'" She glanced at the newsprint again. "They received over thirty-thousand suggestions and presented one hundred of them to either the Army or the Navy. You aren't mentioned at all."

"That's no surprise," George said wryly. "Exactly what I predicted. The Council's using you to get publicity. I don't blame them."

"But it's not fair. I'm sure the Colonel knows you're the co-inventor."

"No reason to cry about it."

"I'm not. It's Spunky, the kitten Reggie gave me." She picked up the mewling creature and smoothed its fur. "If I'm contacted, I'll give you all the credit you deserve. Equal partners!"

Before she celebrated her November birthday, she received formal consent to Jamesie's adoption and they moved into their new home. Fritz made his usual telephone call from Argentina to offer best wishes.

Reggie stopped by her house for the same purpose.

"Whose mongrel is that?" He backed away from the dog curiously sniffing his trouser cuffs.

"Ours. This morning I found him at the back door, without any collar or tag. I tied washing line around his neck and led him all over this neighborhood, thinking he'd take me to his house. Or his owner might spot us."

"A fruitless effort, apparently."

"I regard him as my surprise birthday present." Kneeling down, she stroked the object of her mercy. "I showed Jamesie how to pat him on the head, so now that's his name—Pat. At first Spunky was unsure about him, but now they're firm friends. Toni is a bit jealous."

After she showed him around the property, he agreed that it suited her perfectly.

While they sipped lemonade beside the pool, she asked, "Have you been to Monterey?"

"A time or two. Why?"

"My next picture, *Tortilla Flat*, is set there, and it sounds so interesting. I wish I could see the bay, and the fish factories."

"You might want to read Steinbeck's novels before you go."

Like King Vidor, director Vic Fleming was adept at drawing from Hedy a spirited portrayal of a strong and independent personality. As Sweets Ramirez, the prickly Portuguese cannery worker, she was costumed in a plain blouse and skirt in most of her scenes and wore her hair in braids. The rustic setting appealed to her, as did the presence of chickens and a goat and many dogs—including Toto from *The Wizard of Oz*. No fancy drawing room or boudoir in this picture, but a weedy shantytown occupied by eccentric lowlifes.

On this third film with Spencer Tracy their characters had few interactions, and hers disliked his. Hedy's favorite scenes took place in the processing factory where she energetically chopped fish while delivering her lines. Her fondness for John Garfield, her romantic interest, proved problematic when the script required her to slap his face. She wagered him that she could do it in a single take—and with her winnings she treated him to a hot dog dinner.

On the first Sunday in December, the principal players were called back to the studio. Puffing on their cigarettes, they waited for the lights to be positioned.

A teamster barged onto the set and rushed over to the director. After a brief, strained dialogue, Fleming took up his megaphone and ordered the enormous doors to be pulled shut.

To his perplexed cast and crew, he announced, "The Japanese have bombed our naval base at a harbor in Hawaii. The radio bulletin reported that many vessels are destroyed, and the number of fatalities won't be known for some time. Ladies and gentleman, looks like we're at war. But we've got a picture to finish. So we will."

Hedy clutched John Garfield's elbow. "The California coast could be their next target!"

Her anxiety increased when she thought of George and Boski and little Peter, living so exposed on Manhattan Beach. Carole Landis and her mother, and Donner the dog, occupied a house on the shore in Santa Monica.

Gene, serving on a Navy ship, might be in grave danger.

When she'd left her house, Ann Sothern had been swimming laps in her pool. Had she heard the news bulletin?

Where was Reggie right now? And Greer and Nina Garson?

She was trapped inside this soundstage, prevented from racing home to hold her son and seek shelter. If the Japanese attacked today, she didn't want to die in Culver City.

"Places," Fleming called to his male actors.

Hedy retreated to the area where her make-up girl was standing by. "Hand me a tissue," she choked, as tears gathered and fell.

America would certainly retaliate against Japan for this tragic and deadly act of aggression. Hedy hoped her adopted country would also join the Allies in their struggle to save the Western Hemisphere from Hitler.

Chapter 27

Asustained blast from the Super Chief signaled its arrival at the Pasadena train station. With a hiss of steam and a squeal of brakes, the engine pulled up at the platform. Hedy fidgeted with the clasp of her handbag, impatiently waiting for her mother to appear. After a five-year separation, she was seconds away from the longed-for, long-delayed reunion.

A gentleman passenger helped Mutti exit the carriage, and a Pullman porter handed down a sleek black Scottie dog. Breathless with emotion, Hedy rushed over to hug them both.

A dozen cameras clicked.

"Turn this way, Hedy!"

"How does it feel to see your ma again?"

"Will you introduce Mrs. Kiesler to John Howard first, or, Reggie Gardiner, or George Montgomery?"

"What do you think about America, ma'am?"

Unfazed by the attention, Mutti answered, "It is wonderful to be here."

Never had Hedy been more conscious of her parent's remarkable fortitude. After enduring her daughter's scandal and her husband's sudden death and her country's invasion, she'd experienced London's devastation by Nazi bombs and a journey across the ocean during wartime. Yet here she stood, small of stature, so refined and ladylike in her dark suit and pearls, as though she'd arrived at a garden party.

In the car, they held each other tightly, chattering away in German.

"I see how famous you are, Hedl, with reporters following you even to the train station. Who are the men they think I will be meeting?"

"Reggie is my friend, and I dated John. But that was before I fell in love with Georgie. He's divinely handsome and makes me so very happy." She petted the terrier, asking, "Was Chérie a good traveler?"

"She didn't care for the train but was quite happy on board the ship. We could walk on the deck for exercise, and the Greek sailors spoiled her. For me it was worrisome, I would be always looking in the sky for a German warplane. California weather is so warm! Canada in January is colder than Austria." She gave Hedy a keen look. "Tell me more about the handsome lover."

"He grew up in Montana, where he was a rodeo cowboy. But his parents came from Sebastopol, so we all speak Russian together. He's an actor now. And an award-winning painter. And he builds furniture. We met a few weeks ago, but I'd elope with him tomorrow. If he asked me."

"You give your heart away so quickly, Hedl."

Mutti had flung the first criticism within minutes of their reunion—and not the last, Hedy was certain. Disregarding it, she said blithely, "You'll meet Georgie tonight, because we don't let a day go by without spending time together. He visits me at the studio, or joins me for supper, or takes me to out for dinner and a movie."

Compared to the palatial Mandl residences, and the Kieslers' home in Döbling, the rented house in Beverly Hills must seem small to her mother. She noticed the Austrian touches Hedy incorporated—cheerful chintz and black oak furniture—and looked forward to using the swimming pool. Pat the mutt befriended Chérie the Scottie, and together they trotted happily around the property.

Mutti doted on Jamesie. She won him over with a stuffed toy of a Mountie purchased during her stay in Canada. Hedy provided her with a glass of fresh-squeezed orange juice and an aspirin and took her up the stairs to the cozy guest bedroom for a nap. She went to the kitchen to help her cook prepare a celebratory dinner.

George Montgomery soon appeared, tall and blond and tanned, and eager to make a good first impression.

"I've loved your daughter ever since I saw *Algiers,*" he told Mutti. "I went more than once. Eventually I found out where she lived. In hopes of meeting her, I sometimes watched for her when she drove to her studio."

"And then one day," Hedy interjected, "some friends invited me to their house to play tennis. Georgie was leaving at the moment my date and I arrived."

"Everybody in town believed she and John Howard were engaged, or about to be. I was so jealous and downhearted that Fred MacMurray's wife Lily took pity on me and gave me her number. I called and called, but never found her at home. One day I followed her car all the way to Culver City."

"Where is this?" Mutti asked.

"To MGM," Hedy explained. "I agreed to go on a date if we could have dinner at Little Hungary. But he wanted to impress me, so we went to Mocambo first."

"I never told you," said Georgie, "but I borrowed the money I spent that night from my brother."

"I must remember to thank him." With a reminiscent smile, she went on, "We danced a lot and talked so much."

"And drove all around. I used up the family gas ration."

"The next day you sent flowers," she recalled dreamily. "And every day since."

"Another whirlwind romance," her mother commented. "Like with Fritz. And the second husband."

Hedy's temper simmered at this unwelcome reminder of past mistakes. "This is different," she insisted. "Georgie and I are close in age. His parents aren't rich like the Mandls. He grew up on a ranch. He didn't attend an Ivy League college like Gene did."

"I wasn't sure what to expect," Georgie admitted, "dating a famous movie star. But my Penny turned out to be a real homebody. She cares a lot less about her career than people realize."

"You call her Penny?"

Answering for him, Hedy explained, "Whenever I get very quiet, he says 'penny for your thoughts.' It's an American phrase."

After carrying the coffee tray into the sitting room, she returned to the kitchen to rinse the dishes. Given time, her man could charm Mutti. She was tying an apron around her waist when she heard the slam of a car door.

The Ford Mercury belonging to her other George was in the driveway.

Without removing her apron or putting down the dish towel, she hurried outside.

"We just finished our dinner. You should come in and meet my Mutti. She arrived today."

"When I'm in a better mood. I would've phoned but you deserve to get the news in person." His expression warned her that it wasn't good.

"Something's gone wrong. The Secret Communication System?"

"I'm afraid so." He leaned against the maroon door and lit a cigarette. "Disregarding the Council's strong support and equally strong recommendation, the Navy declines to develop it. The mechanism as proposed, in their opinion, is too big and bulky and heavy to incorporate in a torpedo. But don't worry. Their lack of comprehension has no bearing on our patent application."

"What's the point of having one, if nobody wants to use the device?"

"You never know," he said with a twisted smile. "We'll keep working at it. I don't doubt you've plenty of other brilliant ideas in that busy head of yours. In the meantime, I'll be writing a requiem symphony for my brother. And searching for our next home." He exhaled a cloud of smoke. "Boski wants to move away from Manhattan Beach. We're living in a war zone, she says. The house shakes every time the defense plant tests their anti-aircraft guns, and she's cross about having to remove all her dishes from the shelves to keep them intact. She's also concerned that all the explosions will turn Peter into a nervous child. Actually, he thinks the booms are exciting. But if the Japs invade, I'd just as soon not be living in their path."

"You could have the little house beside my pool." She led him around the back and pointed out the boxy little building at the far edge of the property. "It's furnished. Why pay rent when you can have this for nothing?"

"Don't you go swimming every day?"

"After breakfast, before I go to work. Sometimes Ann Sothern comes over to use the pool, whether or not I'm here."

"Boski won't stand for my regular exposure to gorgeous movie stars, a brunette *and* a blonde, in their bathing suits. My susceptibility is no secret."

"We've been through this before. I plan to marry Georgie. Ann has a boyfriend. It's quiet here, day and night, so you could compose in perfect peace. Our dog hardly ever barks."

"I'll tell Boski about your generous offer, but I doubt she'll accept. Must get home before dark. No headlights allowed during blackout."

They walked back to his car.

Just before he started his engine, she said, "We could overturn the Navy's objection by being more specific about our methodology. The electrical components weren't meant to be large."

Shaking his head, he replied, "Our military is fighting on multiple fronts. Most likely they lack the ability and the manpower to investigate new weapons systems. They're far too busy using the ones they've got."

⎯⎯⊂·◆·⊃⎯⎯

Critical successes in *Comrade X* and *H.R. Pulham,* combined with advance buzz about *Tortilla Flat,* turned Hedy into a very hot property. Every director in town wanted her. Michael Curtiz at Warner Brothers offered her the role of the European heroine in an upcoming production set in Casablanca. Mayer, consistent in his refusal to loan her to another studio, cast her as William Powell's wife in *Crossroads*. After the strong-willed ladies of her recent films, it was another setback. Every time fortune favored her, Mayer made a bad decision and obstructed her progress.

Her home life, at least, provided a measure of contentment. Before breakfast she and her mother swam together. Ann Sothern, who often joined them, helped Hedy tend the Victory Garden that had replaced her flower beds. When strolling through their neighborhood, they signed autographs for the servicemen they encountered along the way.

On a morning when she wasn't in a hurry to get to the studio, she and Mutti lingered at the pool's edge with Jamesie.

"I like so much your Reggie. And that lovely Russian girl he brought here the other day, the fashion model. Your John, whose mother I see at the hairdresser's, is a very good man. But this Georgie, I'm not sure of. I've never known anyone to be so cheerful all the time, always laughing. Last week you told an interviewer you will marry him and go back to your farmhouse in the hills and have twelve children."

"I was joking. About that many children."

"You got no settlement or support from the nice Mr. Markey who visited Jamesie the other day. You receive a check sometimes from Fritz, but as his family grows you can't depend on his generosity. Georgie hasn't much money."

"It doesn't matter. I'm earning a lot. So will he when he's better known, and isn't making so many Westerns."

"If you love him for himself, that is a good thing. But I wish his initials weren't the same as your last husband's. It seems like a bad omen."

"The family's last name is Letz. He changed it. Just like Mr. Mayer changed mine."

The next time Georgie visited her on the lot, his clothes and face were mud-streaked from some outdoor project. She was elegantly outfitted for a scene at a classical music concert.

"Brought you a present, Penny. The nicest one I could find." From his front pocket he removed a ring set with a square blue-white diamond. "You're going to marry me, aren't you?"

"It's so very pretty, I suppose I'd better." Unconcerned about getting dirt on her Irene Kalloch evening gown, she flung her arms around him and kissed him until both of them were breathless.

"Let's tell your publicist right away, so he can get the announcement in tomorrow's papers."

"Couldn't we keep it to ourselves for a little while? My cook will make a special dinner for us, and we can tell Mutti and Jamesie."

Shaking his golden head, he replied regretfully, "They want me on the set at Twentieth Century tonight. People will figure out pretty quick that we're engaged, if you're wearing my ring. Might as well make it public."

She was in love, more intensely than she'd imagined possible, and she couldn't deny anything he asked.

Within a day the press release was issued, accompanied by a photograph taken when he'd visited her *Tortilla Flat* set. At Georgie's urging, they participated in joint interviews, receiving a steady stream of magazine writers and gossip columnists at her studio or in her home. Whenever she stated her strong preference for a speedy, surreptitious Las Vegas ceremony, he declared that he wouldn't deprive her of the big Hollywood wedding appropriate to her star status.

She aired her frustrations to her friends over lunch at the Brown Derby. Each of them had something to celebrate. Hedy was newly engaged and embarking on a new role, Greer had completed *Random Harvest* and purchased a Beverly Hills mansion, and Ann had filed for divorce. Ever mindful of their figures, all three ordered salads.

"I *won't* let Mr. Mayer walk me down the aisle," Hedy said darkly. "It's his dearest wish—he said so after I eloped with Gene. Even if I wanted an elaborate ceremony, I don't have a spare minute to plan it. Not while playing an oversexed mixed-caste seductress, who slithers about in a sarong."

"Good heavens," Greer gasped.

"You haven't heard the worst. I marry a naïve white man, and try to murder him so I can have Walter Pidgeon instead. Your Mr. Miniver," she added.

Ann smirked. "In real life her Mr. Miniver is the younger one, that handsome boy who played her son. Cradle robber!" She crunched a stuffed celery stick.

A rosy blush tinted the redhead's cheeks, and she glanced around the room to check for eavesdroppers. "Mr. Mayer is furious. He's so worried about a scandal that he made us promise to see each other only in private, at my house. With Mother as our chaperone."

Ann muttered, "Your Richard better not turn out to be another George Montgomery, romancing a Metro star to boost his career."

Greer was quick to say, "Did I tell you that Mr. Roosevelt and Mr. Churchill have both previewed *Mrs. Miniver*? They're saying it will be a big boost to morale in America and Britain."

Hedy frowned at Ann. "Why did you say that about Georgie?" Suspecting a conspiracy, she turned on Greer. "You knew what she meant, because you were in such a hurry to change the subject."

"One of us should tell her," Greer said. "Before somebody else does."

Ann wiped a speck of cheese from her cherry-red lips.

"Well? I'm waiting."

Avoiding Hedy's gaze, Ann pleated her napkin. "Your Georgie has a history of attaching himself to the most newsworthy actresses. He started with Ginger Rogers. After she dropped him, his publicist advised him to date you. According to a friend of mine at Twentieth Century Fox."

"Reggie Gardiner works there, too," Greer said. "He told me the same thing."

"Why didn't he tell *me?*"

"I hoped he would." Her voice heavy with sympathy, Greer added, "But Benny Thau and Mr. Mayer didn't want you to find out. They worried you'd have an emotional breakdown, and they needed to keep *Crossroads* on schedule."

"Is there any one in town who *doesn't* know?"

"It might only be soundstage gossip," Ann said in an all too obvious effort to make amends. "Even if Georgie did ask you out for publicity, he fell in love with you. How could he not? And he's going to marry you."

But he'd admitted tracking her route to the studio, watching for her, and visiting the MacMurrays in hopes of meeting her. Before he proposed, he'd taken her to inexpensive diners and even cheaper drive-ins. Now that they were engaged, he escorted her to popular nightclubs and parties. He'd insisted on the press release. Instead of a private elopement, he was determined to have a lavish ceremony attended by Hollywood's most important people.

Hedy stared at the diamond on her finger. "At least I learned the truth before the wedding instead of after."

I listened to my heart, like Papa told me to. And it didn't turn out as well as he promised it would.

All of her prior romances had ended slowly, gradually, as familiarity dulled emotional intensity until she fell out of love. Shattered trust and wounded pride, she discovered, had an instantaneous effect. This, her first severe heartbreak, was devastating. Because her love life was public property, a broken engagement would be aggressively covered, stirring up intense speculation about the cause.

Without referring to her friends' revelations, she told Georgie she wasn't ready to marry again.

"But I'm mad about you, Penny."

"What if it's only an infatuation? So much better for us both if we don't pretend it's something more." Handing over the diamond ring, she wondered whether he detected her implicit accusation.

By the end of the week, he was keeping company with sultry Rita Hayworth.

Hedy shrugged off her misery and made sure she was photographed at the most popular nightspots with her admirers—Charlie Chaplin and Orson Welles and Jean-Pierre Aumont. She resumed her relationship with John Howard, on a purely casual basis.

She found and furnished an apartment for Mutti, set up her bank account, and arranged the deposit of a monthly allowance. She skipped Ann Sothern's Fourth of July picnic to move her belongings, her child, their pets, and the servants back to the Benedict Canyon house she'd abandoned after divorcing Gene. She hired a decorator, who rapturously admired the parlor's antique mantelpiece, attributed to the English carving master Grinling Gibbons. Chairs and sofas were reupholstered. She picked out a chintz pattern with a cheerful yellow background and sewed new curtains. She re-stocked her chicken coops, and once again sold fresh eggs bearing the name Hedgerow Farm.

Her houseboy Mark helped her till a Victory Garden. Armed with a child-sized spade and trowel, Jamesie enthusiastically dug holes for the vegetable plants and herbs obtained from Myrna Loy.

A fresh beginning in a familiar place.

It would do. For now.

———◦•◆•◦———

Over a year after Hedy and George filed their application, their attorney notified them they had received a patent for the Secret Communication System. Official documentation would arrive at a later date.

"What value does it have?" she asked George as they left the lawyer's office. "The Inventors' Council and the Navy rejected our plans."

"It's a rare accomplishment, Hedy. And who knows? Perhaps those numbskulls in Washington will reconsider."

"They might not care about my radio-directed torpedo, but they've asked me to sell War Bonds. And I will. That's how the government want me to help America beat Hitler."

No longer preoccupied with romance, or inventions, she threw herself into the role of Tondelayo in *White Cargo*. Her uninhibited portrayal of the ruthless wanton ought to persuade moviegoers—and Mr. Mayer—of her versatility. But at the preview screening, she was dismayed to see that the African dance she'd spent weeks rehearsing had been drastically edited.

She expressed her frustration to Reggie when they ran into each other at Charlie Foy's Supper Club.

"I worked so hard. All the twisting and lunging gave me a backache that won't go away."

"I daresay your sensual dance was more stirring than the Hays

Office would permit. The verdict would of course be the same if I performed in scanty attire."

She regarded him with affection. "They'll keep you in uniform for the rest of your career. You looked quite dashing in *The Great Dictator.*"

"I'd be wearing a real one, like David Niven and Leslie Howard, if the British Embassy hadn't insisted on my remaining in Hollywood." He tapped the end of his unlit cigarette against the white tablecloth. "I'm signing up for a different tour of duty, a pleasanter and more lasting one. Nadia and I are getting married."

Hedy struggled to interpret her emotions. As his devoted friend, she regarded this as good news. Yet she was conscious of an overriding envy that he'd achieved the contentment and companionship that eluded her.

"What a headline that will make. Hollywood's most popular bachelor, settling down!"

"About time, don't you think? The demands of my social life are extraordinary. And so exhausting."

"I wish both of you all the happiness in the world. When is your wedding?"

"Later in the year, after I finish *The Immortal Sergeant.* Nadia plans to visit her family in New York and arrange for furniture to be sent out. RKO still has her under contract, but she's more interested in being a housewife than continuing as a bit player. You realize, matrimony will require my resignation from this town's most exclusive club, for all the actors who dated Hedy Lamarr but didn't marry her. John Howard can succeed me as president. His first official act will be inducting George Montgomery and Jean-Pierre Aumont as new members."

Hedy sighed. "I ought to start a club of my own. For lonely hearts."

"My poor darling, as bad as that? I was awfully sorry your Georgie turned out to be a bounder."

"So was I." She smiled across the table. "I never quite lose hope that my next romance will turn out better than all the others. I wish I could meet a wonderful man who can complement my life. Without complicating my career."

Chapter 28

Hedy's ruling desire to support the fight against fascism was her primary reason for participating in the Stars Across America Tour to sell War Bonds. She also looked forward to seeing unfamiliar regions of her adopted country. And she was relieved to have a convenient and well-timed escape from Hollywood.

She and other stars, in groups of ten, would fan out across the nation, visiting up to three hundred cities. The tour's inaugural events took place in Washington, a city that seemed to consist entirely of enormous white government buildings. The most impressive one housed the United States Treasury.

"It needs to be this large," Hedy said to the Treasury Secretary as he led the Hollywood contingent on a tour, "to hold all the money we'll bring in. One billion dollars in bonds, that's our goal."

After she and her colleagues addressed citizens overseas via shortwave radio broadcast, they were guests of honor at a luncheon. On the following day, they joined various government officials in front of the vast edifice for the campaign's opening rally.

"Look at us," Greer murmured as they paraded across the platform with Irene Dunne and Bing Crosby and James Cagney, and all the rest. "Who's the fairest one of all? I reckon Secretary Morgenthau would choose you. He's obviously smitten."

The two of them stood on either side of the gentleman at the microphone, hooking their arms through his as he began his address to the tens of thousands of government employees, soldiers, sailors, local residents, and the policemen who had the unenviable task of controlling the crowd.

Morgenthau introduced Greer, who launched into a call to action. "Remember, our weapons of victory—planes and guns and bombs and battleships—must be paid for. Some of us build them. Some of us will fight with them. But each of us has to pay for them. With our War Bonds!"

When it was Hedy's turn to speak, her voice shook from nerves and rising emotion. "I'm proud and happy to do my bit in the war effort." She'd already done more than they knew, with George Antheil's help, but the enthusiastic response to her simple words told her that this contribution would be more effective.

Any star's autograph could be had for the purchase of a bond. Hedy and Greer pinned an orchid corsage on each of the first one hundred women to buy one. At the conclusion of the event, sales totaled more than a million and a half dollars.

Thankful to return to the hotel room, Hedy said "I call that a good day's work." She rubbed the ache in her back. "Next time we'll do even better!"

"It's the public speaking I dread," Greer confessed. "I'm too shy. The crowd went mad over you."

"For both of us. We should write down our speeches and memorize them." She massaged her temples. "I wish we were traveling together."

In the morning, Hedy and her group boarded a train for Philadelphia. Her first appearance took place at a well-attended luncheon. So many people wanted to meet her that she couldn't finish her meal.

At the Navy Yard she gave a brief address that drew cheers from the assembled workers. Stepping down from the podium, she mentioned to her escort that she was extremely hungry.

A shipwright who overheard her opened his lunchbox and handed her a sandwich. She bit off a huge mouthful and gave it back. Holding it up, he shouted that he would preserve it for posterity.

Before leaving the site, she learned that her midday appearance had netted four and a half million dollars.

On to York, where she met with employees at a lock and safe company.

"I've come to you as a gold-digger for Uncle Sam, so we can win the war," she declared. "You came so you could see what that Hedy Lamarr dame looks like. But we should be here for the very same purpose. What you think about my looks doesn't worry me like what Hitler and Hirohito are doing. Each time you reach in your pockets or your handbags, you're telling those two rotten men that the Yanks are coming for them. Buy bonds! I'm a mother. And I say you need to protect America the same way you do your very own child."

She was whisked away to the neighboring state of New Jersey. Anyone who bought a one thousand-dollar bond could ride with her through Newark's Military Park. From there she passed through Orange, New Brunswick, and Elizabeth—where someone offered a thousand-dollar contribution if she sang "God Bless America." No matter how fierce her backache or how stiff her face from constant smiling, she stayed at each location until she'd shaken every purchaser's hand.

The people she met treated her as though she was a friend, based on the information—factual or invented—flowing form Howard Strickling's publicity department. They obtained their knowledge from her films and fan magazine interviews and newspaper gossip columns. Patriots all, they handed over their salaries and their life savings, their grocery money and their children's piggy bank coins. Whether rich or poor, young or old, they were unified in their support of freedom and their determination to secure victory over their enemies.

Portions of her speeches were quoted by press, locally and all across the country. When asked to provide a written account about her tour, she was glad to share her reflections and describe meaningful encounters.

At times I'm sure that I know more about the freedom that we are fighting for than millions who were born in the United States and who have come to accept liberty as their rightful heritage. It must be fought for, won, and then cherished. America is the last stop for freedom. We've got to fight to protect it, and that is why I was glad to help in the government's campaign to sell a billion dollars' worth of War Bonds. It is the least I can do . . .

A great many people ask if selling bonds is a harder job than acting. I wouldn't know. Because I'm not acting on this job. You've got to be sincere to get your message across to the people. They know insincerity when they see it. When I return to Hollywood to start work on my next picture, I'll be grateful for my memories of this bond tour. It has taught me that America is even greater than I thought—and Americans are a kind, generous people who won't give up their freedom.

And that, my friends, is something worth knowing.

Hedy's ten days on the road had taken her to sixteen cities, and her appearances pulled in twenty-five million dollars. She returned to Hedgerow Farm to rest her injured back, spend time with her son, and restore her energy so she could resume her fundraising and pay visits to nearby army bases.

Bette Davis enlisted her support in a new patriotic project, and this one was closer to home.

"*Dar-ling!*" the actress's famously husky voice brayed over the phone. "Bette here. I'm sure you've heard that Johnny Garfield and I are about to open the Hollywood Canteen. It will be a place for our brave soldiers and sailors to cut loose and be waited on hand and foot by us movie people. Johnny says, and I agree, that you're the star our heroes in uniform most want to meet."

"They want to meet you, too," said Hedy diplomatically. Sharp-tongued Bette was notorious for feuding. It was good policy to stay in her good graces.

Not bothering to acknowledge the compliment, Bette charged ahead with her pitch. "Our Canteen is strictly for the enlisted men, no officers allowed. No booze and no rowdiness, just good, clean fun. And plenty of food. Forty-two of our industry unions and guilds have banded together to make this happen. Members volunteered their time to fix up that derelict nightclub on Cahuenga Boulevard. I'm decorating it like our big old barns back in New England, rustic and homey. And we've got financial support from all the studios, so everything we offer the boys will be free of charge."

"I'll be there. As often as you want me."

"Don't imagine you'll simply show up and look beautiful and hand out autographs. You're going to serve the coffee and make the sandwiches and clean up at the end of the last shift. And we ladies will be dancing our feet off, because there's going to be an orchestra every night. Xavier Cougat, Glen Miller, Kay Kyser, Harry James. All the greats. We're setting up bleachers near the entrance so famous people can pay fifty bucks apiece to watch the real stars, our military folk, coming and going. I want klieg lights rotating outside every night, like a premiere. The blackout be damned!"

On the night of the opening gala, the line of uniformed men stretched all the way around to Sunset Boulevard, and the outdoor spectator seats were packed.

Hedy, sporting an Austrian dirndl, arrived at the appointed time with Greer. Bette, who looked ready to drop from exhaustion and illness, gave her volunteers a quick but comprehensive tour of the premises. Murals decorated the walls, and tables surrounded a central dance floor lit by wagon wheel chandeliers. On one side of the room was the stage, where Duke Ellington's orchestra was setting up, and a small control booth was squeezed into a corner. An upper balcony was set aside for servicewomen.

Marlene Dietrich stood behind the snack bar counter, cutting cakes.

Joan Crawford arranged mugs on a metal trolley beside the giant metal coffee urns. Linda Darnell emerged from the kitchen with a tray of prepared sandwiches. Over at the drinks cooler, John Garfield, Hedy's *Tortilla Flat* co-star, trained a group of aproned actors to be busboys.

Bette distributed printed instructions to the hostesses. Her voice rough from laryngitis, she stressed the importance of providing their guests with pleasant memories.

"When you encounter combat veterans who are convalescing from wounds, deal with them sensitively. They may or may not want to talk about their experiences in battle. Listen to them, but never ask any questions. Understand?"

The glossy heads nodded in unison.

"You can go to the lounge and get your name badges. Good luck!" she croaked. "Where are my glamor girls? We've printed up stacks of cards for you to sign."

Hedy started out at the snack bar, serving sandwiches and signatures until Bette ordered her to circulate. Uncomfortable with strangers, she'd always avoided dancing with men she didn't know well. But as the musicians started playing a foxtrot, she tapped a sailor on the shoulder, and would forever remember his amazement when he recognized her. Her next partner turned out to be a skilled swing dancer, and he didn't seem to care that she couldn't match Ann Sothern's expertise. Every fifth number was a slow one, and the sight of so many hostesses waltzing with the warriors brought a lump to her throat.

Before Kay Kyser's band took over, Abbott and Costello told jokes and interviewed members of the crowd, asking whether they were stationed in the vicinity, or on furlough.

"Isn't it wonderful?" Greer cried when they switched places at the counter. "Being here is the perfect cure for loneliness. I've spent too many nights at home, missing Richard and writing long, wistful letters. Here, I can feel useful."

Hedy had no chance to reply. A trio of soldiers crowded around, eager to tell her she was their favorite actress. When she handed the card with her autograph to one of them, he gave it back.

"Kiss it for me," he begged.

"All right. But I'd rather kiss you," she said, and proved it.

By midnight her feet and spine were protesting, and her eyes burned with fatigue. She helped clear away utensils and plates, carrying them to the kitchen. Rosalind Russell was washing the dishes while a newspaper photographer took pictures.

"Well, ladies," Bette croaked, setting down her empty cigarette tray, "we've had a big success. We expected three thousand guests tonight, but the doorman told me a policeman said the number was closer to twelve thousand. No wonder we ran out of food and drinks."

"The men didn't mind," Hedy said. "They were having the time of their lives."

She stayed at Greer's house, so she wouldn't have to drive herself back to Benedict Canyon in the middle of the night. It was her first visit to the Tudor-style mansion

Before following her friend up the soaring staircase, she peeked into the drawing room. "Two grand pianos!" she marveled. "What luxury."

"Richard Ney and I used to play four-hand duets. Before he enlisted." She showed Hedy to the guest room, a bower of floral chintz, and provided her with an elegant silk negligee, trimmed with lace.

"Tomorrow is Sunday, so we can sleep late. I won't bother washing my hair tonight."

"That's a disappointment. I wanted to find out whether you really do rinse it with champagne."

"You'll have to take my word for it. Or Mother's. Sweet dreams, dearie."

Hedy slept soundly through the night, until roused by a tap on the door. Greer, accompanied by her two large poodles, was delivering a tray with tea and toast.

Hedy tried to sit up. "I can't move," she wailed. Her back was stiff, and the slightest motion produced piercing pain.

"I'm taking you to the hospital."

She stared at the ceiling. "I should go home. Jamesie will wonder why I'm not there."

Fortified by pain pills, she struggled through days of screen tests and singing lessons in preparation for a role in a musical, until desperation drove her to her doctor. Diagnosed with a damaged nerve, she spent several days in the hospital. The specialist refused to discharge her unless she agreed to a period of treatment and a rest cure at a sanitarium in the mountains.

Reggie picked her up and drove her back to Benedict Canyon.

She was thinking how handsome and debonair he was, this Englishman she'd gently but firmly discarded, and how reliable and caring, when he spoke of his marriage plans.

The timing, he explained, was now uncertain. "We wanted to have the wedding at a Santa Barbara church. But because of gas rationing, it would be inconvenient for our friends. Now we've got to find one in Los Angeles. I'll let you know as soon as we set the date."

"I can't be there," she told him. "Not because I don't want to be. During my time away, I made up my mind. Everything must be perfect and special for you and Nadia. My presence will be a distraction."

"Not to me. I'll be standing up front with the padre, quaking in my shoes."

"Don't joke about this, darling. Did you and Nadia find a house?"

Eyes still on the road, he replied, "A very small one, but it's close to the studio. Five rooms. I'm hanging your portrait in one of them."

"I can save you the trouble. Name your price."

"I've told you a dozen times, I'm not selling my beautiful 'Scorpie.'"

On Friday, she returned to the Hollywood Canteen as designated hostess for the weekly "Hedy Lamarr Night." Entering through the volunteers' door at the back of the building, on Cole Street, she passed through the kitchen where an assembly line of senior hostesses prepared baloney sandwiches. In the dance hall, the junior hostesses arranged tables and chairs. They checked each other's makeup and hair. For the rest of the night they would be diverting "the boys" from the uncertainties and hardships of military life during the weeks, months, perhaps years to come.

When the doors opened at six o'clock, the first batch of servicemen was admitted, five hundred of them, for their hour of entertainment and refreshment. Many had arrived on the liberty buses making the rounds of military installations. Others had hitchhiked. Inside, the men banded together in packs of three or more, companionably smoking and joking. The majority were white, and those who weren't stuck together. The women in uniform, aware that they were less desirable partners than the stars and starlets, watched the dancing from seats in the balcony.

Standing at the microphone, Hedy offered a warm welcome, introduced the bandleader, and announced the raffle for a day pass. She spent the rest of her shift dispensing autographs and kisses.

A marine, painfully young, wanted her to sign his cap.

Before applying her pen, she hesitated. "Does your dress code allow that?"

"Miss Lamarr, some things are worth getting sent to the brig for!" His pals laughed and punched his arm.

During the brief break before the second shift, she visited the lounge where the men made long-distance telephone calls to family members and sweethearts. The message boards attached to the walls were covered with their penciled notes to hometown friends or basic training comrades who might be passing through.

Waltzing with an Infantryman, Hedy spied George Montgomery in a busboy's apron, clearing a nearby table. Their eyes locked. She was the first to look away, laying her cheek on her partner's broad shoulder. By the time the music ended, her former fiancé was flirting with Carole Landis.

Bette, also eyeing the couple, grumbled, "He shouldn't be sparking our hostesses, it's against the rules. Carole makes a habit of consoling your castoffs, doesn't she? For a while it looked as though she'd become the third Mrs. Gene Markey."

"I hoped she would be. I like her."

"That's generous."

"This horrible war is making me a better person," Hedy confided. "Volunteer work has become much more important to me than my career. When we're selling bonds or working here, we're with all those people we're making the movies for. It helps me understand America, and all the reasons these men are fighting."

Bette released a cloud of cigarette smoke. "Would you consider sponsoring another weeknight? I'd love to have you here on Wednesdays, if you can manage it."

"I can. I will."

Seeking a brief respite from the frenzied atmosphere, she retreated to the cleanup station. Marlene Dietrich, who relished tasks behind the scenes, was hard at work. They chatted in German, Marlene washing dishes and Hedy drying them, until Bette, an efficient and omnipresent manager, stuck her brassy head through the door.

"Get those two Krauts out of the kitchen!" she yelped to no one in particular. "I want them on the dance floor."

Apart from occasional *Lux Radio Hour* and Edgar Bergen broadcasts, Hedy wasn't working. Her studio identified and rejected several projects as they raked in profits from the classic mystery *Crossroads* and the sensational, scandalous *White Cargo*.

In the closing weeks of the year, she hosted meetings of disgruntled fellow workers at Hedgerow Farm. President Roosevelt planned to cap annual salaries of film industry employees at twenty-five thousand dollars, regardless of their contract stipulations, for the duration of the war. The unpaid amount would go to the government, with disbursement to occur at some future date. Her colleagues lobbied her to serve as both spokeswoman and test case. Conflicted, she thought long and hard.

She supported her adopted country in many ways, public and private. She'd offered the Navy her frequency-hopping technology, which she and George had handed over without expectation of payment or credit. Her appearances during the War Bond campaign had raised millions of dollars. Two nights every week, she danced and served at the Canteen. And she welcomed soldiers to Hedgerow Farm, offering them hospitality and respite from the rigors of life on a military base.

But at the same time, Hedy resented involuntarily contributing a punitive percentage of her income. Those who labored to create the films that reinforced morale and promoted American values deserved compensation. For three months, her salary had been docked by five-hundred dollars per week.

On a Wednesday evening in December, Bette cornered her. "I know it's a lot to ask, when you're already hostessing for us twice a week, but can you come tomorrow night, too? For the first or second shift, or both. It's our holiday party, our biggest event yet. You're so popular with the boys, and I'm going to be short-handed. I'd be ever so grateful if you could put in an appearance."

She'd planned a traditional *Heilege Abend* with tree lighting and carols and Austrian food, but she was willing to make an adjustment. "I'll get here as early as I can and stay till closing."

"I've begged and pleaded, and so many people have excuses. Now I know who the real patriots are. And which of my friends are actually Jewish," Bette added with a wink. "The ones with no plans on Christmas Eve."

The next afternoon Hedy taught Jamesie the words to *"Stille Nacht,"* and they sang to Mutti's piano accompaniment. After dinner, she changed into her most festive and formal dirndl and called a taxicab.

"You are an *an*-gel to come here tonight," Bette cawed, giving her a hug. "I'd stick you on top of our tree, but that wouldn't be fair to our brave men. Here's a chap you should meet. My *dar*-ling John Loder, the only actor as generous with his time as you are. You'll remember him from *Now, Voyager.* We spend our days together at Warner's, shooting *Old Acquaintance.* He plays the husband of that bitch Miriam Hopkins. But he's in love with me."

"Of course," Hedy said, amused. Before she could exchange words with the actor, neither a complete stranger nor yet an acquaintance, a sandy-haired, red-cheeked sailor boy invited her to dance.

It wasn't long before Bette directed her to the snack bar to serve food. While there, she also signed her name on whatever was shoved in front of her—napkins and paper scraps, postcards, and dramatic, high contrast black and white photographs of her own face. Green boughs and red bunting and glittering white stars decorated the walls, and the orchestra played all the most popular Christmas songs, many of them crooned by Bing Crosby and his sons. A man wore a Santa Claus suit, and dog-loving Bette received a large pup as a gift.

John Loder, tall and distinguished, with medium brown hair, was a most handsome busboy. Every time he passed Hedy, she received a warm smile and a friendly nod. When he stopped coming by, she assumed he'd already left for the night and was sorry she hadn't been able to talk to him.

After closing time, she swept the floor and helped Bette stack the last of the dirty dishes.

"There are hundreds more in the kitchen. Any chance you can stay to wash up? I'd help, but I *des*-perately need to go over the accounts with our office manager before we close for the holiday."

John Loder stood at the sink, a bib apron attached to his tall frame.

"Reinforcements!" he greeted her. He handed her a dish towel. "No reason to mar those pretty hands. You can dry."

"I don't mind washing."

"I reckon I've got more experience than you. I did my share of kitchen patrol when I was a prisoner of war, in Germany."

"You couldn't have been very old."

He handed her a dripping plate. "After Sandhurst, I was commissioned an officer in the Fifteenth Hussars, a cavalry regiment. I was the youngest." His accent was as purely British as Reggie's, but with a cadence of its own. "I survived Gallipoli, and the Somme. About six months before the Armistice, I had the bad luck to get captured by the Germans on the road to Amiens, and they shipped me over the border in a cattle train. I was in three different camps before the Peace. After my release, the British army kept me in Germany. After resigning my commission, I started a factory with a close friend."

"What type of factory?"

"We bottled and sold pickles."

"Pickles!"

"Very successfully. Until the change of currency and revaluation bankrupted us. I was at low ebb when Alexander Korda hired me. I made several pictures in Berlin."

"Which studio?"

"Staaken."

"I was with Sascha-Tobis-Film. One picture in Berlin, the rest in Vienna."

"By then I must have returned to England. I would remember you if we'd met."

Clearly flattered by her interest, he told her his real name was John Lowe, and he'd planned to become an actor since his school days at Eton. One grandfather was a Sicilian nobleman, and his mother descended from Scottish baronets. His British father rose through the officer ranks to become a general. Out of consideration for his upper-crust relatives, he used his mother's surname professionally.

Fluent in languages, he'd performed in German and French plays and movies. He knew Salzburg and Vienna from working on a picture about Mozart, shot at Schönbrunn, during the period when she'd been married to Fritz. He told an amusing story about displeasing Frau Sacher with a complaint that his steak was tough and too dry.

"You should only ever eat her schnitzel and the torte." Hedy's voice dipped and wavered from regret when she said, "I don't imagine either of us will return to the Sacher. Even if we could, it wouldn't be the same."

His grown son by his first wife, a German, served in the British Army. John was separated from his second wife. "When the divorce legalities are completed, and after the war ends, Micheline will return to Paris. She hates Hollywood. Our daughter is four years old."

She wondered if he was as devoted a father as Gene was to his Melinda. John was probably aware that she'd also had two marriages and divorces. "My son turns four in a few weeks." Returning to the topic of filmmaking, she asked how he liked working at Warner Brothers.

"Performing with Bette is a nice break from war movies," he

replied. "I used to be at Twentieth Century. Long ago, before you arrived in Hollywood, I was at Paramount. MGM, in its earliest days. And Pathé."

She couldn't tell whether or not he was ambitious, but he seemed not to take his profession too seriously. And he was very obviously enraptured by her.

When Bette barged in with the night watchman, intent on locking up, she found them seated side by side at the worktable, fully absorbed in one another.

"Well, well," she said. "Sorry to bust up the party, but it's high time we all went home. Shoo!"

John helped Hedy into her coat and followed her through the dark dance hall. It was an hour till midnight.

"Almost Christmas," she said.

"Would it be too bold of me to ask for a present, on such short acquaintance?"

He's about to kiss me, she told herself, and he'd better be quick or Bette will catch us.

"I collect autographs. Might I have yours?" He handed her his card.

She rummaged in her purse for a pencil and scrawled her signature on the back. Below it, she added her unlisted telephone number. "If you're free for dinner next week, I'll serve you my wiener schnitzel. And you won't have to wash the dishes."

Chapter 29

After a five-month courtship, Hedy and John Loder were married at a friend's apartment, with her mother and two others as witnesses. Their first congratulatory telegram came from Lieutenant Commander Gene Markey. Because both newlyweds were committed to their respective studios, they postponed the honeymoon.

In protest of MGM's non-payment of her full salary, Hedy had been on strike while her romance with John blossomed. This left her with plenty of leisure time for dinner dates and quiet cinema nights with her new love, who chauffeured her to and from the Hollywood Canteen.

Her bridegroom was sentimental and thoughtful. Every Friday, as a reminder of the day they met, she received a bouquet that contained at least one red rose.

Their compatibility, in and out of bed, was reinforced by shared tastes. His love of literature and music matched hers, and he added many more books and records to the house at Hedgerow Farm. Devoted to home and hearth, he enjoyed quiet evenings by the fireside, reading the newspaper and puffing away on his pipe. He was kind to Jamesie, who called his new stepfather Papshi. Hedy, preferring that son her

bear the Loder surname, urged John to adopt him. As a former caval-
ryman, he envisioned a military career for the boy. He still enjoyed
riding, and insisted on giving his bride instruction in proper English
equitation. Knowing Hedy's love of dogs, he added a Belgian Shepherd
to her menagerie.

After she resolved her latest dispute with MGM, the studio paired
her with her *Crossroads* co-star William Powell in a romantic comedy.
It didn't provide the meaty role she'd wanted. Walter Reisch, the
scriptwriter, had served her better with *Comrade X*. But an astronomer's superstitious wife was a welcome contrast to the sleazy, scheming, sexually-charged Tondelayo, and a lighthearted picture might
repair the damage done by *White Cargo*.

Her new dressing room, which she decorated in the same cottage
style that prevailed at Hedgerow Farm, could function as an apartment, with a bed, a sofa, a bathroom, and a small gas stove. Her secretary dealt with the mountains of fan mail from soldiers and sailors,
and she spent hours personally signing photographs for her devoted,
distant admirers.

The studios struggled with the effects of rationing and the military's heavy demands, as performers and writers and technical staff
either enlisted or were drafted. A large percentage of scripts put into
production featured various theatres of war. Those that didn't depicted
wartime on the home front.

Ann Sothern, recently married to an actor serving in the Air Force,
was Hedy's most frequent dressing room visitor. She usually arrived
from her set in the Army volunteer uniform she wore for her current
role.

"Everyone's making war pictures," Hedy observed, sticking a straw
in a cola bottle and handing it to her friend. "Except me. Your character is stationed on Bataan. Mine flirts with an air raid warden who
tells her to turn out her bedroom light."

"The public needs escapism. That's why my Maisie movies are so
popular."

"Even Maisie went to work in an aircraft factory, building warplanes,"

Hedy reminded her. "She did her part. So does your husband."

"He's training to be a flight instructor, and I'm thankful he won't be sent overseas. But planes scare me. They can be so dangerous. Think of poor Carole Lombard." Ann sighed heavily. "I wonder if Clark will marry again."

"For now, he cares only about dropping bombs on the Germans."

"Maybe he has a death wish. He was an awful mess of a man after her air crash, when he signed up for active duty. I think of Carole whenever I'm peddling War Bonds. She died during a a bond tour, not in battle. But she was a war casualty just the same, wasn't she?" Ann's fingers fluffed her golden mane. "Richard's leave was so short, we had to honeymoon at home. When do you get yours?"

"After our Mexico trip. Mr. Mayer and Mr. Disney are receiving awards there, and we're part of the entourage. As soon as we come back, we're going to Big Bear Lake. It will be heavenly. Staying in a sweet little woodland cabin, wearing a shirt and dungarees all the time, watching the sun rise and set. With nobody around but the birds and the squirrels."

"And the bears."

"John will keep me safe." Hedy glanced at the wedding portrait on her make-up table. "He's so romantic, and quite funny, but it doesn't show on screen because he always plays stuffy English officers. If Warner Brothers won't give him better parts, he should come to MGM. And he'd better leave behind that hideous bathrobe he keeps in his dressing room. It's made out of scraps from all his leading ladies' costumes."

Ann got up. "I expect I'll find you at the Canteen tonight, holding hands with your sweetie."

The delayed honeymoon met Hedy's high expectations of low, casual living. She and John returned to Hedgerow feeling refreshed and very much in tune with each other.

Every morning they walked their dogs along the canyon road. Hedy had named her shepherd dog Oscar, since she wasn't likely to receive the statuette handed out by the Academy. Greer won hers for

Mrs. Miniver. Bette now had two of them and seemed likely to get more, because she was nominated every year.

Hedy and Jamesie gathered eggs from the henhouse and marked them with the Hedgerow Farm rubber stamp. At dusk, she sat with John on the terrace, watching the deer wander down from the hills.

Her days weren't entirely without strife. While gardening, she came upon a rattlesnake at rest near the ducks' enclosure and killed it herself with a well-aimed shovel. A raccoon found its way into the storage room and had to be lured out with dog food and sardines. One day, Jamesie found her sewing scissors and gave himself a trim, cutting off the curls she treasured.

"Hide your scissors from Peter," she advised Boski Antheil when they shopped together along Sunset Boulevard in smart suits designed by Adrian. Hedy had purchased hers from his atelier, and her companion wore one of Janet Gaynor's discards. With a glance at the child clutching his mother's hand, she said in a low voice, "My Jamesie gave himself a crew cut. John is terribly cross and wants to enroll him in the kindergarten at Black Fox Military Academy in Burbank. Don't you think he's too young? He's not yet five."

"Being with other little boys his age can only be good for him."

It wasn't the answer she wanted to hear, but Boski was a firm disciplinarian—of son and of husband alike. "What's George working on these days?"

"He finished his Fourth Symphony, the one you and I agonized over. Leopold Stokowski will conduct the premiere—eventually. Where *is* that man?" Boski muttered, glancing at her watch. "When I phoned him from the shop, he promised to pick us up straightaway. I suppose he's lost in whatever music he's composing."

Hedy studied the flow of passing cars. "Let's try and get a ride. Lots of people do it, because of gas rationing. Anybody heading up the Canyon could drop us at your house."

A rare smile crossed Boski's face. "All right. Who wouldn't stop to pick up a hitchhiker, if she's Hedy Lamarr?"

They positioned themselves, at the corner of Laurel Canyon

Boulevard and Sunset, across from Schwab's, and held up their thumbs. After fifteen minutes, nobody had pulled over. Drivers sped past, stirring up dust that dirtied their shoes and clung to their skirts.

"This is ridiculous," Boski complained. "The world's most famous face can't stop traffic long enough to get a lift. Wait here, I'll go to the drugstore and phone George again."

When he picked them up, they told him what happened. He laughed all the way to the Antheils' house in Laurel Canyon.

In February she joined them to hear the premiere of her friend's Fourth Symphony, featured in a coast-to-coast broadcast.

George, cigarette in hand, fiddled nervously with the radio dial. "No one's going to like it," he moaned. "It's too modern. Too radical. Stokowski fought like hell to get it on the air."

"Why hasn't it started yet?" Hedy demanded, pacing the tiny living room.

Boski entered from the kitchen with an alcoholic drink for her husband and Hedy's Dr. Pepper. "You two won't be stomping around there during the entire performance, will you?"

They did.

At the conclusion, as waves of applause poured through the speaker, everyone collapsed on the sofa in relief.

In his current paying job as a news analyst on a radio program, George offered his interpretations of the war's progress, and his predictions.

"Are you more optimistic about this year than last?" Hedy asked him.

"Much more. The next twelve months will determine the outcome."

"I can't bear another year of soldiers getting wounded and killed. Or people being herded into concentration camps. What use was the National Inventors' Council? It was created to discover wonderful new weapons that would defeat our enemies. We worked so hard for so long on our Secret Communication System, and the magnetic anti-aircraft shell. But it didn't matter at all."

Firmly he told her, "In our different ways, we've done our part to

bring about the end of tyranny. I write books and articles and pontif-
icate over the airwaves. You dance with the boys at the Hollywood
Canteen, and pose for the photos that decorate their bunkhouses.
You've sold I don't know how many millions of War Bonds. When
victory comes, you'll deserve as much thanks as any battle hero."

——◇·◆·◇——

The cast of Hedy's next film referred to it as "Reunion in Vienna,"
despite the fact it was set in Lisbon and titled *The Conspirators*. On
loan to Warner Brothers, she joined expat Austrian actor Paul Henreid
and Peter Lorre, the composer Max Steiner, and Rudi Rohr the editor.
Most of her castmates came from countries afflicted by the Nazis.
Several had appeared together in *Casablanca*. If Mr. Mayer hadn't
refused to loan Hedy, she could have played Ilsa, the part that went to
Ingrid Bergman.

She was back in the glamor game. Her character, an alluring resistance fighter, was married to the villain and in love with the hero. The
studio spared no expense on set decoration, which included a genuine
Versailles tapestry and a massive pair of European cut-glass chandeliers. Some of the action took place at a grand European casino,
thrusting Hedy back into the world she'd known as Frau Mandl. A
change of director pushed the schedule several weeks beyond expectations, adding to the costs and providing Hedy with a healthy boost
to her salary for overtime.

Warner Brothers had transported her portable dressing room
from MGM, with its furniture and the all-important radio and record
player. Between takes, she listened to war bulletins or to George
Antheil's music. John had given her the first pressing of their friend's
latest symphony.

After years of coaching from language expert Ruth Roberts,
Hedy had earned a certificate for Mastery of English Speech. When
she pondered whether she would ever be cast as an American, her
husband declared that her accent was utterly enchanting and expressed

disapproval of her painstaking effort to eradicate it.

"If you sound like every other Hollywood actress, you'll lose too much of your charm. And your uniqueness."

His calm yet pointed method of criticizing frustrated her. And she was picking up the habit from him.

We're both working too much, she warned herself. If we aren't careful, our marriage will suffer.

The Allied invasion of Normandy unfolded in the final days of shooting *The Conspirators*. Rejoicing at the prospect of a free Europe, between bouts of celebratory lovemaking she and John discussed returning to places they had lived or visited in the past and longed to experience together—London, Paris, Venice—Vienna, most of all.

"Not even Nazis could destroy the beauty of the Wienerwald forest," she declared, as they dined by candlelight at home. "The Lipizzaner horses will return to the Spanish Riding School at the Hofburg. And I'll visit Döbling cemetery to lay flowers on my father's and my grandmother's graves."

After a month's rest she started *Experiment Perilous*, a period piece for RKO. John gave in to her insistence that he cut his tie to Warner Brothers and joined her there. He received a higher salary, and they enjoyed the convenience of working at the same studio.

"At last I'm playing an interesting character," she told him when they met for a commissary lunch. "I've made fourteen films. I've played women who were similar to each other, and some that were unusual. But I didn't much like any of them. The worst was that dumb creature in *White Cargo*—I'll never forgive Mr. Mayer for making me do it. It's very devious of him, inviting you to go riding with him so often. He wants you to persuade me to finish out my contract, doesn't he?"

Wearing a pained expression, John replied, "All evidence suggests Mayer genuinely likes me. I'm the one he invited to Mexico. And he gave me excellent advice about investing my inheritance."

"He's the most self-centered man on earth," she maintained. "It appeals to his ego, keeping company with a well-born Englishman, who is also a cavalry officer and a veteran of the Great War."

Ignoring her spiky reply, he asked, "Why are you having a second serving of everything? You won't leave any room for your ice cream."

"Yes, I will, because I'm starving. All morning I felt faint. It was a fur coat scene. Why do they always film them on the hottest day of summer?"

Not long afterwards, when she was sidelined by a sudden attack of nausea, John was called over from *The Brighton Strangler* set.

She sat on a Victorian-era chaise longue, unsure if she'd lost all her breakfast, or whether more would come up. She blamed her tightly-cinched bustle gown.

"Hadn't you better go home and rest?"

"They expect me to finish the scene."

"You don't look as though you can."

"I will. I have to."

The next day she felt dizzy when she woke up, and her stomach was swimming. He insisted that she remain at Hedgerow Farm and go back to bed.

"You'd better tell them I've got flu."

"But it's not flu season."

"When actresses report symptoms like mine, the rumors start."

He kissed the top of her head, just before she leaped up from the breakfast table and dashed to the nearest toilet.

After several quiet and restful days, she resumed her work. As the date of her next period approached, she felt conflicted. She wanted a daughter. Jamesie mustn't remain an only child. He should have the companionship she'd missed while growing up. So many of her faults, Hedy believed, resulted from her overly attentive parents' contrasting styles of childrearing. Too often Papa had indulged her youthful whims, so on rare occasions when his anger or disappointment surfaced, she'd been confused and hurt. Mutti's unrelenting effort to restrain her impulses and regulate her behavior was still a source of insecurity and sensitivity.

But pregnancy, for an actress, could be a problem as much as a blessing. Her contract stipulated that she owed MGM another picture, not that Mr. Mayer was concerned about her just now. While at his ranch, riding his favorite horse, he'd suffered a bone-shattering fall. When discharged from Cedars of Lebanon he had a relapse, and his slow recovery kept him away from the studio.

Their RKO projects completed, John and Hedy planned a two-week holiday at the same cabin on Big Bear Lake where they spent their honeymoon. On the day of their departure, they visited her doctor's office to initiate the test that would confirm pregnancy. Lacking a telephone at their mountain hideaway, they wouldn't learn the results until they returned. During their long, lazy days, she spoke often of her plan to become an independent producer, selecting the scripts that most interested her and hiring compatible directors.

"Bette created B.D. Productions so she could be her own boss."

"She'll say and do anything when she's fed up or doesn't get her way," John responded. "Since her husband died, her behavior has been erratic. Jack Warner should put her on hiatus and give her time to grieve."

"She prefers keeping busy. That's why she's at the White House right now. Probably bossing her beloved Mr. Roosevelt and telling him exactly what she wants him to do."

On their drive back to Los Angeles they stopped for gas. Leaving John to settle with the attendant, Hedy used the pay telephone to contact her doctor. Next, she put in a call to her publicist to give him the news.

Climbing back into the car, she said simply, "Sometime in May. Or June."

"Darling!" He turned to embrace her. "How do you feel?"

"Different. The same. I was already sure." Looking down at her middle, she gave it a pat. "I wish baby and I didn't have to go back to work."

"You don't."

She shook her head. "Mr. Mayer will demand his due. One more picture."

"Ask for a medical leave of absence. He's so unwell himself, he might agree."

But by delaying her inevitable return to MGM, she would also postpone the professional independence she was increasingly desperate to attain.

Chapter 30

Louis B. Mayer retained his extraordinary power and influence, within his own industry and in the halls of government, but his riding accident had diminished him physically. The pudgy face behind the round glasses was pale. His hand quivered when he switched on the recording machine beside his white telephone.

"You make tapes of your meetings?" Hedy asked.

"Your colleagues sometimes try to renege on the agreements we make. This way, I have proof of what transpired, in case of a dispute."

"If you don't turn off that recorder," she said coolly, "I'm going to scream out loud, 'Don't touch me Mr. Mayer! Take your hands away! No, I won't sleep with you!' What will Ida and your secretaries think? Or perhaps they're accustomed to overhearing that sort of rebuke."

"Ingratitude is an unattractive quality in a beautiful woman." But he switched off the recorder.

"I'm not ungrateful. You wanted to make me a success, and sometimes I was," she conceded. "But in the future I'll be making fewer pictures. And they'll be of my choosing. Not yours."

"You were nothing when I discovered you," he snarled. "An actress from Austria who was foolish enough to run around the woods in the buff. For years I've tried erase that scandal. I groomed you, spending a fortune to make you the most famous female star in the world. I deserve to make back every dollar I've spent on you. And then some."

"If you compare the profits of my films to the costs you incurred, I expect you'll find you came out ahead."

"I'm holding you to the terms of your current contract. In a few weeks you'll start *Her Highness and the Bellboy,* with Robert Walker and June Allyson. We'll get you in front of the cameras before you start showing."

"And then?"

"You want to negotiate right now? For this next picture, I'll pay you seven thousand, five hundred dollars per week. Give me three more pictures over the next five years, and I might pay as much as a hundred thousand for each one. You won't get a better deal from any other studio, contracted or freelance."

"After the baby comes, I'm taking a six-month maternity leave. When I start work again, I'll be producing my own films."

"A big mistake. That's what I told your husband. He's very doubtful about your going independent."

The sting of betrayal momentarily unsettled her. John shouldn't have undermined her, it was an act of disloyalty. Reaching for her purse, she replied, "My agent will let you know my plans."

He got up, and with halting gait crossed the white carpet to open the door for her. "What are you naming the kid?"

"John Andrew, if it's a boy. For a girl, I like Gretel or Gretchen. John prefers English names like Mary or Susan."

She left the enfeebled lion's lair feeling degraded and depressed. Mayer had never figured out how best to use her, and his choice of project confirmed it. Her successful pictures were inevitably followed by mediocre ones.

If she committed to three more, there was no certainty she'd receive quality scripts. However, as the primary earner for her expanding family, she fully understood the significance of Mayer's offer.

Greer, the studio's reigning empress, was similarly frustrated. Her marriage to Richard Ney hadn't dulled her luster in Mayer's eyes, but she was rebelling against his dictatorial ways. After playing a series of dignified, suffering women in costume dramas, she vented her displeasure directly to him, to the press, and to her friends. To placate her, he permitted her to make revisions and improvements to her scripts. He gave her Norma Shearer's former suite in the Star Building, the best dressing room on the lot. Somehow her wry, self-deprecating humor survived all the attention and accolades and awards she received.

If Greer wasn't so warm and funny and genuine, Hedy thought, it would be easy to hate her.

Entering her fourth month of pregnancy, she began wardrobe fittings. Designer Irene Kalloch relied on Grecian style dresses, floating peignoirs, and a full-skirted ballgowns to conceal Hedy's swelling abdomen. Sydney Guilaroff trimmed her hair and curled it to draw attention to her face and away from her waist.

Not only was Hedy saddled with a shallow character—the princess wasn't even the primary romantic interest—she performed opposite a dispirited co-star whose estranged wife was sleeping with David Selznick, Mayer's son-in-law. Her dramatic role in *Experiment Perilous* was earning strong reviews, but she was stuck in a comic confection that had nothing to recommend it.

Out of concern over her spiking blood pressure, her doctor ordered her to avoid exertion. When she described her routine—leaving Benedict Canyon before dawn and returning after dusk—he advised her to alter it until she completed the film.

With the studio's permission, Hedy took up residence in her apartment-like dressing room.

On many evenings, John joined her for dinner and occasionally stayed the night. He shared Jamesie's school reports with her, and dialed the home number so she could wish him good night. Sometimes he took her to the preview screenings MGM offered their directors and producers and publicists.

She had to cope with inconveniences. One night the water in her building was turned off. Another time a janitor came to clean and was startled to find her toasting bread on her little gas stove. Constantly hungry, one morning she visited the commissary at half-past five and discovered breakfast service didn't start until nine o'clock.

Very late at night, after the production personnel and cleaning staff departed, a rare calm settled over the vast studio complex. Hedy stretched out on her bed to read the popular novel *Forever Amber* and munch her way through a box of cookies. Lying alone in the dark, she thrilled at the occasional faint flutter of new life.

Please be a girl, she pleaded.

She had time to read through the fan letters that arrived daily, from everywhere in the world. Some of the writers penned their admiration of her looks. Most congratulated her on the baby. Many of them sought her advice on how to become a movie star. She learned of domestic woes, romantic conflicts, losses from the war. Her secretary answered the majority of them, but Hedy responded to those that touched her most deeply.

She was particularly moved by one from Denise, a teenager whose sweetheart was serving in the Coast Guard.

> *My family says I have a duty to marry him when he comes home, but I'm not sure about it. My grades are the best in my class, and our science teacher says I could get accepted into any of the best universities—without having to pay. Physics is my favorite subject. I dream of becoming an astronomer, even though I am a girl. Did you know that stars and planets make radio waves? Dr. Jansky discovered this. He is the person I would like to meet the most—except for you. I read about your torpedo in the newspaper."*

After she dried her tears, Hedy composed a heartfelt reply. *Dear Denise, I am living proof that dreams come true. Don't abandon your education. Continue to work hard to increase your knowledge. Believe in yourself always. I hope that you will be able to make many wonderful discoveries. Good luck, Hedy Lamarr.*

She could have shared a great deal more of her hard-won wisdom.

Parents don't always know what's best. Men will disappoint you. Marriage brings out the best and the worst in a person. Mindful of the fact that her correspondent was an intelligent, idealistic young girl, she dispensed gentle encouragement instead of a strong dose of reality.

On the day Hedy had to film a ballroom scene, Margaret Wood helped her into a white gown of lace and gauze, worn off-the-shoulder, and tugged long evening gloves up past her elbows. Sydney arrived to arrange her hair himself, not trusting the assistant to make it perfect. Decked out in ersatz diamonds and glittering tiara, she was driven to the soundstage.

The extras, elegant in their finery, had already received their instructions. Hedy's waltzing partner was Carl Esmond, an Austrian actor who had stirred her teenaged heart in films and plays. Like her, he'd fled their homeland before the *Anschluss*.

They took their places, waiting for the music to begin.

"Action!" called the director.

Her head swam from the repetitive motion of the waltz, and there was a ringing in her ears. The other revolving figures blurred.

She was back in Vienna, laden with jewelry, trapped in a broken marriage, desperate to escape.

Choosing to embrace the present and plan for the future, she avoided dwelling too much on the past. On her arrival in Hollywood her history had been edited and altered by studio publicists, written and rewritten, and presented to the public as truth.

What was real and what was fabricated? Would she ever feel able to reveal the worst facts about herself to her children? Could she accurately remember them?

"Hedy?" Carl's worried face stared down at her.

She blinked. "You used to be Wally Eichberger. A long time ago, when I was Hedwig Kiesler. Before the Nazis destroyed everything."

"That's right. But we're far away from them now," he soothed her.

Close to tears, she said shakily, "I want to sit down. May I have a glass of water, please?"

He drew her away from the false columns and fake floral displays.

Fifteen minutes passed before she regained her composure and felt well enough to continue the scene.

The pregnancy affected her in other troubling ways. Her temperament had always shifted from calm to mercurial, but her former placidity was obliterated by anxieties and emotion. Conscious of a shift in her feelings about John, she harbored an unexpressed fear that this marriage would prove no more durable than the preceding two. She loved him still, but she wasn't sure that he was capable of being the strong protector and supporter that she wanted for herself and her baby and her son.

Many actors and actresses turned to psychiatric treatment. During her youth, after Sigmund Freud and his daughter Anna had visited her home, her parents had been critical of weak and mentally unstable people who needed therapy. In Hedy's mind, there was a stigma attached to seeking help. Acknowledging her frailties and speaking frankly about her past would be difficult, but she began to accept that it might become necessary.

When the production wrapped in mid-February, she reached the end of the seven-year contract she'd negotiated for herself on board the *Normandie*. With her secretary's help, she packed up the personal items in her dressing room, and the many gifts her fans had sent for the baby.

With mixed feelings, she passed through the imposing gated arch. She departed as one of the studio's highest-paid stars, and the most recognizable. Crossing the employees' parking lot, she noticed a woman inside a car, her flame-red head slumped over the steering wheel.

Lucille Ball was weeping.

"What happened to you?" Hedy asked, and passed a tissue through the open window.

"L.B. Mayer," the actress rasped. "He demoted me. Instead of top billing for my next picture, I get a supporting role. And when it's finished, so am I. He called me a pain in the ass and said my husband is a prick. My career is over. Everyone will call me a failure."

"No, they won't. Once a star, always a star. You can prove him wrong."

"When I left RKO and came here, he promised he'd be a father to me, and I believed every word. I signed his contract, and now I'm stuck."

"Get a lawyer and find a way out. We're both better off without that monster. You'll see!"

———◦•◆•◦———

A month after President Roosevelt's sudden death from a stroke, Germany unconditionally surrendered to the Allies.

"It's so sad that he didn't live to preside over our victory celebrations," Hedy said on the public holiday. Her folded hands rested on her massive belly. "I was hoping and praying we'd see peace in Europe before the baby arrives."

Mutti sipped her champagne. "He'll be a large one, so late he is." She had moved in to help prepare the nursery and soothe Hedy's anxieties about the ordeal ahead.

"*She.* I'm having a girl, I've said so all along." Her mother's greatest regret was her failure to bear a son, but she would prefer a daughter.

Mutti pushed the ottoman closer to Hedy. "Keep your feet up, Hedl. It helps with the swelling of the ankles."

Watching John's attempt to hang new curtains, she said, "I'm afraid Jamesie will be jealous. The baby is going to take up so much of my attention."

"We can send him to the overnight summer camp out at Catalina," her husband replied. "The number of places is limited, so we can't wait any longer to enroll him. He can take an archery class. And learn to ride a horse."

"You could teach him that," Hedy pointed out.

With great reluctance, she'd agreed that their son would benefit from the discipline and academic rigor of Page Military Academy, "the big school for little boys."

Mutti said, "I hope he won't have to wear his uniform at the camp. It makes those children look too much like Hitler Youth."

Before the issue could be settled, Hedy was admitted to Cedars of Lebanon hospital. Her hopes for a swift and painless labor receded as the hours dragged on. The baby didn't budge.

When the medical team determined that the birth would be breech, which her narrow hips made even more difficult, she received repeated spinal injections. After hours of unrelieved agony, through a haze of anesthesia and exhaustion, she heard the doctor call the nurse over.

"A beautiful daughter," he declared. "Weight?"

"Seven and a half pounds, exactly. Twenty inches long. You can sleep now, Miss Lamarr."

Residual pain, partly physical and partly mental, kept her awake and restless. On her release from the hospital, her suffering persisted. The infant was precious, exquisite, a miracle being, but bringing her into the world was a torture that Hedy continued to re-live.

"What is to be her name?" Mutti kept asking.

"Denise," Hedy answered, stroking her infant's rosy cheek. She hadn't forgotten the aspiring astronomer.

"So very American for a half-Austrian, half-English child. You should make her other name Hedwig."

"If John agrees."

Her delayed recovery from labor trauma and her deep depression were worrisome to her family and her doctor. To lift her spirits, John gave her a diamond ring and a matching bracelet.

When she read in the paper that Gustav Machatý wanted to remake *Ecstasy* with Linda Darnell, a young and popular brunette, Hedy burst into tears and locked herself in her bedroom. An international scandal in its day, the film had forever tarnished her, and the title obtruded in almost every newspaper or magazine profile. How puzzling, and unfair, that nowadays it was an acceptable vehicle for a rising Hollywood starlet.

Mutti knocked on her door. "Denise is crying, she was supposed to eat an hour ago. Feeding from the breast was your decision. You cannot stop after you've begun."

Nursing her child, Hedy let her mind wander back through the years to that woodland where she'd run naked, and her chilly swim in the lake. She remembered her parents' dismay. Her own shame. Fritz's revulsion.

Seeking a means of expressing inner turmoil, she returned to drawing and painting. One afternoon she went to the orchard at the edge of the property with her watercolors. Seated on the ground, she began an impressionistic recreation of the hilly landscape. For a soundtrack, she had birdsong and buzzing bees.

John found her there. After a watching her for a few minutes, he suggested that they dress up for an evening out.

"Where would we go?" Reluctant to put down her brush, she kept her eye on the image before her.

"It's a surprise. I promise you'll enjoy it."

Giving in, Hedy carried her unfinished picture back to the house, and John followed with the paint box. She changed into one of the elegant dirndls she used to wear at nightclubs and the Canteen.

Their secret destination turned out to be the Hollywood Bowl, where a crowd was assembling for the weekly Sunday night concert. She was pleased to see some favorite pieces listed on the program, and Leopold Stokowski would wield the baton.

"George and Boski are here," she observed, waving to them. "I haven't seen them for such a long time. Not since the baby."

A Grieg piano concerto performed by Percy Grainger was followed by a Bach toccata and fugue and Stravinsky's "Afternoon of a Faun."

After the intermission, the conductor moved to the microphone for an announcement.

"As a special treat for our patrons, tonight we present a new work, a debut performance. My great friend Mr. George Antheil composed this modern American symphony to honor the heroes and heroines in our midst, and their many patriotic efforts of recent years. 'Heroes of Today' and this premiere are dedicated to Miss Hedy Lamarr."

Never in her life had she witnessed a standing ovation before the musicians began to play.

Hedy blew a kiss to George. Undeterred by Boski's ever-watchful and jealous presence, he returned it.

———◇·◆·◁———

Giving in to her doctor's repeated recommendation that she try psychiatric therapy, Hedy conquered her prejudice against the couch. In weekly sessions, she delved deep into long-buried childhood recollections as well as her adolescent sexual history, including an early pregnancy scare and her young lover's suicide. She admitted to conflicted relationships with each of her parents. She described her years with Fritz, whose extreme possessiveness and domination that pushed her into flight. She questioned whether proximity had made her complicit in his morally dubious actions. She confessed her extra-marital affairs. She revealed her sense of displacement on arriving in Hollywood, confusion about her identity, and her ambivalence about the beauty on which her fame was established. She shared her fears for her children, and how haunted she was by the knowledge that hydrogen bombs could blast entire cities from the face of the earth.

After months of analysis and self-discovery, she felt able to cope with the myriad responsibilities of movie making, unfettered by a studio contract. Working independently was also therapeutic, combining her creativity and her inventiveness. She conferred with producers and directors, honing and improving the scripts she'd chosen for her initial independent productions. Her characters in *The Strange Woman,* based on a Ben Ames Williams novel, and *Dishonored Lady,* adapted from a popular play, were strong and aggressive risk-takers.

As I am, she acknowledged.

Returning home from a tennis date with Ann Sothern, Hedy found a large, thick, and very official government envelope on the hall table. Tearing it open, she found several papers clipped together.

The first one, stamped *August 11, 1942,* bore the number 2,292,387.

Beneath *H.L. Markey et. al.* at the top was the title SECRET COMMU-
NICATION SYSTEM.

Three years after obtaining her United States Patent, she held the
document in her hands. Diagrams of the radio-control torpedo guidance mechanism covered the first two sheets. Five additional pages
presented the typed, two-column description, credited to Hedy Kiesler
Markey and George Antheil.

One branch of the government, the Patent Office, deemed her idea
worthy and had approved it. Yet it had been discarded by the Navy officials to whom it had been donated. She and George had devoted their
ingenuity and a considerable amount of time and energy to design an
accurate and undetectable torpedo. In a saner world, its value would
be higher than the fame and beauty and sexual allure that persuaded
her fans to purchase War Bonds.

Going to the workroom where she'd begun her project, she stuffed
the patent into the envelope. Briefly she held it to her lips in a kiss of
homage, leaving a bright red imprint. Then she slid it between two
scientific volumes in the bookcase.

The Hollywood Canteen, a far more public and successful war-
related enterprise, had outlived its usefulness. The directors formed a
foundation to continue supporting the armed forces, but the storied
venue on Cahuenga Boulevard would be shuttered.

On Thanksgiving Day, Hedy and John joined the singers, come-
dians, and movie stars who had tirelessly performed and volunteered
during the past three years. Actors and other studio personnel recently
returned from military service were present for the Canteen's final
hours of operation.

John resumed his familiar task of turkey carving while Hedy signed
autographs. During her break, she spied Jimmy Stewart, a decorated
war hero, and invited him to waltz with her. His skill on the dance
floor hadn't faded during his time away flying bombing missions over
Germany. She'd forgotten how tall he was. Even in her heels, her head
barely reached his shoulder.

Afterwards he told her, "I was hoping to see you here. I wanted to ask about this." He removed a folded paper from his uniform pocket and brandished it. "From the latest issue of *Stars and Stripes.*"

Accepting the creased sheet, she confronted her own face—darkened skin, sensuously full lips, bare shoulders—and the accompanying headline.

HEDY ADDS NEW TWIST TO WAR: ACTRESS INVENTS REMOTE CONTROL DEVICE.

"If I'd known they'd use a Tondelayo picture," she muttered, "I wouldn't have given the interview."

"When did you develop this thing?"

"I started while we were shooting *Come Live with Me* and continued throughout *Ziegfeld Girl.* Then my friend George and I spent months and months figuring out the technical part."

"I always knew you were a remarkable girl. But I sure underestimated you."

"So did lots of people." She shrugged. "I got used to it."

Hearing her own words, she realized their inherent truth. She accepted that faulty or incomplete perceptions of her would always exist, no matter what she did. Rather than constantly striving to prove her worth to other people, she was putting her skills to use for herself and to provide for her family. She'd severed her relationship with MGM to make movies under the banner of her very own production company, Mars Film Corporation. She was a wife and the mother of two precious children.

A few weeks ago, on turning thirty-one, she'd expressed the wish that this new decade would be more fulfilling than the preceding one. She planned to make it so.

"How about another dance, Hedy?" Jimmy asked. "This could be my last chance to partner a famous inventor."

Bette Davis was charging about the place, her energy undimmed as the evening wore on. Hedy and John succeeded in cornering her just long enough to request a favor.

"We're having Denise christened sometime next year," John explained. "We hope you'll agree to be her godmother."

"Oh, my *dar*-lings, of *course* I will. She wouldn't exist if I hadn't introduced you. Our first Canteen Christmas, wasn't it? You tell me when, and I'll be there."

By midnight, the Canteen's indefatigable co-founder had removed her high heels. Standing barefooted at the microphone, she announced that three million men and women in uniform had been fed and entertained at the Canteen since its inception.

"But what we have done for them is nothing compared to what they have done for all of us," Bette declared, before leading the crowd in an emotional rendition of *Auld Lang Syne*.

The fascist movement that drove Hedy out of Austria was as dead as Adolf Hitler. She fingered the scrap of paper in her pocket, grateful for proof that her contribution, patented but never implemented, wasn't entirely forgotten.

George Antheil had titled his autobiography, *Bad Boy of Music*. As soon as it was published, he presented Hedy with signed copy. Devouring it, she envied his gift for words, his humor, and his frankness.

"I learned so much about him that I didn't know," she commented to John, who held a flickering match to the bowl of his pipe. "And even about myself."

"How do you mean?"

She laid Denise on the sofa and reached for the volume. Thumbing through the pages, past the description of their first meeting at the Adrians' house, his assessment of her breasts, the succinct description of their torpedo, she came to the most gratifying words she'd ever read.

"The Hedy we know is not the Hedy you know. Hedy is an intellectual giant."

Epilogue: 1949

"I would like the privilege of a private life."
—Hedy Lamarr

The mature height and thick trunks of the trees marked the passage of thirteen years since Hedy first came to the Thalberg Building. On that distant day they had been spindly saplings, and she'd been a fugitive Austrian actress who barely spoke English.

Outwardly, the stark white modernist palace was unchanged. The Stars and Stripes fluttered on the rooftop flagpole. The lawn, well-watered and fertilized, was lush and green. Precisely trimmed hedges, with round-topped topiaries placed at intervals, hugged the foundation of the structure. The sidewalks were spotless. The windows gleamed. Sharply-dressed employees entered and exited through the main doors.

Louis B. Mayer still ruled here. But as Hedy and the rest of Hollywood's film colony knew, his grip on power was no longer as firm as it used to be.

Antitrust suits were dissolving corporate monopolies, mandating separate ownership of the theatre chains and the major studios. Block booking, which had previously ensured the distribution of

MGM's entire output to Loewe's cinemas, was eliminated. Movies, so essential to morale during the Depression and throughout the war years, faced competition from the entertainment programs available on commercial television. Production costs had escalated, along with the risk of unprofitability as audience tastes shifted. Blacklisting had diluted Hollywood's talent pool. Many of the most gifted screenwriters, producers, directors, and actors were indelibly tainted by their association—actual or alleged—with communism.

Hedy was confronting her own challenges. Thirty-five was a precarious age for an actress whose looks were valued more than her talent. She never ceased to regret that her paymasters hadn't provided the complex characters or comedic parts that might have extended her usefulness to them.

Since leaving his studio four years ago, she'd encountered Mr. Mayer at social events. He treated her with his habitual combination of paternalism and lechery, claiming full credit for her successes and ascribing her failures to her stubbornness and poor decisions. Despite her efforts to thrive beyond his orbit, she remained bound to him.

Prepared to do battle yet again, she wore her most figure-flattering New Look dress and several rows of pearls.

Ida Koverman, in her seventies, retained her position as guardian and gatekeeper on the third floor. "They're waiting for you upstairs, in the executive dining room. It's good to see you again," she added. "You've been missed."

Whether it was true or not, Hedy appreciated that small kindness.

Does Ida's boss feel the same, she wondered as she arrived at her destination.

"Come in, sit down," he greeted her, flashing his teeth. He hooked his arm in hers and pulled her into the room. "Gentlemen, here she is. Delilah in the flesh."

Cecille B. DeMille's Technicolor Biblical epic *Samson and Delilah* was potentially the biggest money maker since *Gone with the Wind*. Advance publicity and praise from those who had previewed Hedy's performance had catapulted her into the stratosphere of stardom.

She recognized only half of the men assembled around the table. All of them shook her hand, offering effusive congratulations. Her long-time champions Howard Strickling and Benny Thau, grayer than they'd been so many years ago on the steamship *Normandie*, came forward to kiss her cheek. She was saddened to see so much evidence of physical decline. Mayer was fragile after various surgeries. Benny, survivor of a near-fatal automobile crash last year, walked with a limp.

"You must remember Dore Schary," Mayer said.

Studying him closely, she said, "We never worked together during your scriptwriting days."

"I wish we had," he said gallantly. "You would have been an inspiration." He had a prominent nose, and his short, side-parted hair exposed oversized ears.

An executive vice president and producer, Schary was regarded as Mayer's likeliest successor in the event of retirement—or removal. His liberal politics and inclination towards message films didn't mesh with his superior's conservatism and established preference for comfort movies and musicals. Theirs was a tense but crucial partnership, she'd heard, and its survival was wholly dependent on the balance sheet.

When everyone was seated, Mayer began. "Thank you for meeting with us before you return to the East Coast."

Restless and lonely, Hedy was often drawn to New York in search of excitement and stimulating company. The diversity of the social scene appealed to her, and she met people who were cerebral, artistic, or both. Prominent men took her to the theatre or nightclubs. Important producers offered her roles in stage plays or invited her to appear on television. By comparison, Hollywood now seemed sleepy and dull, entirely focused on its sole defining industry.

"As I reminded you on the phone, we terminated your last contract with the understanding that you'd do three more pictures for us. The first property we've reserved for you will out-gross *Samson and Delilah*, I'm sure."

She raised a skeptical eyebrow. "So much depends on the script. And the director. And the casting."

"For this project, we want a foreign actress. Garbo and Dietrich are too old. Besides, they aren't interested in working. Bergman is box office poison. She deserted her husband and kid, ran off to Italy, and got knocked up by her director." Turning to Dore Schary he said in a tone of command. "Tell Miss Lamarr about the picture."

Schary referred to a printed synopsis. In a low, sonorous voice, he began, "The setting: Cuba. The heroine: a Hungarian refugee."

"Of course," she murmured.

"Marianne speaks three languages."

"Hedy speaks more than that," Howard interjected. "Five." He'd always inserted that detail into her studio bio and press releases, to be reprinted in numerous magazine and newspaper profiles.

"She's determined to enter the United States," Schary went on, "by any means necessary. Her father, an unlawful asylum seeker, is already there. Her love interest is an American immigration inspector."

"Of course," Hedy repeated.

"Working undercover."

When he finished, each of his associates chimed in. Howard promised a vigorous promotional effort. The casting director assured her of top quality talent in supporting roles.

Nothing about their pet project, a bundle of elements from at least three pictures she'd done previously, tempted her. One of the least appealing aspects was the decision to shoot on location in Havana.

Mayer, alert to her lack of enthusiasm, dismissed his brain trust and invited her into his inner sanctum, the familiar site of so many past skirmishes. She interpreted their withdrawal to the all-white office as a sign of his determination to win her over. If he needed her, then advantage was already hers.

The female stars Mayer had created and nurtured had either flickered out or flown to other studios. Judy Garland, completely unreliable, was a victim of her personal demons and over-dependence on drugs. Greer Garson possessed indisputable talent but her recent pictures were neither profitable or popular.

Wasting no time on preliminaries, he said, "You were making

seven thousand, five hundred a week when you deserted our family. I'm willing to pay you ten thousand a week, with a four-week guarantee. And script approval."

"When I left MGM," she reflected, "I was dissatisfied."

"And how satisfied were you making movies for yourself? More work than you bargained for, wasn't it?"

"I would have received an Oscar nomination for *The Strange Woman,* if there hadn't been so many actresses in contention that year."

"You screwed Ulmer, your director. Isn't that what busted up your marriage to John Loder?"

"No. I was bored. He was boring."

"After your separation, you cast him in your picture. You let him get you pregnant. And then you demanded a divorce. Gotta feel sorry for the guy, the way you used him."

"You needn't. John recently married a rich New York socialite, twenty years younger than he is."

"You've got an enormous house. Must be expensive to run."

Too busy producing and acting to enjoy or maintain Hedgerow Farm, and anticipating her third divorce, she'd sold it to the Bogarts. Her Spanish-style mansion in Beverly Hills had ample servants' quarters, the requisite swimming pool, and a pool house.

"You're a single mother," Mayer continued. "Think of all you could do for your kids, making forty grand per picture. Doesn't the oldest boy go to that fancy school where Joan Crawford sends her children?"

She nodded. "Chadwick."

The little ones had a nanny. Denise was four, bright and articulate. Two-year-old Tony had arrived in the dying days of Hedy's marriage to John. Mutti, more casual and complaisant as a grandmother than she'd been as a mother, enjoyed swimming with them and teaching them Austrian songs and games. With her job at the Lanz of Salzburg garment factory and her own apartment and a circle of friends, she led a busy life. Recently she'd been invited to make a lecture tour—her topic, "Hollywood As I See It." Although her mother never requested financial assistance, Hedy made sure the bills were paid and provided money for little luxuries like a vacation or new furniture.

Mayer folded his hands on the sleek white desktop and leaned forward. "How about fifteen thousand per week? With script approval."

They had played this game before. How many times?

"I prefer a flat fee. One hundred thousand."

"No deal."

Relying on the tactic that had proved successful during that first negotiation in his London hotel suite, Hedy stood up. "As I said to Samson, no man leaves Delilah. But she left you. And she's doing it again."

"Wait!"

"Well?" She looked down at him, fingering her necklace. She'd worn pearls to every one of their meetings, since the beginning of this long and complicated relationship.

"Seventy-five thousand. We'll work on the script. It could be better. And that's going to cost me, you know. Production budgets aren't what they used to be."

"I'll accept ninety thousand, guaranteed, without approval of the scripts, if you promise they will be excellent. You will pay my agents outright instead of deducting their percentage from my salary. And you won't make me go to Cuba."

After a long pause, he said, "My board's going to have my head for this. And probably my balls." He got up and reached across the broad white desk.

She took his hand, dry and papery, and shook it firmly.

"You drive a hard bargain. You always did. If we could've packed your determination and stubbornness into a bomb or a torpedo, we'd have won the war a lot sooner."

His statement was more accurate than he realized.

Pride and ambition, far more than her agents' prodding, had overcome her reservations about dealing with Mayer. She still possessed qualities he wanted to exploit, as her role as the sexy, scheming Delilah had reminded him.

But her heart really wasn't in moviemaking. It hadn't been, for a long time.

Her career was a habit, one that she had sometimes considered breaking. The long hours on the set were tedious—and painful, when her back acted up. She was more acutely aware of the privacy that stardom had stolen from her. She stubbornly refused to do publicity for the DeMille picture, apart from posing for stills in full vamp makeup and her skimpy seductress costumes.

Years ago, over the span of a few months, she recalled, she'd starred in three major pictures—with Gable and Stewart, Judy and Lana—while working with George Antheil late into the night. How had she managed it? Along with her enthusiasm, her energy had ebbed.

After Hedy exited the building, she paused to lean against the white wall. Heat radiated from the stone blocks, soothing the persistent ache she felt low in her spine.

I'm going to begin the new decade the same way I spent this one, she thought. Struggling to fulfill other people's expectations, wrangling with my boss and his henchmen and my directors. Seeking true love from actors and inevitably suffering its loss.

But when I've completed Mayer's films, I'll be free again. And rich enough not to work, unless I choose to.

She imagined her father's voice, repeating advice he'd often given. *Think with your heart, Hedl, and you'll win in the end. Even if sometimes you seem to lose.*

Bathed in the unrelenting sunshine, she surveyed buildings where her burdensome and unshakable image had originated. In that moment, she knew beyond all doubt that her desire to invent a new life for herself would eventually lead her far from Hollywood.

Author's Note

n 1997, on learning she would receive the Electronic Frontier Foundation's Pioneer Award for her spread spectrum and frequency-hopping technologies, Hedy Lamarr responded, "It's about time." She wasn't able to attend the ceremony, but her son was there to play her recorded message of acknowledgment and gratitude. The late George Antheil was her co-honoree.

The exact correlation between frequency-hopping and the knowledge Hedy acquired at Fritz Mandl's pre-war meetings and dinners in Austria, remains a mystery. She acknowledged a connection but offered few details, other than a reference to her encounter with Hellmuth Walter at the Hirtenberger factory Christmas party.

Her collaboration with Antheil and their patent for the "secret communication system" gave rise to various technological advances. The basics of Hedy's invention have served the U.S. military (remote control rockets, radio guidance for missiles) and national security agencies (spy satellites, surveillance drones). Consumer applications developed from spread spectrum technology are enmeshed with our daily habits and activities: wi-fi, cellular telephones, Bluetooth, and geophysical positioning systems (GPS).

Hedy returned to MGM a year before L.B. Mayer was forced out and replaced as chief executive by Dore Schary. His departure symbolized the demise of Hollywood's Golden Age.

In 1951, Hedy announced her retirement from filmmaking to marry resort owner Ted Stauffer. She auctioned all her accumulated belongings—clothes, furs, artwork, even wedding rings from former husbands. Her next and longest marriage, to Texas oilman William Howard Lee, placed her and her Loder children in a Houston suburb. A sixth marriage to her divorce lawyer, Lewis J. Boies, lasted two years.

After a 1961 shoplifting charge, and her acquittal, she left Los Angeles for New York City. The decades that followed were characterized by frequent lawsuits and ill-advised plastic surgeries prior to her move to Florida. According to acquaintances during her reclusive final years, Hedy retained her keen intellect and sense of humor, flexibility (mental and physical), and an ability to re-invent herself.

At the close of her tumultuous life, she had a final ambition—to witness the dawn of the Millennium. Not quite three weeks after doing so, on the morning of January 19, 2000, she expired in bed, her face fully made up. Her death was attributed to heart failure. She was eighty-six.

She had outlived her friend and co-inventor, composer George Antheil, by nearly forty years. He succumbed to a heart attack at age fifty-eight, survived by his wife Boski and son Peter.

Hedy's mother, Trude Kiesler, continued to reside in California and was employed by Lanz of Salzburg for thirty-six years. She died in 1977, aged eighty-six. Hedy, then living in New York, did not attend the funeral. Her son Tony Loder handled the arrangements.

The various colorful and contradictory accounts Hedy and MGM concocted to explain her final break from Fritz Mandl are at odds with contemporaneous press and court records. In May, 1937, Fritz introduced his architect to a prospective third Frau Mandl. His July meeting in Carlsbad with Dr. Joeden was cited in the Nuremberg Trials. According to one report, that summer Vienna was buzzing about the Mandls' plans for a swift Riga divorce. Hedy left her husband's house in late August, very likely with his knowledge, taking money and clothing and jewelry. (A favorite evening gown worn in Austria accompanied her to Hollywood, to appear in a studio glamor portrait and at a New Year's Eve celebration.)

During Fritz's Argentina years, he maintained contact with Hedy. He augmented his fortune in the usual way, supplying weapons to dictators, and was a firm supporter of Juan Péron. With his fourth wife, he returned to Austria in 1955 and successfully reclaimed his properties. Fritz was laid to rest in a cemetery near his factory in 1977. The Hirtenberger Group continues as an engineering and defense products firm.

Gene Markey's distinguished service during World War II earned him the rank of Rear Admiral, a status of which he was extremely proud. After his four-year marriage to Myrna Loy, he wed Louise Parker Wright, owner of Calumet Farms racing stables. He spent his later years primarily in Kentucky, breeding thoroughbreds and dogs.

Actor John Loder had two other wives after Hedy (his third), and died in his native England in 1988, aged ninety. Their daughter, Denise Loder-DeLuca, became an artist, specializing in celebrity portraits. Son Anthony Loder was briefly an actor before going into business. Like his sister, he contributes to biographies and documentaries about his mother.

Hedy's permanent estrangement from her adopted son James Lamarr Markey Loder (Jamesie), took place during his schooldays. Forty-one years after he ceased living with her, they met again but never reconciled. Excluded from her will, he sued the estate, eventually receiving a $50,000 settlement from his step-siblings. Irregularities in his birth certificate convinced him that he is a natural child of Hedy and John Loder, born prior to the Markey marriage. To date he has not submitted to the DNA testing that would prove or disprove a blood relationship. For this to be true, his birth would have occurred at a period when a very slender Hedy was on film sets and at industry events, constantly photographed. The chief MGM fixers, Howard Strickling and Eddie Mannix, were masters at concealing stars' inconvenient pregnancies. No such efforts appear to have been necessary during Hedy's first two years with the studio.

Reginald "Reggie" Gardiner, the British comedian and character actor whom Hedy declared she *should* have married, transferred his talents from movies to television, working throughout the 1950s and 60s. Reggie died in 1980, survived by his wife Nadia and their son.

For my research into the complexities of Hedy's life and career, I relied on two major biographies, three documentaries, and an ever-increasing number of scholarly examinations of her cultural and scientific significance. I'm especially indebted to Richard Rhodes for *Hedy's Folly*, and its detailed yet comprehensible exegesis of her collaboration with the self-proclaimed Bad Boy of Music.

In addition to autobiographies by George Antheil and John Loder, I trawled through reminiscences of the actors, directors, producers, publicists, writers, and photographers who worked with Hedy or encountered her. The richest primary sources were the newspapers and fan magazines that documented her rise to stardom and her impact. Some of the most interesting facts contained in my fictional work are those that either eluded her biographies, or which they considered less interesting than I did.

For Hedy's life in Austria I relied on contemporaneous press accounts and histories of the pre-*Anschluss* era, several of which tested my limited ability to read German. Other sources were Prince Ernst von Starhemberg's memoir of that time (containing no references to Fritz and Hedy, or any allusion to his affair with Nora Gregor). Kurt von Schuschnigg, son of the Chancellor, is more forthcoming. He describes his boyhood meeting with Hedy and admits to smacking her bottom.

Hedy supposedly told Howard Hughes that a member of the Krupp family offered her half a million dollars' worth of jewels if she would give him "one night of ecstasy." No one currently living can confirm whether or not it's true. In choosing a Krupp for the proposition, I picked Alfried. Because he was charged with crimes against humanity for using slave labor in the factories during World War II and imprisoned, I doubted I could damage his reputation.

The greatest visual records of Hedy Lamarr are the multitude of glamor portraits and her films. I repeatedly watched the ones that fit within the framework of this novel, from *Ecstasy* (two versions) through Cecil B. DeMille's Technicolor epic *Samson and Delilah*.

Any writer, whether of fiction or history, who recounts Hedy's life faces difficulties. Partly because much evidence is missing, and also because MGM so often presented a manufactured narrative for public consumption. But mostly because Hedy's own accounts, entertaining and rich with detail, are as variable as they are unreliable. Not only do her stories change with every telling, many are contradicted by the factual record. Especially the ones in her autobiography. She disassociated herself from it and sued her collaborators, who countersued. *Ecstasy and Me*, however dubious a source, presents her opinions and experience of Hollywood, illustrated with anecdotes that might or might not be faithful. Conversations with other people, after a gap of twenty to thirty years, can hardly be accurate in the details. The sexual escapades she recounts veer from the possibly possible to the highly improbable.

And yet . . . in fact-checking her romantic depiction of her stay in Malibu immediately after the *Algiers* premiere, I discovered that yes, indeed, there was a full moon that night.

<hr/>

I extend my gratitude to all involved in this project, directly or indirectly. The brilliant Deborah Bradseth was a wonderful partner on the production side, creating a glorious cover. BKR Editing was enormously helpful, as usual, and I'm indebted to Maryann Miller for her proofreading skills. Many friends—especially Hazle Hamilton, Kate Atkinson, Fran Gardner-Smith, Leslie Carroll, and Virginia Macgregor—were supportive in their individual and very special ways. And to my husband, I offer infinite thanks for his patience, helpfulness, and companionship while my mind and attention were occupied with my compelling main character and her labyrinthine life.

From my teenage years, I was aware of Hedy Lamarr. I suspect she was my father's adolescent crush. When he grew up, he married a more attainable brunette beauty—my mother. But he never forgot Hedy. Whenever I paraded before him in an evening gown, or played an ingenue in a play, his highest praise was, "You look like Hedy Lamarr." I didn't, but I appreciated the compliment.

As a graduate student in film studies, I learned about *Ecstasy* and its place in cinematic history but without realizing its impact on Hedwig Kiesler the person, or the extent to which it clouded her life and her reputation. Golden Age Hollywood has always fascinated me, but for a long time Hedy Lamarr was but one of many glamorous actresses who starred in black and white movies.

Now, knowing so much more, I marvel at the intelligence that was inevitably outshone by her memorable face.

About the Author

Margaret Porter is the award-winning and bestselling author of more than a dozen works of historical fiction. A former stage actress, she also worked professionally in film, television, and radio. Other writing credits include nonfiction, newspaper and magazine articles, and poetry. She and her husband live in New England and return annually to Great Britain and Europe. Information about her books can be found at www.margaretporter.com.